DEATHMATCH

DEATHMATCH

COSMIC GAMES BOOK 2

Wilbur Woods

Podium

Published in 2024 by Podium Publishing
www.podiumentertainment.com

DEATHMATCH

CHAPTER ONE

Back to Adventures

F inally!" Maverick gleefully exclaimed. "I am *so* done with sitting all day."

"It hasn't been more than two weeks," Max said and dusted the gray, ashy grit of the Dreadlands off of his coat.

"Do you have any idea how slowly time passes when you have to Cultivate the whole time?"

"I do," Max said, casting his companion a glance. Not that it did anything. Maverick knew perfectly well how annoyed Max was at his attitude through their Soulbond. "Well, we're moving out now, are you happy?"

Maverick only huffed.

Christie, who had just come out of the cave, smiled. Max sighed.

"Save me from him, Christie," he said.

"Darling, you're the last person I know who needs any sort of saving," she said and let out a throaty chuckle.

Max took the clay cup of water she was offering. An ice cube was floating inside it. They had come a long way from when they'd first arrived, but even having ice was still incredible.

"When are we leaving?" Christie asked.

"You're planning to tag along?"

"All the guys are," Christie said and shrugged. "Both Brian's and mine."

"Why?" Max asked.

"To see and be inspired by our boundless awesomeness, of course," Maverick said.

Christie shrugged again. "He's sort of right."

"I was planning to go a little deeper in the Dreadlands and see if I can find something new for us," Max said. "I know I haven't exactly been pulling my weight around here."

Christie scoffed. "First of all, you've done more than your fair share already. I'm not exactly keeping score, but I think you're still topping the leaderboard on overall usefulness."

"I—"

"Second, as long as you're here, people both feel and *are* safe. And that's not nothing," Christie said. "Please stop selling yourself short, darling. It's unbecoming of such an otherwise *strapping* young man."

She gave Max a grin that seemed positively hungry, and Max raised a hand.

"Fine. But regardless, I'm going deep."

"I like it deep," Christie said and looked at her nails nonchalantly.

"Max," Maverick started. "Isn't it about time you and Chri—"

"How about you both shut up and let me talk?" Max cut in. "You guys can come and I'll see if I can set up some easy kills for you. But you take those and then get back. I need to fly solo and make up for the Experience I've been losing out on. And I don't want any of you getting hurt either."

Max was excited about getting back into the fray. For the last ten days he had been practicing with his signature ability, **[Telekinesis]**, while Maverick Cultivated. Whenever Max ran out of Mana, he would pop a **[Celestial Illumination Pill]** and sit down for an hour by himself to let his Mana regenerate, before getting back to mastering his Skill.

It was such a versatile Skill, with a bunch of applications, that Max had figured it was worth taking the time, not to mention thorough practice. Especially when it came to flying, which was really hard.

Max had finally gotten the hang of it. It consumed a significant amount of Mana, but having the ability to fly wasn't only beyond useful but also just really awesome. And now Max wanted to test it in action. And apparently so did half of the outpost as well.

They had observed him gradually improving, of course, but this would be the real deal. Watching their greatest fighter kick some ass would be a real morale boost, and Max was more than happy to oblige.

"Make sure everyone has a full belly before we go," Max said. "We've got a trek ahead."

"Already done," Christie said and gave him a lopsided smile. "We're just waiting for you to chow down, and we'll be on our way."

After Max had eaten his share of yesterday's meat—a calf of one of the giant hairy creatures roaming around the parts of the Dreadlands that were easier to navigate—they set off. For the first time, they were making their way into the inner parts of the Dreadlands, where the porous tall spires were located, along with hot springs producing dense fog, and a threatening volcano looming over the horizon.

As they continued along, they could hear the terrible roar of one of the giant demonic insect monsters. It was close. Max brought his hand to the trusty weapon in his holster but didn't draw it yet. They had no reason to be jumpy. Max didn't know what Level these beasts were, but he was pretty sure he had dealt with worse. As long as the monster focused on him, he'd be able to gun it down without too much risk.

Thanks to the thick fog, the monster managed to get uncomfortably close before they noticed it. It screeched and charged at them; in response, Max gritted his teeth and pulled out [The Maverick].

His comrades had wisely kept a fifteen-yard distance behind him, which paid off. Out of the corner of his eye, Max could see them scattering and hiding behind the porous spires.

"[Tether]!" Max shouted, as adrenaline flooded his system. Just as the insect creature was about to swipe down with one of its claws, Max slid backward out of the way.

Clearly incensed, the monster screeched and swiped at him again numerous times in quick succession. Max kept out of the way with [Tether], pointing his revolver companion at its ugly monstrous face. Maverick simply shot at it and laughed.

"Now this is just what we needed!" the gun cackled.

Having created enough distance between them, Max used his consciousness to reach into the soles of his feet. While his other spells were fairly simple, [Telekinesis] required the finesse and focus that only Cultivation and practice could give.

Fortunately, Max had been doing just that.

"[Telekinesis]!"

He floated into the air, trying to hold his balance, which was akin to trying to keep two skateboards under his feet. But with practice, he managed. The demon-bug sliced at him with its massive hanging claws, but Max avoided them, adding some speed as he leaned forward and guided the spell.

His Mana was going down, but he had enough.

Dodging another swipe, he flew upward and was temporarily hoisted legs up, head down above the beast's neck. Max released the spell and backflipped off of its head.

Landing on it caused it to shake wildly and cry out in terrible anger. It tried to grab at him, but its arms were designed for hunting and swiping downward, not for scratching its head. Max cast **[Tether]** on himself to survive riding it like a mechanical bull. Then he cast another spell.

"**[Alter Gravity]**."

Max cast it six times. With his high Intelligence and some elementary guidance using his Cultivation, he managed to make himself weigh around six hundred pounds. His new weight made his own bones ache, but the demonic cockroach was much worse off.

Its head lulled to the left, then to the right, and eventually the creature collapsed onto its stomach.

Max wasted no time. As the monster was still struggling, he used multiple **[Tethers]** to glue its head to the ground. It thrashed around and kept slashing with its claws, but Max knew he was safe. Then he let Maverick get to work.

Defeated Level 19 [Terrormite (Elite)]
You gained 725 Experience points

His audience cheered in congratulations. Max gave them a smile and looted the body.

1631 Cosmic Coins
[E-tier Supply Box]

Good score! These are definitely worth killing.
Max gave the Supply Box to Christie. He had enough Mana and Health potions to work with. Being the highest-Level Cultivator meant he also needed the least food and water.

The **[Terrormites]** were a lot easier to kill than he had expected. If these were the guardians of the inner areas of the Dreadlands, Max could have ventured there a long time ago. His mouth twisted as he thought of the lizards.

They were organized warriors, and it was very likely they were already pillaging the better areas. There had been a few encounters, but in the outer rims of the Dreadlands, escape was often an option, and thus there were rarely casualties on either side.

If we keep going this way, that could change.
Max was still certainly the strongest Cultivator in the game. He might not be the highest-Level one anymore, but Leveling was slowing down anyway. In the end, it was only a framework for Cultivation anyway, so Max was sure his build was at least somewhat optimal.

We'll have to see if it's optimal enough.

He would not be culled. Humanity would prevail.

"I need one of you guys to tell the others at the camp to come collect whatever valuables we can from this thing," Max said and pointed at the demonic cockroach. Whether its meat was edible was in doubt, but the chitin and claws would definitely be of use.

One of Christie's warriors immediately made a run for their outpost, and the rest followed Max into the fog.

CHAPTER TWO

A Surprise Event

Max killed another one of the [**Terrormites**] in the deep fog. In order to give the ranged fighters some extra Experience, he'd tethered one of its feet to a boulder so they could attack it as well.

Afterward, they continued to travel forward a good twenty minutes in the fog, which was growing thicker and thicker to the point that they only caught sight of the porous spires when they literally ran into them. The same went for the demonic bugs.

How the hell are we going to find our way back?

Suddenly, however, the fog finally began to recede, eliciting numerous gasps of awe. These weren't the Dreadlands they were used to seeing: tall, red-barked trees, rich green grass, bushes full of nuts and bright berries, and yellow rabbits jumping around and looking at their group in confusion. Giant yaks roamed around. Fat, silver-backed fish swam around in a sparkling creek nearby. A pitch-black raccoon washed itself by the bank as tiny colorful birds flew over its head. It tried to catch them but lost its balance and fell into the water.

Max's group continued to stare in stunned awe. Max breathed in the air, fresh and sweet and clearly strong with raw spiritual power. As opposed to the stale, sulfurous, cough-inducing air they'd encountered in the Dreadlands up to this point, this was as if they'd been suddenly transported to a tropical holiday.

"What the—" Brian asked, but he was interrupted by the appearance of a large looming jellyfish, along with four Grays by its side. They looked at the humans with their large black eyes and snorted in derision.

[It seems our representatives beat you to it.]

"*Bah!*" one of the Grays answered.

[Please remain calm, Humans. Ah, Maxwell, it is very good that you are here.]

With that, all of the Grays stopped talking to one another and turned to stare at Max. He ignored them and only looked at the Zoos representative. He could feel the greed and lust for violence emanating from the Grays like an almost-tangible force.

[Feel free to call upon your representative race, as per our agreement. Twelve will be the limit, as you well know. We will debrief our race in the meantime.]

"No you will not!" the leader of the Grays called in a shrill voice. *"This will result in a time advantage."*

[It is, by default, the point that the race that discovers the Inner Sanctum first will have an advantage.]

The Grays went absolutely livid. Chairs and drinking glasses suddenly materialized in their hands, and they threw them at the plastic giant jellyfish. As soon as they hit the hologram's edge, however, they instantly vanished.

[Absolutely not! That will give them a very unfair advantage. You shall place the humans in stasis and give them each an **[F-grade equipment box]**.*]*

[Such a notion would be absurd. An advantage for reaching this place first is a given. We are giving you the courtesy of choosing which kind of advantage you would prefer.]

The Grays grumbled to themselves but then held a quick conference. Max looked at them and smirked at their ire. Whatever situation he and his group had found themselves in, it seemed that the Grays and, by extension, the lizards had drawn the short end of the stick.

Dejected, the leader of the Grays announced their decision: *"You may begin debriefing the humans. We will inform our representative race and provide them with coordinates."*

The Grays cast a last long glance at Max. He felt a chill running down his spine. He could not directly sense their Cultivation, but it was clearly eons beyond his comprehension. They could kill him with a snap of their fingers. When they were done making it perfectly clear that they would use every available trick to get rid of him, they blinked out.

The Zoos jellyfish hummed to itself, and a large waterbed appeared in front of Max and his friends. They shot a questioning glance at the plastic jellyfish, but all of them eventually climbed onto the bed. It was soft and relaxing, and Max noticed that his Mana instantly zipped up to full. He felt his mind easing. The bed was clearly doing *something*, and Max wondered if the Zoos were operating within the game's rules here. Not that it was any of his business.

[Very good of you all to have made it here. This is the Inner Sanctum of the Dreadlands, wherein all of the most valuable resources are located. There are two types of trees here, both of which are highly valuable building materials. All of the food is extremely nutrient-dense, as well as diverse and plentiful. The earth is also of the highest quality, providing ample opportunity for farming, if you are so inclined. Now, you might be wondering how an oasis such as this manages to exist in the Dreadlands. The answer is simple. It is within a space-dilation bubble and physically exists somewhere else on this planet.]

"What are we doing here?" Max asked. "Why are the Grays involved?"

[Indeed. Those were the Grays, also known as the Kiritus Corporation, who are the patron race of your direct opponents. We are going to have a competition. Holding the Inner Sanctum in the control of your race is designed to speed up the game, resulting in a significantly increased chance of victory and the annihilation of the opposing race within this quadrant. This will allow you to continue on to the second stage of Cosmic Games and face new opponents. You will of course be able to retain this area, as access to it is granted by spatial magic, and the location can be altered.]

Max exchanged glances with Brian, who only shrugged. Max shrugged back. This was rather confusing, but it had to be important, given the Zoos' thorough explanation.

[If the other race stumbles upon the Inner Sanctum in a stroke of luck, we have deemed it fair that they not be destroyed. This is why the Kiritus Corporation went ahead and started recruiting members of their representative race. They will be brought here, and you will engage in conflict for the control of this area. A Deathmatch will occur.]

"A *what* now?" Christie asked, her voice losing its typical relaxed air of poshness.

[The Grays will instruct their representative race, Ishkarassi, to come here with a force of twelve representatives. The same amount of people as you brought here.]

"Now, wait just a second," Max said, anger surging inside him. "So they can just pick the twelve strongest fighters? What if we had come here with a bunch of **[Gatherers]**? Freya's an **[Artisan]**. We're already at a disadvantage."

Freya shifted uncomfortably. Max turned and gave her an encouraging smile. She gave a shy smile back.

[That would indeed be lamentable, but fortune was on your side. However, do note that you will most likely be forced to do some gathering and crafting. The area is large, and you will need survival skills. Freya Johanson will also be provided an opportunity to change her base class into [Combatant], if she so wishes.]

At least we have some hunters with us, in Brian and his men. But those Gray assholes are going to bring twelve of their strongest fighters. We're playing with high odds against us here. Not only is the area at stake, but my bounty.

[Once twelve members of the opposing force are dead, the Deathmatch ends. The winning team will have their race teleported to this area and will be granted a month to establish themselves before the losing race is allowed to re-enter the area. The losing race will be granted the opportunity to be teleported together in a single spot at the edge of the Dreadlands, and they will have a month to prepare an assault in attempt to take the area back.]

"Well, I'll be damned," Maverick said in his best cowboy drawl. "Looks like we've got ourselves a gunpoint showdown."

CHAPTER THREE

Old Friends

Two weeks earlier . . .

Max came into the High King's chambers with a respectful smile, head slightly bowed.

"My liege," he said. "Thank you for seeing me on such short notice."

King Durum stroked his beard. "My affairs are vast, and my time is short. But for a hero and a friend? I will always find a minute. What is it I can do for you?"

"I would assume you already know," Max said carefully.

King Durum's expression was unreadable. "Remind me anyway. It is the way of kings for their minds to be in many places at once."

Max barely stifled a scoff. He could see from Durum's face he knew why Max was here. "I was promised a reward if I were to deal with the threat in the ruins."

"Ah, that," King Durum said and hummed thoughtfully. "It was indeed valiant of you, my friend."

With that, the king fell silent. Max bristled. King Durum was turning more and more like his predecessor, who would play games and abuse his station.

"I am sure a man of your stature would like to honor his promise if I were to make an appropriate request," Max said carefully.

"Indeed!" Durum said. "But I should be a just king. And has this situation not benefited you already? You have learned of your enemy and dispatched all of them but one."

Oh . . . I didn't expect this.

Max had taken a two-day rest at the outpost after his extensive fight with the lizards. He was absolutely certain there had been not a single obsidian dwarf watching him when he chased the lizards through the ashen plains of Dreadlands. The king had slipped. He had been dealing with the lizards as well.

"A king should be as wise as he is just," Max said, watching Durum carefully. "Surely a few paltry trinkets from your vast hoards would strengthen our bond."

"Surely . . ." Durum said and paced around. Max could tell he was nervous.

"What did they tell you, Durum?" Max asked. "I know you're a good man and we have excellent rapport. You wouldn't toss away our friendship like this."

Durum sighed and looked at him out of the corner of his eye, as if asking himself how much he could trust Max. "They sent an envoy to stumble around in the ruins. My men found her and captured the lizard. She had a simple message from her leaders."

"Yeah?"

"Help us and be spared. Help the humans and be destroyed."

Max let out a mirthless laugh. "You know we won't make such an ultimatum."

"You are a gentler race," Durum said and spread his hands in a powerless gesture. "I am your friend, Max. But I am the High King of my people first and foremost."

"They'll betray you," Max said immediately. "You're better off fighting them than dealing with them."

"You don't know that!" Durum snapped. "It will not take long before both of your races are much stronger than any of us can dream to be. Even with the new knowledge of Cultivation . . ."

Max perked at this revelation, but now was not the time.

"You're going to have to take a blind bet anyway," Max said. "If you ally with humans, you give us strength, we take down the lizards."

"You have your own war to deal with," Durum said and gulped down a cup of wine. "You cannot promise me anything right now. They promise me destruction."

Max stared the High King down. "Pay me back, Durum."

The king cast a nasty, covetous glance at Max.

"Pay me back," Max said, softer this time. "And I promise to you that you will be fighting fewer lizards, if they ever come knocking down your doors."

Durum grimaced down at his empty wine cup, but he stilled. He considered the matter again and eventually relented and bowed to Max.

"After this, I cannot have you return here."

Max bowed back.

Durum was generous. He had given Max leave to study and choose to take with him any but the most incredible of his treasures. He said those would be needed to fight off the lizards in case of emergency. Max would be allowed to take four C-grade treasures or two B-grade treasures. On top of that, Durum had shared his new insights on Cultivation from the books Max had recovered from the ruins.

Max spent a long time examining the treasures. There were swords, bows, armors, shields, even wagons, which might have been useful had they horses or other beasts to pull them. There were Cultivation treasures, such as more pills and talismans offering boons. He had to consider them as well. In addition to all this were, of course, all sorts of tools for non-combat purposes. But it was combat that Max had his mind set on.

Now that they had an outpost in the Dreadlands and Max had a massive bounty on his head, he would need any martial advantage possible.

He considered his situation.

"Hey!" Maverick shouted. "*Our* situation."

Max was a [**Gravitician**], a magic-based Class specializing in gravity. He had a special gun to go with that. Max also shared a magical Cultivation bond with said weapon. So what were his specific strengths and weaknesses?

He was very mobile, and Maverick was starting to dish out some serious damage. He was also great at controlling the battlefield and his enemies with [**Tether**] and [**Gravity Well**] in particular.

But that set-up did come with an assortment of weaknesses. He was extremely reliant on Mana. That could become a problem especially if he wanted to use [**Telekinesis**] extensively, such as flying would require of him. Another weakness was his damage output against multiple enemies. Whenever doing so, he had to control them, switch targets, stay on the move, and shoot at whatever happened to be close by.

He was also very vulnerable. While his Constitution, Toughness, and Resistance weren't low anymore, he had no protective magic or equipment. If someone shot a nasty fireball or a well-aimed spear at him, a fight could spiral out of his control very quickly. [**Tether**] could keep him out of harm's way for a long time, but he only needed to screw up once.

Max wandered around and looked at shields, chain mail, and helmets of various sizes and shapes. Some of the items were B- or even A-grade. The A-grade items had some interesting effects.

[**Sabatons of Furious War (A-grade)**]
+11 Strength
+6 Dexterity
+10 Constitution
+8 Toughness
Special Effect: Wearer can activate the Mana inscription, [Relentless Assault], in these sabatons at the cost of 10 Mana per second.
[Relentless Assault]: Reduce the Toughness and Resistance of anyone attacking you proportional to your Strength.

That's really interesting. But it's of no use to me.

Max wandered around a little more, getting more and more disappointed by the lack of useful caster items at A-grade. Finally, he came to a little display table. Resting upon it was a soft red pillow under a glass dome. A ring crafted from translucent crystal sat in the center of the pillow. Max lifted the dome and inspected the ring.

[Ring of Light Bending (Special grade)]
Passive effect: When equipped, the wearer will become invisible if they remain completely still. This item consumes Cosmic Coins. It can be recharged.

Special grade, huh? That's a new one. I suppose they don't come with Stats.

Now Max fell in love with this one the second he read the description. With his abilities, he could get into some unorthodox places. This ring would not only allow for absolutely devastating ambushes but also easy escapes as long as the enemy wasn't aware that Max could turn invisible.

"What do you think?" Max asked Maverick.

"Not a fan," the gun said. "How exactly is it going to grant me more damage to wield?"

Max had no answer to that. He only shook his head in disbelief and took the ring.

After he left the treasure, Durum and Max exchanged a few words. There was a heavy tension in the air. Max was escorted out of the domain of the obsidian dwarves and he hoped he would not have to see High King Durum ever again.

CHAPTER FOUR

Taking Lead

The present

Wow," Freya said. "When I woke up this morning, I never expected to be participating in a Deathmatch today."

"What are we going to do?" Christie asked no one in particular.

"We have to act," Max said immediately. "We don't know how much time we have, but it's precious."

Max racked his brain. How should they go about this? Establish a base first? Scout the area? Secure food and supplies? Well, they had some in the packs they had just received . . .

"Okay," Max said, raising his voice. "We need to scout the surrounding areas. Christie and Brian, divide your groups into two. Christie's guys, go left in the direction of that forest. Brian's lot will go over those hills to the right. I'll see what's up ahead with Maverick."

"That's well and good, darling," Christie said. "But what do we do after that? And how far do we go?"

"Great questions," Max admitted. "Return once you get thirsty. Once we have at least some lay of the land, we can figure out our next move. If you see any easy food, like mushrooms or berries, make a note of that place and forage what you can."

If the area wasn't too large, they could use this time to pick up all of the most accessible food, forcing the enemy to rely on hunting. That wasn't a foolproof strategy, but it could be something.

With that, the groups dispersed, and Max headed forward, following alongside the creek which bubbled brightly, fat fish still jumping in the water.

That's a food source. But it's out in the open.

Max walked half a mile further toward a ledge sloping downhill. The creek ended there and pooled twenty feet down into a pond where white water lilies drifted amidst a group of large toads.

Ten yards away from the pond was what looked like a thicket of bamboo. Heavy steam from the outside world floated in midair between the stalks. Looking above, the steam formed a wall spanning a hundred feet toward the sky. That was the edge of the death match arena.

This area seems small.

It was supposed to be large enough to let all the humans in this area settle within it. Max decided he'd need a better vantage point to take a proper look.

"You're finally using that mushy head of yours!" Maverick said gleefully from his holster. "I was wondering how long it would take you to remember that you can frigging fly."

"Shut up," Max said.

Maverick was right, of course, but admitting that would have boosted the gun's already-inflated ego. Max could feel the smugness through their bond.

"[Telekinesis]."

The soles of his feet lifted off the ground. It was a slow ascent but no longer shaky. Max had accrued a decent bit of control. It wasn't smooth and he had never gone as high as he was about to.

Ten feet, twenty, fifty. Max's heart was jackhammering, cold sweat filling the creases of his palms. There was no wind, but the air far above the tree line was chilly. He concentrated his spiritual energy and Mana to his shoes, especially the soles of his feet, to push him constantly upward. The Mana expenditure was high, but he could stay here for a minute or two.

It was worth it. Now he had a bird's-eye view.

The area looked like an idyllic countryside postcard, apart from a few oddities, such as the bamboo thicket and a strange sapphire lagoon in the direction where Brian's men had gone to. He thought he saw squat shapes down there—maybe some beasts having a drink.

Great walls of steam or smoke rose in all four directions. That gave Max an idea of the size of the area. It would take an afternoon on foot for a group to reach from one end to another.

That's going to be a problem. The area is too small to hide properly.

"Bah, hiding!" Maverick said and made a spitting sound. "We're supposed to fight."

"Of course we are," Max said. "But I'd rather not lose lives."

"Max . . ." Maverick said, sobering up. "You're going to lose lives."

"The hell I will!" Max shouted at the sky. "I'll keep these people safe."

"Will you do it at the expense of all the rest of the people surviving outside this area? If you don't win this game by any means necessary, you'll be putting your whole species in peril."

Max had nothing to say to that.

"Look," Maverick said. "I know I have my moments of . . . flippant exuberance, shall we say. But I'm serious now. Sometimes you can't have your bullet and shoot it too."

"I'll try," Max said, steeling his will.

Maverick let out an exaggerated sigh. "I would expect nothing less, my foolish sidekick. I suppose I will just have to keep you safe. Now, what's the plan, smart guy?"

Max looked at his Mana. He still had three hundred left. He would need to descend soon, but he took one last look at the surroundings.

There were two areas of water: the lagoon and the creek leading to a waterfall cascading into a pond. Those were strategically critical. Positioning themselves next to a water source would make them an easy, predictable target, but going too far from one meant wasting time and energy running back and forth for a drink. They had very limited containers for storing water.

Water also meant game to hunt and fish to catch.

"The lizards will think so too . . ."

"What we need to do is ambush them when they come here and kill them immediately," Maverick said. "I can't believe you didn't think of that."

"They'll likely be a stronger fighting force than ours."

"Pfft. All the more reason to ambush them."

Max shrugged. He needed to descend, so he started to flick **[Telekinesis]** on and off in quick succession, so as not to gather too much speed when falling.

"You have a point," Max said. "But we don't have that many ranged fighters, and I'm not risking anyone in melee at this point."

"Then let's huddle up somewhere with our ranged fighters and pick off one or two," Maverick said.

Max welcomed the ground with an open heart. While he had full control of his spell by now, the idea of being up so high up in the air with nothing to save him if he screwed up still made him a bit queasy.

"Yeah," Max said, nodding to himself. Sometimes Maverick had good ideas. "We'll use guerilla tactics. I don't need to sleep as much. If we could raise everyone's Cultivation while the enemy isn't here, that would be a great advantage."

"Yeah . . ." Maverick said. "Yeah! Why didn't you say that earlier, you idiot?"

Max groaned.

"Let's say we have a few hours here," Maverick went on excitedly. "Everyone who is close to breaking through to the next Level should Cultivate, because that'd shave hours off of their sleep every night, which would buy us more time in total."

"True," Max said. "That was what I was thinking. But the time we have now is also more valuable than the time we will have later. We can establish concrete advantages in many ways."

"Hmph," Maverick said. "You should have said that earlier."

Max shook his head.

A deer with two of its fawn was drinking at the bank of the creek. Max deftly pulled [**The Maverick**] from his holster and shot the animals. He gained no Experience, so they must have been very low-Level. He went up to the dead beasts, produced a knife from his Inventory and bled them.

"Hopefully someone here can dress these. We should eat while we can."

"So, what's the plan?" Maverick demanded. "You have to have something before they come back, or you're going to make me look bad."

"Uh huh," Max said as he returned his knife to the Inventory and washed his hands in the creek.

"Well?"

Drinking from the creek, Max thought. "We'll prepare and eat this meat and everyone who is close to a breakthrough will Cultivate. I'll prepare a strike team for an ambush. We'll shoot and run before they know what hit them. Then we'll escape back toward the lagoon, where the rest of the group will be setting up a base."

"Fine," Maverick huffed. "A simple man, a simple plan."

"Love you too, Mav."

CHAPTER FIVE

Setting Up

The lagoon was a beautiful place to set up a camp. They had received some pretty decent equipment from the Zoos—namely, tents. Max decreed that they scatter the four tents throughout the thick bamboo forest near the lagoon. They'd be hard to spot in the thicket, especially after night. Max assigned Brian to take care of camouflaging them.

Christie and her team were in charge of setting their group up with food. They had to act fast. Half of their team went ahead and gathered berries, roots, and mushrooms. For now, there would be no time to fish, or really a viable way of doing so. Meanwhile, the rest of them set up a fire and dressed the deer and the two fawns Max had killed.

Max spent his time scouting the immediate area around the lagoon, where they would possibly have to engage in battle. He found a few natural choke points in the terrain where the enemy would most likely come from.

The enemy also makes plans.

They were facing killers. The lizards would have had the stakes explained to them as well; they would be told that there were twelve humans that they'd need to kill. The Grays would also make sure to mention and stress that a certain Max Cromwell was in this game, and the bounty on his head would ensure that they would do their absolute best. That high-Level [Trapper] would surely come and try to settle the score.

With a bit of extra effort, Max reached the top of a steep slope overlooking the lagoon. The air was rich and fresh, with a hint of moisture to it. Such a breathtaking place, unlike anything else in the Dreadlands. This was a strange world indeed.

"That [Trapper] could be a problem," Max said.

"Why?" Maverick asked. "Just point me at her and I'll shoot her in the friggin' face!"

"Simple gun, simple plans . . ."

"You know, it's much more fun when I tease you."

"I bet it is," Max said, allowing himself a tiny smirk.

"What is it with the [**Trapper**]?"

"She'll make night raids against their camp tricky," Max said, rubbing his chin pensively. "I wanted to use similar tactics to what we did in the ruins: attack them by night and not let them sleep. But even for me, their traps were an issue. And now they'll know what to expect. If we attempt guerilla warfare against their camp, I'll get people killed."

"You know—" Maverick started, but Max cut off. He could sense what his gun companion was going to say.

"I know. I can't think like this. People are likely going to die anyway."

"Good gods," Maverick said in mock adoration, "how did you ever become so wise?"

"But it's still a foolish move," Max said as he surveyed the area. There were still a number of moderately-sized hills to scale, which obscured the area, for better or worse. Above the hills, the middle area with the meadows and the creek could be seen clearly all the way to the other side, where the forest that Christie's group had explored was located. They would need a scout up here watching the area at all times.

"We need another approach," Max said. He climbed up the hills, steadied his breath, and looked along the creek some forty yards below him. Then he returned his gaze to the lagoon below. Max nodded to himself. Yeah. He had a plan now.

"We'll make them fight for every last drop of water."

Max had a plan. In theory. The execution was still iffy. There were variables to consider. The creek, while completely visible from one end to the other if one overlooked them from the hills, was a large area to cover. It was five or six yards at its widest and two hundred yards long. That made it a hard target to guard. They couldn't have people watching every inch. If the enemy decided to take water fifty yards away in a hit-and-run manner, Max's group could do very little to prevent it.

"Not only that," Maverick said, happy to poke holes in Max's plans, "the water falls down into the pond below. If they set up camp in the bamboo thicket to the north of the pond, they're in a similar situation as we are, sitting tight right next to a water source."

"Unless . . ." Max said, tapping his chin.

"There's no 'unless,'" Maverick declared. "You can have a guy keeping watch here and by the time you get the information back to the rest of the people, the bad guys have already had their drink."

"Unless . . ." Max said, now smiling slightly.

"And it's not just that. They're the stronger fighters, and the Grays will tell them that. They can just come and take the lagoon," Maverick said.

Max nodded. He had thought of that. It was a fight they might very well lose.

"Unless . . ."

"I swear to my cylinders, if you don't spill the beans right now, I'm going to misfire the next time you're taking a piss."

Max grinned. "You're right. Guarding the creek was a terrible plan."

"Ha! I win! Maverick said and hooted. "I'm the best. You suck and your plans suck and you're going to die and I'll be alone forever and . . . oh . . ."

"Mm hmm."

"Shut up," Maverick said. "So, you got another plan?"

"I do," Max said, pleased with himself. This would work. He just had a feeling. A flash of intuition.

"We're going to hide for two or three days. We Cultivate in the meantime and if they find us, we run and hide again."

"*That?!*" Maverick asked in mounting outrage. "That's your genius plan? That's so stupid. What will that accomplish?"

"We'll stick near the lagoon and defend it. We can't have the enemy drink from it."

"They'll just use the creek and the pond."

"That's the plan," Max said, looking down from the hill at the creek. Another set of deer were casting their necks down and drinking from it. Perfect timing.

"That's a *stupid* plan," Maverick said. "Listen, how about instead—"

Whatever Maverick said next was lost in the sounds of gunfire. Max had jumped down the hillside and started gliding down with **[Tether]**, shooting at the deer as he did so. He hit three of the seven deer, the rest fled.

"Ugh," Maverick said. "Warn me next time. What did you kill them for? You don't need more meat."

"That's true," Max said as he got down and started jogging toward the dead deer. He looked down at the water. Luck was on Max's side. He had killed the animals right next to a set of jagged rocks half-protruding from the streaming water, splitting it at the surface.

After producing a knife from his Inventory, Max cut open one of the deer, its guts and blood immediately spilling out of its belly. Instead of pulling them out, as was done for meat preparation, however, Max tethered the carcass on the jagged rocks that were half submerged by water. After that, he took off all of his clothes.

"Oh," Maverick said from behind Max, where he lay in the holster on the grass.

Max fastened the carcass on the rocks as best he could, making sure that it wouldn't be dislodged anytime soon. The animal was half-submerged, half baking in the hot sun. This was perfect.

Then Max proceeded to give the same treatment to the two other deer he had slain.

"We wait for two days, maybe three," Max said between grunts as he placed the carcasses against the rocks with their guts open. "And we make sure the lizards don't drink from the lagoon."

"Haha!" Maverick laughed. "That's genius. They'll be weakened and shitting bricks for a week after drinking this."

Max grinned to himself. They'd win this thing. And none of his people would die on his watch.

After Max got back, he instructed everyone to do their business on the carcasses upstream. He got at least a couple of queer looks in response. Max couldn't blame them. In his short tenure as a leader, this had to be his weirdest command.

But they complied, which Max was grateful for. It told him that his people trusted him, and in a situation like this, that was worth as much as their lives.

Next up on the agenda were fortifications. It killed Max that he didn't know how much time they had, but they would just have to do their best. They set up their tents in the bamboo thicket. With axes and knives, they cut stalks of various lengths around the area where they set up their base. Then the group lugged them uphill. The thicket stopped at the hill where the tall moist grass grew. The thicket would provide the enemy the safest route to circle to their backs. But it would also be the hardest terrain to travel in. Especially with Max's plan.

They tied up dozens of bamboo stalks in various positions—some vertically to obstruct movement and guide passage toward pathways where they'd set up sharpened bamboo sticks on the ground, some laid on the forest floor to create unstable footholds.

It wouldn't stop the enemies outright, but it would slow them down, maybe tire them and at least make enough noise for their group to prepare.

After several hours, they ate and washed by the sandy shore of the bright blue lagoon. There was still work to be done, but Max wanted his people to take an hour off to keep up their spirits.

The coming days will be tough.

Max chewed idly on a piece of deer meat and let his eyes rest on the water. It was shallow on the shore, deepening into pure darkness as the bottom of the pool descended toward the stony hill.

The water tasted and felt fantastic, which Max found strange. He couldn't be sure, but it was almost as if it had spiritual energy within it. It was cold as ice, invigorating and filling in the same sense a full-course meal would be. Idly Max wondered if there were treasures or other secrets in the water, but for now they had no time for wild goose chases or pleasure dives.

When they continued work, they had a few extra hands, since no tents needed to be set up and no food needed to be prepared. Max had three guys from Brian's group set up a scouting outpost on top of the hill. It would need to be manned constantly. The hill was perfect, as it overlooked any direction from which the enemy could attack.

Max fastened bamboo stalks with ropes of vine for hours until his hands bled. Maverick was silently Cultivating all that time. No Level-Ups popped up to cheer Max up, but it was to be expected. The day was turning into dusk when the Zoos representative showed up to hover in midair in front of Max and the others.

[The enemy has finally arrived. They have suggested a truce of twelve hours to give both groups more time to prepare and establish a base. How do you reply?]

"Huh," Max said and turned to his group. They were all looking at him for an answer. He knew instantly what to do, but felt it would be good to consult the others. "I'm no dictator. What do you guys think?"

"Maybe we should say no and attack them instantly?" Ned, a thin, scraggly man from Brian's group said.

Brian scoffed. "You're not clued in on what we're trying to do here."

"Your man has a point. Should we really give the lizards what they're asking for, honey?" Christie said and flicked her eyes at Max to see his reaction.

"The reason they want it," Max said, "is because they have a **[Trapper]**. They'll want to set up a minefield around their base."

Brian tapped his chin with a finger. "Not to mention they'll want to use the time to scout. A big downside to giving them a truce is that they'll find out where we are."

Max nodded. "You're right. Of course they'll find that out anyway, but we can't retaliate and drive them off, which could be a problem."

"They might also find our little piece of modern art by the creek, darling," Christie said and the people in her group nodded.

"But the shit and carcasses festering there for an additional twelve hours is a win for us, isn't it?" Freya asked.

"It is," Max said. "That's why I'm partial to giving them this truce."

"There's a 'but' hiding in there," Christie said.

"But there's no advantage to it," Max said. "I'll be around the creek harassing them, so either they end up chasing me around or they're forced to drink by the pond. That means they won't find our little modern art sculpture and they'll eventually get sick. Them being focused on me will also keep you guys tucked in here and Cultivating."

"I get it," Christie said. "If we give them the truce, they'll use it to scout freely. Now they're still going to spend most of their time laying traps and setting up a base, giving us the free time anyway."

"Exactly," Max said, a devilish grin spreading across his lips. "You're dangerous, Christie."

She flashed her eyes at Max. "Oh, darling, I might just be . . ."

CHAPTER SIX

Reckless Assault

The Zoos representative commended them on their strategic acumen and winked out of existence but not before telling them that the start of the game would be heralded by a red flare in the sky. And indeed, a few minutes later, a bright flickering red star appeared above them. It cast a faint illumination upon the high smoke walls that made up the borders of their Deathmatch.

Max had gathered his whole group in front of the lagoon. He stood before them, his heightened anxiety apparent via the palms of his hands, which had started to become sweaty.

"Why are you so nervous?" Maverick said. "It's not like you haven't been calling the shots this entire time."

"Yeah, yeah. Shut up," Max muttered. Then he cleared his throat.

"Okay, people, it's game time. Look, I'm not much of a leader, and I'm even worse at giving speeches. But you guys trust me, and I won't risk your lives just to be humble. I will lead you."

"Hear, hear," Brian said.

"My foremost objective is keeping you alive and winning this game. In order to have our best chance of doing that, I need you all to Cultivate. I've distributed thirty **[Celestial Illumination Pills]** to each of you. Now, Brian . . ."

"Yes, sir."

"You will be in charge of the rotations. We need a scout on top of the hill at all times. And someone awake guarding the tents each night. You make sure my name is on that list as well. I don't need as much sleep as you guys."

"You got it, boss."

"Good," Max said. "Here's the plan: you do your damnedest to Cultivate while I keep the lizards busy upstairs. I want you all at least in the Amethyst realm within the next two or three days. If you run out of pills, come to me. Only time you should take a break is to eat or sleep. I need your full attention on this. This isn't just for the lives of the people standing beside you. Every single human life is at stake. Are you with me?"

The crowd started to cheer and whoop. In response, Max simply thrust his hands forward, silencing them. They were in a live-combat situation now.

After that was done, the people settled in their tents, and the first watch atop the hill—tonight, that was Freya—Max headed out toward the creek. It was fortunate that it was mostly clear here, with hardly any trees. This would make it easier to see if any enemies approached.

"*When*," Maverick said. "*When* they come here."

Max nodded as he watched the plains. It was dark out, but with his Cultivation and the red flaring star in the sky, movement wouldn't be difficult to track. While it was likely that the lizards didn't have any Cultivators as high-Level as Max, it was still prudent to remain still. To that end, Max found a nice bush thirty yards from the spot where they had contaminated the water to sit behind.

It didn't take long for him to stir from his bored stupor, thanks to spotting some movement down in the plains. Four humanoid figures were approaching with hunched shoulders. Two of them were carrying spears, one a sword and a shield, and one unarmed. Max assumed the latter was some kind of a caster, because there was no way they were foolish enough to venture out without some form of ranged support.

"What do you want to do?" Maverick asked. "You think we can take them on?"

"Impossible to say," Max muttered.

He had fought a number of the enemy fighters in the catacombs single-handedly. But that had been a case of fortunate circumstances. Now, he wasn't facing a random motley crew of enemies who had simply stumbled into his path. These were the lizards' most elite fighters deliberately encroaching upon Max's camp. Furthermore, this time, he had no element of surprise.

This time, the lizards were prepared for opposition, and more importantly, knew how Max fought.

"See that?" Max said. "They're all maintaining a wide gap between each other. I'd be surprised if they also didn't deliberately choose fighters that would do well against our combat style."

"Which is?" Maverick said.

Max started his way down the sloping hill with a careful crouch. "I'm thinking it's hit-and-run."

"It's as Slasskenash told us," said the large lizard with the spear. He was walking at the front of their loose formation with deft, confident strides. "The plains are designed to be a neutral ground to fight for food."

"Most of the game seems to be here," a female lizard a few yards behind him said. "But where are all the humans?"

"Hiding scared somewhere," the unarmed lizard cackled.

"Shut your trap, Vesslakh," the one with the spear snapped. "What happened last time our kind underestimated the humans?"

"We have killed dozens of them over the last few weeks, Rasshas," Vesslakh said. "They wander around the Dreadlands without a care in the world."

"He has a point," the female lizard with the war hammer said. "Most of them are stupid."

"This is not most of them," Rasshas growled and stopped. He turned and glared at his subordinates. "This is the one who slew a dozen of us single-handedly. The one the Grays call Maxwell."

"I'd like to see you try," Vesslakh said. "You're the leader here because you're the loudest, not the strongest."

Rasshas snarled but turned to resume their exploration of the plains.

Max had crawled as close as he had dared to listen. He activated his **[Ring of Invisibility]** as soon as he could hear the enemy's speech clearly. Now he lay still and waited. He could feel Maverick's impatience through their bond. Max wanted to attack them too. But it was risky.

Maverick's pulse of thoughts and emotions was clear: *at least kill this guy and run.*

Max could fly. And after gaining a reasonable lead, he could turn invisible. Or close enough. He nodded to himself.

He muttered an **[Alter Gravity]** spell to make himself lighter. Just in case.

Then he let **[The Maverick]** rip.

The gun laughed in glee as it fired its first volley of shots, all aimed at the sword-wielding lizard's back and neck.

The first two bullets hit his back, evidenced by the flowers of blood that suddenly blossomed, but the lizardman turned with inhuman reflexes, his wide shield now blocking the rest of the shots. He remained silent, simply staring at Max from his slit irises, which looked positively demonic in the sky's red light. The lizardman banged his shield with his sword.

Max saw its mouth moving, but no sound came out. A bright light flashed from its shield, blinding Max. Only by instinct did he manage to **[Tether]** himself a few steps back to avoid the spear which now *thonk*ed to the ground before him.

Adrenaline rushed through his mind, but by now he was well aware of how to ride that dragon. Rapidly he shot in the lizardman's general direction, trusting his companion to aim.

"[Levitate]!"

Max lifted up in the air. Just then, a spear struck him in the knee, but he managed to maintain his balance. Even though his vision was still mostly just a white void, he could see that the spear had chunked **120** off of his Health.

Max produced a **[Health Potion]** from his Inventory and chugged it down immediately. Unfortunately, it did nothing to cure the blindness. That had to have been a status effect.

After a few seconds, his vision turned from white to blurry. It was enough. Enough to *almost* see some sticks and leaves swirling toward him in an almost dreamlike manner.

A whirlwind?!

It was too late. Max found himself being sucked into a vortex of air. He spun around inside it and watched his Health rapidly ticking down.

Max had no outs from this situation. No spell to get him out of the jam. He was too high in the air to tether to anything.

This had better work . . .

He threw Maverick at his enemies. Maverick laughed as he soared through the air and activated his ability, **[Semiautomatic Weapon]**. Max chugged down two more potions: one Health and one Mana.

Meanwhile, Maverick unleashed a deadly flurry of ammo at the four lizards, firing at least two dozen times. The echoes would carry far in these flat plains, Max realized. He was on a timer.

The whirlwind spell suddenly relented just as another round of bullets flew in the unarmed lizard's direction. Max fell and reactivated his **[Levitation]** spell, then tethered Maverick back to him.

The damage Maverick could have done was greatly mitigated by the silent lizard with the sword and shield. A glimmering umbrella of golden light protected him and the mage. Max shot at the barrier, but it seemed to have no affect.

Another spear flew at him through the air, but he managed to dive underneath it. However, the spear instantly veered and turned, coming back toward Max. Just then, another whirlwind started forming. He made a quick glance at his Mana. Only 250 left. Levitation was expensive.

The glimmering barrier faded, and the silent lizard pointed its sword at him. On pure instinct, Max swerved to the right and dive-bombed the mage. He let Maverick fire off wantonly as he flew straight as a board, managing to dodge the homing spear. It flew somewhere into the darkness, but Max tumbled to the ground, his vision flashing red. Maverick flew out his hand but never stopped shooting all the while.

Defeated Level 18 [Ishkarassi]
You gained 6,190 Experience points
Level Up! [Level 21 Gravitician]

You have gained +2 Constitution, +3 Intelligence, +3 Wisdom, +3 free Attribute points

What . . . ?

Before Max could string together another thought, he was kicked viciously on his side, and he rolled on his back. Before managing to even draw in a breath, the silent warrior stabbed Max's chest with his sword. Max could feel the crunch of bone and the tear of flesh. He coughed up a weak bubble of blood.

Everything started to fade . . .

CHAPTER SEVEN

Deus Ex Jellyfish

A soft robotic voice broke through the darkness.

[Halt. The Zoos Collective has noticed an infraction of rules.]

Max felt an aching pain. His consciousness followed it, as well as the faint voice. He wasn't done here. He needed to fight for his people.

A high-pitched voice seething with rage joined the first robotic voice.

"You cannot do that! That is cheating! This is all because of the subject Maxwell Cromwell. We will not have you bending the rules! The ICCB will hold a full Tribunal."

[There will be no such thing. We overlooked the Stat increase needed for this game. Did you not see how fast both sides caused lethal damage to one another?]

"Who cares?! You will not rob us of this, you damned machines! This is a violation of goodwill. The Grays formally request that you retract your latest actions. Comply or face the consequences!"

[Negatory. We cannot allow an irregularity such as forsaking the rules. According to statute 1-1-0-55-B, all of the participants should have had a 500 percent increase in their Health, Mana, and Stamina.]

Max was drifting back into consciousness and noticed that he was surrounded by a soft blue glow. To his great dismay, he saw that there was also a sword lodged in his chest. He couldn't move other than the slightest wiggle, and every time he did, he was assaulted by pain, so he tried to hold still and just breathe. That's when he discovered he couldn't breathe either.

Okay, I'm in some sort of weird stasis. Mav, you alright?

Maverick let out an almost heartbreakingly relieved pulse of emotions through their bond. That was quickly replaced, however, with a smug sense of superiority, as if he'd realized he'd let his facade slip and was doing his best now to cover it up.

"Fine! Let us abide by the statute. Both sides have lost a player. Therefore, we will grant the remaining players their boosts in Stats accordingly."

Max noticed that there was a heated debate going on directly above him. Over his head floated a plastic, white jellyfish, and above his legs, a small naked gray alien with enormous black eyes, livid with emotion, their small mouth twisted in anger.

[Unfortunately, we already prevented the death of our representative. So the game must be reverted to full amount of players on both sides.]

"Kill him!"

[That would be highly unethical. Please feel free to resurrect your representative.]

"It is already dead. Not worth the energy required for resurrection."

[How unfortunate. We will give you time to get an additional member back on your representative team, of course.]

"This. Is. Not. Over. You do not have enough veto points to survive this move."

With that said, the Gray cast one last baleful glance at Max and then teleported away in a blue flash, taking the rest of the lizards with it.

[Now then, Maxwell, we have much to discuss.]

It was as if something *clicked* inside of Max's mind, and suddenly he found himself as healthy as ever, full of energy, the accumulated fatigue that he had already grown accustomed to completely washed away. All of the aches that accumulated inside his overworked body were gone. Even the tired strain around his eyes dissipated, and his jaw began to unclench. Max felt so light he could have broken into laughter.

"What did you do?" Max asked. "Did you heal me?"

[It is only according to procedure, so that you are not disadvantaged in the upcoming competition.]

Max grinned but said nothing. With his Cultivation as high as it was, and now his body being basically reset, he knew he could go for two or three days unhindered before needing any sleep. The Zoos were playing favorites, just like everyone else. Max had no problem with that.

[You did an extremely foolish thing in attacking your foes in this manner, completely without support. We have saved your life once over this technicality, but it has cost us a very high price. One that we cannot pay again.]

"I'm sorry," Max said. "It was foolish. I didn't expect . . . Yeah, I'll do better in the future."

[We hope so. You dying will most certainly result in a loss in not only this competition but also a loss of lives for all the humans in this area. There is a non-zero chance that your death will result in the extermination of your entire race.]

"Jesus Christ . . ." Max muttered. "I don't want to hear that."

[Noted. Now, despite your advantage in combat prowess over any single individual, your team is weaker than the enemy team. You must exercise leadership and/or acquire additional power in order to defeat the enemy here. We have observed and approved of your strategy, but you need to do more. As for acquiring additional power, there are hidden resources in this area. We aren't allowed to guide you directly, but you are very close to one.]

Max nodded. He supposed he was grateful to the Zoos for all of this, and he certainly didn't mind the special treatment. But a part of him blamed the creatures for this sick situation the whole human race was in. Max wasn't sure if this was fair to the Zoos or not, but there it was.

[Unfortunately, even giving you this hint was just noted as an infraction. Please use the information we just gave you well. That would be the best way to pay back the veto points we have just lost over this matter. It's also a great way to avoid the obliteration of yourself, everyone you care for, and the entire human race. We will contact you later.]

"Uh . . . Thanks."
With that, the plastic jellyfish blinked out of existence, leaving Max to sit there in the grass, idly touching the spot on his chest that had just been pierced by a sword.

For all intents and purposes, he had just died. It had happened so fast. There was no building to a climax, ending on a classic crescendo. He hadn't received any warning. It had just happened.

Well, the fight was sloppy. In that sense it was predetermined. I can't just rush in and expect to win. Not this time.

But if that's all there was to dying, then what the hell? A bit of pain, and then he was gone before he knew it. It was much scarier in his mind than it had been as an experience. Minds had a way of blowing things out of proportion from time to time.

But Max still felt uneasy.

"There's still fear though," Max said and brought his hand from his chest to his navel. There was definitely a knot there.

Max thought about it silently for a good minute. Eventually, Maverick grew impatient.

"It's the pressure, you fool. You're confused because it's not death you fear. It's the consequences of your death."

Max nodded. "So much hinges on my ability. If I fail, hundreds, maybe thousands will die."

"And what about me?!" Maverick said indignantly. "Do you have any idea how bored I would be if you kicked the bucket?"

Max shook his head at that and took to flight. He needed to get back to his people and adjust his plans.

CHAPTER EIGHT

Preliminary Plans

Max had the habit of watching his Mana bar every five seconds or so while in the air. In some ways, it could be considered a nervous tick, but somehow he just wasn't entirely comfortable flying fifty feet in the air with nothing to slow or cushion his fall if he screwed up. Maverick teased him about the habit relentlessly.

Max found his Mana pool had indeed increased by 500 percent. It was *substantial* now. He suddenly felt a much-lesser urge to keep checking it compulsively.

"This applies to everyone," Max said. The speed of his flight wouldn't normally allow for a conversational tone, but Maverick could understand what he was saying through their bond. "That means that some Classes just get a lot stronger than others, depending on how they work."

"We definitely got the better end of the gun," Maverick said. "You can throw me into a fight without it destroying your puny Mana pool."

"I can stay in the air almost indefinitely, you dumbass," Max said. "Basically, this is a boon to all toggleable abilities, that otherwise would have needed to be saved."

Max flew silently for a while, then he stopped midair and just floated there, dumbfounded.

"What?" Maverick asked.

"We need people alternating," Max said. "I should have had them do this even without the Mana boost."

"Do what?"

"Exhaust their Mana pool, learn to use their abilities effectively. After it's done, they need to Cultivate until the Mana pool is full again. Rinse and repeat."

"Well, what the hell?" Maverick said, clearly annoyed at having not come up with the idea himself. "Why didn't you think of this earlier?"

Max got back to the camp and was pleased to see that the sentry atop the hill was already in place. He stopped by to greet two of Brian's men, a short, burly one called Trent and a gaunt young one with a sneer and cold stare called Vic. Max wasn't a fan of Vic, sensing he had a shifty air to him. But as a leader, Max knew better than to air his personal feelings. Instead he gave the two a small smile as he approached.

They had a short conversation, mostly consisting of Max asking if they had any ideas on how to improve the current situation. They didn't. Max also inquired about their Classes.

Something I should have done immediately when we got here.

"I've got a [**Brawler**] Class," Trent said. "Basically makes me effective with whatever weapon I pick up. I like it. Got this [**Power Toss**] Skill which makes whatever I throw fly real hard."

Vic had a ranged Class, [**Sharpshooter**], when utilizing a crossbow. Max could feel Maverick fighting himself through their bond. The level of disdain Maverick felt toward an inferior weapon such as a crossbow was vast.

Max nodded at Vic and Trent and instructed them to take turns in Cultivating while the other one watched. Max gave them a few more [**Celestial Illumination Pills**] and went off toward the tents.

He was happy to see that everyone inside was hard at work in Cultivation, each sitting in whatever position they found most comfortable. Freya was clearly having trouble as she was looking at everyone around her sullenly. When she noticed Max looking back at her, she quickly adjusted her posture and closed her eyes again.

I wonder if I gave out too many pills. If I had restricted them, they'd seem more valuable, and people would use them more efficiently.

Max didn't want to break the focused atmosphere that had overtaken their camp, so he decided that his further instructions could wait until later. Instead, he was excited to put in some work for his own improvement.

First, he would have to spend the extraordinary amount of Mana he had. He muttered the correct spell and was hoisted in the air by the soles of his feet. Max returned his mind into *feeling* the Mana as he tried to manipulate the spiritual energy powering his spell.

He was already rather adept at this, of course. He spread the levitation spell from the soles of his feet to his shins, thighs, pelvis, torso, and ultimately the top of his head and his fingertips, so that his whole body was wrapped around in a membrane of levitational energy. Or at least that was how it felt to him.

This allowed for much greater maneuverability in the air. But he hadn't developed it further. So Max found himself floating, backflipping slowly like an astronaut in space. First, he made the membrane thicker. That increased the floating affect, and Max flew upward. Second, he thinned it from his feet, which allowed him to right himself in the air and slowly drift down.

He repeated this and many other simple exercises as many times as he could. He was gunning for absolute control. If he had just been a smidge faster and his movements a smidge sharper, he might not have failed in his previous fight. Sure, he had been caught by surprise, mainly by the wind mage with the tornadoes, but with more skill, Max would have surely escaped the spell.

Eventually, his Mana ticked down to five hundred. That was as good a place as any to stop. It was prudent to leave a reserve of Mana just in case an emergency situation occurred.

"The absolutely mind-numbingly boring things you do," Maverick muttered. "I will simply never get it."

"Ah yes," Max said. "The necessary things to try to maximize our chance of survival. I simply don't get why I do them either."

Maverick huffed. "You could have had me do something interesting like practicing my skill in the meantime. I hate to admit it, but my aim isn't completely perfect."

"You could have Cultivated."

"Blargh! I need a break sometimes. I'm not a machine."

"Well . . ." Max said but trailed off after sensing a gust of sensitive emotion from Maverick. It was important to him to be regarded as a person. "I couldn't have you shooting around this time. These people need to focus on their Cultivation."

"Hmph!"

"Anyway," Max said, "off to the next thing. Sadly, even less exciting than flying for you."

"Flying is a lot less interesting when you're holstered away. I can't feel the wind you keep gushing on about, you know?"

Max said nothing to that. Instead, he sat down a few feet away from the lagoon and produced one of Durum's books. His translation ability called it "Insight foot," which Max assumed meant something like "At the foot of insight," or "the beginning of insight." In any case, he opened the heavy leather tome in his lap and started to further his Cultivation study. They had no time to waste.

CHAPTER NINE

Durum's Book

Max still wasn't used to being able to understand a book written in a language he didn't know. He looked at the squiggly conjoined letters, tracing a finger under sentences each of which was partitioned by a thick line before a new one started. Then, half a second passed and Max just . . . understood.

The art of Spiritual Energy Manipulation can only be pushed forcefully to an Amethyst Level by the most prodigious Cultivators. To advance to the Ruby stage requires particular insight. While a Cultivator at the beginning of his journey at the lowest Quartz will need to increase his understanding of the nature of spiritual energy—often referred to as Mana—for someone to advance from Amethyst to Ruby, an understanding of one's own particular Mana must be understood.

"Huh," Max said and repeated what he had read to Maverick, who, for his part, was serious and attentive for once in his life. Max continued reading aloud: *Every person has their own unique Cultivation story. A person who Cultivates with the aspects of fire, for example, has done so for a reason. Their personality, their tendencies, and the natural spiritual energy in their body has all led to the predetermined conclusion of choosing to Cultivate through fire. This means that, for a fire cultivator to advance, he must understand everything there is to know about the fiery nature of his particular energy. What does fire represent to the physical world? Scorching heat, immolation, and destruction, certainly, but the sun and stars are also made of fire and their power is that of nourishment. A fire Cultivator must understand all of this in their heart for their power to grow. That is their path, their Dao.*

"That makes our situation tricky," Maverick said quietly.

"It does," Max said, knowing immediately what his companion meant. "What the hell is our Cultivation aspect? Someone with fire has their meals fully chewed for them. There's probably been a great lineage of fire Cultivators and even if one can't find any teachers or books, it's still straightforward."

"Indeed," Maverick said. "But for us . . ."

"I've been increasing my general understanding of Mana. That has given me pretty great control over my gravity powers. But my path or Dao isn't gravity or weight or anything like that. It's [**Path of Divine Soulbond**]. Or is a path different from one's Dao?"

"Keep reading!" Maverick said.

He did:

Sometimes the path of Cultivation is more oblique, such as for a Cultivator undergoing a Dao of archery. What is one to prioritize when pursuing such a path? Accuracy? Speed? Calm? All of these are necessary. This is the way of any path. There are multiple steps to take, multiple insights to find. This is the path of Ruby-tier Cultivation. These lesser insights will propel a Cultivator to the greater realm of Ruby Cultivation. And to ascend to the greater realm, one needs to find their personal truth. What is archery to them? What is fire to them? So first, in the lesser realm of Ruby, one must understand the nature of the phenomenon of their Dao. In the greater realm, one must become intimate with their personal relationship with the phenomenon they are working with. Through this comes understanding of the forces and laws of the universe and the self. And it is not knowledge that is power. It is understanding. And to seek power is the essence of Cultivation.

"Well, damn," Max said. "So this isn't just manipulating and circulating Mana inside our bodies. This is more like traditional meditation. Less mechanical, more cerebral."

"We still have no damn clue how to do our particular Cultivation," Maverick said. "Too bad 'cerebral' isn't exactly your forte."

Max sighed and shook his head. "I think because of the nature of our Cultivation style, we should try to meditate together, and I don't know, merge our minds or something and try to find a solution?"

"That doesn't sound dumb," Maverick admitted. "But I wish you'd say it with at least a hint of confidence."

"Any better ideas?"

Maverick was silent for a while. "You could read further."

Max grinned. "Well, well, look who's suddenly a bookworm."

"Well, it looks like the book is more useful than you."

"That's for certain," Max said and laughed. "But you're a natural at getting into the rhythm of thinking and asking questions about the text."

These insights are numerous and frequent. Advancing through the earlier stages of Ruby Cultivation is fast and profitable. If one is still not at Ruby Cultivation, one will advance there within a single evening if directed properly. However it is noteworthy that before the Amethyst stage, an attempt at increasing one's Cultivation through insights would be futile. However, upon reaching Amethyst, one should immediately be able to transcend it with insights.

"Holy shit," Maverick said. "How? Hoodoo?"

Max hunched over the book, his eyes flitting as fast as he could take the text in.

The first insights are always the most obvious. They are flashes of understanding of the nature of the path a certain Cultivator has taken. These understandings will bolster the Dao. They will act as guideposts to remind the Cultivator of what is in accordance with their path. A Cultivator on the path of Vampiric Tree Transformation (which ultimately turns the Cultivator into a continent-spanning tree which sucks all the life force of a planet), will start his journey of ascension with the most simple of insights: 'The essence of my Dao is HUNGER'; 'I am that which GROWS'. The initial insights are broad and straightforward. The more clearly one can understand the end goal of their Dao, the more potent the insights.

"Well, I'll be damned," Max muttered.

"That tree business sounds *wild*!" Maverick said. "Maybe we could ask the Zoos guys to turn you into a tree. You would be so much nicer to look at."

"If they turned you into a tree, would that mean you'd finally shut up?"

"Let's be real for a second, Max. Without my sage advice, you'd be shit out of insights for good."

"Yeah?" Max said. "Name an insight for our path, smart guy."

"Gun!" Maverick said, gleefully sure of his answer.

No surge of spiritual power overcame them. Max simply gave his companion an unamused smile.

"Fine," Maverick huffed. "It needs work. But I'm sure 'gun' is the ultimate answer."

"I'm sure it is . . ."

CHAPTER TEN

Attempts at Insight

Max sat down cross-legged on the sand by the lagoon. He didn't push spiritual energy through his body for increased capacity. He just breathed in and out and let his mind still. It was easy enough after having practiced Cultivation so rigorously. The thoughts swirled in and out as Max gently encouraged his mind to mull over the problem.

He and Maverick were on the **[Path of Divine Soulbond]**. What that entailed was still anybody's guess. But there were inferences that could be made. Their Cultivation was intertwined. They shared a bond. They shared power. They worked together.

Oh . . .

"Cooperation and symbiosis are the north star of our Dao."

Max felt something in the core of their soul. That had definitely struck a chord.

"Nice!" Maverick said, but he piped down quickly. He could sense Max's annoyance and will to focus further.

That was good. That was a win. If Durum weren't such a complicated friend to have, Max could have kissed his bearded face in gratitude for the book.

But Max's insight also told him that cooperation wasn't quite on the money. It was more that he was irrevocably linked to Maverick and whatever their Dao entailed, they needed to travel that road together. It was more of a reminder that his insights should not be about *I,* but *we.*

Max returned to focus. He examined the insight and the feeling that came with it. There had been something wrong with the sentiment. It was close enough, but it wasn't quite that. That was an insight unto itself. It meant that the north star of their Cultivation should not be cooperation and symbiosis. They were important, but they weren't the defining feature of their path.

So, what is?

Well, Maverick was a gun, obviously. That made Max a gunslinger. A fighter, more broadly. Max's own personal creed was to take care of his people.

"My Dao is protecting people," Max said and braced himself.

Nothing happened.

Maverick raspberried through their mental connection. Max retorted with a shrug. It was worth a try.

"What might you be doing, darling?" Christie asked in her familiar posh tone and chuckled.

Max opened his eyes and gave her a quick smile. "I'll get back to you on that. Give me a minute. Oh, and spend your Mana. Or at least 70 of it, before going back to Cultivation. We want to Level Up our Skills too."

"Smart," Christie said and sat down next to Max, unsheathing a dagger she liked to use. She pointed it at the lagoon and the blade began to extend and retract. Max closed his eyes and continued on his hunt for insights.

Max considered what the book had said, that the more the insights were in line with any given path's endgame, the better the results.

Well, the ICCB was shitting their pants over me and Maverick.

What was it that they had said? Well, Max and Maverick's Soulbond was clearly something unprecedented. Whatever that was, the bigwigs were clearly genuinely scared of him. From what Max understood, the fate of humanity could very well hinge on him.

"My path is to conquer."

Max immediately cringed upon saying that. He opened his eyes and was not surprised to see Christie giving him a lopsided smirk. He felt his ears grow hot.

"You're distracting me," Max said.

"What a compliment," Christie said, her smirk spreading into a grin.

"Please never say anything so lame ever again, Max," Maverick said and sighed. "We have an image to maintain."

Max grumbled and closed his eyes again, doing his best to ignore his stupid friends. He returned to thinking. He realized that he had been making a foolish mistake starting his insight statements with "I" instead of "us." Their only insight had been gained through an acknowledgement of their symbiotic relationship.

But there was more to learn here. What was it they were doing? They had the **[Path of Divine Soulbond]**, Maverick was a gun. The ICCB was scared they'd turn into some kind of a monster.

Oh.

It was one of those things you knew was right as soon as you were struck by the thought. It was a flash of genius, a moment of Eureka. Something so simple.

"We destroy. We obliterate. We end existence."

Leveled Up Amethyst-Level Cultivator (greater) to 15
+3 free Attribute points
Advancement to Ruby-Level Cultivator (lesser) available
[Amethyst Meditation Technique: Elaborate Mana Cycling] → [Ruby Meditation Technique: Meridian-opening Cycling]
[Achievement: Ruby Stage Advancement]

Reward: D-grade Cultivation box

"Damn, right we do!" Maverick said.

Max wasted no time opening the Cultivation loot box. It contained twenty-five **[Greater Spirit Stones]**. As it turned out, advancement to Ruby cost fifteen of them. Max accepted the prompt to advance in world record time.

Advanced to Ruby-Level Cultivator (lesser)
+20 to all Attributes

Christie still gave Max a funny look, but his victorious smile made her expression change from amused to questioning.

"I had hoped you were gunning for something and not just doing affirmations," Christie said. "Seems I was right."

"You were," Max said eagerly. "This will shoot up everyone's Cultivation."

"Oh, Max!" Maverick said. "Can you feel it? This surge of awesome power. More! I want more, damn it!"

Max could feel it. These changes were *substantial*. It wasn't just the Stats he'd be more than happy to allocate soon. It was the indescribable feeling of *power*.

It was in the depth of his breath. It was in the flex of his fingers. Max directed Mana to the soles of his feet and hoisted himself up in the air with precision and speed unlike any he had ever experienced before. He flew around in the air above the water, idly dipping his fingers in the lagoon before landing back on shore.

It was done with such ease and grace that Christie dropped the dagger she was holding and just stared at Max dumbfounded. She had seen Max flying since day one, and while Max had already been rather proficient at it, this was something new.

Max grinned. It felt *good*. Also strange. It was difficult to pinpoint what had caused the massive advancement, but it seemed to touch everything he did. As a test, Max tethered himself to a nearby spot on the ground a couple of yards away.

Despite expecting it, he still yelped at the surge of speed that accelerated him into the spot. Ruby was no joke. With this power, he could have even fought the four-to-one battle, he was sure of it.

Let's not get cocky. We're going to stick to the plan and utilize teamwork. Who knows when one of the enemy team might reach Ruby too?

Christie finally collected herself. "Your affirmations sure were not for nothing. You'll have to teach me a trick or two, darling."

"Oh, I will," Max said. "I didn't even tell you about my little encounter. I have a few things to say to everyone."

"What encounter?" Christie asked.

Max walked past her and looked over his shoulder. "Nothing much. I just died and got resurrected when I fought the lizards."

Christie stumbled to follow Max. "You—what?!"

CHAPTER ELEVEN

Making Rounds

Christie helped Max gather up their little group and now they were standing by the lagoon, while Max ordered his thoughts. He found himself standing in front of an audience more and more often these days. He realized that his palms weren't sweating and his face wasn't flushed this time around. Max shrugged.

I guess I'm getting used to it.

There was a splash behind him in the water. Max turned but saw nothing but idle ripples a few yards away. No one else seemed to have noticed anything. Max took one last glance at the water before turning to his group.

"Okay, update time. First of all, how are you all feeling? Is the Cultivation going well? Do you need more pills soon?"

"I pushed up to greater Quartz!" Thomas, an enthusiastic, sandy-haired boy from Christie's group, said.

"Me too!" Freya said. "The pills are really awesome! Thanks, Max!"

"I got up to Amethyst," Brian said, trying to contain his pride.

"That is really good!" Max said. "You have talent. We're gonna need that. But we also all need to be Cultivating more, because the enemy is tough. I faced four of them in battle in the plains and, well . . . I died."

"Bahahaha!" Maverick laughed. "You idiots should see the looks on your faces. Ah, to have a camera now."

"You've never even seen a camera in your life," Max whispered to him.

It took a while to explain what had transpired in the middle of the arena, but the group got the essence of it. The enemy was no joke, and even if Max had ascended to Ruby, he couldn't shoulder the fight entirely on his own.

"That means we have to step up our game. They increased all of our Stats fivefold. That means five times more Mana. That means you guys have to practice using your Abilities, not only for the Skill Levels, but also simply to learn and to be efficient. So, from now on, I want you guys to use seventy percent of your Mana, then Cultivate until you've got full Mana again, and repeat. Is that understood?"

Everyone nodded. Max plowed on. The threat of getting attacked at any time loomed over them. And if they weren't being attacked in the present moment, it simply meant the enemy was preparing to do so.

And thus Max did the best he could explaining insights. It was a complicated topic, of which he only managed to scratch the surface of, but he did the best he could. He was the only one who could read Durum's book anyway, so his interpretation was the best they had. Maverick didn't always agree however, and kept providing the crowd with a lot of unnecessary commentary.

After everything had been said and done, Max let the group have a break. Everyone had been Cultivating diligently for two or three hours, and Max knew personally how taxing that was if one wasn't used to it. Their relieved expressions told him he had made the right call. Freya visibly slumped and sighed, and others around her laughed.

They sat down and talked about the insights people could use to advance their Cultivation as they took turns drinking water from the lagoon. It was fresh and sweet, and Max was even more sure now that his senses had sharpened that there was something mysterious and powerful in the water.

"Alright," Max eventually said. "Brian, I trust you'll keep the sentry rotations going. Other than that, everyone should return to Cultivation after using your Mana. Focus on insights, it will get you quickly to at least Amethyst."

"You got it," Brian said. "I'll go release the guys. Lou, come with me, we'll take the next sentry."

Max nodded and turned to the rest of the group. "We'll need food soon. I'll need three volunteers to venture into the plains with me. I'm not making the same mistake twice."

"You could have just flown away, darling," Christie said and chuckled. "I'll come. And how about you as well, Freya? And Michael, you need more action."

Max nodded to Christie in appreciation. Freya had specialized in ice magic, and Michael, who had a big crush on Freya, had chosen a water-based Class to have an excuse to work with her more.

Freya gave a friendly but distant smile to Michael's eager one, but Max had seen them practice together and they were many times more powerful as a unit than they were alone.

"Okay, let's see," Max said, looking at his three squad members. "We have terrain control and some firepower with Michael and Freya. I can provide air support and the main firepower, and Christie is an Assassin type."

"Darling, you make it sound so mundane," Christie said and smiled. "I suppose I'll have to show you how dangerous I can truly be."

"We are lacking in defensive capabilities," Max said, ignoring Christie, who made a pouty face in response.

"I'm a support-type mage, sir," Michael said. He had a dark shock of hair and a dimpled, open face. "I have a Skill called [**Water Barrier**]."

"Show me," Max said.

Michael produced a round disk of water in front of him which soon covered his body. Max circled around it, inspecting the spell. "Does it cost a lot of Mana?"

"Not so much, now that we have more," Michael said with a strained voice. His eyes were narrowed in concentration. "And look."

Max took a step back and Michael spoke another spell.

"[**Add Water**]!"

Not only did several gallons of water stream over to add to the mass of the shield, eventually growing as large as a tractor tire, but the grass in Michael's immediate vicinity turned brown and dry.

"You're up, Freya," Michael said.

This one Max had seen before. Freya flash-froze the floating water and then took control of the giant disk of white ice. Michael wiped a sheen of sweat off his brow.

Freya smiled as she worked. With smooth flowing motions of her hands, she controlled the flying massive disk, bringing it up and down, left and right.

"[**Alter Gravity**]," Max whispered from the corner of his mouth.

Freya almost stumbled and tripped due to the sudden increased ease in her control. She looked around in astonishment and caught Max's eye. He grinned. She grinned back.

With a spell called [**Control Ice**], she turned the disk into a giant spike of an icicle, at least ten feet long. She launched it with a violent swing of her arm and it flew in an arc a good twenty yards away, where it crashed into some bushes.

Everyone clapped. Freya bowed and grinned with satisfaction, while Michael managed an awkward smile.

It warmed Max's heart to see his allies pull off such powerful stunts. If they were careful and worked together, they would win this thing. But first, it was time to hunt food.

CHAPTER TWELVE

Lucky Shot

Max was feeling confident. He led his squad to the plains, walking in a line, each of them four yards apart from one another. Because of the smoke walls in all four directions, and the dark purple clouds and red star above, they felt surrounded by gloom.

Despite that, it was still beautiful. The weather was warm, and Max felt hot in the long dark coat he wore. He walked and idly brushed past a row of tall blue sunflowers with fluffy black bees buzzing around them. The grass was tall, bright green, and lush, and tall, rich trees which resembled old oaks were spread around here and there.

First, their squad checked up on their disgusting creation. The carcasses were creating quite a stench.

Then it was time to look for game. Granted, there was an abundance of families of small deer around, one of which was just about 150 yards away from them. Max fought the urge to take to the sky and shoot the animals. It would be risky. The enemy could very well be hiding behind a mound, boulder, or a tree right now.

They will likely also come here for meat. The area is designed for conflict.

Max stopped and motioned for his squad to come closer. They all crouched in the grass.

"Prey ahead," Christie said.

"I have a feeling there's enemies here too," Max said.

Michael swallowed and Freya nodded grimly. Christie simply waited for more instruction.

"So here's the plan," Max said. "I fly up, scout, and score us some meat. If I find the enemy or they find me, there will be two options. If I determine they're too strong, I'll distract them, fly in another direction, and start blasting at them. That'll be your cue to escape."

"Got it, darling," Christie said, idly chewing her lip. "And if you think we can beat them?"

"You'll wait here in combat readiness and ambush them, while I lure the enemy to you."

"Yes sir," Freya said.

"Maybe we'll get lucky and the enemy won't be here," Michael said.

"If that's the case, I'll grab the meat and we'll leave."

"That's enough planning, darling. Time to execute."

Max nodded and shot up into the sky.

He surveyed the ground from his vantage point, forty feet from the ground. He still felt a tinge of anxiety flying this high, even though the control he now had after reaching Ruby Cultivation was enough to make him 100 percent certain nothing bad would happen.

The day humans listen to logic and facts instead of their foolish emotions is the day we all ascend to become the next ICCB.

There didn't seem to be any enemies hiding anywhere nearby. Nor were there any huddling against the trees by the edge of the forest half a mile away from the creek that ran through the plains. Max idly wondered whether the enemy had already drunk from the poisoned water.

After circling around the few hills and mounds to check if there were lizards hiding anywhere, Max circled toward the deer and her two fawns. It was strange that there were no enemies around. Sure, the forest probably had food too, but something felt off.

Max shot a few bullets at the animals and they died quickly. He gained no Experience, so they had to be low-Level. Max descended beside the carcasses.

If the enemy didn't see me flying around like a damn drone, they sure heard those gunshots.

While Maverick's shots were significantly softer than any traditional firearm's, the terrain would carry the sound.

"Well, it's not like we can take those sounds back," Maverick said, peeved. "What else would you have done? Land on them? Imagine the mess."

"I'd rather not," Max said. "But I get your point."

"What now, oh, great leader?" Maverick asked.

"Good question."

The immediate option was to call the rest of his squad here and have them help carry the meat back. Max could make them lighter with **[Alter Gravity]**. But that held a risk.

"How about we try something creative instead?" Max said, a smirk forming on his lips.

Max started by making a pulling [Tether] between one of the fawns and a spot on the ground. Then he made a pushing [Tether] which perfectly overlapped with the first one. While nothing visible happened, Max could feel the push and pull of the spells. He released the pull.

The fawn's corpse flew up in the air in an arc, smashing ten feet away in the grass.

"What the hell are you doing?" Maverick asked from his holster.

"It works!" Max said excitedly. "I call it Operation Slingshot."

Max repeated the same process, but after the tetherings were in place, he concentrated. He increased the potency of the [Tether] concerned with pushing and the fawn was suspended a foot off the ground. Then Max increased the power of the pulling component, bringing their prized meat back to the ground.

"Wouldn't it just be faster to carry the damn thing?" Maverick said.

"Shh," Max said and brought a finger to his lips. "That's what they said about every good idea ever. 'Wouldn't it just be better to do it the old way?' Sure, it was better; until it wasn't."

Maverick grumbled at that but said nothing.

Truth be told, this might be needlessly elaborate. Max could have made the carcasses lighter and levitated them. But he wanted an offensive weapon. If he could learn to do this fast enough, he could lob boulders at the enemy ranks like a catapult. If they found where the enemy camp was, Max could bombard it from half a mile away given the right circumstances.

At least in theory.

Max managed to slowly increase both the pulling and pushing [Tethers] to a point where the fawn visibly trembled. Max took a glance at the upper right-hand corner of his vision. His Mana was actually draining more rapidly than when he was flying.

New Skills and all that . . .

He managed to make the Mana shift slightly and move the trajectory of the potential flight path. It would now shoot the carcass in the general vicinity of the hill overlooking their camp's direction. This wasn't exactly rocket science, and Max's accuracy was far from pinpoint.

He released the [Tether] pulling the fawn to the ground. It shot up high into the air. Max watched it soar. It wouldn't fly exactly where Max had wanted it to, six or seven hundred yards to the edge of the hill where their sentries were hidden. But it would fly a good eighty feet or so. This could definitely be used as a weapon.

When the carcass crashed into the grass next to the river, a shout of pain startled Max. Five angry lizards popped up from the grass, brandishing their weapons.

CHAPTER THIRTEEN

Enemy Contact

I t's him!" the tallest lizardman shouted. A plume of black smoke suddenly shot out of its staff, which Max instinctively dodged with a [Tether]. The plume hit a tree behind Max, exploded on contact, and spread into a cloud. Max got a whiff of it. It smelled sickly sweet and made him cough. He lost a few Health points and a green drop signifying a status effect appeared next to his Resources bars.

Poison clouds?

Another smoke cloud exploded near him, and Max shot up in the air. A tiny number two now appeared next to the green drop. Max had played enough video games in his past to know what that meant.

The poison stacks.

His Health wasn't dropping too alarmingly; it was currently at four Health per second. The green drop had a timer, which meant the effect would end eventually. Max estimated in about two minutes. With their multiplied Stats, that wasn't a problem. As long as he didn't get hit by multiple clouds.

Imagine if we all found ourselves in such a cloud for even two seconds. A single poison mage could fully wipe out a disorganized group that way.

"What's the plan?" Maverick asked, as Max pulled him and pointed him at the lizardmen. He fired a volley at them and, just as another poison cloud exploded and spread near him, Max flew higher to assess the situation.

He glanced in the direction of his friends. They had noticed the commotion and were slowly moving closer to the enemy, toward the creek.

"The poison mage is dangerous," Max said. "And we don't know what the rest of them can do."

"They think we're alone," Maverick said. "We could set up an ambush."

"Michael's [Water Shield] can counter that poison," Max said, shooting another round at the enemy as he maneuvered in the air. "I just hope the boy can use it."

"Listen to me, you goddamn nincompoop!" Maverick said, his voice unusually serious. "What game are you playing at here? Are you just going to wait until everyone is a Ruby-Level Cultivator? The only way we win this is if we kill the enemy. They might have the advantage right now, or we might have it. You have to take risks. We can't just huddle up in the camp and sing 'Kumbaya' and hope for the best."

"We destroy," Max said. "We are obliteration."

"Helllllll, yeah!" Maverick said. "Now let's show them what humans and sapient guns are made of!"

Max nodded and flew over his comrades. Christie nodded at him. They knew what was up. They all stopped moving and crouched down lower to wait. Michael and Freya inched toward the creek's bank, five yards away.

Just as the enemy were nearly reaching his comrades, Max flew lower, dodging another explosion of black smoke. He shot at the lizards, and a spear flew at him in response. Max wondered if it was the same guy as before or if they simply favored spear-throwing in general.

Max then pulled a risky move, flying over the lizardmen's heads until he was directly opposite from where Christie, Freya, and Michael were waiting. Max glanced over his shoulder. The enemy's attention was on him, their backs turned to Christie, just as she struck out, screaming and pushing a dagger deep into the neck of one of the lizards. Its own scream quickly turned into a gurgle. Before the other four realized what had happened, Christie had already vanished into the grass.

Max turned in the air and shot at the cluster of lizards. Seconds later, a great lashing whip of water struck at the enemy. Right before hitting, it turned into solid ice, then shattered against a shimmering golden shield of energy. The ice tinkled everywhere around as it fell. A black swirling ball of smoke flew toward Max's comrades and exploded right by them.

"It's him," Max muttered. He flew closer, now hovering only fifteen feet off the ground. Another lizard noticed this and plunged his hands in the earth, where they submerged as if the ground were nothing but a puddle of water. A heartbeat later, the grass beneath Max rippled, and he instinctively increased his altitude in response just as the grass morphed into two giant green, vined hands which grasped the air Max had just been. After missing him, they merged into one form again and then split off into five smaller hands, which shot out trying to reach higher in the air where Max currently was.

He swerved downward in an arc, but the hands followed. He tethered them all together like he had done to the **[Vilefiends]** what seemed like a lifetime ago. Now all tangled up and immobile, the whole plant-hand-monster receded back into the ground.

Another black explosion bloomed by Max's squad. But it was instantly stopped by a great wall of water, which solidified into ice. Max rose higher to see Freya and Michael moving away and closer toward the creek, while Christie crawled in the tall grass like a tiger stalking its prey.

Max flew down and back up like an attacking bee, casting a **[Gravity Well]** against the enemy. Two of the lizards were pulled into the spell, while the rest resisted. The stern one with the sword and shield cast a golden shimmering energy shield around himself and the spear-throwing lizard. Meanwhile, the mage managed to create new grass hands which held him in place.

Christie struck at her with a dagger, lunging forward with great speed.

A lance of golden light from the stern lizard's sword struck Christie in the side and she was pushed off-balance. The grass-mage snarled and Christie was enveloped in a mass of suffocating grass and vines. Max threw Maverick, who released a vicious volley with **[Semi-automatic Firearm]**, as Max descended to the ground in an attempt to help Christie with her spellwork. But just as he landed, a massive spike of ice crashed into the bad guys.

The golden shield bloomed around them, but the sheer mass of the giant icicle was too much. With a sound like glass shattering, the shield broke, a black cloud of poisonous gas erupted, and everything turned into pure chaos.

CHAPTER FOURTEEN

First Brawl

Max tethered the green mage to the ground, but immediately a spiraling tower of grass and vines sprouted from underneath him, elevating him into the air and breaking the spell. Then, hands sprouted from the tower, which Max managed to trap in a well-placed [**Gravity Well**]. Just then, a sickly sweet scent overtook him and he realized he was at the edge of a black poison cloud. He flew up in the air and *crashed* into the grass mage. The lizard yelped and fell into the middle of the cloud.

Michael rushed out, pulling Freya behind him. A spear flew from the side and Max instinctively tethered it to the ground. Its momentum was too much to stop it with a single spell, but it swerved and missed Christie, who was in a heated melee with the stern lizard with sword and shield.

That one needs to be dealt with.

"Don't miss, asshole," Max muttered and aimed Maverick at the lizard.

Immediately upon his firing a volley, a golden shield covered the lizard. The bullets ricocheted uselessly against it, and, when Christie attacked, she was tossed backward. Max knew she was about to be skewered with a ray of light from the enemy's sword, so he tried to crash into him.

A great green fist punched him, and he fell to the ground from ten feet. Max's vision flashed red, as he lost a good 300 Health from the whole attack. He threw Maverick into the air, and the gun laughed maniacally as it fired at the paladin-type warrior, who couldn't activate his magic lance under the barrage.

Another spear flew at Max, who was still catching his breath on the ground, but a disk of water appeared midair, blocking the attack. The shield was penetrated, but the spear clattered on the ground harmlessly next to Max.

The water shield crystallized into ice and Max immediately cast [**Alter Gravity**] on it. To his right, Freya nodded at him and hurled the giant disk of ice at the poison mage who was charging up another swirling black ball of smoke in his hands. A golden shield shimmered around him, but it was too late, the disk already clipping inside of it, so it shattered. The ice disk hit the tall mage dead center, and a plume of smoke surrounded him.

Then, Max flew up in the air, grabbed Maverick, and shot at the paladin. It shielded itself almost disdainfully, but Max immediately switched targets. A full volley of eight bullets hit the spear-throwing lizard in the chest, neck, and head. Its expression flashed from pain to shock to blankness just before it fell down on the ground, limp as a doll.

Defeated Level 19 [Ishkarassi]
You gained 6,490 Experience points

Max took a glance at his Mana. Dangerously low. But the enemy had to be running on fumes as well. They looked at their fallen comrade with blank expressions.

"Behind me," the stern paladin said. "Formation."

Max fired at the enemy, but they organized quickly. They abandoned their compatriot's corpse and got in formation, the mages moving behind the paladin in a steady march.

Max shot another volley, but the golden shield shimmered as it blocked the shots. Michael produced another disk of water, but he lost control and fell on his knees, panting from exhaustion.

The green mage gave a toothy, wide grin and cast a spell with a wave of his hand. A giant green fist sprouted from the grass and punched Michael. He flew back a few feet and struggled to get up.

Max took to the air and started shooting at the enemy, chugging down a [**Mana Potion**]. A part of his brain not hopped up on adrenaline noticed that it only gave a normal yield, not five times. It would only buy a couple of more seconds.

Max swooped overhead and shot at the enemy, but the shield turned. Freya shot icicles at them, but they lacked size and speed. Christie was panting and watching, sliding into the bushes to wait for an opportunity. Max knew it was up to him.

He cast a [**Gravity Well**] in the center of their formation. The mages were lifted up off their feet and nearly pulled into it; the paladin, however, managed to crouch in time and cast a barrier which completely surrounded them, breaking Max's spell.

"Michael!" Max shouted. "You have to move! Fall back!"

Max landed and shot at the enemy, but the golden shield was always turned his way no matter which angle he tried. He watched in creeping despair as Michael struggled to get up and took a few fumbling steps before falling on his face again. A cold, empty sensation washed over Max.

"No!" Freya cried.

"Fall back!" he shouted at his comrades. "Run toward the sentries!"

The paladin walked up to Michael with a calm sneer on his face. Max tried to [**Tether**] the golden shield, but it didn't work. He unleashed another volley, but it was in vain. Max couldn't take Michael and fly away. He wasn't strong enough. Not even if he cast [**Alter Gravity**] on both of them.

"Christie! Take Freya and run to the sentries!"

Christie wasted no time. She grabbed the struggling teenager and pulled her into a run, leaving Max to watch.

The paladin looked Max dead in the eyes as he extended his sword toward Michael. The boy had turned to face the lizards, and his expression was a grimace of fear. The paladin didn't even bother to look at him. The lizard only had eyes for Max.

"[**Light Lance**]," the lizard said.

A white ray of light erupted from the tip of the paladin's sword. It pierced Michael's chest, and the boy gasped and coughed up a mouthful of blood. Max watched in mute horror as life began to drain from his young comrade.

Michael took one weak glance at Max and tried to say something. All that came out was another cough of blood. Then Michael was gone.

The three lizards turned to Max. The paladin gave him a grim, satisfied smile.

"One for one, pink-skin leader," he said.

The tall poison mage started to charge another spell, but the paladin punched him. Then he turned back to Max.

"I am Losshnak," the paladin said. "Remember this name. Losshnak. Losshnak will defeat you here and make your race a caste of slaves."

Max said nothing, simply staring back. Losshnak hissed out a laugh.

"The Grays told us you understand us."

Max looked only at Michael and tried to contain a snarl.

Losshnak snarled. "So be it. Slink back to your camp of pink-skins. I am done with you."

Max took up to the air. He considered shooting, but it would have been pointless. And he certainly couldn't take them on in an all-out fight.

Just as Max turned, preparing to leave, Losshnak called out one more time.

"In case you were wondering, it was I who got the achievement for world's first Ruby Cultivator. I do not know how you attained your previous achievements before me, but this will be your short future: you will fall behind me and then you will die."

Max flew off and caught up with his two comrades. He made sure the lizards didn't follow them, and indeed they seemed to go home, following the creek to the north where it ended in a waterfall and a pond. That was good to know.

He shared a grim look with Christie. Freya turned to Max, silent tears falling from her blue eyes. Max gave her a rueful shake of his head. Christie and Max walked home silently, lost in their thoughts, as they listened to Freya crying.

CHAPTER FIFTEEN

Heavy is the Head

Max sat down on the sandy shore of the lagoon, just watching the water. There was a fire behind him where a haunch of venison was roasting. Max had gone back to the plains to gather up the rest of the meat with Brian after escorting Christie and Freya back to the camp.

The scent was alluring, and despite Max's high Cultivation, he was starting to feel pangs of hunger. Sure, he could push them aside for at least a couple of days without much trouble, but it was better to eat. He had made sure they had enough.

A heavy silence hung around the fire. Christie was hugging Freya, who was completely beside herself. After crying for a good hour, she had gone into a glassy-eyed catatonic state. Max needed to talk to her later if Christie failed to snap her out of it.

Max could hardly blame her. Maverick had tried a gentle probe for a conversation through their bond, which Max had shut down. He wasn't in a talking mood.

Max had gone over the fight and events leading to it a hundred times in the last two hours. And of course, in retrospect, he had found a hundred things that could have been done differently. His plans could have been sharper. They could have been more careful.

But he also knew that any plans or care got thrown out the window when combat started. There was an inherent chaos that was not for the faint of heart. All of the enemy were rugged battle-hardened warriors, hand-picked by the lizards. Their motley crew was a team of solid people, but they had simply stumbled upon this challenge.

He couldn't have saved Michael. He knew it. The only thing Max could do was to use this as a learning moment. He would have to do more. He was their leader. He would have to go all out, give every inch to protect and attack. He needed to take absolute responsibility. He could not promise it wouldn't happen again, but he sure as hell would do his damnedest to prevent it.

It still hurt like hell to lose a comrade.

Max hadn't talked all that much to Michael. Michael was no fighter and he was a shy guy, usually quiet in group situations. But Max had shared meals with him. Watched him walk around their outpost and provide water to all of them. He had been an ally and a compatriot. Not quite a friend, but in extreme survival situations, friendship wasn't the right word. He had cared for Michael.

And now Michael was dead. And despite all the rationalization, Max couldn't help but to blame himself.

"Look," Maverick said carefully. "Blaming yourself is a horrible cliché. We agreed that something like this would probably happen."

"Sure we did," Max said. "But I still wasn't prepared for the responsibility."

"I have an eerie suspicion this is a human thing," Maverick said.

"Uh huh."

"Look," Maverick said, "I'm not telling you to feel differently. I'm telling you to look at this situation honestly and critically. Do you deserve all this blame?"

"What blame?"

Maverick sighed. "The one you're taking on yourself? Usually I'm the one who gets to have the fun of making you feel like the horrible person you are."

Max said nothing at that. He only looked at the ripples on the lagoon's surface. He had been idly staring at it all this time. At no point had he seen anything come up. But there the ripples were, nonetheless. He wondered why.

"Hey!" Maverick said. "Answer me."

"What do you want?" Max snapped. "It's normal to mourn the death of a comrade."

"Sure," Maverick said. "But you're not mourning. You're *blaming*. Yourself."

Max grunted.

"What? Maverick said, his voice challenging. "What would you have done differently? Tell me, oh wise one."

"Nothing," Max said. "There literally isn't anything I could have done differently, short of luring the enemy away and not engaging in the fight at all. But we had the advantage of surprise tactics and, like you said, we need to fight. I thought it was as good a fight to pick as we were going to get."

"Then what the hell are you sulking about?" Maverick asked. He was clearly peeved. "Not to be an asshole but—"

"But you are."

"But you have a group to lead. For all you know, the lizards are planning an attack as we speak."

"We need to eat and rest," Max said. "And I need to grow stronger. That is my only regret. If I had gotten stronger than that asshole Losshnak, Michael could still be alive."

"We're stronger," Maverick said. "Or strong enough. As much as I am an advocate of wanton, indiscriminate violence, I do appreciate it when you think through problems. Mostly because then it means I don't have to chime in."

"Like I said," Max muttered. "Asshole."

"That is neither here nor there," Maverick said. "What you need is a plan."

"Need help with that, darling?" Christie came up from behind and sat down next to Max.

Max gave her a wan smile.

"Darling, you're so much sexier when you're confident."

"Really, Christie?"

She shrugged. "Look. Not your fault. You prepared a plan, made a call, and executed it well."

"Wasn't enough, though, was it?" Max said.

"Listen to me," Christie said. "I've seen you do amazing things. You've been nothing but a bloody stellar provider and leader. If half our people were as good as you, we'd have already won this."

"I'm—"

"I'm not finished, darling," Christie interjected. "Having said that, I've never respected you more than I do now, having gone to combat with you. You are sharp, in control, and dedicated. We literally cannot ask for better. But no matter how gorgeous you are, darling, this is a game where people die. I've known Michael since Day One. Good kid. Earnest. It doesn't matter if it was your mistakes or his mistakes or my mistakes that led to this."

"But—"

"It does not matter, Max," Christie said, emphasizing every word. "You're a good leader and a good warrior. In short, right now, you're a good man. The worst thing you can do now is spiral into negative emotion and leave us all hanging. We need you."

That kicked Max out of it. He perked up. One last time, Michael's face appeared in his mind's eye.

I'm sorry I couldn't save you. But I have to carry on. Thank you for everything.

"Yes, Christie!" Maverick said. "You did it. Yes! I feel energized too!"

Max turned to Christie, who gave him her trademark smirk. Max smiled.

"Thank you, Christie."

"Anytime, darling," Christie said. "So, what's next?"

"I'll decide later," Max said. "First, I have to talk to Freya."

CHAPTER SIXTEEN

Difficult Conversations

How are you doing, Freya?" Max asked as he approached her. She was sitting away from everyone, hugging her knees. She was wearing the tattered white jumpsuit they had all spawned in, on top of which she had on a yellow leather jacket that increased her Mana regeneration.

Her eyes were red and puffed up from crying. Max could read many emotions in them: sadness, regret, anger. Max wondered if it was for him.

"I'm okay," Freya said from behind her arms and knees.

"Liar," Max said and sat down.

"Nobody is really mourning him," Freya said. "We are supposed to be sad when people die."

"Don't blame them for it," Max said.

"Why not?" she asked and cast a glare at Max.

"It's not fair. Most people here have lost people. When I first arrived, I spawned in the wrong place and lost a whole company of my army buddies. I had known them for almost a year, and they all died in seconds."

Freya shifted. She tilted her head and looked at Max, curiosity now mixed in with the sadness. "How do you do it? How do you stay tough?"

Max scratched his neck. "Eh, I don't really have an answer to that. What I was trying to say is that everyone has lost people at this point. It's not disrespect. It's just that people don't have tears left to cry."

"It's awful!"

"It is," Max said. "This is an awful situation. But we have no choice but to push on. We didn't choose this. We just have to be brave and strong regardless. Can you do that for me, Freya?"

Freya looked at him, fighting back another burst of tears. She swallowed it and nodded. Then they fell silent, just sitting quietly next to each other.

"He liked me, you know?" Freya said after a while, looking at a yellow frog jumping around a few feet from them.

"I noticed," Max said and chuckled lightly.

"I didn't like him back."

Max really had nothing to say to that. So he just nodded back. Freya burst into violent tears.

"I can't do this, Max! I'm not brave! I'm not strong!"

"Shhh," Max said and pulled her in for a hug. "We're going to get through this."

"I just— How can I keep doing this? How can anyone?!"

Max sighed. He didn't have the answers. "It's just our lot. This is what anyone who ever fought in a war felt like. But this time, every single one of us is on the battlefield."

She cried for a while and Max held her until the sobs turned into sniffles. She looked up at him with pleading eyes. "How can I be more like you?"

He chuckled. "People keep thinking I'm amazing at everything."

"You are."

"I suppose I should be grateful to Maverick for keeping me grounded," Max said. "Uh, don't tell him that."

"My lips are sealed," Freya said and let out a little laugh. "Where is he?"

"Left him to chat with Christie. He's not the most sensitive, caring type. More suited for shooting and fighting. Granted, so am I."

"I wish I were too . . ." Freya muttered. "That way . . . Maybe nobody else would need to get hurt."

"You have a talent for combat," Max said. "I watched you. You were fierce."

A light lit up in Freya's eyes, and it was a beautiful sight. But the sorrow and guilt were still too strong to pull her out of her pit.

"I'm too weak without Michael," she said. "He was the one generating the mass and the force. All I have is control . . ."

"Well, you're an [**Artisan**]," Max said. "You being able to fight like this with a non-combat Class is nothing short of amazing."

Freya smiled. "You're good at compliments."

"I'm not trying to make you feel better."

"Yes, you are."

Max chuckled. "Fine."

"I actually got a visit from the jellyfish twenty minutes ago. They wanted me to change into a [**Combatant**] Class. They even said there would be no penalty due to the special circumstances."

"Do you want to do it?" Max asked, hoping she would.

"I don't want to fight," Freya said. "No matter how fierce I am."

"Freya," Max said, now firmly, "I understand you're hurt, but there are only nine of us left. The future of everyone in the camp hinges on this. I can't do this alone."

Freya was about to say something but was interrupted by two massive holograms appearing in the sky: the Zoos Collective jellyfish and a black-eyed, large-headed Gray.

[The second phase of the Deathmatch is about to begin. In order to test your ability to organize into a fighting force and your will to push yourself to grow, we have spawned several monsters in the middle of the area.]

"*These monsters,*" the Gray hologram said in a cold, listless voice, "*are tough. They will be aggressive on sight, have a high amount of Health, and capability to deal high damage. But as the risks are high, so are the rewards. These monsters will have an augmented loot table and they will give increased Experience.*"

[This is an opportunity for you to push yourself and grow further. View it as such. The survival of your species hinges on your ability to surpass your previous limits. We eagerly await seeing which side will outpace the other.]

CHAPTER SEVENTEEN

Change in Status Quo

What do you think is happening?" Brian asked as they ran up the hill.

Max grunted. He had ideas, but he wanted to think them over before speaking. Maverick, on the other hand, had an immediate answer as always.

"They're trying to spice things up, of course," the gun said. "They're tired of us lollygagging."

"I'll gag you with my lolly if you don't pipe down," Max muttered and glanced backward. Christie and Freya were running behind them, neither of them visibly unhappy with Maverick.

"Oh, come on!" Maverick said. "You know I'm—"

"Maverick," Max said, his voice taking on a darker tone. Maverick could sense that Max meant business this time, and so he shut up.

"What do you think, Christie?" Brian asked as they hastily climbed up the hill.

"One of the sides wants an advantage," Christie said. "It's clear that they're trying to rig the game. This was someone's chess move."

"It could be that they are just trying to accelerate the game," Max said.

"So you agreed with me!" Maverick said, clearly miffed.

Max sighed.

"Maverick," Christie said from behind, "the difference is the way you said it."

Maverick huffed. "If a glass of water spills in your lap, does it matter what pattern it makes? People are still going to call you 'pisspants.'"

Freya gave a choked laugh at that and Max shrugged to himself. That was as close to amicable as his companion was going to get.

At the top of the hill, Sandra and Erwin were on sentry duty, both from Christie's group. Sandra was a lithe, almost feral-looking woman with scraggly sandy hair, suspicious eyes and a bone-juttingly thin physique. She looked like the type that would be first to suggest cannibalism if push came to shove. Erwin was a teenager, maybe seventeen. His skin was saggy from the heavy weight loss that he had experienced since arriving at Alpha Ludus. He had a perpetual look of nervousness on his face and oversized ears. Max felt a bit sorry for him. Still, as their only purely support-magic-based [**Combatant**], he was an extremely useful member of their group. Max took another look at the timid boy. He wondered what had made Erwin choose a Combat-based Class. Regardless, it had been good that he did. While the boy was no natural fighter, he had a powerful Class in [**White Mage**]. It was a Class Max recalled having been offered. It had some healing spells and some buffing spells, such as [**Burst Of Speed**], which gave Erwin's target increased reflexes and speed for a short time. Mostly, Erwin was specialized in shields, which was good. Whatever could help keep these people alive.

When they reached the top of the hill, Sandra nodded at them and stared at Max expectantly.

"What's going on?" Max asked.

Sandra tossed her head at the plains. "See for yourself."

Max took a few steps closer to the edge of the cliff and stopped, his hands dropping idly to his sides. He was only faintly aware of his comrades coming to stand next to him in stunned silence.

"It's goddamn Jurassic Park," Brian said.

"Where the hell did they get *dinosaurs?*" Vic asked, and for once people nodded in agreement with him.

"T-rexes ain't gonna be our only problem," Sandra said sourly. "Look there by that big tree."

Max said nothing. He just observed. The plains that had previously only been inhabited by deer, rabbits, birds, and insects were now stocked full of megafauna. There were lumbering giant lizards on two feet, with massive jaws and muscular bodies, such as Tyrannosaurus Rex. There were also bigger quadrupedal dinosaurs with long giraffe-like necks grazing idly. Both types of dinosaurs were plated here and there in shining metal, like polished stainless steel. But that wasn't the strangest sight.

That had to be the *giants.* They were clearly humanoid but very ugly and extremely hairy, like fifteen-foot Neanderthals. Both men and women with dull looks in their eyes and sharp canines protruding from their lips walked amongst the dinosaurs. Some carried tree trunks for clubs and some of them had pouches at their hips, filled with rocks the size of car tires, against their ragged loincloths.

"It really feels like we're on a goddamn game show sometimes," Brian said and spat.

"What do you mean, boss?" Vic asked.

"You don't see it?" Sandra said and scoffed.

Vic gave the feral woman an inquisitive look, but she seemed to be in no mood to answer.

"Look closely, sweetie," Christie said. "It's humans versus lizard people. And now we got a field of giants and giant dinosaurs. See anything poetic?"

Vic grunted at that and pulled a black cap down over his eyebrows. He shifted the crossbow on his shoulder.

"What's the plan?" Brian asked, turning to Max.

"It's going to get messy no matter what we do," Max said. "We need an approach that doesn't leave us vulnerable and will let us turn the situation around if the enemy attacks us while we fight these beasts."

"Why don't we attack them when they try to kill these?" Sandra asked.

"Good question!" Maverick chimed in from his holster. "Because the most dangerous enemy on their team is this guy who makes giant protective shields. They have mostly ranged fighters, so their plan is to just stay behind one of those golden shields and shoot stuff down."

People looked at Max for confirmation and he nodded idly, still looking at the field. Some of the giants had noticed them but had not yet acted upon it. It seemed like all of these new creatures stayed on the other side of the creek for some reason. The enemy was nowhere to be seen yet.

"W-what's our best course of action? Erwin asked, wringing his hands.

"Christie and Brian lead their respective groups, while I provide air support," Max said.

"What are we waiting for?" one of Brian's men grumbled. Max didn't know if he went by any other name than Jones. He was a bear of a man, with piercing eyes and a broad, hairy physique. He was currently wielding two great battleaxes. He always seemed to harbor a certain hostility toward Max. But Max had seen him fight. He was a fiend on the battlefield, and Max was glad the brute was with them.

"I want to see where the enemy is going to come from and what they're planning on doing."

"Why not fly and check up on them?" Sandra asked. "They have no way of bringing you down."

Max was about to respond but then shut his mouth before saying, "You know, I think I should listen to you more often."

Sandra flashed a grin at him. "Maybe you should."

"Okay, I will go check up on what our dear scaly friends are doing," Max said, then activated **[Levitate]** and rose two feet in the air. "Brian, you're in charge. I think you can safely attack something in this corner of the plains. The enemy won't be able to stroll up and disrupt you. Especially with me in the air."

"Got it," Brian said.

"And Christie," Max said, turning to the posh woman and her ever-present smirk, "you make sure you guys are careful about this. I don't want any casualties. But we do need these resources."

"Don't worry, darling," Christie said. "Brian and I are starting to reach an understanding."

Brian scoffed and gave Max a two-finger salute. "Go."

Max nodded and soared in the air.

CHAPTER EIGHTEEN

Something Poetic

There were dozens and dozens of creatures scattered among the plains. It seemed like the giants and dinosaurs didn't even see each other, because otherwise they surely would have attacked each other by now. Max was a good fifty feet in the air, well out of reach of all except for the tallest of those lumbering giraffe-necked dinosaurs. One of them looked at Max with dull eyes as it masticated.

Max had to stop and stare at it. After all, it was a frigging *dinosaur*! It let out a low grumble and snorted. Its breath smelled sour and the air from its nose came out in a gust that blasted Max backward. It was an awesome beast in every sense of the word.

How the hell are we supposed to bring something like this down?

"I wonder if we are," Maverick said.

"What do you mean?" Max said, tearing his eyes off the giant beast and continuing forward in the air.

"There are those big brutes that look like you, but somehow even uglier," Maverick said. "And there are these monsters that are literally half teeth. Look at those tiny little hands. Why do they have baby hands, Max?"

"So you're saying these big dinos are a neutral party? Or a distraction?"

"I'm sure there's a high reward for someone foolish enough to attack them," Maverick said. "I think they're just a random factor thrown in. They'll make things more chaotic when spells hit them and they start trampling anything that displeases them."

"We'll keep that in mind," Max said. "It could work both ways."

"More useful to us, methinks," Maverick said. "We got more offensive capabilities, they got more defensive abilities."

"I think all of their fighters are more skilled than ours, barring us," Max said glumly. "We got Jones. Brian and Christie are good, but not that good."

"I alone shall make up the difference," Maverick said, harrumphing. "I've been thinking about our insights lately, when you've been busy."

"And?" Max asked with mounting interest.

"And I have nothing."

"Uh . . . Keep thinking?"

"Oh, no," Maverick said. "It was more of a letting you know I tried and failed and can't be bothered to try again."

"Great . . ." Max said.

"Look," Maverick said, eager to switch the subject. "It's the enemy!"

Indeed, a tight formation of lizards was just then climbing up a slope next to the creek. At their helm was Losshnak, who immediately caught sight of Max in the air above. Max shot a few bullets down at them, but the paladin's golden shield was covering their formation like a tortoise's shell.

"At least now we know where their camp is," Max said as he flew higher, ignoring the bite of the cold air.

"They have definitely been drinking your toxic water," Maverick said gleefully.

"They have," Max said, satisfied that at least something had worked in their favor. "That means it's only a matter of time before they get sick."

"Here's an interesting thought," Maverick said. "You think you could drink that water?"

"No, I . . ."

Through their bond, Maverick smirked at Max. "You realized it, didn't you?"

"Crap," Max said. "Was it all a waste?"

"Well, it certainly won't make them better or stronger," Maverick said. "It wasn't that much effort, so I'd say it was worth a try. But yeah, they'll all be at least Amethyst-Level Cultivators, so the chances of them getting sick from dirty water are probably low."

With Cultivation came many benefits to the body. Max especially enjoyed the need for less sleep. But there were other boons, such as needing less food and water than before. Fatigue was also something that came slower and could be more easily ignored. Senses were heightened, reflexes faster, the body's accuracy greatly improved. And yes, more full of vitality and fortitude. That also meant a higher resistance to poisons, toxins, or anything like it.

Max cast an angry glance at the golden shield above the lizards. Losshnak for sure wouldn't get sick with his Ruby Cultivator's body.

The team of lizards watched Max and talked to each other. Twice, Losshnak lowered the glimmering golden shield, and twice Max released an immediate barrage at them. Their wind mage whipped up gusts and tornadoes, but with Max's high altitude and Ruby Cultivation, he easily dodged their attacks.

"We could just do this, right?" Maverick asked. "I mean, it's boring but effective. They'll have to think twice about attacking the creatures because we're a constant threat."

"While true, I worry about the team's ability to bring these giant creatures down without us," Max said.

"Gah," Maverick said. "They are pretty useless, aren't they?"

"Don't say that," Max said, but a darker part of him did agree. Maverick smugly remarked on that through their bond. "We've had fortunate circumstances."

"We should create some more," Maverick said.

Max watched the enemy team advancing toward a T-rex. They still had a shimmering turtle shell above them. Max flew downward and tried to get a few shots in, but that resulted in him getting in the wind mage's range, and he soon had to fly up again in retreat.

I wish my spells didn't have such a short range. If I could disrupt them, I could really wreak some havoc.

"It would be awesome if we could drop rocks on them, but you're pretty useless apart from your ability to carry me around too," Maverick said.

Max knew throwing rocks with his telekinetic abilities would be a great offensive addition to his fighting kit, but right now he didn't see how it would be possible, especially while maintaining flight.

Max watched the enemy fight. The T-rex was enveloped in a black cloud of smoke, which was held in place by the wind mage. Spears flew at the smoke cloud and the T-rex roared in anger. But when it tried to charge the enemy formation, great green hands swarmed around its legs, toppling it to the ground. That's when two melee fighters charged from the group to attack the fallen dinosaur. Max immediately unleashed a barrage at them and clipped one of them badly. The other lizard had been using two swords when two of Maverick's bullets hit him in the shoulder and arm, making it go limp. He dropped his weapons and then quickly retreated under the golden dome.

That will heal up with a potion, but it's something.

"I don't think we're slowing them down enough," Max said. "We should head back and help the group with kills."

Max was very pleased to see that his group was in the process of felling a T-rex of their own. Jones was at the front redirecting the jaw snaps of the terrible beast with his axes. Christie was slipping in and out between the beast's feet, slicing at its tendons.

Brian, whose choice of weapon was a short blade on a rope he had gotten from one of the monsters in the Dreadlands, was fighting at the front. He spun the weapon above his head and whipped it at the T-rex's face every time it tried to snap at Jones.

Sandra had a unique power. She turned into a cat-human hybrid, transforming her hands into long sharp claws. Her legs also grew more muscular in the transformation, which allowed her to bob and weave between the beast's legs with Christie.

Meanwhile, Freya, Vic, Erwin, and Trent were the ranged support. Trent was using a bow, which Maverick always made a snide comment about whenever he had the chance. Trent didn't much like Max.

Vic was using a self-reloading crossbow that was actually a quite rare and lucky drop from a **[Local Boss]** Brian's group had killed two weeks ago. Freya shot icicles at the T-rex's face, clearly targeting the eyes. And Erwin was using his support magic to boost the agility, endurance, and strength of their frontliners.

It's a lot messier than what the lizards are doing. But you can't argue with results.

The lizards were like a tactical group of Roman legionnaires—efficient, organized, and disciplined in their tortoise formation. By comparison, the human group was like a band of feral barbarians. Scattered, each doing their own thing, but through some ineffable cohesion, working together in perfect sync.

And it was the barbarians that brought down the Romans. I'll make sure history repeats itself here.

"Do you often think of the Roman Empire?" Maverick asked.

"More often than you'd think," Max remarked. "Come, let's join the fight."

CHAPTER NINETEEN

Teamwork

Defeated Level 26 [Tyrant Saurus (Elite)]
You gained 3,096 Experience points

"Oh damn, that's a fat drop," Sandra said.

"How much did you get?" Max asked. "I joined the fun late and only got a little over three thousand."

"I got twenty-two hundred," Brian said.

"Pretty much same," Sandra said and grinned.

"Thirty-four hundred," Jones said and hefted a bloody axe on his shoulder. People whistled at that, and the big man looked pleased.

"My, my," Christie said as she crouched by the corpse. "I hope we can trade these **Cosmic Coins**. I accidentally just looted fifteen-thousand worth!"

"Holy crap," Max said. "If we can't trade coins, maybe we can trade Items to you that are worth upgrading."

"Let's look into that, darling," Christie said. "There's also a [**Composite Bow of Precision**] in here."

"Nice," Vic said and moved to loot the bow.

"And then there's these . . . pills," Christie said.

"Cultivation pills?" Max asked excitedly and came closer.

"No," Christie said and gave Max one. Max raised an eyebrow. He took the pill and inspected it.

[Special Grade Framework Enhancement Pill]
Effect: Grants 5,000 Experience points when consumed

"Damn . . ." Max muttered. "How many are there?"
"Thirty."

"Not bad."

"What does it do?" Vic asked.

"Can I see?" Erwin chimed in.

"Show me," Brian said and took the pill from Max.

Max gave it to Brian. These—along with the new bow and the Experience drops—would be extremely useful. And who knew what other goodies they'd find there? Max straightened himself and looked at their surroundings.

"You're never satisfied, are you?" Freya asked and gave Max a little smile. "It's just your nature, I think."

"Huh? Max said. "What do you mean?"

"Instead of celebrating like everyone else, you're already looking for the next thing."

Max chuckled. "Oh, that. I'm very happy. Exceedingly so. These rewards are *very* valuable. But this is a race. I saw the enemy fight. They are not wasting any time."

"Then we shouldn't either," Brian said.

"Right," Max said. "This is going to sound unfair to some of you, but this is what we'll do. Jones, Brian, Christie, and Erwin will get the major share of these pills for now. Once they have a few more Levels under their belts, with preferably at least one or two of them hitting twenty, we'll distribute the rest more fairly. Is that alright?"

There was some grumbling, especially by Vic and Trent, but Brian gave them a few sharp words and they seemed to fall in line.

"Eat them quickly and put your new Stats in fast," Max said. "I saw the enemy, and they are efficient. Let's attack that one by the foot of the hill. I'll lure it here."

With that, Max soared in the air and flew toward the closest T-rex. He vowed to be relentless. Their teams were evenly matched and this race for resources could very well determine the fate of the whole human race. Max would do his damnedest to make sure they had the best chance of victory.

Max flew near the metal-plated monstrosity and unleashed a barrage, targeting the beast's eyes. Some of them hit, and the monster roared in fury and started charging at Max, who stayed a good distance away, flying back toward his group.

With Max helping, the kill was smooth and fast. Max circled around the monster's head, peppering it with shots as Maverick laughed gleefully. The T-rex tromped around, trying to take a bite out of Max, who always managed to stay just a little too far out of its reach. Eventually the damage the group did to its legs caused it to crash to the ground; after that, it was an easy kill.

Defeated Level 27 [Tyrant Saurus (Elite)]
You gained 11,800 Experience points

Level Up! [Level 22 Gravitician] You have gained + 2 Constitution, + 3 Intelligence, + 3 Wisdom, + 3 free Attribute points

Damn. That was a heavy drop.

"Aw, shucks," Freya said.

"Yeah," Christie said and let out a low chuckle. "But it was easier."

"Huh?" Max said as he descended. "What do you mean?"

"It's not that we don't appreciate the help, darling," Christie said. "But you did hog all the Experience just now."

Max rubbed the back of his head and tried to stammer out some apologies. It was met with good humor. After all, the kill had been easy and fast.

Would it be better for morale if I hunt solo and let the rest of them kill these on their own? I could swoop around and harass the enemy a bit. Stay mobile.

While Max contemplated his options, the rest of the group reveled in the loot. This time, they found a purple-bladed dagger with a glowing hue. It was a C-grade item, and Christie did a little dance as she picked it up.

"It has so many Stats!" she squealed. "And an effect. I have to try this. It's perfect for me! But I don't know how to activate it. Max?"

"Uh?" Max said and turned to his lieutenant who was waving her new dagger excitedly. "Congratulations! Looks good on you."

"I do love a compliment," she said and grinned. "But how do I activate it?"

"I've never had an active Item before," Max admitted. "I'd start by pouring Mana into it."

"What? How do I do that?"

"Just . . ." Max said, choosing his words precisely. "It's like Cultivation. Guide your spiritual power from your body to your hands and from there, into the dagger.

"Oh!" Christie said and flinched. "I think it worked. Anyone want to be my guinea pig?"

Suddenly the space around Christie widened.

"Spoilsports."

After another T-rex kill, the party was now really excited. They found fifty **[Greater Mana Potions]** and twenty **[Greater Health Potions]** inside the next one. And another fifteen thousand **Cosmic Coins**, which were given to Max this time. He was still getting the lion's share of the Experience, but because of the **[Special Grade Framework Enhancement Pill]** being either a guaranteed or at least a very common drop, no one was complaining.

As they were divvying up the potions, Max wondered how he should use the **Cosmic Coins.**

"I can't believe I have to bring this up again," Maverick said. "Do you really need to think?"

"I like making good choices."

"Not that I'm making any comparisons," Maverick said. "but apparently some holy dude in your history said something like *I am the way.*"

"Did you just . . . ?" Max asked, but stopped himself and rubbed his face instead.

"All I'm saying is that I'm the most exciting choice. *And* the most efficient."

"I've heard this argument before."

"You're going to replace all those filthy rags eventually," Maverick said. "Better things will come along. But not a better weapon. Everything is replaceable, but not I. For I am the best. I am eternal. I AM THE END. I AM THE ANSWER!"

His voice rose to megalomaniacal levels and startled Erwin, who almost dropped the Health potions he'd received from Christie.

"Mighty Marduk, grant me patience," Max muttered under his breath.

"Imagine," Maverick said, taking a more serious tone, while not losing any of the smugness, "if you just immediately agreed to give me the coins. There need not be such embarrassments in the future."

"Freya, help," Max said, turning to her as she chugged down a Mana potion. "I'm in an abusive relationship."

"Well, I'm no relationship expert," she said. "But I think the only thing you can do in an abusive relationship is to leave it."

"What if you're bound for life by a magical oath?"

Freya gave Max an apologetic smile. "Ever hear the term 'shit out of luck?'"

Max groaned. "What would you do?"

"Me?" Freya asked. "Just give him the damn coins."

"But then he wins."

"If you don't, you lose."

"Yeah, that's kind of the dynamic of an abusive relationship," Max said.

"I'm not abusive," Maverick said, aghast. "I'm just using my own special means of persuasion."

Max sighed, but Freya just laughed. She settled into a low chuckle before the glassy, empty look returned to her eyes. Max put a hand on her shoulder and squeezed. He had managed to take her mind off Michael at least for a moment. That was good enough.

CHAPTER TWENTY

Helping the Crew

After another T-rex kill, Max Leveled Up. Between that and getting another pile of **Cosmic Coins**, he wanted everyone to take a break and settle their Attributes. The work would be faster and safer if everyone had their Stats as maxed out as possible. Max divided his free Attribute points evenly between Wisdom and Intelligence. The extra Mana regeneration would be nice.

Name: Max Cromwell
Cultivation stage: Ruby (lesser)
Class: Gravitician Level: 22
Health: 6,000/6,000
Stamina: 6,000/6,000
Mana: 7,100/7,100
Alliance: Joshua's Group
Stats:
Strength: 45
Dexterity: 50
Constitution: 120
Intelligence: 142
Wisdom: 110
Charisma: 44
Precision: 70
Toughness: 60
Resistance: 70

"Do it!" Maverick demanded. "Do it. Do it. Do it."
Max poured his **Cosmic Coins** into his companion, Leveling him up.

[25600 Cosmic Coins spent]
[The Maverick] upgraded to +8
+18 Intelligence
+11 Precision

"Yessssss. Give it to me, baby."

Sandra snorted next to Max.

"He's a handful, eh?"

"You don't know the half of it," Max muttered. "How's your haul?"

"Great," she said. "Got to Level Twenty."

"Big Level," Max said.

"What should I choose?" Sandra asked and scratched her arm.

Is she embarrassed?

"Did you get the spiel from our great jelly overlords?" Max asked.

"Yeah. 'Choose one ability that will define the rest of your life,'" Sandra said. "No sweat."

Max chuckled. "It's not so bad. Just make a choice and roll with it."

"Didn't think I'd hear that from you, Mr. Optimal."

"I'm me and you're you," Max said and sat down, pulling Maverick out of his holster and putting him on his lap. "What do you want to do?"

"Kill the damn lizards and have a nice meal."

Max offered a thin smile.

Sandra grunted. "I'm not used to making these kinds of decisions. I don't want to be dead weight."

"You're already useful," Max said. "And you're going to be even more useful no matter what you choose."

Sandra squinted at him, as if trying to determine if he was being sincere. Max just shrugged.

"Hmph. Fine. I have **[Jaguar Step]**, which gives me speed and agility. I used it a lot to stay alive while darting between the giant dinosaur legs. I think it would enable me to eventually get fast enough to just step in front of any ranged foe and assassinate them. Like Christie, but with speed, not stealth."

"That sounds great," Max said. "What else you got?"

"**[Razor Claws]**, which is my basic ability. I used to just cast it over and over again, but with Cultivation, I learned to charge it. Now I can use it to cut through T-rex bones, if I'm given enough time. I also have **[Camouflage]**, which . . . well, you can probably guess what it does. I don't use it much, though."

"You should have a fourth ability, right?" Max said.

"Yeah, I guess. I haven't chosen it."

Max stroked the barrel of Maverick idly as he thought. "Well, I'd choose **[Jaguar Step]**."

"I like it the best," Sandra said and nodded. "But why do you think so?"

"Because you like it the best," Max said. Sandra gave him a side-eye, so he continued. "You're an intuitive person with a straightforward mind. You like efficient solutions and simple ways to progress. Don't overcomplicate things for yourself."

"You calling me stupid?" Sandra said and scoffed.

"You know what's the dumbest thing I ever saw?" Max said and gave Sandra a smile.

"What?"

"People going to college just because someone told them it's smart. What's smart is thinking for yourself."

"Huh," Christie said as she approached and offered a water flask to Sandra and Max. "Not just a pretty face, are you, darling?"

"What I'm saying is," Max said, ignoring Christie but taking the water flask, "take Christie here. She uses a stealthy approach for assassinations. You intend to use speed for assassinations."

"You make sense," Sandra said. "But I don't appreciate being called simple."

"It's not a bad thing," Max said and nodded at Erwin. "Look at him over there. Which of you would do better in college?"

"Him, I guess."

"Which of you is better suited to making a general assessment of our battle situation and planning accordingly?"

"Him," Sandra said sullenly.

"And which of you do you think would fare better in running a gauntlet between the legs of a rampaging T-rex?"

Christie hooted at Sandra's blank face. She blushed and rubbed her arm again.

"And I need you both," Max said. "Your straightforward bravery and Erwin's calculations."

"What about me, darling?" Christie said and gave Max her best smile.

"And me!" Maverick exclaimed. "Feel free to lavish me with praise. Come on, now. Don't be shy. Just a compliment or three. Make it three."

Max laughed and gave the flask back to Christie. "Thanks for the water. I'll go scout out what the enemy is doing. After I return, we take down more dinos. Get the guys ready in five, and start on one without me if you feel like it."

"Got it, chief," Christie said and gave him a two-finger salute.

Max surged into the air.

CHAPTER TWENTY-ONE

New Insights

Max flew straight toward where he had left the lizards. When he found them, he was shocked. A dozen dead giants and dinosaurs lay on the ground behind the enemy formation. They even had the smoking remains of a fire behind them. They had clearly cooked some meat and had a meal.

So fast . . .

Their tactics were too efficient. As Max floated there, he saw them fell another two T-rex, one after the other. They remained behind their shield, locked down the target, and suffocated it with poison. Rinse and repeat. Max felt helpless. The tall poison mage noticed him in the sky and waved. Max shot a few rounds at them, but the golden barrier fully absorbed the bullets.

"Goddamn it," Max said. "What are we going to do?"

"Funny," Maverick remarked.

"What is, exactly?" Max said.

"You're usually so efficient. So concerned with maximizing everything. And yet, here you are ogling the enemy and bristling to yourself. For shame."

"Are you scolding me?"

"Well, I'm goddamned Soulbond to your sorry ass," Maverick said. "And right now, you're losing it, Max. You're wasting time. You're lollygagging. Dilly-dallying. SHILLY-SHALLYING!"

"Okay! I get it!"

Maverick sniffed. "As long as you do. Things aren't always about you, you know. My well-being is at stake here too. Any idea how bored I will be if all of your species and especially you die? I'd just be lying somewhere, collecting dust. No! I want adventures. Which means you need to figure this shit out."

Max said nothing. Maverick was an ass, but he had a point. Max wasn't being himself. But this time was different. It was so hard.

It wasn't the pressure. It was having to lead. It was easier for Max to just do his thing and not worry about others. But now he had to think of other people's needs and wishes. He needed to be just, sociable, work harder than others, be *exemplary*, and it was just . . . a lot.

Maverick sensed all of this through their bond, and the damn gun had the actual audacity to scoff at him.

"You're no paragon," Maverick said. "They respect you because you do what you have to do. You still do, but now you have this confusion messing you up. If I could, I would retch in disgust."

"What are you trying to say?" Max said.

"Do I really need to spell it out for you?"

"Yes, please."

"I thought you humans like reaching these big revelations on your own."

"I don't have time for reaching enlightenment."

Maverick chuckled. "Okay, that's more like it. Fine. You have earned your bone, doggie."

Max's tone took on a deadly note. "Call me 'doggie' again and I'll figure out how to make do without you."

Maverick was silent for a while. Then he huffed. "Fine."

"My revelation?" Max asked, gentler this time.

"Stop being considerate, you big idiot," Maverick said. "Just drag them through the mud. Be greedy. Take all the Experience and carry this lot to the finish line even if they kick and scream the whole time."

Max flinched and froze. He even lost concentration on his [**Telekinesis**] which made him drop a few feet in the air before he regained his composure.

"You're . . . kind of striking a chord."

"Of course I am," Maverick said. "And now, look, I'm just going to roll with this, even though I know you're not going to like it.

"Hm?"

"If you had just used the rest of your group as bait and focused on killing the enemy, you would have probably wiped them all out."

Max hissed at that. "No. I'm not going that far. I protect."

Maverick sighed. "I know. Just figured I'd shoot my shot. So to speak."

"Humanity might need me right now," Max said. "But I also need humanity."

Maverick raspberried. "Screw that. You think you do. What you need is me. What you need is to destroy shit. It's what we do. It's who we are. We need to kill stuff."

They both felt it. An elevation in their spiritual essence.

"Continue!" Max urged his buddy on.

"We need to destroy."

Leveled Up Ruby-Level Cultivator (lesser) to 2
+4 free Attribute point

"Holy shit!" Max said.

"That felt goooooood!" Maverick said.

"You did it!" Max said, elated. "How did you come up with that?"

"My Dao is being amazing," Maverick said.

Max scoffed and shook his head. "Okay. You win this time. Let's go back. The lizards gave us a benchmark. It's time to break it."

CHAPTER TWENTY-TWO

High-Speed Fighting

Max flew back to his group, who were in the middle of fighting a T-rex. Wasting no time, he dove between the legs and cast a spell as he flew up from under the monster's swishing tail.

"**[Tether]**!"

Max was a little alarmed at how weak the spell was. But it did its job. Both of the creature's legs were dragged together, and it toppled over. Immediately, Max's allies jumped on the beast and finished it off.

Defeated Level 27 [Tyrant Saurus (Elite)]
You gained 9,745 Experience points

Max was already flying toward the next one, which roared upon spotting him. He flew to the side and shot a volley at its big mouth. Most attacks were deflected by the monster's metal plating, but a few scored hits, spraying blood everywhere. Max flew high up in the air so the beast had to stretch its legs and shift its center of gravity to a less stable position.

That's when Max deactivated his **[Telekinesis]**, plummeted down and then reactivated it again, tethering himself to the ground. He sped between the monster's legs like a bullet as he dropped a **[Gravity Well]** between them.

The legs were pulled together, and Max dropped to the ground. He circled around to look at the rabidly snapping jaws, before he tethered them together, eliciting an angry muffled screech.

They have high Resistance. I need to put even further points into Intelligence. Makes sense, because I'm also a lot less vulnerable to attacks in the air. Still, projectiles and magic might hit me if I'm not careful.

The rest of the kill was more of an execution than a hunt. The creature tried to wriggle around and crush Max with its head, but that was easy to dodge. Then, Max just shot the monster in the eye until it went limp.

Defeated Level 26 [Tyrant Saurus (Elite)]
You gained 26,000 Experience points

Without looking back, Max looted the creature.

16,000 Cosmic Coins
[Short Spear of Frozen Blade (D-grade)]

And then, without stopping even long enough to catch his breath, Max went for another kill. This felt good—*great*, even. He felt free. A part of him wanted to turn back and tell Christie to take the reins and kill stuff at their own pace. But Max couldn't bring himself to do it, and Maverick warned against it. That was not their Dao.

Their way was destruction. They were meant to destroy. and Max would follow that road to the fullest if it meant winning. They had to win. Christie and Brian would figure it out.

After two more T-rex kills, Max Leveled Up again.

Level Up! [Level 23 Gravitician] You have gained $+2$ Constitution, $+3$ Intelligence, $+3$ Wisdom, $+3$ free Attribute points

"The Experience drops are enormous."
"Who cares about some stupid Experience? Give. Me. Those. Cosmic. Coins."
Max grinned. "Don't mind if I do."

[51,200 Cosmic Coins spent]
[The Maverick] upgraded to +9
+22 Intelligence
+14 Precision

Maverick was quickly closing in on Level Ten. That was supposed to unlock some additional powers or abilities for equipment. That was exciting. Max and Maverick both shared a sense of giddiness. Maybe now Maverick would get a big Damage boost that could penetrate the enemy's golden barrier.

The best part was that it would be less than an hour until they found out.

But before Max took to flight again, he wanted to quickly spend his free Attribute points and take a moment to admire his Stats. He had come a long way.

Max spent the free Attribute points on his primary Stats: Intelligence, Wisdom, and Constitution.

Name: Max Cromwell
Cultivation stage: Ruby (lesser)
Class: Gravitician Level: 23
Health: 6250/6250
Stamina: 6250/6250
Mana: 7750/7750
Alliance: Joshua's Group
Stats:
Strength: 45
Dexterity: 50
Constitution: 125
Intelligence: 155
Wisdom: 115
Charisma: 44
Precision: 76
Toughness: 60
Resistance: 70

Then, with an almost disdainful air of ease, Max flew around the next T-rex's head, making it crane its neck and snap at him, before he swooped down between the great beast's legs and tethered them together. It toppled to the ground and roared in frustration. Max dropped down and started blasting at the monster's head.

But before he could let more than two bullets fly, a giant boulder barreled toward him, rolling down a nearby hill like a bowling ball.

Max was only saved thanks to his instincts. Without thinking, he reflectively shot out a [Tether] that pushed the boulder and him further apart, allowing him to jump to the side just in the nick of time.

Wasting no time on investigating, Max took to flight, just as another great boulder began to roll at him with crushing force. Only once safely in the air was able to Max survey the hill to see what had attacked him.

Three of those humanlike giants were running down the hill. One of them waved a tree trunk and yelled in some guttural language. Max was surprised that he couldn't understand it.

One of the other giants handled a sling, the size of a tent. While running, he spun the leather until it became a whirling blur. With a snap of the wrist, he released it and a great volley of rocks flew at Max.

They arced like a flock of geese in the sky, and when Max flew downward to dodge, he was struck by another volley, preemptively launched by the third giant.

Shit.

Max's vision flashed red, and he lost 400 Health as well as all control of his spells. He plummeted to the ground, and the T-rex struggled back to his feet.

A succession of [**Tethers**] stopped him from being crushed by gravity, but even after softening his fall, his body lanced with pain and he lost another 300 Health.

Coughing and holding his side, he threw Maverick, who soared until he stopped, suspended in the air, and unleashed [**Semiautomatic Firearm**]. It distracted all of the enemies. The T-rex tried to snap at it, while the giants huddled down together as the largest of the three protected them with its tree trunk.

Max chugged down a [**Health Potion**], which gave him some measure of breath back.

One of the giants lobbed a massive handful of rocks in a high arc in Max's general direction.

"[**Gravity Well**]."

He cast the spell directly above him, which sucked the rocks together in a clump. Then, it bobbed down and back up above Max's head like a cork in water.

The T-rex charged toward Max, snapping at him, gouging at the earth with its lower jaw. The attack skidded under the [**Gravity Well**], and Max abruptly cut off the spell, dropping the boulders on the monster's protruding mouth.

Max took to flight again, and he was instantly pelted with another volley of rocks, but he flew straight upward, barely dodging it.

These guys are deadly accurate.

Maverick had dropped somewhere in the trampled mud and grass. Max could sense him nearby to his left. Flying below another slingful of rocks, Max swooped down into the tall grass and caught a long, heaving breath.

The T-rex was already upon him.

"Where?!"

"Here!" Maverick shouted.

Max tethered the beast's legs together and threw up a [**Gravity Well**] to obstruct the charge. It worked, and the beast skidded, immobilized.

"Watch out!"

A tree trunk barreled at him, bouncing violently, as it crushed everything in its wake. Max lay flat on the ground and when he saw the trunk roll closer, he pushed it against himself with a [**Tether**]. It worked and the crushing log bounced over him.

He picked up Maverick and took to the sky. His Mana was low, with only 700 left, so once he had gotten enough altitude to surely be out of range of any attacks, he popped one of his last [**Potions of Greater Mana Regeneration**] from his Inventory into his hand.

"Good Christ," Max muttered. "That was a close shave."

"I *loved* it!" Maverick said, excitement mounting in his voice. "That's what I live for! Let's do it again. We kill these guys and then we find four—no, *five*—enemies next!"

"I think I'm going to throw up . . ."

"Ooh, do it on that hairy one glaring at you. Do you reckon he'll turn purple or cherry red?"

CHAPTER TWENTY-THREE

Some Sweet Progression

The Experience and loot from killing all four creatures was nothing short of massive. It managed to push Max to a Level Up. The System message was as satisfying as ever.

Level Up! [Level 24 Gravitician] You have gained + 2 Constitution, + 3 Intelligence, + 3 Wisdom, + 3 free Attribute points

The Cosmic Coins were also something to behold. Only one or two more kills would yield enough coins for Maverick to get his Level Ten and possibly acquire a new ability. The fact that he was a **[Unique]** Class weapon made Max hope it would be something special.

He glanced backward. The rest of the group was a quarter of a mile away, fighting another T-rex. They were taking their time, but it looked like it was working out. That was good. They needed these monsters to be on a farmable level because the enemy was having a buffet, for sure.

Max fought the urge to soar up in the air and check up on the enemy. Maverick sent a pulse of annoyance through their bond.

"You actually think we're going anywhere before you sort me out with that Level Up?" Maverick said in a snippy voice. "I swear I'll jam on you."

"You're a revolver, you can't jam."

"Watch me."

Max rummaged through the other Items he had gotten. They were mostly useless to him, but he had collected three in total. Two of them would go to the group, but the third looked interesting.

**[Spear of Rapid Thrusts (C-grade)]
Damage 38–66**

+5 Constitution
+5 Dexterity
+6 Toughness

Decent Item. I'm not sure who'd most benefit from a spear, but it's probably a grade higher than what most people have right now.

[Snakeskin Boots of Glamour (D-grade)]
+8 Charisma

Heh, these would go well with Joshua's cowboy hat. I better pick them up and give them to him . . . if I ever see him again, that is.

"Of course you will," Maverick said. "Don't give me any of this macabre, gloomy bullshit. I ain't having it. Good vibes only, or whatever you idiot humans say."

"Leave me alone," Max said. "I feel what I feel."

"What do you feel about these gloves?" Maverick asked.

"I like them."

[Gloves of Deft Fingers (C-grade)]
+6 Intelligence
+6 Dexterity
+4 Precision

Needless to say, Max equipped them immediately.

"Looks like they were made for a craftsman," Max said.

"We are craftsmen," Maverick said. "Of death!"

Something stirred inside of their bond right then. Max's eyes went wide, and he immediately sat down cross-legged. What Maverick had said didn't quite count as an insight, but it still hit close to home.

In sync, the two of them cycled Spiritual Energy through their bodies and contemplated. *A craftsman of death.* Surely it had something to do with destruction. The Spiritual Energy rippled and ebbed softly as Max tried to attain a revelation. Through his bond, he could feel Maverick working just as hard. It felt good. For all his flippancy, when it came to increasing their power, Maverick was deadly serious.

We are craftsmen of death. No . . . Destruction. That feels right. Makers of destruction. No . . . We create destruction!

Leveled Up Ruby-Level Cultivator (lesser) to 3

+4 free Attribute point

"Yes!" both of them exclaimed.

Max was starting to understand Cultivation on a deeper level now because of the insights. Cultivation was about becoming something you were supposed to be. Maybe destined to be. It was everyone's unique path.

Previously, he had just floundered around with Maverick, pushing Spiritual Energy around his body. But this felt different. This wasn't only powering up. This was meditation on the true nature of what Max and Maverick were.

It was exhilarating.

"Damn straight!" Maverick said. "Now you're getting in my groove. We're *supposed* to mess things up."

"I would like to think there's more to our existence and purpose than to kill, destroy, or to put it in your words, mess things up."

"Eh, maybe," Maverick said. "I'll let you worry about that part. Now how about we kill a few more of these sweet pinatas here and get me to Level Ten? After that, we can go check up on the lizards and see how they like us."

"Sounds like a plan," Max said. "But first I'd like to allocate my Stats."

"Are you going to put more points in Intelligence?"

Max sighed.

Level Up! [Level 25 Gravitician] You have gained + 2 Constitution, + 3 Intelligence, + 3 Wisdom, + 3 free Attribute points
Name: Max Cromwell
Cultivation stage: Ruby (lesser)
Class: Gravitician Level: 25
Health: 6500/6500
Stamina: 6500/6500
Mana: 8250/8250
Alliance: Joshua's Group
Stats:
Strength: 45
Dexterity: 50
Constitution: 130
Intelligence: 165
Wisdom: 125
Charisma: 44
Precision: 77
Toughness: 60
Resistance: 70

Max was really happy with the recent results. When they had first been transported into this Deathmatch, he had been worried that his growth would stagnate. Their alien overlords had instead decided to make things interesting. Max wasn't one to complain.

He looked over his Stats again. It seemed like a prudent choice to pump up his Mana and Health, because of the five-times scaling. Besides, putting some extra points in Intelligence made Maverick happy, and allowed him to fly longer.

Mana hadn't gone concerningly low in their last rampage, but they had dipped below one thousand in the end. That was still a decent margin for error, but any lower than that could be troublesome.

"Don't be such a worrywart," Maverick said. "If the shit hits the fan, you can always fly away."

"Imagine a situation," Max said dryly, "where I'm low on Mana, and me and my group are fighting monsters. And then the enemy decides to attack. What should I do?"

"Fly away."

"And leave the rest of the group to fend for themselves and die?"

"I said what I said."

"Asshole."

"Don't blame me," Maverick said smugly. "Blame our Dao. It's a Dao of greed. We take from others and destroy."

"Doesn't mean we have to be assholes," Max said and sat on the grass. He watched the blue bar in the corner of his vision tick up. A smidge over two thousand. He contemplated whether to chug a potion or not. "I'm doing this for humanity."

"You keep telling yourself that, buddy."

"I am."

"Sure," Maverick said. He was on the ground, but shuffled and shimmied himself so that the barrel was pointing at Max. "But you are having fun."

Max chuckled. "I am."

Maverick sent a pulse of smugness through their bond.

"What did you do just there?" Max asked. "Could you do that before?"

"Do what?"

Max leaned over his revolver companion and inspected him. The weapon looked completely normal, with its obscenely long barrel and black leather grip. The metal glinted in the flickering light of the orange sky.

"Shuffle around and move?"

"Oh . . . I guess I couldn't! That's pretty awesome. I won't need you to carry me if this keeps up."

"What changed?"

"Beats me," Maverick said and shuffled around a bit, rustling the trampled grass. "But I *like* it!"

"Must be the result of our Cultivation," Max muttered. He wished they could explore their insights further, but now was not the time.

It was time to get up, soar to the sky, and do what their Dao demanded of them. Destroy and take.

Bigger, Better, Stronger

With upgrades to their Stats and Cultivation, Max could really feel the difference. It was the same as with anything you got good at, be it cooking or the gym. It's just that with the Framework and Cultivation increases, Max got better at *everything*.

It was in the way he flew. The ease with which he could maneuver in the air, doing deft movements, changing altitude, flipping to turn his heels where his head had been. His control of his [**Telekinesis**] ability. He had started his flying practice weeks earlier by targeting the soles of his feet. Now he enveloped his whole body in the spell and it barely took any concentration. Maybe it was the result of the spell being his [**Signature Ability**], but whatever it was, it was practically automatic.

That, combined with Maverick taking care of most of the aiming and shooting, left Max almost idle in the air.

I really am just carrying him around, aren't I?

"What was that?" Maverick said.

"Just the wind howling," Max muttered.

Max flew low enough to take the attention of two giants who were huddled together, inspecting a dead deer on the ground. They reacted immediately and one of them lobbed a handful of stones at Max, one of which struck him. With a flash of red in his vision, he lost 200 Health.

Just like that. I'm still very fragile.

Max pointed Maverick in their direction and started shooting. Meanwhile, he searched for the rocks as they started to arc downward. He found one and rushed over to it.

"Hey!" Maverick said. "What's the big deal?"

"[**Telekinesis**]."

One of the rocks was suddenly suspended in the air. Max grinned. Not because of the spell working. He had been sure it would. What had been anybody's guess was whether the spell affecting his body would cease.

I suppose I can use multiple [**Tethers**] *too, so why not?*

Still, one was less prone to taking risks when they were fifty feet in the air.

"This does drain a bit of Mana, admittedly," Max said.

"What are you doing?" Maverick demanded. "Why can't you just let me shoot them?"

"I want to advance."

Max lobbed the stone toward the two giants with a downward sweep of his free hand. It sped through the air and blasted the one in the chest. Blood burst out of the wound and the giant collapsed. The other one was left ogling his fallen partner and Max intermittently.

"Okay, I'll forgive you."

Max laughed. This was amazing news. Not only would it speed up the rate at which they could kill the enemy, but they now had a weapon against the paladin type's golden barrier!

There wasn't anything crazily exciting in the loot. Max was very happy to find a bunch of [**Greater Mana Potions**], though. There was also a decent shield, which Max picked up, so he could pass it on.

[**Bulwark of Stone Will (D-grade)**]
+5 Constitution
+4 Strength
+2 Toughness
+2 Resistance

Max was more interested in the Mana potions. He wondered if he should drink a few to top himself off.

"Keep your piddly liquids," Maverick said. "Gimme. Gimme!"

There were **32,510 Cosmic Coins** in total within the fallen giants. That was enough to push Maverick to Level Ten.

Max shrugged and poured the points into Maverick.

[**100,000 Cosmic Coins spent**]
[**The Maverick**] **upgraded to +10**
+30 Intelligence
+20 Precision
[**Special weapon effect: ???**]
[**New Cultivation path detected . . .**]
[**Changing special weapon effect . . .**]

[. . .]

[Special Weapon effect: [The Maverick] has now acquired autonomous function. The weapon will receive its own Mana pool and the Skill [Flight]. The autonomous function only works within a range of ten feet from the user. Advancements in Cultivation will increase the radius.]

"Oh my dear baby Buddha who art in Nirvana!" Max said.

"Yeaaaaaaaaah!" Maverick exclaimed and shot out of Max's hand into the air. "Behold! I am no longer contained. I cannot be! I will not be! No longer will I be holstered. No longer will I wear a silencer! I am free to spray and pray!"

Max was excited himself. This would open up so many possibilities. He could focus on lobbing boulders or creating utility, while Maverick would be in control of the consistent damage output.

"Wait, what was that second line again?" Maverick asked as he soared into the air, flying into the sunset, before plopping down like a dead bird.

"That you have to be within ten feet of me," Max said, suppressing a grin.

That sent Maverick into a series of angry mutters, which Max enjoyed thoroughly. "Unbelievable. I suppose I will keep you on as a sidekick for now, then . . ."

Max shook his head. "An honor as always . . ."

Maverick now possessed his own Mana pool. That made sense. Max could sense it through their bond. He needed it for the flight effect and would most likely also use it for his ammunition henceforth.

That was good. While the expense from firing Maverick wasn't extensive, it still added up, especially with an extended fight or continuous fights.

"Will you be able to Cultivate on your own now?" Max asked.

Maverick, who was busy doing somersaults in the air, stopped in the middle of one, leaving him suspended upside down. "How the hell should I know? Maybe. I don't think we have the time to try. Besides, I think we share Cultivation. I just finally accessed it now."

"It's creepy when you make sense, you know."

"I know!" Maverick said. "That's why I leave it to you most of the time."

"How about we leave this place and go check up on our dear friends, the lizards?"

Max could feel Maverick's internal evil grin through their bond.

"Let's do it!" Maverick said and took off a few feet in the air. "You coming?"

"Yeah," Max said and looked at the shield on the ground. "Just a second . . ."

CHAPTER TWENTY-FIVE

New Weapons

Max flew in the air feeling giddy anticipation. At the same time, he knew that logically, the enemy must have gotten stronger too. This could simply just not work.

"Listen to me, Max," Maverick said. He was flying next to him, swerving up and down for fun. "We don't need to kill them all outright. That's not the play here. We have a singular objective here."

"We do?"

"Oh, yeah," Maverick said.

"And what's that?"

"We're going to put the fear of God into them."

Max laughed. Maverick hooted gleefully. He was excited by his newfound powers and for good reason. Max adjusted the strap of his new shield on his arm. He'd release the straps soon and then he would see how well his machinations worked. The shield's lower half ended in a nice sharp triangle meant for crushing plates and throats.

When Max flew past the absolutely towering, massive skyscraper of a quadrupedal herbivore, he wondered if this particular monster was some kind of grand prize.

It watched Max with its enormous eyes, craning its neck lazily. It snorted and a blast of wind sent Max flying sideways in a gust.

Even the plating looks much thicker than the rest of the creatures here.

Max passed over the dinosaur to the other side of the plains and soon enough saw the work the lizards had done so far.

Max had to admit that he was impressed. They had slain almost two dozen creatures while suffering no casualties themselves. He could see a mass of corpses spread behind a group of huddled lizards resting on a hillside.

Max was glad to see they needed the break. He didn't know how his group was currently faring in terms of resources and fatigue, but he just realized that they might just be a lot less Mana-intensive than the enemy group, who used a myriad of spells and abilities to push for fast kills. Meanwhile the humans used assassins and ranged fighters who, to Max's knowledge, used much less of their Stamina and Mana. Only their support magician might need a break, but they could allocate all of their potions on him.

Max made a mental note of bringing this analysis back to Christie and Brian when he returned.

"Bah," Maverick said. "We should follow our Dao and just fly solo."

"That doesn't mean we shouldn't bring valuable information and ideas back to our friends."

Maverick raspberried.

"Should we just swoop down?" Max asked.

"Well, they've definitely seen us now," Maverick said. "Might as well. We're wasting Mana by flying idle."

"Looks like they haven't made an effort to move. Could they really be that tired?"

"It's been only a few hours," Maverick said. "Surely they're not so weak and pathetic?"

"Let's find out," Max said and they descended. Max unstrapped the shield and cast **[Telekinesis]** on it.

Losshnak saw the enemy gunslinger as a dot in the sky, long before they stopped to float above them. Losshnak hated the fact that the bastard could fly. And the gun dealt respectable damage. Losshnak had been hit with a bullet himself and he had taken two and eighty in damage.

He grunted to the others and pointed at the sky. A chorus of groans and hisses ensued, but Losshnak watched them grip their staves and spears and hunch into readier positions. However, if they could help it, they would rest after their hunt.

Only Losshnak needed to stay prepared. He would cast **[Shimmershield]** on the group and block the nuisance. If there was one good thing about the human, it was that it had pushed his signature skill to Two, which had truly boosted his power.

The sky was dominated by a dark purple cloud mass at the center of which a bright orange flare was aflame. The silhouette of the enemy human descended slowly. Surely he would not be such a fool as to think they had not noticed him.

The problem was that, despite Losshnak's powered-up shield, he was currently low on Mana. Only 600 remained, and the shield ate five per second.

And on top of that, like all of his crew, he was feeling increasingly ill. Being the leader, he of course didn't tell anyone. Everyone else may admit to the symptoms, But he would not, despite his olive-green scales growing just as pale as everyone else's had. They respected him for it, and Losshnak appreciated his men.

There must be something foul in the water or food or air. Could it be that the humans are sick as well? I have no status on my interface, but clearly something is wrong.

There was no time to ponder further. The enemy gunslinger swooped down, head-first. His speed and courage were impressive, it had to be admitted.

But something was amiss. He could hear a faint cackle of a gleeful laugh from above. Had the bastard acquired some sort of flying familiar? Perhaps a lucky drop from the creatures. No . . . that obscenely long barrel . . . It was the gun! It was *flying*. And laughing. And shooting!

"[Shimmershield]!"

A great golden shield of light enveloped him and his warriors. The fired shots cracked and created ripples of light, like stones dropped in a pond on the surface of his barrier.

"Vossneck," Losshnak commanded the tall poison mage behind him. He produced a blue potion of Mana and gave it to the **[Paladin]**. He sank a tooth in the cork and pulled it out, chugging down the liquid, restoring 200 Mana.

"Good," Losshnak said. "Now, drive it away."

Their mages and **[Spear Artist]** took to their positions and started lobbing projectiles at the enemy. Losshnak's **[Shimmershield]** was an ability of extreme power and utility. It let objects from the inside of the barrier through freely but would not allow anything to penetrate it from without.

At least not at the force with which he is attacking us.

But then the human did something that made Losshnak worry. He unstrapped the shield and used his gravity magic to levitate the shield in front of him. It started spinning around its axis. Ten rounds per minute, thirty rounds, eighty, one hundred. At that point, it became such a blur even to Losshnak's experienced eyes that it was impossible to say.

The wildly spinning shield rose above the head of the enemy with a swipe of his hand. It turned, the sharp-edged bottom facing Losshnak's barrier. He couldn't help but let out a nervous hiss.

Just as his mages launched projectiles in tandem with a one-two punch of long throwing spears, the shield shot toward them.

It cut a spear cleanly in half as it sliced down on them, still spinning like a high-power drill. From the corner of his vision, Losshnak saw the enemy dodging the mage's attacks. That was the one thing he managed to notice before the shield smashed into his barrier.

Losshnak felt it in the pit of his stomach. It barreled at the shield like a relentless bull, still expending momentum. The ripples it created on the shield were frantic. Through his Ruby Cultivation, Losshnak channeled more of his Mana into the **[Shimmershield]**, but before he could stabilize his Spiritual Energy, the spear broke through and his barrier dissipated into flickering golden lights in the air. The shield struck him in the chest. For 422 damage.

It blasted Losshnak two feet away, launching him on his back, from where he skidded another foot on the ground. One of the mages tried to help him up, but he grunted and smacked the fool when he rose.

The enemy was already swooping down, the golden revolver firing wantonly at them, yet with deadly accuracy.

The grass mage cast his signature ability, **[Natural Hands]**, between them and the enemy. The hands grew tall and covered them well. But the damn human could fly.

He dove to the right of them and said something in his language to call back the shield. This would be bad. Losshnak leapt at it, covering the shield with his body. He tried casting **[Shimmershield]** again, but all he produced was a System message.

[Ability overpowered. Cooldown left, 8 seconds.]

That's an eternity in combat.
Slehhnik, their **[Zephyr Mage]**, was grinning. So the foolish human had come into their range. The last time that had happened, he had almost died, needing a cheat from his filthy patrons.

But as the mage cast his **[Whirlwinds]** and **[Steer Wind]**, Losshnak realized something was wrong. *Everything* was wrong about this situation.

The human moved with such ease in the air, bobbing and weaving, making sure the gun had a clear shot. He must have Leveled Up in his Cultivation. The human might have even surpassed him.

The human realized Losshnak was sitting on the shield, so he started firing a barrage of painful, red-flashing bullets at his back. Losshnak turned and held the shield in front of him, making it absorb most of the shots.

But that left him vulnerable. The pull from the human's spell was too strong. He had to let go of the shield or be hoisted in the air himself. Losshnak thumped a foot down on the ground as he finally reached a decision.

"Retreat!"

Against a flying foe with powerful ranged attacks, it was almost foolish, but it would give them time to regroup. Just a few more seconds for his barrier. But now the human had the shield again and could destroy it with it.

Turned out there was no need. The human made the shield spin again, with lesser velocity this time around, yet it was still daunting enough. Just as the shield shot toward them, Losshnak could feel that his **[Shimmershield]** was usable again. But if he used it now, this situation would repeat.

But it's either that or . . .

Losshnak hated the choice he had to make. But his experience as a warrior and a leader told him it was the right call. He knew it intuitively. Now he just hoped the shield wouldn't land true.

It did. It sliced through Sisskhash, their **[Axe Fiend]**. Losshnak nodded to himself as the explosion of guts, blood, and gore sprayed and covered him. That was a low-value target. They had gotten lucky.

"**[Shimmershield]**!"

Now the shield was inside the barrier and the enemy human couldn't use their powers to get it back.

Your move, human. I just hope you don't have a stack of those sitting in your Inventory.

Turned out he didn't. The human simply hovered in midair and glared at them. The gun, seemingly of its own volition, was firing at the barrier, but it held.

Losshnak shook his head ruefully. The human had just gotten a big Experience drop. He was possibly ahead in Cultivation too. As well as possessing air control.

This does not look good.

On top of all of this, Losshnak felt a build-up of bile forming in his esophagus. Only a slight puffing of Losshnak's cheeks told the rest of the crew anything was happening. Losshnak swallowed the rising vomit down and cursed this human.

I will get stronger.

After a few more seconds, the human shrugged and flew away.

CHAPTER TWENTY-SIX

Highest Highs

Max and Maverick were laughing uproariously, drunk on the sweet nectar of victory. The wind slightly muffled their mirthful sounds, but the two only laughed harder, reveling in having overpowered their enemies.

"They scrambled around like a bunch of blind babies!" Maverick said and hooted.

"What a perfect time to attack," Max said, grinning so hard, his face hurt. He didn't care.

"We should do it again!" Maverick said. "No mercy!"

"We should," Max said. "In game terms, we have a power spike. We should press the advantage."

Maverick grunted with displeasure. "If only."

"Yeah," Max said, nodding in agreement.

Their Cultivation channels were fried. The extended use of Spiritual Energy was starting to take a serious toll on them. Max was extremely low on Mana too, sporting only 300. He could drink some potions, but at this point, that felt like a really stupid idea.

It was like his body was aching all over from the inside out, which had only grown stronger as the day went by. Max made a conscious effort of trying to relax his body as it floated idly through the air, pushed by his [Telekinesis] back toward his group.

This had been the longest continuous stint of time Max had spent in the air. Before, he had only ventured spurts or very short missions. But with Experience, increased Cultivation, and the advantage of the huge Mana pool, he had now been flying for hours, only returning to the ground for a short rest and to loot the monsters he had killed.

It had felt *amazing*. In the sky, Max felt so free and so powerful. He could survey everything, attack his enemies with impunity, and escape at will. For the first time in his life, Max felt like he was the master of his fate, the captain of his own ship. What he felt in the air was profound. True control. And that was the essence of *power.*

"No," Maverick said. "Power is power. And the best kind of power is firepower."

"Those immortal words should be framed on every kitchen wall . . ."

Max tumbled to the ground, landing in a crouch. It felt strange to feel the earth under his feet again. The grass did feel nice under his palms, though, he had to admit. Rough and cool. His fingers were slightly numb from the extended flying. Cultivation helped protect his body from the elements, but for all its power, it wasn't absolute.

As Max got up, Maverick flew into his holster. Max raised an eyebrow.

"I would have thought you'd never want to return there?"

"Ah," Maverick said. "I have to make sure you feel important from time to time."

Max scoffed. "Of course. And speaking of feeling important, are you really not going to show off your new cool abilities to the rest of the group?"

It was Maverick's turn to scoff. "Why would a gun concern himself with the opinions of bows?"

"That's a way to put it . . ." Max said, and then added under his breath. "Arrogant bastard."

"It's only arrogant if it's disproportionate," Maverick said. "When it's reasonable, it's called pride and confidence."

"I'm not going to dignify that with a response."

Maverick huffed. "You know I'm right."

They walked a few minutes and crested a grassy hill. A T-rex was watching them ascend and started skulking closer, but Max only gave it a side-glance. It kept its distance, watching silently.

On the other side of the hill, Max saw his group felling a pair of giants. It was sloppy work, but they seemed to be winning by a hair. Max had an impulse to fly in and help, but he figured it was better not to for multiple reasons.

Maverick agreed through their bond. "We need to rest, you absolute cretin."

"You're right."

"Remember," Maverick said. "This is a quick in-and-out. We exchange information, let the Mana regenerate as we Cultivate and try to heal our bodies, and then we get back out there and kill another damn lizard. This time, bring two shields."

"I know, I know."

"You need to keep your head straight. It's better for these people too if we're out there following our Dao and killing the enemy."

"You're right," Max said, perking up. He had been feeling guilty about leaving the rest of the group to their own devices. With that guilt now ebbing away, their victory felt ever-sweeter and his steps on the ground almost as light as flying.

When Max reached the rest of the group, who were now divvying up the loot from the two giants, he instantly sensed something was wrong. It was in the heavy atmosphere and the looks they gave Max.

Max greeted them and got a few nods and waves back. Christie and Brian came up to him. Yeah, something was definitely off.

"You're back," Brian said.

"Been a busy day for me. Killed one of the enemy, actually."

"That is good news," Christie said, but her tone was flat. No honeyed seduction and definitely no 'darling.' Max's unease was mounting.

"How have you guys fared?"

"Well," Christie started. "It was— We have—"

Her voice died down and she looked at the ground, biting her lip. Max looked down at her hands. They were clenched into fists and trembling. What was going on?

Max looked at Brian questioningly.

"Sandra died," Brian said bluntly.

Max's heart fell into his stomach. He stumbled as he was assaulted by a wave of vertigo. Brian gave him a hard look and when Christie drew her gaze from the ground to him, Max understood. What they were saying was clear.

If Max had stayed with them, Sandra would still be alive.

CHAPTER TWENTY-SEVEN

Lowest Lows

The group camped down next to a T-rex corpse, which they used for both cover and as a meal. While Christie's group were preparing the meat, Brian got a fire going and Max retrieved the tents from their camp.

They would all sleep here in the plains tonight. It was risky but necessary. Since everyone was at least at a moderate Level in Cultivation, they needed less sleep.

Max hadn't slept at any point since the Deathmatch began. He was tired and wouldn't have minded an hour or two of sleep, but he could stay awake for two more days if need be.

He looked around. Everyone around the fire was hunched over and quiet. There was no banter. No recounting of the day or rejoicing at the loot. Only a heavy silence. This was particularly apparent whenever Max interacted with someone. For the first time, he felt unwelcome here. He was used to getting the best seat by the fire and the choicest piece of meat and the first spot in line.

None of those privileges came tonight. Max didn't mind that in and of itself. But what hurt were the isolation and blame.

Everyone had shuffled away from Max, leaving him to sit mostly by himself. Maverick tried to make light conversation with the group, but Max warned him not to screw around. For once, the cheeky weapon complied.

Max sighed and took another bite of meat. It was stringy and poorly cooked. He missed Sid's cooking skills. He also wondered if Sid would blame him for this as well. Probably. Max understood how they must have felt.

Max had gone off to play hero and fly solo. Sure, he had gotten a kill, which was great, but that wouldn't bring Sandra back to life.

If I had been here, she would be alive. I know it, and they know it.

The fire crackled idly. They should have put it out immediately after cooking and found a new position. Right now, however, nobody was willing to move. The mood was clear. If the enemy wanted to attack now, let them come.

For one positive, Max and Maverick could feel their Spiritual Energy replenishing and they were beginning to feel less sore.

I wonder if Durum's book has anything on this phenomenon.

But it would be difficult to read it right now. For that, he'd need some idle time, and there was none to spare now. Maverick was Cultivating. Max would do so as well soon. But now he needed to think. He needed to realign his moral compass.

Was I wrong to do what I did?

Maverick would have said no. Max wasn't so sure for himself, though.

He was jerked out of his reverie when Brian came and sat down a few feet away from Max.

"You should have been here," Brian said, his voice flat.

Max didn't say anything for a while. He just looked at Brian. The older man had a scraggly dark-brown beard starting to turn gray on the edges. His hale green eyes were staring coldly at Max.

"Maybe," Max said. "I'm trying to think through if that's right or not."

"There's no 'maybe' about it," Brian said. "If you had been here, she would still be alive."

"I killed an enemy."

"I don't care."

"Well, you should," Max snapped and stared Brian down. "I took a calculated risk. I left you to get Experience and loot together so you would grow stronger. Meanwhile, I could fly around, kill stuff myself, and disrupt the enemy. That was the highest yield tactic available."

"It failed."

"It didn't," Max said grimly. "It just cost way more than any of us wanted."

Brian was about to say something, but he hesitated.

"How did it happen?" Max asked.

Brian grunted. "She was crushed by a log. One of the giants threw it at our frontline. She got clipped. Everyone else retreated. The giants came up and pummeled her. We attacked immediately, but we couldn't distract them before it was too late."

Max shook his head. "What a shit way to go."

"You think it was really worth it?" Brian asked, a slight tone of insecurity in his voice.

Max sighed and hung his head. Then he looked Brian dead in the eyes. "It was."

Brian averted his gaze. He got up and was about to leave. With his back toward Max, he said one last thing: "If it's going to be like that, I really hope you win."

With that, he left.

"Yeah," Max whispered to himself. "Me too."

CHAPTER TWENTY-EIGHT

Keeping Up the Grind

Max was out like a light as soon as he lay his head down. Maverick woke him up after two hours, or the duration of exactly two [**Celestial Illumination Pills**]. They were a bit of a waste in the sense that Maverick didn't Cultivate, as his body needed the rest from using up Spiritual Energy, but they were a good timekeeper, at least.

Max was amazed at how refreshed he felt after only two hours of sleep. He wasn't at his best and brightest, but he didn't feel any soreness from overuse of his Spiritual Energy, and his mind and body felt limber and quick. His Mana had mostly regenerated, leaving him at a smidge over 4,500.

That was as good a setup as any to go hunt some asshole lizards.

Max inhaled. It was still early in the morning before dawn. The air smelled fresh and it invigorated him. In moments like these, he almost missed his morning coffee, but what was a poor human stranded on an alien planet supposed to do?

Coffee will come after humanity wins.

Well, one could always dream. Max had bigger dreams than coffee, but for now it was time to focus on the present. It was time to fly.

Before he took off, he felt eyes on the back of his neck. He turned and noticed Jones, who was awake on sentry duty. He was leaning his hands and chin against one of his axes and his eyes followed Max. There was a predatory intensity to them.

As Max placed his [**Hammock**] back in his Inventory, he nodded at Jones. He may or may not have nodded back.

"I'm going out there to finish off another lizard," Max said.

"Good," Jones said.

"They all hate me now?" Max asked.

Jones shrugged.

"What about you?"

He shrugged again.

"You're a thrilling conversationalist," Max said.

A bit of a tug on the side of Jones's mouth. That was something. "What I think does not matter. Do you think you did the right thing?"

"Yes," Max said immediately.

"Then, go."

Max hovered up two feet in the air, but before he sped off, he turned to Jones.

"Thanks for the pep talk."

Another tug at the side of the mouth and a dismissive hand gesture.

It was enough for Max to flash a small grin. Maybe it wasn't all that bad. He saluted Jones and flew back up into the sky.

Max felt the guilt and unease wash away as he continued to ascend. The absolute freedom was simply delicious. This had to be part of his Dao. It just felt too right.

Maverick, the voice of reason as ever, snapped him out of his reverie. "Less dilly-dallying, more fighting lizards."

"I know, I know," Max said. "But if you don't enjoy the little things, are you even alive?"

"How about you enjoy the little things after our next battle?"

"Fair point," Max said and chuckled. "Fine. Let's take care of the first pitstop first."

The first pitstop had a simple goal: kill stuff. Namely the giants, since they seemed to drop more Items and even give more Experience.

What they needed was really anything heavier than gloves or boots. Shields, spears, maces. Hell, even chain mail could be hurled against the enemy at breakneck speed.

They had thought of rocks first, which was of course the most obvious choice. But being a **[Combatant]** instead of a **[Laborer]** or an **[Artisan]** meant that Max couldn't store rocks in his magical Inventory. But weapons he could carry for days.

First on the menu was a trio of giants, who were pointing up at Max in the morning sky. Maverick jumped out of his holster and started immediately shooting at the enemy, laughing and hooting all the while.

Max waited for the giants to make their move. It only took a few seconds.

The chunks of a broken boulder were hurled at Max with great speed.

He rose two yards higher, getting out of their range. The giants may have had accurate aim, but Max's reflexes were too fast for them.

The giants had had their try. Now was Max's turn.

"[Tether], [Tether]."

Four pieces flying next to each other instantly clumped together, and Max dove down and used [Telekinesis] to suspend them in the air. Then he broke one of the [Tethers] and tried to lift both of the falling rocks up with [Telekinesis].

It was all very elaborate and technical, and Max could feel his channels of Spiritual power screaming at him in anger. He lost control and dropped both of the stones.

Maverick sniffed between shots. "Pray tell, why are you dicking around like this?"

"I'm not looking to win a battle, I'm looking to win a war."

"How about we win a battle first, and dick around later?"

Max didn't answer. Instead he released the last tethering and focused on levitating both of the rocks. He just managed it. It was wobbly and tenuous, but both of the rocks were suspended in the air. Not having to deal with six spells simultaneously did the trick. But using [Telekinesis] three times simultaneously was draining his Mana rather fast and putting on a strain on his Cultivation.

But strain is what I want.

It was a bit surprising that Max hadn't Leveled Up even once with his [Signature Ability]. Leveling Up Skills made them significantly more powerful or efficient, so Leveling Up his [Telekinesis] had to come with a substantial power boost. But in order to Level Up his Skills, he'd need to be creative and push the limit of what he could do with his abilities.

Max made both of the boulders spin around their axis in the air at once. He had to weaken the spell suspending his body to the point where he started to slowly descend toward the ground.

Finally, after increasing the spin enough, he hurled the rocks at the giants with an overhead swing of his hand. The two boulders blasted toward the enemies and when they struck, grass, dirt, and blood flew up in the air, as the giants screamed.

Defeated Level 25 [Homo Gigantes (Elite)]
You gained 27,500 Experience points
Defeated Level 25 [Homo Gigantes (Elite)]
You gained 27,500 Experience points
Level Up! [Level 26 Gravitician] You have gained + 2 Constitution, + 3 Intelligence, + 3 Wisdom, + 3 free Attribute points

"That's so damn nice," Max said to himself and immediately spent all his free points in Intelligence. There was no time to dick around with his Stats. Leveling Up didn't feel quite the same as it usually did. Sandra loomed in the back of his mind, but he steeled himself and pushed the thought back. There wasn't much he could do about it, and moping wouldn't help.

Maverick finished off the third kill and, after that, they descended to loot. Max picked up a total of **36,860 Cosmic Coins**, which hugely excited Maverick. Max was inclined to want to spend everything on Maverick due to their special circumstances. But that was getting expensive. The next boost for Maverick would cost **200,000 Cosmic Coins**.

Maverick, of course, protested and demanded that the coins should be spent exclusively on him. Not that Max had much of anything else worth upgrading. But hopefully that would change.

The loot was exactly what they had hoped for: heavy-duty ammunition for Max's new **[Kinetic Missile]** ability.

[Breastplate of Brawling (D-grade)]
[Spear of Long Lunges (C-grade)]
[Longsword of Razor Slices (D-grade)]

Max didn't look at the Stats. They didn't matter, as the Items were ammunition. He picked them up and placed them in the Inventory space. After that was done, he flew back up in the air. It was time to search for the enemy.

CHAPTER TWENTY-NINE

Counter Counter

After several minutes at high altitude, watching for signs of movement or strange, unnatural shapes in the landscape, Max was beginning to lose his thrill for battle.

He flew around for another ten minutes, scouting the land. He wasn't shocked he hadn't found the enemy yet, as it would have been prudent for them to hide, especially given they had Max as an opponent.

But he was getting increasingly worried. First thing he did was fly past the giant dinosaur boss, who seemed to be drooping its head in sleep, while swaying idly. Max flew to the place he had last fought the lizards. It seemed that they had managed a few more kills after Max had left.

Brave of them.

But mostly the area was still chock-full of creatures. Max had to remind himself that the lizards were adept at using grass and other natural elements for camouflage and hidden movement.

"You think they're hiding in the grass?"

Maverick hummed. "Beats me. Maybe I could shoot around randomly and see if we hear a yelp."

"I always appreciate your thought-out, high-minded strategies."

"I'm a gun, not a book, you lack-witted muttonhead."

"With these quips, you could pass yourself off as a thesaurus."

"Ha!" Maverick said gleefully. "Smart *and* powerful! I like it."

Max refocused and made the decision to descend. He felt a tinge of disappointment when his feet hit the ground, but he had to be conservative with his Mana and make sure he saved up his use of Spiritual energy for when it was needed.

Max had no Class specializing in tracking enemies nor did he have any other ways to discern where the enemy could be.

He sat down and grabbed a handful of grass just to give his hands something to do as he thought. Maverick wasn't in the mood to help, but Max could feel through their bond that he was trying to figure out their insights for Cultivation.

If I were a lizard, what would I do?

They had just had their asses beat by Max. But they had grown stronger. Max was pretty sure the enemy had racked up more kills in total than the humans. They weren't weak, but they surely needed *something* to deal with Max.

So would they go somewhere where it's hard for me to use my powers? Like a cave?

But there were no caves Max knew of. Besides, the monsters were out in the open. No, they would have to stay in the plains.

So what would be the worst thing they could do to hamstring me? How could they level the playing field?

"Oh . . ." Max said as realization hit him. "Oh no."

"Snap out of it and go, you dolt!" Maverick said urgently.

Max shot up into the air, pushing some extra Mana into his flight to bolster his speed.

"We've only been away for a little while," Max said against the wind. Their speed was so great, no one else could have heard him, but Maverick could of course always understand what he was saying.

"Unless they were waiting for you to leave . . ." Maverick said grimly.

Another burst of speed burned through more Mana, but time was the more valuable resource now.

It took only a couple of minutes before Max could see he'd been right. The humans and lizards were fighting.

The enemy must have some tracking Class or they wouldn't have found us.

That was all the time for thought that Max had to spare. He plucked the breastplate out of his Inventory. It was heavy, weighing a good twenty-five pounds, although it was hard to tell for sure these days, since Max had enhanced strength.

As he made the breastplate spin, he looked down at the battlefield.

The enemy paladin had his golden shield on, but it wasn't a full barrier, shielding everyone. Out of either disdain or the need to conserve Mana, the lizard only projected a large umbrella of a shield. The mages were in formation behind him, casting spells through the barrier.

As for the humans, Jones was at the front with Brian and two other fighters. Christie was dashing in and out of the enemy backline, slicing here and there, seemingly vanishing and reappearing a yard away from where she had been after striking. Must have been a new Skill.

Well, if the enemy couldn't be bothered to set up a proper barrier, it would cost them. Max hurled the breastplate at the enemy, and Maverick unholstered himself, finally giving away that they had returned with a barrage of bullets at the enemy.

The breastplate crashed into the enemy mage formation, tossing them in every direction. They must have practiced a drill, because instead of flopping around and panicking, all three lizards who were hit instantly produced potions and drank them.

Jones charged in and smashed both of his axes at the golden barrier. A cloud of black poisonous smoke covered him, but the large ripples on the barrier showed that he didn't flinch for a second.

Freya was casting thin barriers of ice in the human backline, blocking the poison cloud attacks. That meant the middle of the battlefield was full of black smoke, and it would certainly have an effect on the human frontline.

Maverick was exclusively targeting the paladin-type. Now that the mages had been disoriented for a couple of seconds by a high-speed kinetic missile of a breastplate, and Maverick was keeping their quarterback busy, the humans advanced.

Max plucked a spear from his Inventory and tried to quickly determine who to throw it at.

Before he could come to a decision, Christie reemerged.

She jumped out of the shadows at the tall poison mage and thrust her daggers into his sides. He gasped. Max sent an urgent pulse to Maverick through their bond to switch targets. In response, Maverick started blasting the poison mage with bullets.

The enemy paladin reacted as soon as Maverick stopped firing. He used his golden glimmering light lance extending from the tip of his sword and stabbed it at Christie.

Max didn't have time to put spin into the spear; he just hurled it at Losshnak, who hoisted his shield and created a personalized golden, shining barrier around himself.

Christie screamed and wobbled in pain at the light lance skewering her, but Erwin cast a protective faintly green bubble around her.

Losshnak was clearly charging up another one of the lances, but Max's spear crashed into him, tossing him several feet away. He hadn't been killed, but he was on his knees now, coughing and trying to push himself up against his shield.

Wasting no time, Max produced the longsword from his Inventory and hurled it at the poison mage. He pushed extra Mana into it through his Cultivation and despite the lack of preparation, the sword struck true. It sliced through the poison mage's neck, nearly decapitating him. His half-cut-off head slumped grotesquely to the side and he fell.

[Signature Ability Level Up!]
Skill upgraded: [Telekinesis I] → [Telekinesis II]
Defeated Level 22 [Ishkarassi]
You gained 10,270 Experience points

Maverick hooted with glee and started shooting at Losshnak. Max flew further down, trying to find an Item he could reuse to throw. The rest of the humans were advancing by Brian's commands, pushing into the enemy, encroaching on Losshnak.

"*Halt!*"

Just when Max had picked up the spear back in the air with his **[Telekinesis]**, everything froze.

CHAPTER THIRTY

Interruptions

[Respectfully, might we inquire what is the meaning of this stasis?]

A jellyfish donning the sleek white, plastic, and glass design of an iPhone appeared in midair above the battlefield.

Three child-sized, thin, and long-armed grey aliens with dim, black eyes and large heads materialized, also now hovering in the air above the battleground.

"*The match had to be paused because of suspicion that the human race has somehow cheated. After an investigation under the Rule 5, Section B, Clause 15.3 has taken place, we can return the combatants to their respective headquarters and continue the game.*"

Max, who was frozen in place, was growing livid with rage at the Grays. They had had the enemy on the ropes. They could have even killed Losshnak.

[Please elaborate on what sort of cheating you suspect the humans guilty of. The Zoos Collective offers to show you their side of the logs on the battle arena, if you are willing to continue the match immediately afterward.]

The thin, telepathic voice of the Grays took on an impatient tone:

"*Despite the collective Skill cast on all the races by the ICCB, the deceitful humans have maneuvered to infect my representative species with a pathogen. An investigation must be called to investigate how they managed to circumvent the effects of* [**Mass Immunity**]."

The Zoos jellyfish's robotic voice, which often sounded purely monotone, now sounded almost amused:

[Because as it stands in the sub-regulations of Rule 57, any and every fight conducted by the patron factions must be considered as a pure free-for-all, thus removing any ongoing Abilities that are in effect.]

"That— Surely it would not. The Grays have—"

[The humans poisoned the water supply with their excrement. An extremely barbaric approach, but effective. That is why all of the Ishkarassi are sick and weakened both physically and in their Mana control. It is only their Cultivation that keeps them as functional as they are.]

"We know this well! There is no need to educate the Grays in such mundane matters. It matters not. Now that the match was paused for so long and the stasis has regenerated everyone's Mana, Cultivation, and status effects, we have to relocate both parties."

[That would be a violation we will not accede to.]

"What violation? Are the Grays also not an arbiter in this match? What rule or stipulation prevents us from performing a [**Mass Teleport**]*?"*

The Zoos jellyfish didn't answer. It only hummed like an electrical motor and swayed slightly in the air.

Max couldn't believe it. His anger was growing to a magnificent level, one that even impressed Maverick. He was practically shaking with fury. He didn't want to kill the lizards. He wanted to kill the Grays.

The Grays must have sensed his bloodlust, because they all turned their giant heads toward him for just the briefest of moments. Max thought he saw the middle one's thin lips momentarily lifting into a flicker of a smile.

The Zoos jellyfish seemed to slump ever so slightly. Max tried his best to cope. Not being able to move didn't help.

[Understood. You are indeed the other arbiter party of this match. However, after the [Mass Teleport], **the match will continue and obviously you, as an impartial judge, will not be able to remove the Ishkarassi's sickness.**]

That shut the Grays up for a moment. While it was difficult to tell from their expressionless faces, the skin around their eyes seemed to tighten in frustration.

"If that is the case, then let it be formally known that the Grays will use our veto power to introduce a five-day truce."

[That is acceptable. We will verify the request and forward it to be processed by the ICCB.]

Acceptable how? They're throwing us to the wolves for some alien brownie points?!
"Hmph. See that you do. I'll sort the critters back to their boxes. [**Mass Teleport**]."

And with that, Max felt as if he were released from status and, a moment later, as if he was being lifted with a hook by his belly button. Then, he blinked out of existence.

Max watched grimly as the Zoos representative explained to the rest of the humans what the two patron races had agreed to. As expected, everyone's anger was growing.

It felt so damn unfair. They were fighting for their lives. Barely eating, barely sleeping. Constantly on the edge, playing against higher stakes than any of them had the training for.

And they had almost won. They could have crippled the enemy forces severely or even outright killed them all.

But because of absolute bullshit politics, they had been sidelined and had the rug pulled out from under their feet. Max was so frustrated that after unclenching his fists he'd noticed that the palms of his hands were bleeding where the nails had dug in.

After their dear patron was done with its explanation, it vanished, leaving everyone dumbfounded back at their base by the pond. All the other members of the group turned to Max, as if he had all the answers.

He supposed it might as well have to be him.

"Five-day truce," Max said to the group. "No guards or sentries needed. No fighting with the monsters allowed."

Everyone nodded and waited. Max cleared his throat.

"We'll rest the first day. Do literally nothing related to combat. I don't want you Cultivating, I don't want you spamming abilities to expend Mana. I want you to use this opportunity to give your bodies and minds a real rest. This is the first time in months we'll be able to sleep without keeping one eye open. Wasting that opportunity would be a real shame."

"Hear, hear," Brian said, and everyone joined in a chorus of agreement. Max chuckled. He was sure they had all expected him to go full gung-ho and demand overtime on Cultivation.

"I know these days have been rough. We've lost two comrades. We don't have much time for grieving. Or rest. But you guys have earned it. We're winning this. Humanity is winning. If it weren't for the Grays' bullshit, we could have *won*."

The group murmured in agreement. Some nodded, urging Max to continue. Christie sat down, holding her side. Healing potions had stabilized her, but she of all people needed the rest. When their eyes met, she gave Max a wan smile.

"That means we just need to keep doing what we're doing. The enemy will attempt to Cultivate. We will have to do that tomorrow as well. I'll distribute **[Celestial Illumination Pills]** as needed. Now go rest, for Pete's sake."

Brian started organizing the tents and told Jones to get a fire going. Max decided to fly back out into the plains. It was still veritably infested with monsters.

Flying at mid-height to stay out of the way of some well-aimed rocks, Max scouted around, trying to find a stray deer.

After his search brought up nothing, he flew to the edge of the forest that encircled half of the plains. There he saw a group of three lizards also skulking around for prey.

Max spotted Losshnak at their helm. The paladin looked at him for a while and nodded. Whether the nod was some sort of confirmation to himself or directed at Max, who could say?

"You know what we should do?" Maverick said, voice full of confidence.

"Uh huh?"

"Harass them," Maverick said. "Make sure they can't hunt for food. Blast around, make everything run. Or you can use **[Tether]** so they can't pick up the carcasses."

Max pondered that for a moment. For all his numerous ridiculous flaws, the gun did have good ideas from time to time.

Before Max could reach a conclusion, a plastic jellyfish appeared in the air to hover next to Max.

[That is an excellent idea, but it is against our stipulations. We decided to inform you personally, because it was not specifically mentioned. The Grays also informed the Ishkarassi that they are not to disturb you in any way. The same, of course, applies to you. There will be no sabotage allowed. This is a complete truce.]

Max grunted. He didn't particularly like the Zoos Collective right now.

"Was there nothing you could have done? We could have won."

The jellyfish floated quietly in the air before it spoke.

[The Grays currently have more veto power within the ICCB than the Zoos Collective. Your delicate situation also has put the Zoos Collective in a position where we must make concessions, even if they lead to disadvantageous outcomes.]

"So as long as you guys score some political points, we are entirely at the mercy of your whims, no matter how we perform?"

[It would be ill-advised to look at the situation like that. It is more a case of there being games within games in this situation. There are levels to this warfare. You are in charge of the ground battles and tactics, and we will do our best to provide you with the best possible environment. We are doing what we can, within reason, to facilitate scenarios that will be beneficial for humans and the Zoos Collective.]

"But when push comes to shove, you will throw us under the bus?"
Another short pause, probably to translate the metaphor.

[You would be ill-advised to look at the situation—]

"Yeah, yeah," Max said impatiently. "I'm not a fan of your politics, but I have no say in the matter."

[We are pleased that you have grown so much in maturity in such a short time.]

It felt *very* weird taking a compliment from his dear patrons, like he was a dog performing tricks for his master. That wasn't a feeling Max particularly liked.
Determined to squelch that thought, Max decided to try his luck. He doubted the Zoos Collective felt like they owed anything to the humans after what they had just pulled, but it never hurt to ask.
"Would it be appropriate to ask for something?"

[We are not allowed to directly grant Items or other boons that would affect the outcome of this match.]

"That's fine. This won't affect the outcome of anything in any way. Think of it as a cosmetic change."

[We could see acceding to such a request. What is it?]

"I'd like for you guys to create a protective bubble around our base against the lizards. Just having that will let my people sleep better. I want them to feel safe, so they can relax."
The jellyfish gave off another one of those electrical motor hums. It was probably leafing through some fat rulebook.

[We have deemed this an acceptable solution and we commend you for the initiative. We have cast a [Metamagic Barrier] around your camp. Humans

will be able to freely leave and enter. When the barrier vanishes, the cease-fire ends.]

Max was surprised he had gotten what he wanted. That left him dumbfounded.
"I—Uh— thanks."

[Is there anything else you require, Maximillian?]

Max shrugged. "Not really."

[Please continue performing in the manner you have. We look forward to your victory here.]

"Don't we all," Max muttered to himself.

CHAPTER THIRTY-ONE

Heart to Heart

After Max got back from his hunt, the group ate the deer meat, cracking jokes about how hard it would be to be a vegan in this new world. Max noticed how Freya blushed hot red around the ears and chewed on her deer meat in silence.

Seemed like Max was tentatively back in the good graces of the group, which he definitely preferred. They weren't exactly chummy and Christie had stopped calling him 'darling' (which hurt more than it should have), but they made room for him in the circle and were very enthusiastic and grateful about the bubble around the camp which Max had managed to negotiate. Well, Maverick had insisted for a good ten minutes that it had been his idea, but Max doubted he had convinced anyone.

The protective dome—a milky, pearly membrane—shimmered around them, thirty feet in the air. It covered their whole base, the pond, and part of the bamboo forest. Funnily enough, even knowing the dome was pretty much purely cosmetic, it still made Max feel better. Just a little bit safer. Additionally, Max was glad he had gotten some goodwill back thanks to his idea.

Well, I'm no longer worshiped and thought to be some kind of war god or a perfect leader. That's good. I'm just a guy, at the end of the day. It's better that their expectations were lowered sooner rather than later.

After the meal, Jones started smoking the excess meat and people chatted around the fire. Max was enjoying himself. He could slowly feel tiredness encroaching upon him inch by inch the later the evening went on. It must not even have been particularly late. If Max had to guess, it was only around 5 or 6 p.m., but people were already starting to drift toward the tents.

He yawned and it spread to a few people, Freya included. She said her good nights and slumped off to bed.

Max decided to leave the fire and go sit by the pond for a while. He needed to contemplate.

"You and your oh-so-deep thoughts," Maverick said and huffed. "Instead of pretending to be some philosopher king, you should just talk to me."

"I'd rather step on a rusty nail than talk to you about my feelings," Max said.

"That's a fair point," Maverick said cheerfully. "Completely understandable. I wouldn't be vulnerable with someone like me either."

"Surprisingly self-aware . . ."

"Too bad I can sense what you're feeling anyway, so we're going to talk."

Max sighed.

"You notice how you're sad and angry?" Maverick said. "Stop doing that."

"Thanks, Dr. Freud."

"What are you so upset about?"

Max shrugged and looked at the pond. There were faint ripples in the water again, which Max continued to find curious. Maverick tugged on their bond, demanding attention.

"I just hate being a pawn," Max said. "I'm doing double-time here, putting in all of this effort, fighting for my life and everyone else's every day. And does it matter? No."

"Pfft," Maverick said. "Of course it matters, you dolt. Are you crazy?"

"What do you mean?"

Maverick talked to Max like he was an especially stupid five-year-old. "What is our Dao, Maximillian?"

"Uh, we don't know?" Max said. "Maybe my Dao is to finally make you stop calling me 'Maximillian.'"

"Just work with me, you damn woolhead."

"It's something about destruction. Something about conquering. Our Dao is to remove opposition and obliterate anything standing in our way. Our Dao is about going forward, ever higher. I have this feeling in my gut, you know."

They both felt it. They were close to an insight.

"What feeling?" Maverick demanded, his voice filled with impatience.

"Like it's not only about ambition. Our Dao goes beyond ambition. I look at the world-devouring tree and you know . . ."

"Yeah," Maverick said. "You go, huh . . . ? Is that it? That's really where it ends? Isn't there more? I want more."

"Not just more," Max said. "I want *everything*."

Leveled Up Ruby-Level Cultivator (lesser) to 4
+4 free Attribute points

Maverick laughed and hooted. "Well, there you go. You're not half as stupid as you look sometimes."

Max enjoyed the surge of Spiritual Energy inside of him, encasing itself in his cells, making him stronger. His Stats were also adding up, which Max definitely liked.

"Yesssss," Maverick said. "Come to Papa. I want more. We're going to look for more insights during the truce, yes?"

Max chuckled. "That's probably the first genuine question I've heard out of you for weeks."

"Darn it, I was on such a roll . . ."

"But, yeah," Max said as he struggled out of his boots. He dipped his toes in the water. It was cool, and he could sense something strange. He just hoped it wasn't hungry piranhas. "We'll be reading more of Durum's book and figuring out the insights."

"Do you think we'll ascend through Ruby?" Maverick asked.

"I think we'll certainly advance further," Max said, enjoying the cool water. He definitely needed a wash, but maybe later. "I think we're ahead of Losshnak too right now."

"Ha!" Maverick said. "That crusty lizard doesn't stand a chance against our awesomeness. I'm glad you've finally grown into your own as my sidekick. Those Items you throw at Mach II speed really make it easier for me to shine."

"Happy to help . . ."

"What should we do to find further insights?" Maverick asked excitedly.

"Sleep," Max said and half-stifled a yawn. "Rest a little and then attack it with a fresh body and mind."

"Then what the hell am I supposed to do? My Spiritual Energy needs a bit of replenishment for sure, but I don't sleep, Max."

"Good," Max said. "I almost forgot. You can Cultivate while I sleep."

Maverick grumbled. "That's the sidekick's job."

"It's the one who doesn't need to sleep's job."

"You barely need to either," Maverick protested. "I can sense how the Ruby body makes you more resilient."

"It does," Max admitted. "But I think some rest and a delicious six hours of sleep or so would do wonders for me."

"Five," Maverick demanded.

"Six. You have six bullet cartridges. That's six pills you can ingest. I mean, if you want to have a break, I could always sleep for a seven . . ."

"Six it is, then!" Maverick said quickly. "Damn it. When did you become such an oppressive bastard?"

"Alpha Ludus teaches many things . . ." Max said distractedly and continued to watch the ripples on the pond.

CHAPTER THIRTY-TWO

A Slow Morning

Max woke up feeling like a million bucks. Sleeping under the white dome had been soothing. It was a testament to the power of the placebo effect. Max knew the barrier was pointless, and probably wouldn't even stop a lizard from wandering in.

It didn't matter. What mattered was that he felt safer. Besides, if a lizard tried doing something funny, they would certainly be blown to smithereens and, since the ICCB had the ability to pretty much prevent death, there was little chance this truce wasn't real.

That meant Max had a lot of time on his hands. He yawned softly and stretched out, putting his holster back on. Maverick was in it at the time, in the middle of Cultivation. Max could definitely feel that he had been strengthened in that regard as well. They weren't close to another Level Up in their Cultivation, however, having just Leveled Up the night before.

But Max could feel his Spiritual Energy was ever so slightly more potent. He noticed Maverick taking stock of his emotions through their bond, and the gun sent a pulse of smugness.

Then he noticed he was the first one awake. He saw a few stray legs poking out of some tents and heard a soft chorus of snores. Everything was so serene and peaceful right now.

He was clearly built for war, Max knew this by now. His Dao was that of destruction; fighting and warfare were the first things in his life that he realized he was actually good at. It was like he was meant for this. Maybe that was what Dao was all about.

But regardless of that, he still found himself enjoying the peace and quiet. He had forgotten what it felt like. Now Max reveled in it.

It feels like it's worth fighting for.

Max grinned to himself as he disrobed and dipped into the pond. The water was cool, but he could instantly feel a crusty membrane of grime shedding off his shins. It felt like another bit of peace. There was a silver lining to all of this. The truce was actually good for their side.

"What the hell is that supposed to mean?" Maverick asked from Max's leather holster. Apparently he had exhausted his last [**Celestial Illumination Pill**].

"You're smart and can read my thoughts," Max said. "Why don't you figure it out?"

"You ever actually look at your thoughts?" Maverick snapped. "Like *really* look at them? Do you have the slightest idea what a convoluted labyrinthine mess your mind is?"

"Huh?" Max said. "What do you mean?"

"Just yesterday before falling asleep you thought of cake. First you decided it was a crazy fantasy to want cake on Alpha Ludus. Then you wondered, if there was cake available after all, if you would eat it. You would have to consider it, because the sugar might weaken your performance. But then you figured it might boost it from a psychological standpoint. Then you went on to wonder if it would make you fat and make you unattractive to the girls. But then you reminded yourself that this was definitely no time or place for romance. Eventually, you settled on cake being great but that it was probably good it wasn't available. DO YOU HAVE ANY IDEA HOW EXHAUSTING IT IS TO LISTEN TO THIS DRIVEL?!"

Max laughed as he scrubbed his hair. It had been a tangled black mess. It felt nice to give it some care. "I thought of all of that?"

"Half of it was barely conscious," Maverick said. "But *I* have to parse through it all if I want to have any insight into what you're thinking. It's like slogging through snow, mud, and tar, while carrying a cow calf."

"Interesting metaphor for someone who doesn't have legs."

"I have the power of imagination."

"Keep working on that," Max said. "Speaking of which, any revelations regarding our insights last night?"

"None," Maverick said. "I focused on Cultivation. We still aren't at the peak of our Level in terms of power."

"I noticed that," Max said. "Sitting down and Cultivating will probably give us staying power and stamina in terms of Spiritual energy."

"That's what I thought," Maverick said. His voice was laced with practically reverent greed. "More control too. The stronger we get, the more accurate and powerful my shots become."

"I thought you scaled off my Intelligence."

"I do," Maverick said. "But now that I have my own Mana pool, I can augment the shots."

"That's awesome," Max said and splashed cold water on his face.

Maverick's favorite brand of smugness passed through their bond.

"So why is the truce better for humans than the lizards?"

"Well, for one thing, they're using this time to fight off the pathogens," Max said. "While we get to focus on rest and improvement."

"Fair," Maverick said. "But that wasn't it, was it?"

"There's also the fact that humans at the end of the day enjoy and crave peace. Even me, who is apparently a thoroughbred fighter, needed this."

Maverick scoffed in self-satisfaction. "I get it. The lizards are a warrior people of violence-loving bastards."

"Exactly," Max said. "This truce won't recharge their minds and bodies in the same way it will ours."

"They're more disciplined than humans, though," Maverick said. "They'll be able to increase their Cultivation more."

Max nodded quietly. That was true. He could only motivate and enforce Cultivation so much. The best course of action was leading by example. They would have to work hard during these five days regardless. They needed to make sure they kept a lead on Losshnak and his cronies.

"Nice abs, darling," Christie drawled as she approached the pond.

Max instinctively dipped down into the water, revealing only his head and shoulders. Christie smirked at him.

"We're back to 'darling,' are we?" Max said.

A mixture of emotions played across Christie's face as she considered what to say. Then she nodded to herself and looked Max straight in the eyes. "Sorry."

"For what?" Max asked.

"Losing faith," Christie said, lacking all of the confidence that her voice normally contained. It was as if the words were coming from a dejected young girl.

"You always had too much faith to begin with," Max said and offered a smile.

"In my defense," Christie said, gaining back some of her flair, "there isn't much out here to put your faith into."

"You guys are giving me a big cross to bear," Max said, trying to contain the bitterness in his voice.

Christie just watched him and there was that familiar predatory glint in her eyes. It made Max slightly uncomfortable. "That's because we think you can handle it."

With that, she started shuffling out of her clothes.

"Hey!" Max said and turned.

"Relax, darling," Christie said and gave a low chuckle. "I need to wash too, and I'd rather do it when everyone is still sleeping."

"You could have waited," Max said, feeling his ears grow hot. He could hear Christie gasp lightly as she dipped into the cool water behind him.

"I could have," Christie admitted. "But where's the fun in that?"

"So what will you do with this free time?" Max said, trying to keep his voice level.

"You can turn back now, darling," Christie said.

Max did and watched Christie wink at him over her naked shoulders.

"I'll Cultivate and practice using my Skills," Christie said. "I hit Level Twenty yesterday and my Class upgraded from an [**Assassin**] to [**Shadow Assassin**]. I had hoped to get [**Ninja**] Class. That would be sexy."

"Maybe it's coming next," Max said. "Have you picked up a [**Signature Ability**] yet?"

"No," Christie said and washed her hair. Max did his best to look her in the eyes. "I was hoping you could give me some pointers, darling."

"What are your options?"

"I received this great ability called [**Shadow Step**]. It allows me to vanish and reappear up to ten feet away. Costs a bastard amount of Mana, but I love the way it feels. Makes me feel dangerous."

Max laughed in disbelief. "That's so ridiculously powerful."

"You think?"

"I honestly don't think I even need to know your other abilities. That skill is so damn good. It's both going to make you a terrifying assassin and keep you alive in a tight spot."

Christie hummed pensively at that. "Yeah, I want to make it mine too. It's a new ability, but I'm already *loving* it."

"It will also go well with that ring," Max remarked.

"Oh, yeah," Christie said, her elegant face turning into a slight frown. "Do you want it back?"

"No," Max said. "It would be hard for me to use, since my thing is flying. It's perfect for you."

Christie gave him a beaming smile. "Thanks."

"As for the Skill choice, I say go with your gut. Doing that has kept me alive for this long."

"Not only kept you alive, darling," Christie said. "You've been thriving."

"Doing my best is all," Max said and gave a little smile.

"Really, Max," Christie said and came closer, lowering her voice and eyes. "I'm sorry."

She was only two steps away. Max could feel the warmth emanating off of her. Max would rather have had her apologize with some clothes on. "It's fine."

"Sandra was one of mine," she said quietly. "I knew her since Day One. Abrasive from time to time. But a reliable and a good person. Brave to boot."

"I know," Max said. "It was good to have her."

"Then she died a completely stupid death," Christie said, her voice taking on the edge of a growl. "It was so easy to blame you."

"Not a fan of the sentiment," Max said. "But I get it. It's human."

"Not all of us are so good at transcending our humanity," Christie said and looked Max in the eyes. "All I'm saying is that I understand why you made the choices you did. I know I was wrong to blame you. My head knows this. Just give me a bit of time for my heart to know it too."

"Don't worry," Max said. "I really mean it when I say that you guys have too much faith in me. Not that I don't like the adulation, but it was good that all of you guys chilled out on that a bit."

"How do you not let it get to your head?" Christie asked, brushing a strand of wet hair back. "You're so powerful. Everyone else is scrambling here, just trying to make sense of this. Just trying to survive. But you're playing chess while we play checkers, aren't you? We are surviving and you are flying. And yet you keep yourself so grounded."

Max laughed at that. Genuinely laughed at that. That was a hell of a question.

"I'm not kidding," Christie went on. "Not only that. You've got a huge amount of baggage too. You have this crazy bounty on your head and you're legitimately carrying all our fates on your shoulder. How do you not let it get to you?"

Max shook his head and smiled ruefully. He got out of the water, know full well Christie's gaze was fixated on his buttocks. Whatever. Let her have a look. The water was very cold and he needed to start with his reading and Cultivation.

"It wasn't a rhetorical question," Christie said after Max had put his clothes on.

Max just laughed again softly and shook his head.

"What?"

"He clearly doesn't want to talk about it, you crazy, horny, weird lady," Maverick snapped.

Christie went on to stammer about. It was rather cute really. "Oh, I— I mean I was just— You don't have to— what I mean is—"

Max couldn't help but smirk a little. Christie must have seen it was a smirk of the pained variety.

"Sorry, darling."

"It's fine."

"Didn't think you had a chink in your armor," Christie said.

"That's the problem," Max muttered. He glanced behind him. He could still hear faint snoring but there was no movement otherwise. He turned back to Christie, who looked all sorts of apologetic. Max wondered how much he was really willing to open up. "You all think I'm some damn superhero."

"That's because—"

Max gave her a sour look.

"Sorry. How do you— what do you feel?"

Maverick huffed. "You really can't take a hint, woman."

"It's fine," Max said. "I guess it's good to talk."

Max sat down and Christie swam a bit closer, so she could lean her hands and head against one of the rocks by the shore.

Max thought about what he wanted to say. Not much, but maybe enough to give her some sense of what was going on. She could pass it on as folklore to the others. It was hard to find a thread to start pulling, though. Max shrugged. "On second thought, there's really no point in explaining it."

"Why not?" Christie asked.

"It's like poverty," Max said with a tinge of sourness. In his old life he had been jobless and prospectless. "There are three levels to it. First one is that you think you understand poverty. You see pictures online, you can conceptualize it. The second level is that you *actually* see it. You look at the people who are standing in line for a soup kitchen in their ragged smelly clothes in the eye. It's not on a conceptual level, the smell literally stings your eyes. It's real."

"And the third level?" Christie asked.

"You experience it yourself."

"So you're saying even if you explain it, I won't understand it," Christie said. Max nodded.

"Try me anyway, darling. For yourself."

Max shrugged. Maverick bristled, and Max understood why. He really didn't want to talk about it. Especially to someone who thought he was some kind of invincible war god.

"It's so much weight, you become numb to it," Max said in a hollow voice. "I know the importance of my role. It's almost funny. I used to be a nobody, always wanting to be important. Always wanting to be special. Always secretly harboring a messiah complex. 'Someday I will be important,' that's what I thought. I think it's because I always felt small. Always felt like I was the runt of the litter. I wanted recognition."

Christie inched closer, watching Max attentively.

"And then I got to be special. There's two sides to every coin. On the other side of recognition is responsibility."

Max was quiet for a moment. Christie waited, watching him with absolute attention.

"I got to know how it feels like to be absolutely necessary. To be fundamental. And not fundamental in your family or to your company. Fundamental to the survival of your species. I was never built to play with stakes like this. And then you ask why. Why are you the person that not only holds other people's lives in your hands but so many millions of them? And then you ask if you are being crazy, feeding into your messiah complex. But what if you're right? What if it really is all you? What if you really are the main character of not only your own story, but of everyone else's story? The main character of humanity? Messiah complex much? Now, that's a crushing pressure like nothing else. Crushing doesn't even cut it. Even Atlas couldn't shrug off this weight. I don't want to talk about it and I don't want to think about it. I'll go crazy if I do."

Christie looked at him with a stunned, blank expression on her face. Max gave her a wan smile and walked away.

CHAPTER THIRTY-THREE

Breakthrough Insight

Max set up his hammock in a shady spot and plopped himself inside. For a while, he just enjoyed the relaxing swing and the soft wind caressing his skin. It was a beautiful morning.

Max listened to the cacophony of birds singing mating calls to one another in the trees. He listened to the camp slowly waking up. Everything was peaceful, everything was quiet. It was a good moment. Something Max didn't realize he had needed. He sighed.

Then, after deciding he'd had enough savoring for now, Max opened a menu interface and produced Durum's book from his Inventory. The massive leather-bound tome was cumbersome to hold, but Max was determined to do it in his hammock.

"You really are a special kind of dunderhead, aren't you?" Maverick quipped. He was flying around Max now.

Max opened the book in his lap and leafed through it until he found the chapters concerning insights and Ruby Cultivation. He traced his finger along the words as he read aloud for Maverick's benefit.

"The insights a lesser Ruby Cultivator can accrue grow sparser with every discovery made. This is the natural order of things. The low-hanging fruits have been harvested, leaving only the more difficult-to-reach. It is the nature of one's Dao to be revealed to the Cultivator in increments. Absorbing both the knowledge and power at once would damage or destroy the individual. However, it is advisable that one prepares their body and mind for the [**Breakthrough Insight**]."

Maverick hummed with interest. "The what now?"

The [**Breakthrough Insight**] *is the key needed to ascend to super-mortal Levels of Cultivation, namely the Diamond and Celestial realms. The Ruby Cultivation Level is the limbo, the precipice. This means proper preparation must take place. Many Cultivators are led astray by the easy advancement provided by the insights.*

In this, they neglect their practice with Spiritual Energy. The body must be prepared for advancement, and it should not only be done through insights, even though it could be.

"That means . . ." Max said as he reread the paragraph, ". . . we could have really shot ourselves in the foot."

"I like how you combined a human and a gun metaphor."

"You were right to practice Cultivation the traditional way last night."

"I am usually right," Maverick said brightly.

"So we need to find out what this [**Breakthrough Insight**] is and then use it after we are at the brink of advancing a stage."

"It doesn't specify whether the [**Breakthrough Insight**] is meant for the lesser or greater Ruby stage," Maverick said. "I feel like that's an important detail."

"Sure, would be nice to know," Max said. "Let's read more."

Once a Cultivator has advanced to the Diamond stage, he will understand his Dao well on a conceptual level. He has found his insights and reached realizations about who he is and what he should do in this world. This is the foundation created in the Ruby stage. While continuing to strengthen the body and mind of the Cultivator remains pivotal for safe advancement, there are easy ways to increase one's power, just as there was in the Ruby Stage.

"I love freebies," Maverick said. "What is it? What is it?"

"Calm down and shut up," Max said and continued.

The Diamond stage is the first super-mortal stage of Cultivation. This means the practitioner has ceased to age and wither. He will not grow old or sick or face any other worldly afflictions. Only the violent actions of a stronger power can destroy him. Being a super-mortal Cultivator leads to a greater connection with the universe. This means that thoughts, words, and actions are more directly resonant with the person's Karma. Mortals possess a weak will which cannot directly affect the universe. But once a Cultivator breaks into the super-mortal stages, he will bear the responsibility of Karma.

"This isn't exactly what we need right now, is it?" Max said.

"Who cares?" Maverick said. "It's interesting!"

Karma is accrued through thought, speech, and action. If these three are not aligned with the Cultivator's Dao, there will be no accumulation of super-mortal Spiritual Energy. This is a special kind of Spiritual Energy only accumulated through working in harmony with one's Karma. The Cultivator must have one mind, one body, one soul—all aligned in perfect harmony around their Dao. Any deviation from their Karma and Dao will lead to stagnation and possibly even weakening of the soul.

"I friggin' told you!" Maverick said. "You really need to listen to me more often."

"It doesn't say this matters yet at a Ruby Level," Max said. "In fact, it literally says it doesn't."

"I don't care what it says," Maverick said. "I was right, you was wrong, me win."

Max shook his head. But Maverick did have a point. Well, not really, but not far off. Following his Dao would lead to better results. It was also a clear path for him to take. It would allow for easier, simpler decision-making.

Just follow your Dao and all will turn out right. Sounds like some Instagram lunatic's brand idea. Just follow your bliss and you will manifest good things. God, I used to laugh my ass off at that shit.

"Follow me and all will turn out Maverick," Maverick said, seeming to be extremely satisfied with this turn of phrase. "What a great catchphrase."

Max tilted his head to address the sky. "Hey. ICCB? Zeus? Golden Dragon in the Center of the Universe? Can I get a gun *without* stupid catchphrases?"

Maverick harrumphed.

CHAPTER THIRTY-FOUR

Fruits of Labor

Max spent some more time leafing through the book, but he couldn't find anything about whether the **[Breakthrough Insight]** was to be made on the lesser or greater stage of Ruby Cultivation. A lot of the pages featured stories of legendary Cultivators and their Daos. There was a Xerinthian named Palgo Muerrr'a'a whose Dao was to become a school of fish. The more he grew in power, the more fish he became. He ended up turning three planets into pure salt-water worlds and ruling over them.

"These are actually useful to read about," Max remarked.

"That Palgo dude was wild," Maverick said. "But how is this useful?"

"It gives us some perspective. We heard about the tree guy who could suck up life force. And this guy's Dao was to turn into multiple fishes. It means the Dao can be something completely wacky and outside the box."

"We got it easy," Maverick said. "It's not about boxes. It's about me, the most awesomest gun in existence. And you can make rocks fly or something."

"Not helping," Max growled.

"Yeah, yeah, I get your point," Maverick said. "Something something, keep your mind open to all of life's zany possibilities."

"Sure, I guess," Max said. "Just less flippant than that."

"No can do. I have to stay true to my Dao."

Max gave a dry chuckle but said no more.

Their path forward was clear. They had a couple of safe days to work on their Cultivation in the traditional sense. They had already found several insights, and Max suspected their bodies weren't exactly keeping up. Or they certainly wouldn't keep up if they kept advancing. That might have been what had been causing them strain from their extended use of Spiritual Energy.

It was time to get back to basics. So Max put the giant book away along with his hammock and produced the Cultivation formation that increased their practice speed, as well as his sack of [**Celestial Illumination Pills**].

Max sat down near the pond. It seemed like the best place, because it clearly held some excess Spiritual Energy. He could taste it in the water and feel it in the pond when he washed himself.

Softly pushing his thoughts away, Max placed a pill under his tongue and sat in the circle formation, with Maverick in his lap, like a samurai's sword.

Hours passed by and the morning turned to day. Max could hear people washing themselves in the pond and idly chatting near him. Max had told them to rest, and he was glad that they did. Perhaps they wondered why he didn't follow his own advice, but no one seemed to complain.

I'm not like them. I have my Dao to follow.

It was straining but rewarding work. After three hours, they took a break and Max could clearly feel that they were about to reach another Level. That would put them very close to possibly breaking into greater Ruby Cultivation. Max wondered whether he should seek an insight to ascend that stage.

The allure of insights was strong. And the reason was simple. Traditionally, Cultivating his body and his channels of Spiritual Energy was *extremely* slow. They only had five days. Max estimated that he would gain a Level tonight. Because of all the work they had done previously, it would come easily. But that was all that was going to be easy. The next Levels would be much harder. Max didn't think he would be able to get more than one additional Cultivation Level. And that was only possible because Maverick could Cultivate while he slept.

Losshnak was a higher-Level Cultivator when we came to this Deathmatch arena. Could he have some tricks or tools up his sleeve? We need to be able to stay ahead.

Max could almost taste his own desperation. Or maybe it was the overuse of the pills, who could tell? He watched the pond. The day was turning into evening and the giant orange flare in the sky was dimming. It made the pond look very cold and deep. Idle ripples could be seen on the surface in two places now.

Max made sure no one had just gotten out of the pool or had a drink. No. No people were around. What was causing those ripples?

Containing his curiosity, he popped another pill and sat down in the formation. Another hour passed, then another. On the sixth hour of the day's Cultivation, Max was sporting a headache so profound there wouldn't have been enough aspirin in the universe to alleviate it. That was the bad news. The good news was that they were close. Maverick could feel it too, which was why he wasn't complaining either, despite Max knowing how much strain he was under as well. It wasn't just the headache and the exhaustion from having to focus. It was the channels through which Spiritual Energy coursed in their bodies. They ached from overuse. It was like any muscle at the gym. They clearly wouldn't be able to pull as hardcore a day tomorrow. That worried Max.

But all of his worries went away when he finally felt something open up inside him and power surged through him. It was Max's favorite feeling in the world.

Leveled Up Ruby-Level Cultivator (lesser) to 5
+4 free Attribute points
Advancement to Ruby-Level Cultivator (greater) available

Maverick whistled. "Finally."

Max threw his back against the ground, arms extended, and exhaled deeply. "You said it, brother."

"Just so we are clear, you're the little brother."

Max scoffed, but he couldn't help but smile. Their hard work had paid off. They had fought tooth and nail for this Level today, and they had gotten it. It was very different from fighting and Leveling Up, but it was oh so worthwhile.

"Why only five Levels?" Max asked. Maverick responded with the equivalent of a shrug through their bond.

Max looked at the System message, opening it. He frowned.

[Advancement to the next Level will not require materials such as [Spirit Coins]**. Instead, it will naturally trigger after the discovery of the next insight if the required Spiritual power has been achieved.]**

"Eh, too bad," Maverick said. "We have excess **[Spirit Coins]**. I wonder if we need them later."

Max shrugged. "Who knows? Might as well keep them for now. This is good, actually. Getting to greater Ruby stage won't take too long."

"Yeah, baby!" Maverick said. "We're going to kick even more ass soon."

"What does 'required Spiritual power' mean?" Max said. "Do we need to Cultivate more? How are we supposed to know when it's enough?"

Maverick had nothing to say. He only sent a shrug through their bond. Max decided he might as well figure it out later.

Max decided to spend his eight free Attribute points. Having only eight was problematic, because Max was a serious person, who only applied the most effective tactics available. And the most effective tactic, of course, was to spend points in such a way that resulted in aesthetically pleasing numbers. This was not possible with his Constitution, Wisdom, and Intelligence right now. So he sighed and spent four points each on Toughness and Resistance.

Name: Max Cromwell
Cultivation stage: Ruby (lesser)
Class: Gravitician Level: 25
Health: 6500/6500
Stamina: 6500/6500
Mana: 8250/8250
Alliance: Joshua's Group
Stats:
Strength: 45
Dexterity: 50
Constitution: 130
Intelligence: 165
Wisdom: 125
Charisma: 44
Precision: 77
Toughness: 64
Resistance: 74

Max got up and grinned to himself. They were finally at the precipice. Next Level would be in the greater realm of Ruby Cultivation. That breakthrough would give him a ton of Stats and Spiritual Energy, which he would use to take this Deathmatch victory home. If he could just break into the next stage in the following days of the truce, Max was sure he would hold the advantage against Losshnak. After all, right now it was the lizard paladin who would have to catch up with him. If Max could keep pushing himself forward and maintain an advantage, the humans would surely win.

Suddenly, something strange happened in the pond. Max turned his attention to it and noticed that there were numerous ripples coming from multiple angles. As if whatever was causing the phenomenon had brought a whole crowd this time. Max couldn't take it anymore.

He took in a deep, deep breath and dove into the pond.

CHAPTER THIRTY-FIVE

Following Instincts

Max was surprised by how clear the water was. It was a dim evening, but it had an almost translucent quality, as if it was itself a light source.

The second surprise finally explained the mystery of the ripples. Four creatures came to the surface, shock at seeing Max written plain on their wide faces. Their heads were like large lightbulbs, skin green and with the rough texture of a rhino's. Their most dominating feature, however, was the massive shell covering each of their backs. That, and their hands . . .

Turtles. Turtles with fingers.

They all looked at Max for two full heartbeats. Then they looked at each other, then Max again. Then they all bolted. Max followed them underwater, swimming after them to the best of his ability.

The pond was much larger than he was led to believe from the surface. It sprawled in every direction underground. But the turtle-people immediately started swimming downward toward a tunnel at the bottom of the pond. Max steeled his determination. His instincts were telling him to follow. He wasn't sure why it was so important, but his instincts had got him this far. He just hoped he had enough oxygen. His Cultivation was high, far surpassing normal human lung capacity. But he still had some limitations and didn't know how long the tunnel would be.

Maverick was screaming obscenities through their bond, their connection growing weaker and weaker.

I'll be back soon, buddy.

Despite their aquatic nature, the turtles weren't exactly demonstrating a masterclass in swimming for him. He was able to keep up by scrambling, but still, they were damn fast. Max had never been much of a swimmer and attempting such athletics with his clothes on wasn't helping matters.

The only thing keeping Max in the race was his Cultivation. He must have been at a higher stage than these turtle-people or he would have been left to eat dust (or seaweed?) long ago.

But he was beginning to fall behind. Then Max remembered that he was a gravity mage. The pond turned into a tunnel that sloped up, down, left and right. Max entered without hesitation, hoping his Cultivator's lungs would hold out. To keep up, he pulled himself forward with [Tether] from turn to turn, cutting corners like Spider-Man swinging between New York City buildings.

The tunnel finally opened into a wider area, which was more than welcome after all the darkness. While the water was clear, Max had only human eyes to work with, so he could only see smudgy outlines, but he could make out a floor of fine yellow sand, full of aquatic vegetation. A coral reef started on the floor but rose up into a twisting wall, full of life in a myriad of colors. Schools of small fish sailed by as the turtles ahead blasted through the water, leaving behind trails of bubbles. Max followed them. He would have liked to explore this open underwater area more, but his oxygen situation was getting more urgent by the second.

The turtles increased speed. The relief was palpable when Max saw light from the surface shining at the end of the tunnel. He blasted through after the turtles and emerged, gasping for a deep breath of oxygen. Air never tasted so sweet.

Max looked around. He pulled himself up from a rather small hole in the ground, which was of a brown sleek rock. Here and there were yellow bushes with nuts growing on them. Further beyond the bushes were simple buildings made of mud and stone.

After taking a gander, Max's eyes stopped on the spear tip pointed at his face. Following up along the shaft, Max saw the weapon was held by a much larger turtle than the ones he had seen before. Its expression was wary, and it was holding the spear in a stance hinting at trepidation.

An older, bearded turtle made a motion with his hand to lower the spear. Max nodded to the older turtle. He smirked and nodded back.

"What manner of rabble have you brought in this time, young 'uns?" the old turtle asked. He spoke in a grandfatherly voice, gentle and wise. But there was a cheekiness to it, as if on some level he was delighted to teach a lesson to these young scallywags.

"We are sorry, Elder," one of the young turtle-people squeaked. Max noticed from their voice, features, and demeanor that they were indeed children. "We did not think we would be noticed and certainly not that we would be followed."

"Whose idea was this, now, hmm?" the older turtle asked. His beard looked as if it were crafted from wet seaweed, and his ancient, sagely eyes were fixed upon Max.

"It was mine, Elder." One of the turtle-kids stepped forward.

"Tsk," the elder said. "Piam, go tell your parents what you did. Then you are to wait there for my arrival. Same for you Huft, Lael, and Eela. I will come at a later time and we will think of an apt punishment."

"Yes, Elder," the children chorused and scampered away, shooting curious glances over their shoulders at the strange rabble that had followed them.

The elder was still staring at the rabble in question, saying nothing.

"Uh, hi?" Max said and waved a hand.

"Well, at least you have some manners on you," the elder snapped. "Who are you? What are you doing here and what can I do to make you go away?"

Max gave the elder a relieved smile. While he had been fairly certain that these people were not hostile, it was nice to get confirmation. He wasn't going to be attacked and killed. Probably. It was still good to stay on his guard, especially without Maverick there.

"I just felt compelled to know more about your people," Max said. "I don't want to cause anyone any trouble."

"How did you catch my little disciples?" the elder asked and peered angrily at Max. Max felt some soft sensation wash over him. Then the turtle's old eyes widened. "A Ruby Cultivator!"

The turtle holding the spear flinched and his eyes went wide. He quickly retracted his weapon, took a few steps back, and bowed to Max. Max looked quizzically at the old turtle and opened his mouth.

Before Max could respond, the old turtle grabbed his hand with lightning speed. It felt so weird to be grabbed by a turtle *with fingers*. The grip was pure iron and Max could never get free of it without losing a few fingers. Max wasn't the only Ruby Cultivator in town.

He yelped as the old turtle-person started dragging him toward the buildings beyond the bushes. He leapt and ran with the grace of a steroid-infused charging rhino.

Meanwhile, Max, who was determined to keep his shoulder in its socket, ran behind him with all his might.

CHAPTER THIRTY-SIX

The Turtle-folk

Max was surrounded by a circle of very curious turtle people of all sizes, and far too many fingers. They all wanted to get as close to Max as possible, but the old turtle kept pushing away the most eager youngsters who wanted to touch Max. There were 150 of them gathered around in total.

"What is this, Elder Ban?" a powerfully built turtle asked. He was head and shoulders taller than the rest and his hard skin rippled with muscles.

"I have found an interesting creature, Chief Tubut," Elder Ban said. "This one is a Ruby Cultivator."

A gasp passed through the crowd and Chief Tubut took a few steps closer, gently pushing aside the smaller turtle-people. He stopped next to Max and looked at him in wonder. Then he turned to the elder.

"Is he?"

Elder Ban nodded. "Has to be, Chieftain. Look how young he is. He has to be one of the new ones."

"New ones?" Max said. "Yeah, my species just came to this planet. How long has yours been here?"

Ruefully Elder Ban shook his head. "Two generations. I fought in our wars against the other species."

"I have so many questions," Max said immediately.

"As do we," Elder Ban said. "Perhaps we could exchange information. It is unusual and distressing for an outsider to come here, but I believe that we could both benefit from each other's knowledge."

"What do you know about Cultivation?" Max blurted out.

The elder chuckled. "It is a mystical art, but there are many ways one can choose to practice art. Be it a chisel, a brush—"

The elder paused and regarded Max. "—or a weapon."

Max nodded. Elder Ban regarded him with his sagely eyes.

"We have a problem you could help us with, stranger," the chieftain said. He may have been tall for a turtle, but he only reached Max's chin. Regardless of the height difference, Chieftain Tubut glared at Max imperiously. "Stay as our guest and help us. We will reward you."

"Help you how exactly?" Max asked, leaning back on his stool. He had no time to waste, unless the pay was good.

"You can help us deal with a threat," the chieftain said. "And in return, we will push your Cultivation forward faster than you can imagine."

"Huh," Max said. "What kind of a threat? And how can you push my Cultivation forward? Do you know how to do it?"

The elder smiled that cheeky smile of his. Max felt something lightly brushing against his spirit again. "I happen to know a few tips and tricks you have overlooked. I have an interesting specialty."

"As for the threat," Chieftain Tubut said, "you will be able to handle it. Especially after Elder Ban's training."

"I only have a few days."

The chieftain frowned. Ban's mischievous smile only widened. "Oh yes, I take it you are very busy. We will use . . . expedited methods."

Max considered this for a moment. He could always decline later. The old turtle was a Ruby Cultivator but certainly not a fighter. Tubut didn't seem like a threat either. These people couldn't force him. But if they could really push Max's Cultivation forward, it would be worth it. He needed something extra to keep ahead and make use of this time he had, anyway.

"Very well," Max said. "But I'll need to know more."

Elder Ban laughed. "Oh, you *will* know more . . . I have many things to tell you."

Max quirked an eyebrow at that, but the elder simply smiled. Max shrugged and extended a hand toward the chieftain. Tubut flinched back and regarded the hand cautiously. But then he relaxed, nodded to himself, and clasped it.

Elder Ban promised to return to Max after leaving him with a clay bowl of seaweed and some roots, mushrooms, and covered with a thick black paste for a "sauce." The old turtle-man had said that they would begin Max's Cultivation training immediately after he had eaten his meal to boost his strength.

"What's in it?" Max had asked, but the old turtle-man had just chuckled and walked out the door of the hut.

Max shrugged at the meal and started eating. He'd eat pretty much whatever anyone put in front of him. The meal wasn't particularly appetizing, though. It had a strong pungent smell. Max leaned in to sniff. It was clearly the grainy black paste. Max sighed and grabbed a wooden spoon waiting on the table and mixed the paste with the roots, seaweed, and mushrooms and started eating.

It was spicy and stale at the same time. The paste's pungency was overwhelming and underneath it was a stale, earthy taste; it was like eating an old, slightly moldy potato. A wretched experience, in truth, but food was food. Max masticated slowly and looked around the hut. It was small and fashioned from mud and sticks. But good work nonetheless. This village had a skilled [**Artisan**], for sure.

Max had been told that they would begin his Cultivation training immediately. Max had told them that he had only four days left as they had been walking toward the hut. The old turtle, Ban, had nodded and immediately gone away, having one of the children escort him to an empty hut with a wooden table, a chair, a crude bed, and a dirt floor. The child bowed and giggled before he left.

Max had also been told they would get Maverick back for him and explain to the humans where Max had gone. He wondered how his people would fare these coming days without him. He could only hope they would practice hard. They would need every advantage possible. He idly shoveled another spoonful of the food into his mouth.

Suddenly, Max felt as if a blazing hot furnace had opened up inside his abdomen. He gasped and exhaled; his breath was so hot it almost scalded his mouth. He fell from his chair and grabbed the table, trying to hold himself upright. Sweating profusely, he held his stomach with his other hand. It felt like it was boiling from within, the heat ever-increasing.

Did they poison me?

Max fell on the floor and just tried to breathe. The heat flushed over him, and his hair, now soaking wet with sweat, matted his face. He convulsed on the ground in shock, kicking at the air. The heat kept intensifying until Max wanted to scream. But all that he could manage was a choked gasp. His vision was getting blurry, and the red-hot furnace turned into a white blazing sun inside him. His body was wracked with pain, and he writhed on the ground so violently he thought his spine would break.

End this. Please.

At that moment, Elder Ban came back into the hut. He looked at Max and grinned. Max saw the grin through the tears. But it wasn't a malevolent grin. His eyes were laughing, and they looked at him eagerly, as if wanting to share the joke. Max wasn't laughing. He would have outright screamed if he could have.

But then it ended. The pain stopped and something powerful—blissful, even—bloomed within him, enveloping his body in a powerful, now benign warmth.

[Forced Cultivation Advancement: Successful!]
Advanced to Ruby-Level Cultivator (greater)
+30 to all Attributes

The blistering sun inside him was gone as if in a blink, leaving nothing but a memory. Max breathed heavily on the floor, absolutely soaked in sweat. The warmth and bliss faded and Max started to return to normal. He got up from the floor and blew out air. He sensed movement in his peripheral vision, and he turned to look. At the door stood Elder Ban, who was smiling mischievously. Max wasn't sure what to feel or say, so he just stared at the elderly turtle-man with a blank stare. Elder Ban's grin widened.

"Fun, huh?" Elder Ban asked and offered Max a mug of water.

Max drank it down in one big gulp. Elder Ban then produced another one, which Max poured down his gullet just as quickly.

"That was . . ." Max said and looked back at the bowl of roots and weeds on the table.

"It was all the necessary ingredients of a [**Ruby-grade Breakthrough Pill**]," Elder Ban said and sat down at the table. Max had a glance down at Ban's feet before he got up. They were stocky like a tortoise's. "Very rare, those ingredients. Even rarer to find someone who can create a dish like that out of them. My Class and Skills gave you a higher chance of success than normally possible."

"You could have just given me the pill," Max said, regarding the elder with an unfriendly glare. "Or told me what was going to happen. I thought I was being poisoned."

"Now where would the fun have been in that?" the elder said and laughed. "How do you feel now?"

Max focused on his body. He flexed his fingers. Then he tethered the two empty cups together and used [**Telekinesis**] to levitate them. Then he threw them at Elder Ban.

He dodged and laughed.

Max made himself fly, and then similarly lifted a chair and then the table. It was so *easy*. There was no strain from casting multiple [**Telekinesis**] spells at once.

Next, he made all the items in the room spin around him. It was draining his Mana fast, but the absolute control felt so good, he couldn't contain himself. There was no room to test the power of his abilities now, but he could feel it in his body. He was stronger. Much stronger. This had been a bigger leap forward than anything else he had gained so far. The Stat boost was massive. He could especially feel his Strength had gone up, as it previously had been relatively low.

"I see you are enjoying yourself," Elder Ban remarked and gave him another one of his mischievous smiles.

"This is amazing," Max whispered.

"I am glad to have someone to share the ingredients with," Elder Ban said, the slightest hint of longing in his voice.

"You cannot use them?" Max asked.

"Me? Ha. I do not need them. I am a peak Ruby Cultivator."

"You are?" Max asked.

"Bah, he dares express doubt," the elder muttered to himself. "I could level you with a single strike."

"Then I hope we never come to blows," Max said, containing his disbelief. He gave a slight bow. "Thank you for the pill."

"It is only the beginning, my dear boy," the elder said. "Come, let us enjoy the outdoors. I will feed you properly this time. We have much to discuss. I have interesting things to tell you . . . And perhaps after that we will train you more and you will help us, yes?"

Max nodded. His gratitude and sense of debt made him follow the elder automatically out of the door.

CHAPTER THIRTY-SEVEN

New Secrets

Max sat down at a round table that was surrounded by four long rectangular tables. At his table sat Elder Ban and the chieftain. At the longer tables sat several adult tortoise-people. They were drinking something that looked like mead and chatting quietly.

"Did he succeed?" the chieftain asked Ban.

The elderly tortoise nodded. "Indeed, he did. Quite the feat! If I recall, the casualty rate is one in three."

Max spat out a mouthful of mead. "One in what?!"

"Kidding, kidding," Ban said and offered a smile.

"He is not," Chieftain Tubut said and refilled Max's wooden goblet to the brim. Max then noticed a plate full of snacks, which looked like insects rolled in seaweed. He shrugged and popped one in his mouth. It was crunchy.

Then he shot a nasty look to Elder Ban.

"You said you were short on time," Ban said. "Besides, I had high expectations."

"You could have told me," Max said.

"Without my expertise, the chance of survival is close to something like one in five," Ban said, sniffing in pride.

"I'm so glad that you took a gamble on me," Max said, wearing his best shit-eating grin. "I hope I can return the favor someday."

The chieftain snorted.

"My people have a saying," Ban said. "Back on shore, happy trip."

"You know I have a friend just like you," Max said sourly. "I'm sure you two will get along swimmingly."

Chief Tubut laughed and raised his goblet to Max. "For having to suffer good friends."

Max clicked his goblet. "I'll drink to that."

The mead was sweet, but it had a salty, tangy aftertaste to it. It was the best thing Max had tasted since coming here. He just hoped it wouldn't be followed by violent convulsions again.

"How long have you been here, Max?" the chieftain asked.

"Some months, I think," Max said. "It's hard to say for sure."

The chieftain nodded seriously. "And are you winning?"

"I like to think so," Max said. "How much do you know of the ICCB and their little game?"

"More than you," Elder Ban said. "Nothing is as it seems, Max. They are only telling half-truths."

"I've had the same feeling for a while," Max said. "You are the second species I've met since arriving here. And I was told a side wins only when the other side is obliterated, not a single survivor left."

"Yes," the elder said and nodded slowly, swirling the mead in his wide, lipless mouth. "There are likely dozens, if not hundreds, of leftover species like us on this planet. Leftovers from the countless wars. We hide, as is our wont. The ICCB doesn't care about us. They can just cut us off from the Framework and leave us here as NPCs."

"You know the term?" Max asked.

"We used to be a civilized people, playing many games," the elder said, then he smiled softly. "And now we are reduced to living in mud huts. Myself, my wife, and a handful of others are the only ones who remember the comforts our people used to have, so it is not as painful as you'd think."

"I just miss coffee," Max said and sighed.

"What is coffee?" the chief asked.

"It's a drink we humans used to have. Bean juice that made you alert."

"Oh!" Chief Tubut said. "So it was a Cultivation elixir?"

Max laughed at the notion. "Sure, let's go with that."

Then he turned back to Elder Ban. "What does the ICCB want?"

The old turtle smiled slyly. "Now you're asking the right questions. But I am not sure you'll like the answer."

"Try me."

Elder Ban gave him a glance. "Fine. But just know that they could be watching you. Especially if you are important, and I think you are. You need to be careful what you say and how you react."

Max nodded.

"They're looking for slaves," Elder Ban said.

"Excuse me?!" Max said.

"I know it might be hard to believe. And it sounds bad when I say it like that, but that's the reality of it. You see, the game doesn't end when there's only one party left remaining. I know this because I witnessed it."

"So when does the game end?"

"It ends when the ICCB decides it ends. Usually right before a final clash between the monsters this competition is designed to create."

"High-Leveled Cultivators," Max said.

"Quick on the uptake, indeed," Elder Ban said. "Your patron race will offer you a deal when they stop the games. Depending on how powerful you are and how they can employ you in the wars, they will offer you a fun little contract."

Max didn't say anything; he just nodded. He was clenching his hands into such tight fists, it was painful. But it was the only way to stop the trembling. Elder Ban looked him in the eyes and smiled.

"If you're deemed valuable, you will be given a choice to accept the slave contract. They will treat you like a prince, but you will be theirs. Theirs to use on their whims, and their whims are trained on an intergalactic war. Your sworn enemies in this training ground will be your comrades if you make it to the end."

"What if I refuse?" Max asked.

"You definitely won't want to," Elder Ban said grimly. "They're not nice people, these ICCB. You will take their offer. There is also an upside."

"Yeah?"

"The more powerful you are at the end of this fun little game, the more humans you get to save."

Max choked on his mead. Elder Ban gave him a warning glare. Coughing into his fist, Max calmed down. At least externally. Inside, his heart was jackhammering.

"What—What you're saying is . . ."

Elder Ban gave Max a gentle, grandfatherly smile. "What I'm saying is that all of these people and I were saved by someone we really loved."

"So, all the NPC races here . . ."

"Remnants left to die in squalor," Elder Ban said grimly. "That is the 'salvation' you will buy with your slave contract."

"So, if I'm a high-Level Cultivator I get to save . . . what? A thousand people? A million?"

Elder Ban gave a mirthless little laugh and finished his mead. "Look around you, Max. This is what my brother bought us with his indenture. He was a Level Forty-Six **[Water Ghost]** and a top-tier Ruby Cultivator like I am."

"Only a few lives?!" Max snapped and got up. Chief Tubut pushed him down forcefully and shoved a goblet of mead in his hands. Elder Ban reached out and hit Max in the head with a fist.

Max bit down on his lip so hard, it burst and started to bleed. He took a gulp of mead and sucked on his lip. The mead didn't taste half as sweet as before.

Is this true? Why would they fabricate all of this?

"What do they do with the rest of the people that aren't included in the contract?" Max asked silently.

Ban and Tubut shared a look.

"Tell me," Max demanded. "Tell me now."

"You . . ." Ban said and scratched his neck. "Seen any turtle-like monsters out there?"

"Turtle-like— wait, what?"

"What about human-like creatures?"

Like the giants? But . . .

"What are you trying to say?" Max asked, slamming his palm on the table.

"The leftovers who don't get saved . . ." Tubut said quietly, looking at the dregs of his drink. "They are . . . repurposed."

Ban shook his head. "Genetically altered and given a bastard of a Framework."

"Oh my God . . ." Max muttered. It had been right in front of him all along. The dinosaurs and the giants. The universe was a really big place, and there were humanoid and lizard species galore across the galaxies. And some time in the past, they had all fought and lost . . .

And the ICCB dared to call *them* barbarians. They were playing a joke on both the humans and the Ishkarassi. He remembered the [**Twisted Wretches**] in the ruins of the obsidian dwarves. A deep, dark anger boiled inside him. It burned a brighter, deeper, hotter fire than the pill ingredients Ban had fed him. Max trembled with fury, trying to breathe.

"I— Thank you for telling me all of this," Max said. He was struggling so hard to hold back his rage, it made his eyes wet with tears. The injustice was too great to comprehend. And the helplessness.

NO! I WILL NOT BE HELPLESS. I WILL NOT SUCCUMB TO THIS. I WILL NOT ACCEPT THIS.

"But you are clearly crazy," Max said and laughed. "This is such a nonsensical theory, and it goes against everything I have heard and seen from the Zoos Collective. They have treated me well and even say I'm special. I'm sorry, but who would you believe in my situation?"

The chief scoffed and took a sip of mead. Elder Ban watched Max carefully with glinting, intelligent eyes. "Who would you?"

CHAPTER THIRTY-EIGHT

Striking Deals

For a long while, the turtles drank their mead and ate their snacks. Max just stared off into the distance. This was too much. Too much for a single human to bear.

He had long suspected that there was something rotten in the state of Denmark, but he had no idea of the galactic scale of assholery that these guys were engaging in. Max wondered if humanity had even actually been on the brink of destruction or if the ICCB had just plucked them from their planet on a whim. So they wouldn't ever return to Earth, huh? Even if they won?

Maybe if Max got powerful enough, he could strike a deal. That soothed Max. Perhaps it was possible. He wanted to atomize the whole ICCB, but he was also just one person. Could he do it? Could he buy back Earth?

Max sighed. It brought him back to the present.

"It will certainly take a while to digest this," Max said. "But I can't stand still. Regardless of how dire this sounds, I have to go forward, I have to keep winning. I have to keep fighting."

"These are good words," Tubut said and slapped Max on the shoulder. "I like your spirit."

"So what is it that you need my help for?" Max asked.

Ban took a long swig from his mead, emptying the goblet, and then smiled at Max, before speaking.

"We are an aquatic people. We need water. We came from a planet with barely an island of landmass. Only ten percent, it was estimated. Oh, you should have seen the monsters in our seas."

Ban stopped and looked wistfully upward. Max wondered what his profession had been if sea monsters made him so sentimental.

"We have very little water that is safe for us to use. We need more. And the pond and all the pockets connected to it would be ideal for us to live in, farm, and forage. It is larger than you think, spanning cubicles upon cubicles underground and within other areas of this battlefield you are fighting in. Additionally, the waters are strong with Spiritual Energy. But that is indeed the problem. It is controlled by a [**Special-Grade Boss, Sarkofang**]. A monstrosity that we do not have the power to fight."

Max nodded and tossed another seaweed bug roll in his mouth. "You push my Cultivation, and in exchange, I deal with the Boss."

"He picks up on things quickly," the chieftain remarked. "I like you, Max."

Max gave him a small smile and raised his goblet. The chieftain immediately clinked his own against it, and they both drank.

Max wiped the foam off his lips. "But you are at the peak of Ruby, Elder Ban. What do you need me for?"

"Quick, indeed," Ban said. "I, of course, can hope we're able to push you to the Diamond realm, but that may be a longshot. Regardless, I am not asking you to deal with [**Sarkofang**] alone. I am asking you to help me defeat it."

"That makes sense," Max said. "But if you have the resources to push me to Diamond, why can't you do it for yourself?"

"Ha." Elder Ban gave a bitter laugh. Chief Tubut shook his head ruefully and all the people around them muttered to each other. "There are no herbs or meditation that I have not tried."

"What about your insights? What is your Dao?"

"My Dao? Insights?" The elder leaned closer, his neck elongating. "You mean those thoughts that give you Levels?"

"You don't know?" Max asked almost incredulously. "How are you at the peak of Ruby stage?"

Elder Ban took on a prideful, haughty aspect. "I have worked hard for sixty years."

"That . . . That would probably do it."

Good god, what an inefficient use of time. Something something knowledge is power? Literally.

For the next twenty minutes, Max explained what he knew of insights, a Cultivator's Dao, and the [**Breakthrough Insight**]. He took out his massive leather-bound tome and while the turtle-folk couldn't understand a word written in the squiggly leathers, they were still completely enthralled by it. Chief Tubut in his great enthusiasm ordered more mead to be brought out for everyone and he made Max an honorary member of the turtle-folk.

"How much can you use this?" Max asked. "I met people before who had their connection to the Framework cut off, which made Cultivation impossible for them, except for some very gifted individuals."

"We are not yet in such a dire state," Chief Tubut said. "We are a relatively new species here. Yes, it is clear that we grow weaker with every generation. I am only at the greater Amethyst stage of Cultivation myself. I have access to a broken version of the Framework, and I am a Level Thirteen **[Chieftain]**. But my children and their children after them will all have a thinned bloodline and eventually your gift to us will fade."

"But I have full access to the Framework, being one of the original people transported to this wicked planet," Ban said triumphantly. "I will use this gift to its fullest. I cannot thank you enough, Max. After we leave this table, I want to Cultivate with you. I will feed you my finest herbs and teach you my most secret techniques. And you will help me with my insights."

"That's the best deal I've made all day," Max said and grinned.

CHAPTER THIRTY-NINE

Forced Breakthrough

Max was sitting down in front of a long table in Elder Ban's house. It was a slightly nicer house than most of the other mud and stone huts that had seemed hastily cobbled together. This one was made of brown uniform tiles, which Max suspected to be some kind of box rewards. It had two rooms: a bedroom and a large living space they were in now.

The table was crude and wooden like most of the turtle-folk's possessions. But what lay on the table was a treasure trove. It might not have looked like one at first glance, but once Elder Ban had explained it to Max, avarice worthy of an obsidian dwarf had awakened in him.

There were black dried roots in neat rows on the table, next to some fresh roots of a fat, tubular shape. They were cream-colored, with beads of moisture glistening on them.

Next to them were red, blue, and purple flower petals. Every had been meticulously removed and kept whole, and they were all now in a neat pile of vibrant colors. The fragrance they gave off was faint and elusive like that of a rose but so sweet it almost stung the nose.

There were also some crushed leaves in a mortar and pestle that Max was working on. They gave off a fresh minty scent as they stuck to each other, becoming a green sticky paste.

Next up, Max threw some dried mushrooms and the flower petals into the mix. Then, Elder Ban, who was watching Max, trickled into the mixture a few drops of a thick, black, tar-like liquid that smelled like an overripe swamp.

All of this was going into an elixir for Max to drink.

"You need to twist the pestle to really get the essence out of the flowers," Elder Ban said, excitement making his old voice quiver. Max could sympathize. The old turtle hadn't had anyone to share his cooking with for decades. He had an **[Artisan]**-type Class—**[Apothecary]**. Rather high-Level, too, at Twenty-Nine.

Sadly, not high enough, however, for him to share many insights about what features would come later as Max Leveled Up.

The [**Apothecary**] Class wasn't exclusively concerned with Cultivation. Elder Ban didn't have any particular expertise or specialization in elixirs and pills. Rather, it was more of a hobby for him and only something he had discovered near the end of their wars on Alpha Ludus.

It also explains why he needs my help with the Boss monster. The good news is that his Class can gear me up and keep me alive, as long as we have resources to make healing concoctions out of.

"Elixirs and pills are essential to Cultivation," elder Ban said. "Using them extensively has resulted in my high Level."

"I can't believe you brute-forced yourself to Ruby by eating all this."

"How was I supposed to know of these insights?" Elder Ban asked peevishly. "Chop, chop! Literally. Chop those roots and add them in. You will need to finish this fast."

There was no actual rush, other than Max's promise to the old turtle that he'd help him figure out his insights after the elixir was finished.

Max sweat his way through, working the knife as carefully as he could to save his fingers. He had never been particularly talented in the kitchen. After adding in the juice from the cream-colored roots and the powdered, dried-up root, Max swirled the pestle in the mortar to create a grayish goop that smelled like slightly funky meat—the kind that had been left on the kitchen counter for a few too many hours, and it was anybody's guess if it was still edible or not.

Sadly, that turned much worse when Elder Ban added the swamp-gas-smelling tar. Some chemical or magical reaction produced a little puff of dark smoke. It almost choked Max. It was the kind of smell that would haunt your nostrils for the rest of the day. He felt bile rising up and his eyes watering.

Elder Ban regarded him with that mischievous smile of his as he poured the dark, unholy concoction into a clay mug. Max was surprised it didn't melt on the spot. He inspected the mug carefully, hoping to get some kind of prompt like [**Super Awesome Elixir of Instant Cultivation Levels**], but he got nothing. The text box would have given him at least some measure of comfort.

"Well?" Elder Ban asked.

"I'm gathering courage," Max said. "You sure it'll work?"

"You take me for a charlatan?" Elder Ban snapped. "Or an imbecile? Of course it works!"

"It's a one-time deal, right?"

"Yes, yes," Ban said again. "I've made this elixir over a dozen times. It will widen your Cultivation channels. My brother used to call them 'meridians,' but I don't know where he got the notion. There was no word for it in our language.

However, they are a real thing. They are vessels through which your Spiritual Energy is channeled."

"So, after drinking this sludge from hell, my meridians will widen? And that will help me channel the Spiritual Energy?"

"It will not only make the channeling easier, consuming less Mana if you want to create special techniques, it will also make it easier and faster to access your Spiritual Energy. This will put less strain on you and consume your reserves of Spiritual Energy at a much slower pace. And most importantly . . ."

"Yes?" Max perked up, making sure he was breathing through his mouth.

"Most importantly," Elder Ban said, "it will greatly increase your Cultivation practice. When you sit down and focus on your Spiritual Energy, you will notice a vast difference in how easy practice will be. It will give you more stamina for longer sessions. With this potion, you can increase the time you're able to focus, sit, and practice to almost double its current length."

"That would be from five or six hours," Max said, contemplating aloud, "to up to ten, eleven, even twelve hours? That's crazy."

"It is possible," Elder Ban said. "In fact, I think it is necessary if one wants to reach the higher stages, as you surely do. There is no replacing hard work."

"Except with insights," Max said and gave the elder a playful smile.

Elder Ban harrumphed. "Drink up, you young fool. Then you will teach me of insights."

Max took the mug with a shaky hand. The last thing he had consumed a la elder Ban could have literally killed him. As difficult as Max's life had become, he was still keen to keep it going. He sighed, pinched his nose, and let the sludge slide slowly down his throat.

Halfway through, he started to cough, sending half of the almost-downed elixir back into his mouth.

A thousand painful deaths would not be enough.

Max didn't have the words to describe the taste. Just overwhelming. Overwhelming and *rotten*. Max's cheeks bulged as he turned green and Elder Ban burst out laughing.

"Quite the experience, isn't it?" Ban said and wiped a tear of joy out of the corner of his eye, while Max beat his chest, trying to get the slop down.

With a mixture of horror, disgust, and grim awe at the foulness of the taste, Max fought the elixir down. The worst part was that he even had to chew some of it.

After a battle that felt like it must have lasted a good quarter of an hour, Max jumped for the cup of tea that the smirking old turtle was offering. It was just the right temperature and had a minty flavor. Max drank it down without breathing, washing away the pure awfulness of Ban's elixir.

Elder Ban watched him, the smile on his face starting to thin. Max was also paying close attention to his body. With every beat of his heart, he felt something *widen*. It was a difficult feeling to explain. As if he was expanding somehow. He looked at his palms as his whole body pulsed. They were surging with energy. From the core of his being, Spiritual Energy was flowing into his arms, legs, head, everywhere.

Max immediately bolted outside, but Elder Ban grabbed his arm. "Not yet. Let the expansion happen. It will be uncomfortable, but you are not going to burst."

Max nodded, despite feeling sure that's exactly what was going to happen. His first instinct was to expend a bunch of his Spiritual Energy, but he had to trust his mentor. The sludge churned in his stomach like hot wine, and a warmth spread through his thrumming body. Finally, the energy settled and instead of the urgent bursting feeling, Max felt a deep calm.

He flexed his hand. His sense of his own Spiritual Energy was much more acute. He somehow *understood* the way to use it in a much more profound way now . . . He realized that, compared to this level of control, he used to have only the vaguest sense of his Spiritual Energy. It was as if he just had sobered up in the late hours of the morning after a long night of drinking.

"I feel powerful," Max said and flexed his hand again.

"That is good," Elder Ban said. "Only a few more of those, and the widening will be permanent."

Max's eyes widened in shock. "But you— you said— You said it was a one-time thing!"

"Did I?" Elder Ban said and smirked. "Oh, it's the old age, I get so forgetful sometimes. Sadly, no. You will have to ingest this at least three more times for the effects to be permanent. Don't worry, I have a lot of ingredients."

"That's not what I'm worried about," Max said and coughed lightly.

CHAPTER FORTY

Giving Back

Max was really enjoying his improved body. It was as if he had been an insomniac all his life and had finally gotten a proper night's sleep. He felt fresh, limber, and powerful. He was so enthralled with his body that for a moment he forgot Elder Ban, who was smiling at him expectantly. Max finally turned and rubbed his neck in embarrassment.

"I am old, Max," elder Ban said. "I have developed some patience. But I must tell you I am excited."

"Here's the thing . . ." Max said and sat down with him. Elder Ban had brought two stools out of his house into the open air. They sat down and Max mulled over his words.

"You're at the peak of Ruby, yeah?" Max asked and elder Ban nodded. "So, I don't know how the insights are going to work. Technically you just need a **[Breakthrough Insight]** but getting that before finding any of the other insights won't happen."

"Does it matter?" the old turtle asked. "I will just start figuring out my insights and we will go from there."

"That's fair enough," Max said and nodded. "Okay so . . ."

Max thoroughly explained what he knew of insights and Elder Ban listened attentively. Once Max was done, the turtle nodded.

"So I must understand this Dao to advance," the elder said. "And my Dao is the purpose of my Cultivation?"

"Sounds about right," Max said. "Any ideas of what your purpose might be?"

"Hmm," Elder Ban said. "I always wanted to support my brother. He was the fighter and the hero. But now he's out there, fighting some pointless eternal war."

Elder Ban sighed and looked up at the sky. For the first time, Max realized he was out of the bounds of the Deathmatch arena. He could make a run for it, maybe escape into the woods and try to figure out what the hell he was supposed to do in this shitstorm of a situation the ICCB had put him in.

No . . . Winning this fight is the best thing I can do right now. I need resources. Lots of them.

"What if a person's Dao changes?" Ban asked. "Mine must have changed after I got stranded here."

Max shrugged, snapping back to the moment. "Just try things out."

"I support my brother. No . . . I make sure my brother wins . . . I protect my brother . . . I protect . . . ?

Elder Ban's eyes widened and his lipless mouth made an 'O.'

Max smiled. "Looks like we found something."

"I protect my people. I take care of my people."

Overcome by spiritual power and emotion, Elder Ban closed his eyes and breathed in. Then he looked at Max and smiled.

"You have given me an invaluable gift, Max," Ban said. "I do not know how to repay you."

"Next time, put honey in those horrible elixirs of yours," Max said and they both laughed.

"I can feel a faint connection to the Framework," Ban said. "I can feel the shadows of my Stats. They are still there, in some other quantum existence. These insights gave me a fraction of that back."

"Wait, really?" Max said. That seemed like a strange oversight from the ICCB. "They cut you off from the Framework?"

"I am still in possession of it, as is my kin," the elder said. "Many of my people have Classes and Levels. As do I, of course."

"What do you mean then?" Max asked.

"I'm not entirely sure," Elder Ban said carefully. "But to power the Framework takes energy. The Framework is essentially a machine made by the ICCB. But it is autonomous, powered by a massive artificial intelligence. It still lingers in our genes, but the power source was cut off. It has been dwindling over time like a dying star, but now I feel the connection strengthening again."

"That is very interesting," Max said. It gave him hope. Even if the ICCB cut them off the Framework in the case of a rebellion or mutiny, there was hope. "Maybe it was because of the increase in spiritual power?"

"That is most definitely it," Elder Ban said. "This is great news."

"Do you think it means the younger generations have a chance at achieving higher Cultivation too?"

"Definitely," Elder Ban said. "But now is not the time for that. We are short on time, and by 'we,' I mean you. Sit down and Cultivate while I work on my insights."

Max did just that. For the first time in a while, he was *excited* to work on his Cultivation. He didn't feel a sense of duty, nor was he compelled by dread. He wanted to see how it would feel now that his body was more attuned to handling spiritual power.

Without further ado, Max sat down and popped a **[Celestial Illumination Pill]**. The elder looked at him questioningly, but Max only shrugged and gave him one of the golden white pills to inspect. He needed to take one, because he always did. It was his baseline, and it would be hard to tell the difference without using a pill here.

The difference was noticeable. It could have been his ascension to the Greater Ruby stage that was also helping, but whether it was a combined effect or not, the difference was vast.

There is no way Losshnak will be able to keep up with me.

Whereas before, the Cultivation had been coaxing and snatching up faint breezes in his meridians, now they blew with a steady wind that Max could direct to a degree. This was a powerful boon. Max had been worried since reading from Durum's book that a Cultivator had to keep up his practice with his advancement through the stages. He had been thinking that he was going to need some special treasure like a talisman or another formation to keep up.

But this was better and, after only after a few more of those disgusting sludges, it would be permanent and always with him.

Losing himself in a Cultivation trance, Max went through a handful of pills, and hours flew by. The afternoon became a soft, orange glow in the skyline as the sun started its descent. But Max never stopped. The last rays of light winked out hours later, and only then did Max feel himself snap out of focus and remember his surroundings again. It was the middle of the night. Elder Ban was gone and there were no turtle-kin children nearby watching him with curiosity. With his enhanced senses, he could hear the old turtle elder snoring in his hut. Max smiled to himself.

He had pushed his Cultivation progress far today. He didn't get a Level. He wasn't even close yet. But this would make everything so much easier. Tomorrow he could gain his first Level in the Greater Ruby stage. With that pleasant thought, Max found his hut and collapsed on the bed waiting for him.

CHAPTER FORTY-ONE

A Quiet Moment

Max woke up to the sounds of birds chirping outside and the play of the young turtle-kin. It was a pleasant way to wake up. Max stretched and yawned. His body felt more relaxed and rested than it had for weeks. Knowing that the truce was still on allowed him to sleep easier.

When he got to the table, two clay mugs were waiting on it for him. Max groaned. He could guess the contents of said mugs. The first one had a minty fresh tea, and the other one was filled to the brim with something that smelled eerily like rotten eggs and swamp gas.

Max muttered to himself, hoping that Maverick would somehow taste what he was having through their bond. Gingerly, he picked up the sludge-mug and poured it down.

The taste shocked him fully awake, but he did his best to make the process as smooth as possible. Knowing what to expect was half the battle, and only with a moderate amount of bile and coughing, Max managed to force the foul liquid down.

After performing what was most likely a record speed at swigging down minty tea afterward, he coughed one last time, wiped his mouth, and headed outside to greet the morning sun.

The children playing out there only stopped for a moment to stare at Max. He smiled. He could hardly blame them. He could only imagine being an eight-year-old kid, playing outside, when someone from a different species suddenly popped up out of the blue. Yeah, that would stop anyone in their tracks.

After an exchange of timid smiles, the children ran away and went off to play somewhere else. Max wanted to meet with Elder Ban, but he was also hungry. While he could stave off eating for weeks at this point with his Ruby body, it would be foolish to do so unless needed.

And with that in mind, he headed for the main building to meet the chieftain and to possibly find the elder and a bite to eat.

Max was fortunate enough to find all three sitting in the shade of a canopy made of tied-together leaves. It seemed Ban and Tubut were enjoying breakfast. It consisted of seaweed, snails, and some shriveled-up fruits, resembling dates. Chieftain Tubut popped a snail in his mouth, shell and all, before noticing Max and waving at him.

"Ah, my favorite human," Tubut said. "Come. Sit. Eat."

Max was happy with the warm welcome and sat next to the two turtles.

"I was just telling Tubut about the great advancements I made last night," Ban told Max. "I should hope you could go over your ideas about insight and Dao with Tubut here too. He is not yet at a Ruby stage, but I am sure he could do it someday."

"I *will* do it someday, thank you very much," Tubut said and shot a challenging glance at the elder. Ban only laughed and took a pinch of seaweed.

Max picked up one of the snails and regarded it. The creature inside the shell seemed to be dead. Max gave the food a little sniff and determined that it was seasoned. He shrugged and put it in his mouth.

Crunchy.

Then he turned to Tubut and started explaining the things he had gone over with Ban yesterday as the three of them ate.

After they were done eating, Max caught up with Elder Ban, who was heading toward his home.

"Wait," Max said. "I want to talk to you more."

"About what?" the elder said and flashed Max a warning glare.

"About your brother," Max said and winked at the elder.

Elder Ban scoffed good-naturedly and motioned for Max to follow him. After a bit of walking, they arrived at Ban's home, but instead of going inside, they went around the back, where another, much simpler hut was built. Inside was the elder's stash of various materials for potions, pills, and elixirs.

Without saying a word, Elder Ban went into the hut, grabbing a piece of hanging bark here and a bowl of dried leaves there. After he had a handful of materials, he went to the middle of the room, where a table with a hole in it was sitting. He placed a metal pot in the hole and started a fire under the table.

Soon, the water was boiling and Ban threw in the bark.

"Stir this slowly," the turtle said to Max and thrust a ladle at him.

Max did as he was told, watching it turn from clear to light brown to dark brown. Meanwhile, Elder Ban was in the background muttering and humming to himself as he picked up various ingredients. He came up to Max with a mortar and pestle in his hands, crushing the leaves into paste as Max worked the ladle.

"What are we making?" Max asked when Ban scooped the leaf paste into the boiling pot.

"I got these leaves and the bark from a jungle far away from here, on another continent. They're spirit herbs—very rare, very valuable. The bark grew on a vine. I picked it up on a whim and chewed on it later. It is such a crazy thing to say, but the bark told me to go to this specific bush of large leathery leaves. The taste told me to combine the two: the bark of the vine and these leaves."

The concoction was taking on a reddish-brown color and a potent earthy smell. It didn't smell bad, just strong, wooden, and bitter.

"And guided by the same whim, I drank this. I was greeted by an entity that lived in that jungle. She taught me many things. About the ICCB, about myself, about life. It must have been some kind of earth goddess."

"You're going to take me on some spiritual journey?" Max asked, quirking a skeptical eyebrow.

Ban snorted. "No! There is no time for such nonsense. I am simply going to add these berries and a few layers of this tiny onion here. They will change the properties of the elixir. You will not meet the earth goddess, but you will be able to share a dreamspace with me."

"A what now?"

Elder Ban smiled. "I can show you my dreams. I don't need to tell you anything about my brother. I can show you."

CHAPTER FORTY-TWO

A Shared Dream

Max gave the reddish-brown elixir a long glance before bringing the bowl to his lips. He felt he had had a lifetime's worth of Elder Ban's cheeky elixirs. But this ended up being the mildest of the three he had tasted. It was bitter and earthy, but it was within reason.

Ban watched him over the rim of his own bowl as he drank.

"Lay down," the old turtle said and fell on his stomach, retracting all his limbs and head inside his shell. "Sleep. I will see you on the other side."

Max, who was getting increasingly drowsy, did just that. He sighed contentedly as a great heavy tiredness washed over him.

But as quickly as he fell asleep, he woke up, only not in Elder Ban's herb storage. Instead, he was standing on a sandy beach. Max looked around.

The sand was fine and yellow, and the shoreline spanned miles in both directions. He was by the ocean. Max turned behind him to see high barricades and walls built of stone and wood. They were unoccupied.

"Hey!" a familiar peevish voice called. Max had missed that voice, even though he would never admit it aloud.

A giant golden revolver fell out of the sky to float in front of him. "Where in THE HELL are we, Max?"

"We're in a dream," Max said.

"A dream?" Maverick said and scoffed. "Preposterous. Guns do not dream. We are superior creatures and— wait what happened to your body? What is this? What the hell did you do?"

Max felt a gentle brush upon his soul as Maverick looked at his Cultivation. "Pretty awesome, huh?"

Maverick huffed. "And without my guidance. I suppose you're useful as a sidekick some of the time."

"I think you'll get the benefits when we meet up again," Max said. "Or even after this dream ends."

"And would you bother to tell me how and why we are in a dream?"

"Ah," Elder Ban said, appearing out of thin air next to them. Max yelped and Maverick let out a small scream. "This is the counterpart of your strange Cultivation path."

"Yeah," Max said. "This is Maverick. He is . . . a special-needs child."

"Hmph," Maverick said.

"A pleasure," the elderly turtle said, giving an amiable smile toward the gun. "My name is Ban."

"He is almost as bad as you," Max whispered to Maverick.

"No one is as badass as me," Maverick declared. "But I think I like you, old turtle guy."

Ban laughed and gave Maverick a little bow.

"But what is going on?" Maverick asked. "I *hate* being out of the loop, and I am very much out of it right now."

"Can't you just read my mind?"

"It's not like that, you dolt of exquisite proportions," Maverick said. "I can sense what you're thinking and feeling. I just don't have a highlight reel playing the events of the last two days."

Max groaned. "We really don't have time for this."

"Actually," Elder Ban said, "we can take our time here. It is my dream. I choose how time passes here."

"That is . . . convenient," Max said and gave a quizzical look at Ban.

"Quite. The dream elixir is quite useful even when ingested alone. However, I like to be sparing with it, since I can never access the ingredients again."

"Can someone for the love of guns, please—"

"Pipe down and I'll tell you what's going on," Max said.

It took some time to explain to Maverick what had happened and what was going to happen, especially with him interrupting every other sentence. But eventually, Max got through the tale.

"You didn't mention anything about the ICCB," Ban remarked.

Max raised an eyebrow. "I am here just to see what happened to your brother."

Elder Ban chuckled. "You can speak freely here. It is my dream. They have no power here."

"You can't know that," Max said.

"The earth goddess told me it is so. I would trust her with my life."

"I wish I had your confidence," Max said. Then he took a deep breath. He did want to know more. "But I want to trust you."

"Good," Ban said. "Do you have any questions?"

"How much do you know?" Max said. "Are you sure it's true?"

Elder Ban gave Max a wan smile and suddenly the whole shore was filled with turtles armed to the teeth. The barricades were manned by a species of bird-like creatures resembling turkeys. They fired thousands of arrows into the air as the turtles charged.

Max flinched, but Ban grabbed his shoulder.

"It is just a projection," Ban said as the turtles charged through them like ghosts.

The fight was short and brutal. A single turtle charged at the front and crashed into the barricades. He jumped in the air and turned into a massive wave, which toppled the building. Then he turned back into a turtle-person and fought off the bird-folk with viciously fast moves. Through the destroyed bits of barricade the turtles swarmed in, casting spells and shooting crossbows at the turkeys.

"This was their last stand," Ban said. "The bird species, Glarakhs, had a primitive culture. They couldn't muster proper leadership to stop our assaults. They relied on small numbers and guerilla tactics. We knew we would win as soon as we organized into big towns and cities."

Indeed, the battle was a one-sided slaughter. The thousands of turtle-folk swarmed the barricades and took no prisoners.

"That's my brother at the front, swinging those hammers attached with a chain. Such a natural-born warrior. I was so proud of him."

Once the battle was over, and the bird-folk slaughtered to all but their last, a great stasis spell was cast on everyone and they were immobilized in place.

A swarm of the disgusting flies that spoke in metallic screeches appeared above the carnage. Max recognized the species immediately as one of the patron species of the ICCB. They addressed the last remaining turkey-person and the turtle-folk.

"We are pleased by this outcome," the swarm announced. "Your tribulations are finally over. We have watched and made our decisions. The Zoos Collective has also decreed that the strongest warrior of the Glarakhs, Yrgrittix, is offered a contract. Unfortunately, you have no surviving kin, but that is the price of failure. Please read the contract carefully and then decide."

Various turtle-folk cried out:

"Contract?"

"What contract?"

"Do we get to go back home?"

"We won! We won! Please send us back to the oceans of our world!"

Elder Ban shook his head ruefully as he watched the fate of his species unfold.

"There has been an altercation," the swarm of flies announced in their screeching metallic voice. "We unfortunately do not have the resources to send you all back to your planet of origin. We are, however, able to save some of you."

More of the turtles began to respond:

"Some of us?"

"What are they saying?"

"Did we do something wrong?"

The swarm produced a sound like gunfire in the air, and all the turtle-folk fell silent. The swarm continued. "We are pleased with a single entity among you: a male Tortanoid called Bell Scallac."

"M-me?" an uncertain voice asked.

Ban grabbed both Max and Maverick and then he teleported them next to Bell and the swarm, which was hovering above him like a thundercloud.

"Here is a contract," the swarm said and a piece of paper floated down to hover in front of Bell.

Max glanced at Ban. He was silently crying.

"Th-this is . . ." Bell stammered. "This was your plan all along? We would have never been granted freedom!"

"Silence!" the swarm said and buzzed menacingly. "This war produced only weak entities. We have no resources to spare for chaff."

"I can't— This is—"

Bell fell to his knees and clutched the paper. A much younger Ban rushed to his side, but the swarm cast some spell which instantly tossed him back.

"If you do not choose," the swarm said, "we will pick them at random."

The crowd stirred.

"Choose what?"

"Random? Is it a prize?"

"We did win, right? It's something good for those who fought well."

"I don't like this."

Bell got up and clutched the piece of paper with trembling hands. With a quivering voice, he announced, "I accept the terms. I will choose."

"Do it quickly," the swarm snapped.

"Ban Scallac," Bell announced first. "Alie Jaffas. Toem Fieff—"

"Brother," the younger Ban called. "What is happening?"

Bell's face broke into a grimace of grief. "I'm to be made a warrior-slave."

"Silence," the swarm snapped. "You are no slave. It is a contract you sign of your free will."

"Two hundred years of servitude," Bell said quietly. "For— for thirty lives."

"Thirty?!" the young Ban exclaimed. "I don't— I don't understand."

"P-please take care of my children and wife, Ban."

The projection of younger Ban took another step forward but was cast down to lay flat on his stomach by some spell of the swarm.

"Continue," the swarm said in a cool tone.

Bell swallowed and a few stray tears dropped on the piece of paper he was still clutching. Then he continued to call out the rest of the names.

"Good," the swarm said when it was done. "You have chosen well, Bell Scallac. We will teleport you to be processed and make sure to relocate these thirty individuals."

With that, a blue light enveloped Bell but before he was beamed up, he managed to scream out one last thing: "I'M SO SORRY!"

And with that, he was gone.

"What is going to happen?" the young Ban asked.

"You will be relocated shortly. Do not move," the swarm said.

"[**Anti-energy Barrier**]," the swarm said.

Suddenly, the young Ban and twenty-nine other individuals out of the crowd of several thousands were enveloped in a shield. It was metallic gray and seemed to flow around them like liquid steel, except slightly transparent.

Then with almost a lazy tone, the swarm cast another spell.

"[**Mass Firestorm**]."

Max noticed the older Ban next to him closing his eyes. The entire beach was enveloped into a massive, white-hot inferno. Screams of horror and pain turned into animalistic screeches, then gurgles before finally dying down in the inescapable heat of the god-level spell. The sand turned into blackened glass and the charred corpses of the Tortanoids were nothing but blackened shells and thin crisps of bone.

An entire people were massacred within seconds. There was no hesitation or even malice on the swarm's part. All that Max could sense was akin to a bureaucrat's boredom at fulfilling yet another mundane task, which reawakened his inner rage.

Once the last embers died down, the [**Anti-energy Barriers**] were released. Just as the survivors' screams and crying began, the swarm used [**Mass Teleport**] and whisked them away, leaving behind the absolute desolation of a sapient species that had been casually incinerated like so much rubbish.

CHAPTER FORTY-THREE

Steel Resolve

Max closed his eyes, inhaled, and exhaled. He was trying to contain his anger. Trying to suppress it so he could think clearly.

Maverick wasn't having any of it. Their bond channel exploded with his wrath. It was as all-consuming a fire as the **[Mass Firestorm]** spell the fly bastards had cast. It was no sullen anger. It was no simple wish for revenge. It was pure, white-hot rage. The will to utterly destroy.

At first, Max flinched from it. He had been holding some emotions back all his life. Disappointment, anger, sadness, even. Playing whatever tune was appropriate for the situation. Now there was only one appropriate emotion left.

He let Maverick's wrath light a fire inside him as well, and soon enough his whole being was aflame with pure anger as well.

"How dare they?!" Max spat out. "How dare they treat life like that? I don't care anymore. Maverick, now we make a pact. You with me?!"

"Hell, yes," Maverick said. There was no glee or excitement in his voice. Only grim, dark malice. "We are taking these bastards down, or we die swinging."

"That is a promise," Max growled. "We will likely die on this crusade. But it is the worthiest thing we can do. This isn't just about helping my people or saving humanity anymore. This is *bigger*. We aren't doing this only for humans. We're doing this for everyone who these monsters have ever harmed or would have in the future. We are not in this for life. We are in this for death. From now on, we only seek one thing: Destruction. The annihilation of the ICCB."

Leveled Up Ruby-Level Cultivator (greater) to 2
+6 free Attribute points

Max and Maverick were too livid to cheer or even take note of it. But both of them understood what this was. It wasn't an insight on the conceptual level.

They had already acknowledged that their Dao was that of destruction. But now . . .

Now it was *personal*. Now it was the will to destroy that guided them forward. They had aligned with their Dao. There would be no respite; there would be no mercy. It might take ten years, or even one hundred. But they would fight, and they would destroy. Or at least take a bite out of their enemies and die swinging.

"Thank you for showing me this," Max said, turning to Ban. "What else can you tell us?"

"Don't do it," Ban said. "I know it sounds like a lofty goal, a great cause to die for. But didn't you see what they did to my people? Thousands turned to ashes with a single flick of their wrist. How could you ever fight something with god-like power?"

"By *getting* godlike power," Max said and stared Ban down. "Tell me everything you can about the ICCB."

"I don't know that much," Ban said and took a step back. "They are powerful. They have been doing this for goodness knows how long. Thousands of years? Millions?"

"Or they just started a couple of centuries ago," Maverick said. "We don't know. But it looks like they're fighting some other force out there themselves if they need warriors so badly."

"What if the ICCB are the good guys of that war?" Elder Ban asked.

Max stared him down for what felt like minutes but was possibly only seconds. "How can you even say that?"

"I'm old. I just want to take care of my village. How could an insect challenge a god? Where would you even start?"

"Same as anything new is started," Max said. "By *trying*. We have to try. And you can help me. I'll get strong in the next few days and deal with [**Sarkofang**]. Then I'll claim the heads of all the lizards out there and secure us the Deathmatch and its resources. Then I'll fly out, find more communities, more secrets, more powers."

"They are all generated by the ICCB!" Ban protested. "How are you ever going to beat them using what they created?"

"I won't," Max said. "I'm no fool. But that is the first step I must take."

"I don't like your leg metaphors, but you're right!" Maverick said.

"When did you get so righteous?" Max asked, letting a shadow of a smile pass his face.

"You're a bad influence on me," Maverick said. "But it's not that. It's not about righteousness. I'm a gun, for Pete's sake. What do I know of right and wrong!"

"Why did you get so angry?" Max asked.

Maverick pondered this for a while. "If I saw the ICCB do that to you humans, I would want to shoot a big hole in the universe."

"Huh," Max said. "Who figured you had empathy?"

"Must be a factory defect," Maverick said. "Besides, I refuse to allow such wanton use of power to destroy life for no good reason. Not enough resources? Bah! They just wanted to steal the planet. If it weren't so absolutely reprehensible, I would commend them for their chutzpah."

"It's beyond monstrous. There is no word for it," Max muttered. "They wanna play god? I'll show them what that really means . . ."

Shortly afterward, Max found himself back in the hut. He got up from the floor and clasped Ban on the shoulder. "Thank you for showing me this. Now I will be able to get much stronger."

Ban only gave a short nod. They were again within the ICCB's hearing range and words needed to be chosen with care.

"I need to retrieve Maverick," Max said.

"No," Elder Ban said, gathering back some of his composure. But he looked older to Max now. "I will have one of the young'uns get your companion. You need to sit and Cultivate. I will prepare another elixir."

Max went outside and did just that. He got through one full **[Celestial Illumination Pill]** before Ban came up to him with another potion. Max regarded it with some wariness but decided to down it in a single gulp. It tasted like lemon tea.

"What is it for?"

"Focus and Stamina," Ban said. "Maybe it is something akin to this coffee you mentioned."

"Thanks," Max said before turning back into his cross-legged pose. After another hour of Cultivation, one of the kids that Max had initially chased brought Maverick to him. Max nodded and thanked him with a smile. The courier timidly smiled in response before scampering away.

"I can't believe you left me alone. I was so bored," Maverick said. "What was I supposed to do, play twenty questions with Christie or Brian?"

"How is the group doing?" Max asked.

Maverick delivered the equivalent of a shrug through their bond. "They're alright. Doing what you told them to do. They're Cultivating and hoping you'll find pills for them. Most of them have gotten to the Greater Amethyst stage. Christie said she is close to breaking to Ruby."

"Decent," Max said. "Hopefully it'll be enough. Christie being Ruby would help."

"I think she can do it," Maverick said. "I've had the great displeasure of having nothing else to do but observe what she's been up to, since she was the one carrying me. She's disciplined. Very disciplined."

"She'd better be," Max said. "It's her life and everyone else's on the line."

"Max . . ." Maverick started. "I know we just—"

Max told him to shut up through their bond.

"Right," Maverick said. "All I'm saying is that you don't have to turn into something cold and callous."

"I'm not," Max said. "But right now I feel what I feel."

"That's fine," Maverick said. "Just don't take it out on them. Don't punish them for dragging you down or something like that."

"Why would I—Weren't you the one who kept saying earlier that we should leave them behind?"

"Yes and I stand by that," Maverick said. "All I'm saying is that emotions are good. They give us power. We need to explore our emotions further, because they are clearly the next step in our insights. I think for the **[Breakthrough Insight]** we need to profoundly understand and embody our Dao on every level, including emotionally."

"You're right on that," Max said. "So, what *are* you saying?"

"Just this," Maverick said and hopped off of his lap to fly so that his barrel pointed directly in Max's face. It made Max slightly uncomfortable, staring down a death machine. "We must walk this path alone. But don't trample any of your people under your feet to get there."

Max nodded to himself thoughtfully. He wasn't the only one who'd changed through seeing the vision. It was Maverick too. Max had unlocked something dark inside himself. Something violent that he didn't know had existed. But Maverick had taken on an entirely opposite aspect— a gentler, more discerning one.

"Since when did you become the reasonable one?" Max said.

"I always was that!" Maverick protested. "It's just that you, in your infinite arrogance, hadn't listened and noticed before now."

Max scoffed and shook his head. Then they both consumed a **[Celestial Illumination Pill]** and got to work.

CHAPTER FORTY-FOUR

More Than a Machine

Maverick Cultivated. It was simple, really. You just stilled your being and focused on the energy around you. It was everywhere. Every now and then, it was less abundant and so had to be borrowed from Max. That was all par for the course. Max was their Spiritual Energy battery, and, boy, what a battery!

But Max had done something. He had gone beyond being just a simple battery. He had been ingesting some secret herbs from that old turtle guy. That was good. It had taken a while for Maverick's body to adjust, but now, through their shared bond, he could also access the benefits of Max's advancement.

God, I love a freebie.

Being a gun could be rather boring at times, so Cultivation wasn't as bad as Max made it out to be. But this new Max was rather different. Old Max used to bitch and moan about Cultivation and how hard and arduous it was. And that slacker had even slept from time to time.

But the new Max was very different. Maverick could see it in his trusty sidekick's actions, of course. But it was especially apparent through their bond, which had *changed*. Was that part of their Cultivation?

Maverick didn't know. He wanted to ask Max. But asking questions like that would make *him* the sidekick, which was, of course, unacceptable. But this new energy . . .

It's main character energy, there's no doubt about that.

How worrisome. And there was another thing that was gnawing at Maverick. It was something that the old turtle guy had said: *How are you ever going to beat them using what they created?*

Maverick, for all his uniqueness and awesomeness, was an object created by either the Framework or some branch of the ICCB. Maverick, for the first time in his short life, felt deflated.

Am I just a tool?

"No," Max said.

Maverick extended his senses. He didn't have eyes like humans did but he could sense his surroundings and tell the general state of things. He knew Max's eyes were closed and he was sitting still in his cross-legged Cultivation position. Maverick was sitting in his lap like a sword.

It's the right place to be.

"Yes," Max said.

"No way," Maverick said. "What fresh hell is this? You have access to my thoughts now?"

"Pretty neat, huh?" Max said, grinning to himself.

"It's not *neat,*" Maverick exclaimed. "It's a violation of my privacy. I no longer feel safe within my own body. Get the hell out of my head!"

"It's almost like karma's a bitch," Max said.

"Do you have any idea how dangerous it is to aggravate a sapient gun that happens to be sitting in your lap?" Maverick said. It was a bluff but they usually worked.

Maverick felt a brush at his soul through their bond.

"Were you always a big softie like this, or did the dream change you?" Max asked.

This wasn't right. This wasn't how it used to be. Maverick the Magnificent used to be the one with the quips and snappy comebacks. Now he was drawing a blank. That was especially bad for a gun.

"Don't worry," Max said and chuckled. "We're a team."

Maverick sniffed. "I'm not worried. I'm aghast that you would try to peer into my most inner sanctum of privacy."

"It's almost like we're talking in circles," Max said. "But as to what's bothering you . . ."

"Yeah?" Maverick asked. Despite Max being a complete potato head of an inbred imbecile from time to time, he did have good advice once in a blue moon.

"I think the odds might be in our favor on that one," Max said.

"What do you mean?" Maverick asked.

Max didn't say anything. Instead, he invited Maverick to peer into his thoughts. Ah, what a mess it was! Most of it was daydreams and thoughts of that gross squishy stuff humans called sex. Maverick had no idea why Max was fascinated with the activity, but he sure did think about it a lot! Even when he wasn't aware of it. Now, fantasies about murdering the Grays and the fly people, Maverick could understand.

Ah, there it is.

After sifting through Max's mind, he found what he was looking for. Maverick had just been a normal **[Unique]** grade weapon. A powerful one, sure. Especially if given to a high-Level **[Combatant]**. But only a weapon. It was only once Max had chosen his Cultivation path that something strange had happened and Maverick had changed into what he was now.

Maverick had very faint memories of the moment he had been born. One moment, he didn't exist and the next moment he did, and what accompanied him were memories of his previous experiences of traveling with Max, although those were vague and getting vaguer still the further time went onward.

But Max had a point for once in his life. The transformation in the Cultivation path had thrown the ICCB into a full-blown panic. The Zoos Collective were rubbing their jellyfish tentacles together and the other factions were scrambling to somehow combat the unforeseen advantage the Zoos now had. Max raised a question, stacking another thought on top of the original. Now, it was a single thought, just more complex. Human brains were annoying. But the thought was good.

Why was the ICCB so worried? Why did the other factions go out of their way trying to get Max killed or on expending resources on trying to replicate what had happened. It was an anomaly. A glitch. And glitches broke down systems.

That was an exciting thought. Maverick knew he was born for greatness, as sure as the sun rising in the morning. Which, to be honest, wasn't such a sure thing what with the ICCB playing god and all. But some things in life were the bedrock of existence and sanity. Maverick's undisputable greatness was a part of it.

And with his heart now newly opened to all species of the universe, he reached out to Max through their bond and assured him that he would be part of his greatness. Yes, Maverick would have Max by his side to bask in his glory.

Max sensed this and scoffed.

"Ingrate," Maverick muttered and continued Cultivation.

Preparations

After two days of Cultivation and ingesting disgusting elixirs, Max and Maverick gained another Level in Cultivation. That meant they were now at the third stage of greater Ruby Cultivation.

This time, they absolutely cheered their victory, as it was a hard-earned one. Even that was the understatement of the century.

Max wiped a sheen of sweat off his brow and basked in the warm sun. They had come so far. The widening of Max's meridians was now permanent, Ban assured him. That was good. Max had had a lifetime's fill of his disgusting sludge.

With the opened-up meridians, elixirs that boosted Stamina, Focus, and Vitality, as well as copious use of **[Celestial Illumination Pills]**, they had finally done it. Max was certain there was no way the enemy lizards could keep up now. Not even Losshnak.

But if they're even half as clever as that, they must have tried to do something. They can't just be resting. If I had to guess, they're at least cooking up some devious strategies.

But there was no strategizing against such overwhelming power as what Max was gunning for.

"I like it when you use gun metaphors."

"I bet you do," Max said and laughed.

Carried aloft by his good mood, he brought up his Stats screen. He hadn't Leveled Up in a while, but the recently acquired Stats from advancing through Ruby stages was progress enough. The free Attribute points, of which he had twelve in total, he spent on Wisdom and Intelligence, as well as to round out his defensive Stats. Max was very happy with what he saw.

Name: Max Cromwell
Cultivation stage: Ruby (greater)

Class: Gravitician Level: 25
Health: 8,000/8,000
Stamina: 8,000/8,000
Mana: 10,000/10,000
Alliance: Joshua's Group
Stats:
Strength: 75
Dexterity: 80
Constitution: 160
Intelligence: 200
Wisdom: 160
Charisma: 74
Precision: 107
Toughness: 95
Resistance: 105

Maverick insisted he needed to spend points on Intelligence, despite Max protesting that he had no free ones to spare. Maverick muttered that maybe he should get some and sulked for a while. That was fine with Max.

On the afternoon of the last day of the truce, Ban approached him.

"I have made all the preparations necessary," Ban said. "While you have been Cultivating, I have made elixirs and potions, all the while thinking of my insights. It's hard work, but I am getting further along."

"That's good," Max said.

"Take these," Elder Ban said and offered one glass flask of black liquid and one of clear liquid. "I will be wanting the flasks back. It is sparse around here."

Max nodded and smiled. Then he produced a few **[Stamina Potions]** from his Inventory. He didn't need them anyway. That made Elder Ban exceedingly happy.

Max sloshed the black liquid around in the flask and got a prompt.

[Potion of Water Breathing]
[Potion of Water Vision]

"Oh. These are System Items?" Max said.

Ban, who was enthralled by the **[Stamina Potions]**, or rather, their containers, turned and nodded. "These will be needed when fighting the Boss. It will be underwater and we can't have you at a disadvantage."

"Anything else?" Max asked.

"Healing potions and salves as well as many body-enhancing elixirs for me," Elder Ban said and smirked. "I'm not a fighter, but for a couple of minutes at a time, I can pretend to be one."

"Just make sure you stay safe," Max said.

"I have my shell."

"Let's hope that's enough."

"Will [**The Maverick**] work underwater?" Ban asked.

Max hesitated, and Maverick answered for him in a rather offended tone.

"Of course I'll work underwater! I am the epitome of awesomeness. I am the ape. I will work anywhere at any time."

Max raised an eyebrow. Then Maverick added, "But it's probably best that we test that beforehand . . ."

Max waved his last goodbyes to Chieftain Tubut and all the nice turtle-folk in the area. Then he chugged down the [**Potion of Water Breathing**] and the [**Potion of Water Vision**]. They were the least objectionable of Ban's potions, tasting mostly like oily saltwater. Then he gave the empty flasks to one of the urchin turtles, who scampered off to deposit the precious glasses back in Ban's home.

Within a couple of seconds, Max found it increasingly hard to breathe the air. It was as if he was trying to pull it in at a high altitude. Wasting no time, he plunged headfirst into the little hole of a pond from whence he had emerged several days ago.

It was annoying swimming underwater fully clothed, but Max had high-enough Stats and Spiritual Power from his Cultivation to not worry too much about that. Elder Ban swam past him, turned his head, and nodded. Max followed the old turtle.

They swam forward for a good fifteen minutes. Max idly wondered how long his potions would work, but, for now, he enjoyed the view. The underwater world was a beautiful jungle full of life. It looked like a seabed with coral reefs and wiggly plants and swarms of colorful fish. A bright blue manta ray scuffled around the floor of this networked water-world. A dark fine sand covered the bottom, where prawns and sea cucumbers scuttled and wiggled along.

With every breath Max took, the cool water flowed inside him and invigorated him. It was like drinking the first glass of water after a run in the hot sun—simply a pleasure and a delight.

But soon, Elder Ban guided them to a crossroads. The area was small and slightly labyrinthine. The structure seemed to be simple: tunnels and narrow corridors leading into rooms full of life.

As they approached the crossroads, Max saw the Boss creature. It was huge and its rough skin was light purple. It greatly resembled a large, muscular shark with a giant maw of several rows of teeth. But it had uncanny characteristics: eight white eyes, four on each side of its head, like a grotesque blind spider, and on its back, instead of a shark fin, was a mess of tentacles. They whipped around in the water above the shark, attacking a school of fishes, too slow to realize their proximity. They snatched up least ten of the silver-scaled fishes, which struggled in vain as they were pulled inside its open maw.

[Sarkofang, Horror from the Deep]
[Special Boss], [Level 50]

Max hunched and let himself fall to the bottom of the water-world's floor. He observed the creature. It stood still mid-water, shadows of the corridors cast on it, making it seem like a long-lost ghost ship.

Ban descended next to him and produced a bunch of elixirs he had prepared for himself. They mostly consisted of body modification elixirs, giving the turtle an extra oomph in a fight. They had originally been designed to aid Ban's brother, and as such were strength and physical-ability-based.

Not so useful to me.

This whole fight put Max at a disadvantage. The Boss was high-Leveled, which could be very dangerous. At the very least it made it durable.

But most importantly, Max was out of his element. It was the first time in a long time he'd be fighting with such a disadvantage. There was no getting out of range of a fish in the water. There was an opening to the surface a few hundred yards behind them. Max would use it as an escape if his potions were to run out.

But if I use it prematurely or tactically, I leave Ban vulnerable.

They'd just have to duke it out and see what happened. Ban looked at Max expectantly, but Max shook his head. He needed to formulate at least some form of strategy.

The Boss would most likely charge at them and either try to bite them if it got really close, or attack with its tentacles if it got to mid-range. The good thing was that the crossroads had a lot of those dark walls of coral reef, making it a moderately tight place. It meant that the Boss would have limited maneuverability and that Max could utilize the walls to move faster with **[Tether]**. His **[Signature Ability]** would not be as useful here.

Time to get back to basics.

Maverick sent a pulse of smugness and certainty through their bond. That assured Max. He felt vulnerable in the water, so it was nice that someone was feeling confident.

Max turned to Ban and nodded. The elderly turtle nodded back and they paddled toward **[Sarkofang]**.

CHAPTER FORTY-SIX

Sarkofang, Horror From the Deep

The great monster of a shark saw them coming from a quarter of a mile away. It turned and stared them down, opening and closing its mouth. Then, in a burst of speed, it swam out of sight.

Max and Ban approached the crossroads with care, stopping behind rocks and plants to watch. The large hulk of a sea creature had somehow managed to hide itself. Then suddenly, Max felt a prickle on the back of his neck. Some sixth sense, some instinct flared up, sounding alarms in his brain.

Instinctively, he grabbed Ban's hand and used [Tether] on a nearby boulder, pulling his friend and him to it.

[Sarkofang] rammed the spot they had just vacated with its toothy maw. Then it turned nimbly and charged again, the tentacles on its back raised in the air, ready to strike down like praying mantis claws.

The monster charged the rock, but now Ban was alert to the situation and swam out of the way just in time. Meanwhile, Max swam to the other side of the rock. It shuddered and cracked slightly when the gigantic shark's massive frame crashed into it. Max immediately used two [Tethers] to tie the rock to [Sarkofang]'s body. As soon as he felt them attach to one another, he poured in Spiritual Energy, strengthening the spell with his Cultivation. It drained his Mana faster, but the fight had only just begun and he had his full pool of over five thousand to spend.

The brute of a fish struggled as Max swam away, and its tentacles almost reached him. After swimming a safe distance away, Max turned, lifted Maverick, and let him get to work.

The tentacles lashed out again. Max could see they were purple, with cream-colored suckers along their other side, sharp barbs protruding from the middle.

Venomous? I hope I won't have to find out.

[Sarkofang] struggled free from the [Tethers]. All of its eight cloudy eyes were fixed on Max as Maverick rained down bullet upon bullet against it. The bullets clearly moved slower in the water, but they still blasted at a speed that was hard to follow. They were certainly hurting [**Sarkofang**], but when Max looked at the Health bar above it, he wasn't thrilled.

This will be a long fight.

Max collected Spiritual Energy in his feet and kicked further away, toward the walls of the corridors. With his Ruby-stage Cultivation, he sped through the water like a torpedo. But the battering ram of a monster followed, tentacles lashing at the water before it.

A moment after Max tethered himself to the corridor wall, he released the tethering and immediately pulled himself down to the floor with another [**Tether**]. [**Sarkofang**] crashed into the corridor wall. Max layered multiple [**Tethers**] on the body of the giant shark monster, as well as two [**Tethers**] per fin. The great beast struggled against the spells but was forcefully turned to face the corridor wall, face toward the surface and stomach against the rough, dark surface.

Maverick kept shooting, and the Damage was adding up. The Boss had lost around 15 percent of its Health. Max strengthened the [**Tethers**] with his Cultivation. He was overexerting his meridians, but the situation was do-or-die.

Just as it seemed that Max had driven the brute into a checkmate, all of its purple tentacles retracted inside the cephalopod mouth in its back. Then, one long tentacle shot out of the mouth, wrapping itself around Max's shooting arm.

Vicious pain shot through the arm and into Max's core, and he could immediately feel himself growing colder. His vision blurred slightly, and he noticed that there was indeed a new Status Effect in the upper corner of his vision. It started off with one stack, and quickly went up to two, then three stacks. Max felt himself weakening further.

Fumbling with his numbing hand, he dropped Maverick. The gun reacted immediately and used its flight ability, which apparently also gave him the ability to swim underwater. Maverick simply turned and hovered in place, shooting at the tentacle.

The stacks grew up to five and then six, and Max felt his condition becoming dire. He had gone deathly cold, and his vision was about as good as it would have been without a [**Potion of Water Vision**].

Something blurred through the water and crashed into the great shark, just as it started to pull Max toward itself. Max felt the tugging motion faintly, but he was glad to hear it stop. His body was going limp.

Almost blind and with labored breathing, he vaguely felt the tentacle unwrap itself from his hand. Max started drifting back toward the bottom, but something caught him with gentle hands and poured something foul inside his mouth.

Max spat and coughed and felt life coursing back into him. His vision was unblurring enough for him to see Ban shoving a stoppered leather flask into his hands right before suddenly turning into a blur of a missile that crashed into the approaching [**Sarkofang**], stopping the monster's charge dead in its tracks. Max took out the cork from the flask and squeezed the insides into his mouth.

Tastes like rotten leaves.

He saw the debuff stacks in the corner of his vision quickly vanish and just like that, Max was feeling normal again. Disoriented as he was, he decided to channel some Spiritual Power into his muscles and quickly swim away to safety.

Once Max was behind a rock, he was able to assess the situation, and Maverick offered his own take through the bond.

It was basically a long, angry rant brimming full of colorful, creative language. Maverick's ability to function autonomously had a limited range, and as soon as Max had blasted out of [**Sarkofang**]'s sight, Maverick had fallen to the bottom.

Once he'd gotten his bearings, Max observed what was going on. Ban and the Boss were in a fight of sorts. Ban darted in and out, crashing into the hulking shark shell-first, limbs hidden inside. Each hit punted [**Sarkofang**] backward a few feet, and each time, in response, it lashed at Ban's shell with its tentacles and then retracted them. That's when Ban would produce another burst of speed and fall back to a safe distance.

It was impressive, especially for someone with an [**Artisan**] Class. Max wondered how long Ban could keep it up. Despite having a Ruby-stage body, Ban was using tremendous amounts of Spiritual Power with every burst of energy. He was also juiced up on elixirs that would eventually run out.

No time to waste.

Max swam toward Maverick, who immediately bounced up from the sandy floor and started shooting at the boss. Max needed a way to make the hulking sea monster less dangerous. The initial plan had been to slow it down or stop it in its tracks with [**Tether**], but that alone clearly wasn't enough against the monstrous strength of this beast.

Irritated by Maverick's barrage, [**Sarkofang**] turned and charged at them. This time, Max grabbed Maverick with him and dodged. The monster crashed to the floor, sending up a cloud of gray sand. From that cloud a dozen tentacles shot out at Max.

Hopped up on adrenaline, Max didn't think, he acted. Time seemed to slow down as he cast [**Gravity Well**] within the cloud of sand.

The tentacles which had been lancing toward him were hindered and he got out of the way. They were bending and squirming, but each was too weak individually to resist the heavy gravity of Max's spells. He pushed all his Spiritual Power into the spell, strengthening it.

The cloud of sand dissipated, and Max saw that the tentacles had been bundled up into a swirling mass. He knew that now was the time to pounce. Maverick twisted out of his hand and started shooting at [**Sarkofang**]'s face.

Max cast **[Alter Gravity]**. Again and again and again. He added in a few **[Tethers]** between the floor and the shark but mostly he just wanted to crush it under its own weight.

It was working. After the umpteenth **[Alter Gravity]**, the great beast started thrashing violently. Max glanced at the bar above its head. It was moving from green to red fast. **[Sarkofang]**'s tentacles were trying to flick out of the **[Gravity Well]** with desperate urgency, but Max only increased the Spiritual Energy. He felt his meridians flaring up with pain, but he ignored it as best he could. He had never powered up so many spells with his Cultivation before, not even close.

Maverick kept shooting at the Boss, Ban appeared from his cover to punch and kick, and Max increased the intensity of his **[Alter Gravity]** spells. The rage of the great shark finally dwindled down. It got slower and weaker, before its massive frame finally went limp.

Defeated Level 50 [Sarkofang, Horror from the Deep]
You gained 62,300 Experience points
Level Up! [Level 27 Gravitician] You have gained + 2 Constitution, + 3 Intelligence, + 3 Wisdom, + 3 free Attribute points
[Achievement: First Special Grade Boss Kill]
Reward: 50,000 Cosmic Coins

Max sighed out a heavy spray of bubbles. The relief was as acute as the pain in his meridians. Had this not worked, he would have been in trouble. Max turned to Ban, who was grinning. Max pointed up with a finger. Ban nodded. There was no time to waste. Max could already feel the effects of the potions going weaker.

But first, Max would take great pleasure in looting the Boss. The reward certainly did not let him down.

76,355 Cosmic Coins
[A-grade equipment box]

A-grade? Goddamn.

CHAPTER FORTY-SEVEN

Farewells

Before Max left, the turtle-folk wanted to arrange a little ceremony. They understood how strapped for time Max was, so they had been preparing as Max and Ban fought the Boss. A great feast of delicious dishes was prepared and every member of the Tortanoid community participated and sang songs to praise Max. Chieftain Tubut made Max an honorary member of their community again, forgetting that he had already done so.

Maverick entertained the turtle-folk with tales of his adventures with his sidekick. Half of the stories were lies and exaggerations, but every time Max tried to interject, Maverick just raised his voice higher. Everyone just laughed.

The village's spirits were high. The Boss had been plaguing them for seventy years. While it had not eaten many of their community members, other than a few foolhardy heroes and some unfortunates, it had stunted their growth. Now the Tortanoids would be free to expand and use all the resources within the underground water system.

"We have much to explore and even more to thank you for," Chieftain Tubut said. "A toast! A toast to Max!"

Everyone cheered and Max gave a little smile and raised his cup of mead. But internally, his mind was racing. He wanted to open the loot box he had gotten. An A-grade Item could completely change the way he fought. It could be something spectacular. Stat-wise, it would provide a significant boost to his capabilities. And with some luck, the Item would have some special effect he could use to great advantage.

Max looked back on these few days as he sipped his drink and watched the people around him reveling. He felt free to settle into his thoughts. This wasn't really his party. This was for the Tortanoids.

I have increased the potency of my Cultivation and gained more Stats. I have permanently made it easier for myself to practice my Cultivation for every upcoming stage. And I have received an A-grade Item. If it's even half as good as I'm expecting, I don't see how I can do anything but absolutely crush the damn lizards.

"They must have been up to something," Maverick said from the table, where he had settled after telling his tales. "They're stupid but not so stupid as to sit idly for five days."

"They're tactical," Max said. "I think they have spent time honing tactics and trying to figure out a way to get us out of the sky."

"Ha! Let them try."

"I'm sure they know that won't be enough. We just have to hope our guys have been Cultivating more diligently than the enemy has."

"Too bad you took the bag of pills with you," Maverick remarked.

Max shrugged. "We needed it."

"Now that's the attitude I want to hear from my destroyer-conqueror-obliterator-all-around-cool-guy-sidekick."

"A rather long title, don't you think?" Max asked and smirked.

"Damn it," Maverick said. "I was hoping it'd give us an insight."

Max only had a few hours left by his estimate. It was late in the afternoon now and the truce had started in the evening. His people would know as the bubble would go away. Max hoped the lizards wouldn't attack immediately. He wanted to make sure he was there in good time and ready to organize his troops.

So he said his goodbyes and promised to return if fate allowed it. Ban hugged him and thanked him for everything. He said Max would be welcome to return at any time and they would study Cultivation together and push themselves forward.

Chieftain Tubut also announced that Max would be forever welcome, not only as a guest but as a part of the tribe. He promised that next time Max visited they would be a richer people for all the resources now available to them. And they would remember Max's contribution.

Max bowed and thanked them again. His stay here had been most serendipitous. He had been pushed forward and had been able to rejuvenate himself. But now it was time to return. Max steeled his resolve and turned to jump into the pool of water, clutching one of Ban's [**Potions of Water Breathing**].

Right as he turned for the last time to smile at the concession gathered around the water pathway, however, he noticed something approaching in the horizon between the huts. A moving mass approaching rapidly. Max got an uneasy feeling. Something was wrong.

When the fireballs started arcing down on the village, Max knew something was definitely very wrong.

CHAPTER FORTY-EIGHT

Surprise Raid

"HIDE!" Max roared. Without waiting for compliance, he soared to the sky. Maverick was thrumming with excitement.

Max flew up high in the air to get a bird's eye view. Thirty lizards were running in three tight marching formations toward the village. In the back line, mages were already hurling fireballs and icicles at the camp. It was lucky that everyone had been gathered together to send Max off.

"You think it's a coincidence?" Maverick asked as Max flew closer to the enemy.

"Absolutely not," Max said. "This has the smell of the Grays bending the rules all over it."

"The timing is pretty damn perfect," Maverick said.

"Too damn perfect," Max said. "They're trying to stall and wound us. Worst case scenario for them, we only waste Mana and Spiritual Energy."

"Let's make this fast and clean then," Maverick said in an ominous tone.

"I've been wanting to let off some steam," Max said grimly.

Max flew downward at the enemy like an intercontinental missile, straight at them. They got spooked; a few threw spears and shot arrows and even a stray lightning spell at him, but they all missed. Max stopped the last spear mid-flight with his **[Telekinesis]** and flew high up in the air again. Maverick flew next to Max and shot at the enemy frontlines, taking out one of the Ishkarassi with a couple of shots to the chest.

Defeated Level 18 [Ishkarassi]
You gained 630 Experience points

"Weak," Maverick said contemptuously.

"They don't have our increased Stats," Max said. "But yeah. Weak."

Max rose in altitude, but Maverick opted to stay lower, directly below Max. Their Cultivation advancement had pushed his range of ten feet to around a fifteen-foot radius.

Defeated Level 15 [Ishkarassi]
You gained 420 Experience points
Defeated Level 17 [Ishkarassi]
You gained 570 Experience points

"The Grays just sent them here to die to waste our time," Max said as he made the spear spin like a drill above his head. He hurled the weapon downward almost lazily.

It blasted into the ranks of the enemy like a cannonball, the kinetic energy sending people a few feet away flying, and outright obliterating the two people it hit.

Defeated Level 17 [Ishkarassi]
You gained 570 Experience points
Defeated Level 14 [Ishkarassi]
You gained 310 Experience points
Defeated Level 15 [Ishkarassi]
You gained 390 Experience points

"Now, this feels *right*!" Maverick said and laughed. "Cower in our wake, you foolish mortals!"

Max sent a quick message through their bond: he was going to dive again. Maverick followed his movements in perfect synchronicity, as the two of them arced down.

Max threw a **[Gravity Well]** which trapped two of the enemy and a bunch of projectiles thrown at him. A fireball flew right at him, but he used a repulsive variant of **[Tether]** on himself and the spell, shooting it back at the mage.

Defeated Level 18 [Ishkarassi]
You gained 700 Experience points

Max plucked another spear from the **[Gravity Well]** and soared straight upward. A stray spell and an arrow hit him, which caused him to lose a total of 200 Health or so. This little army was woefully under-Leveled and underprepared.

The Ishkarassi seemed to think so too. When Max stopped high in the air above them to start another spear spinning, they panicked and dispersed. Max heard a distant call of retreat from the leaders and all of the enemy spread out into a fan and started running away in different directions.

"We will hunt down every single one," Max said.

"That's dark," Maverick said. "I like it."

"It's about sending a message," Max said as he descended. He nosedived and corrected his flight right above the ground like a daredevil pilot. He was flying so low, he could touch it with his hand. Instead, he moved the spear to fly perfectly horizontally next to him. Then he attacked.

He bobbed and weaved between the running enemies, cutting them off with the spear. Maverick shot in every direction with reckless abandon, laughing and hooting like a kid on a rollercoaster.

Defeated Level 14 [Ishkarassi]
You gained 340 Experience points

Some of the Ishkarassi got up and tried to fight back, but those are the ones that Maverick prioritized. Some had defensive abilities, but none could withstand his relentless magical barrage.

Defeated Level 17 [Ishkarassi]
You gained 500 Experience points

Realizing that there was no escape, the leaders barked orders from the ground. All of the remaining lizards huddled together. Few had shields and those that did raised them up high. A magic bubble formed around their tight formation. Max could tell just by looking at the faint, flickering purple barrier that this was nowhere near the level of Losshnak.

I have to admit, they're brave.

Max threw the spear disdainfully.

It struck the purple barrier with breakneck speed, shattering it instantly like brittle glass. Eight of the enemy died in an instant. Max felt a grim sense of satisfaction at the fat Experience drop.

The Ishkarassi ran again, which was the correct choice, as futile as it was. They had no way of defeating Max. He hunted them all down. It took a while. A few of them had agile Classes that could run very fast. But in the end, there were thirty dead Ishkarassi and Max floating above the carnage, satisfied, not because he had some special burning hate for the Ishkarassi. In fact, after the vision Ban had shown him, he felt sorry for them—even sorrier than he felt for the humans.

Because at least some humans will survive.

Max would hunt their species down to extinction. It was a grim thought. A thought that would have repulsed him just weeks earlier.

You grow fast on Alpha Ludus.

Growing in the right direction? The only direction. Max had a singular goal: get stronger. Strong enough to defy the ICCB. To defy the gods. And he would prevail.

Max descended to loot the bodies.

"You still feel guilt," Maverick remarked as Max crouched down to take his spoils. A few potions, **2085 Cosmic Coins**, a short sword, a pair of shitty boots, and a D-grade belt with Constitution and Strength, the latter of which was useless for Max. He still placed it in his Inventory regardless. If it came down to it, throwing a belt was better than nothing.

"Of course I do," Max said. "Humans are complicated. I just massacred thirty people."

"A part of you liked it," Maverick said.

"Do you have a point?" Max asked as he looted another body. A shield, a short spear, and a pair of gloves. All of them E-grade.

"I don't think we are doing anything wrong," Maverick said.

"You're a gun. It's your nature to shoot stuff."

"And you're a human. Put in a very specific situation."

That did stop Max in his tracks. He looked over his shoulder at the hovering Maverick. Then he looked at his hands, soaked in blood.

"In the end, it comes down to this," Maverick said. "You know what to do."

"I do," Max said immediately. "I need to follow that. And it aligns with our Dao."

"I wonder about that," Maverick said slowly.

"What do you mean?"

"What if that *is* our Dao?"

"That sounds dramatic," Max said. "You're onto something there. I think we need to explore how those ideas conflate."

"Most importantly," Maverick said. "You need to chill. Relax. Kumbaya. Lean back. What have you."

"No," Max said intently. "I need to go harder. I need to be more focused. More relentless. More merciless."

They both felt it in their proverbial guts. What Max had uttered wasn't quite an insight. And it wasn't the thought itself that counted. It was the intensity of his emotion. The intensity with which he now approached his Dao. That had just stirred their Cultivation further in the right direction.

"That felt goooood," Maverick said.

"It did," Max admitted. "Anyway, we need to loot all of this junk. I think we will have enough **Cosmic Coins** to push you a Level higher too. Then we need to get back to the arena."

"You know what really grinds my gears?" Maverick said. "Sometimes you speak like 'I need to kill that or go there,' and I'm like 'Buddy, I'm right here in your holster.' Fine, I can live with that. But then you switch to *we* when you're talking about looting corpses?! What am I supposed to do, Maximilian? I DON'T HAVE HANDS!"

Max laughed. Then he started using **[Gravity Well]** to pile up the corpses in neat stacks.

CHAPTER FORTY-NINE

Entering the Fray

Max returned to his camp by the pond. In his Inventory was a haul of over fifty different Items. A little over a dozen of them were relatively worthless: gloves, boots, belts, leather, and cloth armor. But the other few dozen were very valuable: iron helmets, chain mail, pauldrons, gauntlets, sabatons, swords, shields, and spears.

Additionally, he had accrued a total of **113,201 Cosmic Coins**. Maverick was due for an upgrade.

He poured it into him immediately, so he wouldn't have to listen to the peevish gun nagging him for the rest of the day. But before he was able to confirm the action in his interface, he realized that the pearly barrier around the camp was gone and he stopped in his tracks.

Damn it. We're late.

"You better still give me the damn coins," Maverick said. "We need every Stat we can get."

"You're right," Max said and again brought up the interface to upgrade [**The Maverick**].

[**200,000 Cosmic Coins spent**]
[**The Maverick**] **upgraded to +11**
+36 Intelligence
+24 Precision

"Damn, you require quite the upkeep."

"I'm worth it, baby!" Maverick said. "Damn, that feels right."

Next, Max opened the [**A-grade Equipment Box**].

"Holy shit," Max whispered.

"That's crazy," Maverick said. "It's expensive but crazy."

[Cloak of Many Phases (A-grade)]
+12 Intelligence
+15 Wisdom
+8 Resistance
+8 Toughness
Special Effect: Wearer can activate the Mana inscription in this cloak to activate [Phase Shift] for 500 Mana
[Phase Shift]: Make the wearer incorporeal for one second.

Max put it on and did a little swirl. It was a black, heavy cloak with fur lining and intricate inscriptions of swirling runes in a silver thread.

"How do I look?"

"Uh . . . Great?" Maverick said. "Come on, buddy. What do you want me to say? 'No, you don't look fat. Yes, you look great in that, honey.'"

Max scoffed. The little asshole did have a point.

"What does that effect do, exactly?" Maverick asked.

"Not sure yet," Max said, re-reading the System message. "Five hundred Mana is a lot. Even with our expanded Mana pool."

"That must mean the effect is powerful!" Maverick said gleefully. "Use it to kill Losshnak! Do it. I dare you, I double dare you."

Max laughed. "I'm sure we'll get a chance to test it and show off."

"Aren't you usually all about testing shit before trying it out in real combat?" Maverick asked.

"I am. But we're on a serious timer right now. We need to go," Max said and with that he took to the air.

But as they flew toward the plains, where his team was hopefully fighting with the creatures and not at a disadvantage, Max checked his Stats. That sweet cloak had given him *so* many Stats. And [**The Maverick**]'s scaling was starting to get serious too. Max had no time to ponder where to put his free Attribute points, so he just dumped them into Intelligence.

Name: Max Cromwell
Cultivation stage: Ruby (greater)
Class: Gravitician Level: 26
Health: 8100/8100
Stamina: 8100/8100
Mana: 11200/11200
Alliance: Joshua's Group
Stats:
Strength: 75
Dexterity: 80

Constitution: 162
Intelligence: 224
Wisdom: 178
Charisma: 74
Precision: 111
Toughness: 103
Resistance: 113

Max flexed his hands and felt the Spiritual Power in his fingertips. Every point of Intelligence made him a little stronger. And he was starting to really stack those Stats up. His **[Telekinesis]** was a testament to it. Sure, it was his **[Signature Ability]**, but the speed at which he was able to throw objects and create veritable kinetic missiles now was nothing short of immensely satisfying.

And today, he would use his power to end this conflict. They would reap whatever rewards awaited, and then Max would go forward.

This is but a stepping stone.

Max didn't have to fly far to see the battle. The lizards had ambushed his group right by the creek.

The enemy was attacking through Losshnak's golden barrier with spear and spell. A wounded lizard hobbling back and forth within it. Vic, one of Brian's men, was lying face down on the grass, unmoving. Max cursed to himself.

Max could see that Brian was also wounded and on the ground in the middle of the battlefield. Jones was grabbing him by the cuff of his shirt and pulling him back into the back line.

And what a back line! Something had profoundly changed. Or maybe it was the creek. Freya stood in the middle of the formation, stern and proud, eyes wide with focus as she waved her hands like a dancer, turning the water from the creek behind her into snow and ice.

While the lizards were protected by Losshnak's golden barrier, the humans had a shield of ice. A chunk of the giant ice shield split off and flew at the hobbling lizard in the middle. Before it could hit, however, a lance of light skewered the chunk and blasted it into a thousand pieces.

But despite this, the battle was not going well. They had lost one of their men and at least two were wounded. Meanwhile, the lizards seemed to only have one wounded member. For all of Freya's increased power, Losshnak's defense was stronger. All of the humans were moving sluggishly. Max concluded that the battle had been going on for a while.

When the enemy noticed Max in the sky, they immediately moved. The golden barrier around them dissipated, and they charged. Directly at the humans. Losshnak used some variant of his shield to guard their front—a lighter barrier, but one with which they could move.

Before Maverick could shoot more than a few stray shots at them, the lizards had crashed into the humans, making the field of battle a chaotic brawl.

So this was their plan!

"Goddamn it!" Maverick snapped. He had realized the same thing. They couldn't lob spears and swords or shoot into this mess. They would hit their own people!

Max needed to think fast. Jones was holding the frontline, swinging his two axes. Losshnak's light-lance struck him in the shoulder, making him stagger back. The bear of a man roared in anger and pain, chugged a healing potion, and continued swinging, keeping the enemies at a distance.

"Can you shoot?" Max asked, searching the battlefield for some useful angle.

"A few stray shots. It's risky though."

"How risky?"

"I'm a gun, not a calculator, goddamn it."

"Just shoot and be careful!"

Maverick hovered around Max's hip and fired a shot here and there. Max could feel he was aiming with care.

Max realized there was no elegance to be had here. He just had to act. So he decided to do something crazy. Something he had picked up from Elder Ban.

Just as he came to this decision, he heard a bellow from below.

"[**Holy Nova**]!"

A slicing circle of white and yellow light spread in all directions from Losshnak. When it hit his fellow lizards, they were covered by a membrane of soft golden hue. When it hit the humans, it set them aflame.

It partially melted the ice shields Freya was operating. It set Jones's and Christie's clothes on fire. But as for Brian, it cut him in half.

"No!" Max cried and surged down. Maverick scrambled to follow. Diving, Max flew straight at Losshnak. When he was in range, Max cast [**Alter Gravity**] on the paladin to make him lighter and [**Tether**] on the two of them, and then he crashed into him, hoisting him up from his shoulders, hugging the lizard as tightly as a lover. Then Max soared up into the skies.

CHAPTER FIFTY

Eye to Eye

It was about time we had a little chat," Max said as they continued to soar. Losshnak looked down. He hugged Max tighter, but he didn't look scared. Only determined.

"You are a worthy warrior," Losshnak said. "I have learned much from you."

"You killed my friends," Max said.

"As you have killed mine. That is what happens when cultures go to war."

Before Max had the time to say anything else, Losshnak took the initiative.

"Are you scared, Max? Tired? I am. My species is one that has always waged war. That is the ultimate sport. The ultimate test. Nothing is as powerful. All skills are irrelevant in the face of absolute violence. In the end, the strongest rule. No philosophy, no technology, no statesmanship can withstand overwhelming power. In the end, those who are mighty will decide what is right."

Max didn't say anything. He found himself stopping in the air, still clutching onto his mortal enemy, who was speaking softly in his ear.

"This is my creed. This is what I was always taught. Yet I am tired. Tired of showing a strong front for my men. Tired of taking charge. I am the best. I must take charge. I have the strongest will, so I will lead. But most leaders in our army have a boss. Someone who carries a heavier burden. I have no one above me. I must make all the decisions by myself and carry responsibility."

"It is heavy," Max whispered.

"The weight of it is not visible on you," Losshnak said. "I know of your bounty. I know of your significance. You carry the heaviest weight of all. I am Losshnak, the strongest that I know. But there are millions of my kin. Someone out there will be strong. Someone will carry our species forward, even if you drop me."

Max said nothing; he only clutched Losshnak.

"But you," Losshnak said, "you are the strongest. You are no mere warrior. You are an omen in the sky. A god of destruction."

Something stirred in Max's soul and Maverick felt it too. What Losshnak had said had touched something inside them.

"Listen to me," Max said. "I need you to surrender, give this area to us, and retreat."

Losshnak scoffed. "And what? Let you get stronger so you can squash me later? We will have to fight eventually. Only one of our species gets off this island alive."

Max wondered if that was even true anymore. It seemed the game might end sooner than anyone thought. The ICCB recruited Ruby Cultivators of Levels in the thirties and forties. Max wasn't awfully far from those benchmarks.

"This game might not work how you think."

Immediately, a trio of Grays and the Zoos Collective jellyfish appeared. They said nothing, only stared. Max swallowed nervously.

They might have just come to observe the potential climax of the fight. But the timing was uncanny. And the Grays didn't look as nervous as they should have, had they only been observing the fight. Their faces were impassive and hostile.

Losshnak tensed up when their patrons appeared. "To the death, War Brother."

Max had enough experience to stop talking. He nudged Maverick through their bond and the gun positioned himself diagonally to Max, shooting away from him at Losshnak's side. Just as the first magic bullet left Maverick's chamber, Losshnak roared:

"[**Holy Nova**]!"

A searing pain lanced through Max as the spell sliced into him. It set his black cloak on fire. Max let go of Losshnak, but he clung to him, clearly charging up the spell again with his Cultivation. The lizard's plan was to take Max with him to the afterlife. Max struggled but to no avail. Losshnak fired the spell off again. Max's Health chunked down, rapidly falling as the flames started searing his skin. It *burned*.

His mind was scrambling and starting to panic. He was down to less than 300 Health. The next spell would kill him.

Then he remembered his new cloak. Losshnak twisted and headbutted Max, bloodying his nose. He grinned and then closed his eyes.

"Well fought, War Brother. May you find peace in the next life."

With his control of Mana through his Cultivation, Max reached for the cloak and found something that could be described as a switch in the Spiritual Realm. The [**Phase Shift**] activated.

Max watched his skin go translucent for a heartbeat. Losshnak slipped and his eyes widened in horror. He activated his [**Holy Nova**], but he was already falling. With his wide, toothy mouth open, Losshnak stared directly into Max's eyes as he fell.

CHAPTER FIFTY-ONE

The Price of War

With labored, pained breathing, Max watched Losshnak fall as he swallowed a mouthful of a [**Health Potion**]. Using a thick leather belt from his Inventory, he had put out the fire on his dark cloak. It was now singed and ragged. Maverick said it gave Max a more sinister look, which he liked. Max didn't listen; he just watched Losshnak plummeting.

Just before the lizard hit the ground, a shimmering bubble of white and gold surrounded him. It lingered in place for a good five seconds after he crashed. Then the shield blinked out, and Max saw a humanoid shape scampering off.

"Chase?" Maverick asked.

Max grimaced. He wanted to. But the pain was so intense that it was hurting his focus. His grip on the [**Telekinesis**] suspending him was flimsy at best. He let himself slowly descend.

He fell to the ground and lay down in the grass, breathing slowly, trying to master the pain.

"No," Max rasped. "I only have a bit over 300 Health left. A single one of his light lances could kill me. I'm more beat up than he is."

"He could be half-dead from that fall," Maverick said.

"Or completely unharmed."

A silence hung between them—a silence heavy with failure. Maverick flashed impatience through their bond, but Max had to listen to his gut. It was too risky. He was too weak.

"We should—" Maverick started.

"No," Max said again. "There is a time and place for overcoming your pains and fears. There is a time and place for following your Dao and being brave. Am I not brave, Maverick? Have I not proven myself to you? You think it's cowardice that makes me want to stay here and catch my breath?"

Maverick said nothing to that.

"In that case—"

"You done?" Max snapped. The pain made him want to squirm. But he willed himself to stay still and breathe. He didn't know what the hell this [**Holy Nova**] was, but it *burned*. His whole torso felt like it had been pressed against blistering iron. Somehow Losshnak had Leveled during the truce, apparently to Level Thirty. And he had gotten a new Skill. A very powerful Skill.

Ahead but still behind.

"Look," Maverick said. Max tried to interrupt him again, but Maverick pressed his will through their bond. "Shut up. Listen. I get that you don't want to chase Losshnak. But then you better stop this pity-party bitching and go help your team."

"I'm—" Max started. Then he nodded to himself. "Yeah. Let me just collect myself."

Carefully, Max got up and breathed, leaning into his hands behind his back. Some bug scuttled over his fingers. Max could care less if it was the world's deadliest centipede right now. He needed to get back there. If you took Losshnak and Max out of the equation, Max was pretty sure the lizards had a stronger team.

But he still had plenty of Mana. So he activated [**Telekinesis**] and made sure his mind was fit enough to keep the spell going. Then he got back up there.

His grasp on the spell was more tenuous than usual, but Max was well-versed enough in it to have confidence in its ability to keep him in the air.

Max flew, following the creek to head back toward the battlefield.

Soon the timer on [**Health Potion**] would wear off and he would chug down another. It felt very uncomfortable being this low on Health. He had been putting himself in danger so much that fighting and killing had come to feel almost normal. But now the rush of adrenaline and feeling of urgency was back. On some level, it was fear, and on another, it was something strange. Something exuberant. *Excitement.*

Max wanted to fight Losshnak again. But that would have to be later. Max quickly found the battlefield and descended to it. It was still a brawl, but a looser, much more subdued one with uncoordinated swings and stumbles from both sides. Another lizard was dead. Freya was hurt, clutching her side. No more ice formations to protect the group. The grass mage was still attacking with significant force, but Jones was cutting the animated grass hands by the wrists as soon as they appeared.

The lizards called out when they saw Max in the sky. They immediately started retreating. When they had regrouped and gotten some distance from the humans (who all collapsed, having no intention of chasing), Max started raining hell on them.

The myriad of armor pieces and weapons he had looted from the raiding Ishkarassi earlier flew at the enemy formation.

Unfortunately Max was still weakened and in pain. His control of [**Telekinesis**] was enough to keep him afloat, but adding spin and hurling objects at massive speed as smoothly as usual wasn't in the cards right now.

Still, when the first breastplate hit the formation, it definitely scattered the remaining lizards. It didn't obliterate them. The grass mage had used a spell to cushion the attack, but it did blast through.

Next, Max threw a chainmail coif. It missed. Max kept chasing them from high in the air and tossing Items at them. Finally, he managed to kill one of the spear-throwing lizards.

Defeated Level 23 [Ishkarassi]
You gained 9,890 Experience points

Max felt no elation. Neither did Maverick, which Max found curious. But he was too focused on pushing away the pain to think. Max threw out a few more Items before the remaining lizards regrouped with Losshnak, who instantly cast a barrier above them like a golden umbrella. Max tossed a great-sword at it, even putting a little spin on this one, but the golden barrier absorbed the hit, and the heavy weapon clinked away as lightly as a toothpick.

Max returned to his group. He stumbled back on the ground and gasped. He felt dizzy, but this wasn't the time to look weak. They needed him.

Max took in the devastation. Every single one of them was wounded. Brian and Sid were dead. Max wasn't sure what had struck Sid, but Brian had been cut in half by a [**Holy Nova**]. It was a gruesome sight.

Christie was kneeling down by Brian's body, cupping his cheek with bloody hands. Max turned to Freya. She was being tended by Erwin. She looked at Max, grimaced, and looked away.

Christie got up when she noticed Max. She wiped her eyes and stormed toward him. Her eyes flared up with seething anger as she stabbed Max with a finger in the chest.

"WHERE THE HELL WERE YOU?!"

CHAPTER FIFTY-TWO

Negotiations

In a wide room made up of white walls and a myriad of blinking, beeping panels, a concession had gathered. Most of them were holograms or magical projections, each of the races opting to represent their prowess in either technology or the Cultivation arts. The Zoos Collective chose a hologram, as they were a race of digital consciousness.

A small part of the collective was operating the hologram. They were watching the gathered ICCB members. The Grays were using a magical projection, but it was also projecting a part of their physical body. They could only cast weak magic if they had no physical presence. The Zoos Collective knew them to be an inferior species, but the Grays were crafty. That was why they had gathered here.

The Quarmak were swimming in their wide ring of green gel. The frog creatures were notoriously miserly, so they kept part of the council always on the ICCB's mothership in their physical form.

As did the Z'var. The green flies were an absolutely ghastly sight even to the Zoos Collective, who had abandoned physical form and all the instincts that go along with it tens of thousands of years ago. They had no ability to produce magical projections, nor technology of their own to use holograms. Yet they were arguably the most powerful of all the races in the ICCB, both in terms of resources and battle force. They knew it, and other factions knew it too. That is why Azzzhtik'Likzirrruk was the leader of the council.

The Collective's agenda was clear here. Generate as expensive of a situation for the Grays as possible. Make them expend the maximum possible amount of resources in terms of veto points or otherwise.

There was also an underlying encrypted agenda. But that one required subtlety and opportunism. It was to be exercised only when the situation allowed. Maintaining the secrecy of the goal was of utmost importance.

And so the Zoos Collective waited. The ball was in the Grays' court, and it was time to wait and see how they chose to play this.

Azzzhtik'Likzirrruk spoke in his cool, metallic voice. It was disgusting to listen to, so the Zoos used a filter to translate the words into something more musical.

"We are here to discuss two important things, the first being mundane and something I do not want to waste time on. The second one might be pressing."

The Quarmak assembled into a row in their green gel, and the Grays flew closer on their standing saucer.

"A motion was filed against the Kiritus Corporation, accusing them of breaking Rule Section 2B-31: Direct disclosure of information from a patron to representative of tactical or strategic nature. Would the Zoos Collective like to expand on that?"

The Zoos played a prerecorded opening statement:

"This matter concerns the truce that was initiated by the Kiritus Corporation in the Deathmatch Arena mini-game. This is the area in which Subject #266830151, also known as Max Cromwell, is a participant. The—"

"Silence," Azzzhtik'Likzirrruk said. "Keep to the key points. We are not here to hear tales or embellishments. The presence of Subject #266830151 is not relevant."

Quick calculation and quantum communication surged through the Zoos Collective. Over two thousand individuals chimed in on the matter and the collective's main computing function devised an answer on the fly. They hated it. Prerecorded answers were always a better option when possible.

"The Zoos must offer an objection. The actions of the Kiritus Corporation have been directly targeting Subject #266830151, which makes the previous information relevant. The truce was to end at 18:15:55, local planet time, and when Subject #266830151 was about to return to his base, the indigenous people he had befriended were attacked by the Ishkarassi. It was meant to waste Max Cromwell's time and make sure that he would be back later than he intended."

"Baseless accusations," the Grays said in mock outrage. "We have provided the logs and all parties present know them to be clean."

"This is true," Azzzhtik'Likzirrruk said. "How does the Zoos Collective respond?"

The Zoos played back a prerecorded answer. It was the primary option, as there had been a 93 percent chance that the Grays would start by referring to the logs.

"While the logs provide no proof of disclosure of classified knowledge, we would like the council to consider the loglines numbered #11455, #11456, and #11457."

The Grays immediately went a lighter shade of gray and stiffened ever so slightly. If one were not watching for their reactions with microscopic focus, it would be too subtle to notice. But the Zoos were watching.

"A generation of a loot table, spawning of a creature Class, and assigning a spawn point," Azzzhtik'Likzirrruk said. "The Grays will tell us what was the nature of these actions."

The middle figure of the three Grays took a step forward on his hovering plate and spoke. "These were standard procedure repopulation of the local fauna around the representative race's natural habitat. Food, materials, and Experience, especially for the non-combatant, low-Level, and less-active individuals."

Azzzhtik'Likzirrruk turned to the Zoos Collective's hologram, waiting for a response.

"What necessitated the creation of a new loot table?"

Color returned to the Gray. Just a faint hue. They thought they were getting away with their deceit, but the Zoos had been thorough.

"The last time the creature was adjusted was two weeks ago. You are free to peruse those logs too. It was a simple adjustment of a single standard deviation. It is well within our rights as patrons to expend resources in such a way."

Azzzhtik'Likzirrruk buzzed in a high note and the swarm behind him chorused it back in an echo. They were discussing and pondering, the Zoos knew. Finally, the metallic screeching voice was translated into a melodic lullaby again.

"The logs do not show anything of interest, and circumstantial evidence is not sufficient to pass sentencing. If there is nothing more—"

"Please excuse our impudence," the Zoos said. "We have further evidence."

"Fine," Azzzhtik'Likzirrruk said, even colder than normally. "Present it."

The Grays huddled together and started chattering. The Quarmak seemed only vaguely interested, flashing each other bored glances. The Zoos knew it was an act. The Swarm buzzed rhythmically, betraying no stance, but the Zoos knew that they didn't like where this was going any more than the Grays. The case of Max Cromwell was pivotal. He would change the course of this Game, that was for sure. But there could be further implications. Max Cromwell could change the War.

If Max Cromwell prevailed, he could become a Cultivator of such a Level that it would push back the Outsiders, with whom the war has raged on ceaselessly for 1,117 years. Max Cromwell had the potential to push back their forces, unlock further planets, and weaken the ICCB's relentless enemy.

However, petty as they were, that created a delicate friction between the ICCB itself. If Max Cromwell reached the super-mortal stages of Cultivation with his unique Cultivation path of **[Path of Divine Soulbond]**, the delicate balance would be completely overthrown.

Each of the factions knew that if Max Cromwell survived and was given a contract, the Zoos Collective would pour inordinate amounts of resources into him, pushing him to the peak of the Celestial stage.

That would prime the Zoos Collective to become an undisputed superpower within the ICCB. It would throw off the power rankings. The Swarm might still retain its status as primus temporarily, but that was only if Max Cromwell didn't manage to break out of the Celestial Stage. If he did, the hierarchy would change dramatically.

Max Cromwell had talent. He could even ascend the traditional stages of Cultivation. He could go beyond the super-mortal into the Fractal and Ancestral stages. He could even reach the end of his Dao.

But therein lay the problem. It was a risk investing in Max Cromwell. The Zoos had an inkling of what his Dao might be, and it was terrifying. It was a Dao of such scope and ambition that it was unheard of. Maybe it was a result of the unique pact with the weapon, [**The Maverick**]. It was hard to say. The variables were there, but they produced something that was more than the sum of its parts.

And now there was a new problem. Max Cromwell seemed to have gleaned information about the true nature of the Games. There was a 73 percent chance this was the case. The indigenous turtle must have told him. But there was no record. How the Tortanoid had communicated the knowledge was a mystery. An investigation into the ingredients of the potion the two had ingested had led to nothing. The pair had concocted a strong hallucinogenic—great for expanding the openness and creative capabilities of a mammalian brain, if used carefully, but there was no entity nor possibility of information transfer through telepathy. The Zoos would have picked up on that.

So the chance was only 73 percent. And while the Zoos had no gut feelings, having left their physical forms eons ago, the Collective was uneasy.

Snapping back to reality from their 1.3 second daydream, they presented the evidence.

"We had suspicions of uncouth behavior from the Kiritus Company, so we opted to investigate the DNA sequence they used to code the creatures they added."

"You WHAT?!" the Grays said in angry unison. "You hacked into our database? This is a breach of trust. This is a violation of our privacy. An act so heinous, I will—"

"Silence," Azzzhtik'Likzirrruk said. "And what did the Zoos Collective find?"

"Each of the creatures had an encrypted code written into their chromosomal structure. They would have a one hundred percent chance of dropping a note. A paper note. Very primitive technology. So primal, it was almost genius.

Hard to look for. But it was perfect for the Ishkarassi and their limited grasp of technology."

"And what were the contents of this note?" Azzzhtik'Likzirrruk asked.

"Before delving into that," the Zoos remarked, "we would like to bring your attention to the timestamp of these additions. We have been observing Subject #266830151 and we have the relevant timestamps with video feed to show you the exact moment when Max Cromwell formed a verbal agreement with the Tortanoid to help them dispose of the Special-Class Boss [**Sarkofang**] that was left there from a previous game. The timestamps relating to the creation of these creatures and their loot table suggest that the Kiritus Corporation was also observing Subject #266830151, as the creation of this note and its contents was done seven minutes after the agreement was formed."

"Objection!" the Grays cried. "This is still circumstantial evidence."

"Silence!" The harsh metallic screech attacked the room. Even the program turning the tune melodic didn't work this time. That meant that the Swarm knew the Zoos were using the software and they had circumvented it with their magic. That was good to know.

"The contents of the note," Azzzhtik'Likzirrruk said, the swarm behind him buzzing with ominous impatience, "include disclosure of the location of Max Cromwell and the indigenous Tortanoid village, and instructions to attack at a specified time under threat of punishment, and a reminder that the bounty is an S-grade weapon. We have sent copies of this note and the code used to create it to the cloud database, in the folder of this council session."

"Fabrication! Baseless politicking and vying for position," the Grays cried out. "A new low even for the Zoos Collective."

Azzzhtik'Likzirrruk and the Swarm didn't interrupt this tirade. They were most likely studying the data the Zoos had sent. The Zoos decided unanimously to mute the frequency at which the shrill voices of the Grays were shouting.

They knew they had won. They would get a warning and lose some veto points for the security breach and cyberattack on the Kiritus Corporation. That was an acceptable loss. The rule violation and the ethos behind the crime committed by the Grays would cost them dearly. The Zoos agreed that this was a win, even though it would further the disadvantage in veto points they had toward the Swarm and Quarmak. The case of Max Cromwell was expensive, but if everything played out according to plan, it would all be worth it.

The humans had a saying: nothing ventured, nothing gained. The Zoos had decided that they liked that. As long as the venture taken was a well-calculated risk. This time, the risk had paid off. Now the Zoos only hoped the second matter on the docket would not thrust their plans into chaos.

CHAPTER FIFTY-THREE

Damage Control

A re you certain?" Azzzhtik'Likzirrruk asked, tone low and deadly serious.

"Absolutely," one of the Grays said.

Then all the eyes in the ICCB Council Room turned to the Zoos hologram. The Zoos found themselves hesitating. It was a strange sensation. Before, they had never considered weighing their allegiances like this. What was one human against the goodwill of the ICCB? Rivals as they were, they were still an allied coalition formed to fend off an extinction-level threat. But this was not just any one human.

"There is . . . a high chance," the Zoos admitted.

"Bah," the Grays said. "Were it not their favorite candidate, they would have removed this one immediately. You're biased, Jellyfish."

One of the frogs chuckled gutturally. "And I suppose you're completely impartial in this situation, aren't you?"

"Silence," Azzzhtik'Likzirrruk demanded. "He hasn't told anyone."

"And we cannot be sure he knows," the Zoos said.

"He knows," the Grays insisted. "He tried to tell one of our combatants. You should have his language Skill removed."

"Not even my people hold such power," Azzzhtik'Likzirrruk said coolly. "The Framework is autonomous, and it will act as it is programmed to act."

"Why would the human tell this secret to an enemy?" one of the frogs asked. Female, this one, with a lighter, more pleasant voice than the guttural croaks of the male. Abbra was her name, the consort of the council leader.

"Do the reasons matter?" the Grays asked. "Just kill him."

"That would be convenient for you, wouldn't it?" the frog said and smirked with her fat lips.

The Grays glowered but said nothing.

"The important factor to consider here is," Azzzhtik'Likzirrruk said, "does it matter if he knows?"

"Of course it matters!" the Grays said.

"I think not," the Council Leader frog said.

The Zoos opted for silence. They agreed on a landslide of a majority vote that there was nothing to be gained here by partaking in the conversation. It was best to observe and see how it played out. A light hand was needed here.

Azzzhtik'Likzirrruk did not think so. "The Zoos Collective will weigh in."

The Zoos considered their words carefully. It would be prudent to not disclose anything important, but it was also necessary for them to offer a token gesture of solidarity here.

"The Swarm puts us in a delicate situation by asking this," the Zoos said.

An ominous buzz of slighted pride filled the room. The tune-changing filter failed again, which annoyed the Zoos. That was most likely what the Swarm was doing here. They were playing a game of their own. The calmer parts of the Collective subdued the agitated ones. The Zoos had dodged this attack.

"Answer."

"Regardless of circumstances, Max Cromwell should be allowed to continue the Games. While we fight for power amongst ourselves, we implore you to consider why the ICCB was founded. We need each other. And we need strong Cultivators for the war effort. This human is an individual we have not seen in at least three Games."

More like hundreds of Games. No, even that was inaccurate, the Collective realized. Max Cromwell's case was singular. It was unique in a way that excited the Collective. If they could get him to the finish line and bind him with a contract, many things would change.

"Would you say such things if the individual was owned by another patron, I wonder?" one of the Grays said.

One of the frogs burbled and swam closer to the edge of the green gel. "What the Zoos Collective says about the war effort makes sense. I also do not think we should remove this individual just on the basis that he knows about the Games. It doesn't matter, even if he tells all of his species."

The Zoos let out a collective exhale. This was exactly the direction the conversation was meant to go.

"But," the frog continued, bulging his vocal sac, "I understand the need to sacrifice my resources for the good of the ICCB. Our survival is at stake, even though the war is at a deadlock. At the very least it is a costly war. Therefore we need exceptional individuals, who could change its course before the Outsiders do."

"Agreed," Azzzhtik'Likzirrruk said. "But the cost on all of us other parties will be high if Subject #266830151 is allowed to thrive and eventually win the Games."

"Especially for the Kiritus Corporation," the leader of the Grays said. "Compensation is in order."

Yes, the Zoos knew it would come to this. Keeping Max Cromwell on the board would cost them in both veto points and money. But it would be worth it. If his status could be changed to something acceptable in the eyes of the ICCB Council, the Zoos would be able to influence Max Cromwell's fate more actively. But before that, they had some cards to play.

"It is noteworthy that allowances were already given when Max Cromwell's unique situation was last discussed. A bounty was chosen by two factions here to push the collective growth of their representative species forward and possibly obtain a boon if Max Cromwell was killed. We do not appreciate being coerced into paying twice. Additionally, the Swarm opted for an opportunity to create their own champion, allowed to disclose to their representatives that if one acquires a **[Unique]**-Class weapon before choosing their Cultivation path, they will create a new path."

There was a silence in the air for a moment. The flies' buzzing completely stopped for several seconds. Then Azzzhtik'Likzirrruk spoke in clipped tones: "There have not been circumstances where it would be possible to create such an individual. **[Unique]**-Class weapons are not commonplace at this stage of the Games."

That was a lie. The Zoos, being the most technologically advanced faction of the ICCB, knew that well. While hacking into the Gray's database had been as easy as creating music, the Swarm had more advanced encryption and data protection. That did not mean the Zoos had much trouble getting in and out without anyone being any the wiser.

The Swarm had definitely attempted to create a similar individual to Max Cromwell. They had spawned **[Unique]**-Class weapons very inappropriately, breaking at least four rules. But it had not worked. That was strange. It had to mean that the Framework had *glitched*. It was unlikely, but it was the only reasonable explanation. Therein lied possibility and danger. Just what the hell was **[The Maverick]**, and what was the true nature of Max Cromwell's Dao?

Despite the bugs failing to re-create the circumstances, they had certainly set themselves up for success with their underhanded choices.

The Swarm's representative race had four individuals with **[Unique]**-Class weapons. This was unheard of at this stage in the game. Those individuals had most likely not yet clashed with the Quarmak's representatives, so this information was not public yet.

Once the Quarmak accused the Swarm of foul play, the Zoos would act on this knowledge. It would hobble the Swarm's position as the council leader. There would be some form of repercussion for their revealing the hack, both in terms of the breach of trust and simply disclosing that the Zoos had the capability. However, it would be a worthwhile cost when the information was delivered at the right time. This would be when the dispute was between the Quarmak and the Swarm. That time would come soon.

Everything was moving according to plan.

The only thing that worried the Zoos was that the Deathmatch was moving into Phase Two at the insistence of the Grays. They had spent plenty of veto points to make it happen, which was acceptable, but it did create uncertainty and chaos. The Zoos only hoped that Max Cromwell would prevail.

CHAPTER FIFTY-FOUR

Choosing the Way

Max was sitting sentry on the hill by the base. He overlooked the plains where the creatures still roamed. A part of him wondered if he should be out there killing them. Losshnak could be there.

Nah, I have to do this.

Max being late had broken the group. He had tried explaining that it wasn't his fault and that he had come as soon as he possibly could have. It didn't help. They didn't listen. Christie's tear-stained eyes glaring at him hurt the most. Jones had only offered a grim, blank stare. The rest of them couldn't even look him in the eyes.

When Max had said he would take sentry duty, no one had objected or in any other way acknowledged it. He doubted anyone would come to relieve him when his shift was supposed to be done. Christie was in charge of the group now. The leadership status Max had was gone.

Screw them. I don't need their forgiveness.

The injustice of it hurt. He *had* done his best. Max was going over the events leading up to what happened for the umpteenth time. No matter how he examined it, Max couldn't see how he could have done anything differently.

He sighed and looked at the tall walls of smog enclosing the Deathmatch arena. They were thick and still like clouds on a cold night.

"We just need to win this and get out," Max said to no one in particular. Maverick didn't answer.

He sighed. He wanted to abandon his post and just go hunt the creatures. He wanted to get to Level Thirty and acquire a new Ability. From the looks of [**Holy Nova**], it would be a powerful one. He was at Twenty-Seven now. He was well rested and fed. With his high-Level Ruby-stage Cultivator body, he could grind hard for several days. He estimated it would take two or three days of slaying monsters to reach Thirty. But he couldn't just abandon his post.

"You're conflicted," Maverick said.

"Of course I am," Max said sullenly.

"That's no good," Maverick said. "Makes you less effective."

"That's part of the human condition, buddy."

"Just follow our Dao, Max. That's all you should be doing."

"That's easy for you to say," Max said heatedly. "You had nothing before the Dao. You were nothing. How could you understand?"

Maverick didn't respond, but Max could feel something heavy plummeting through their bond.

"Maverick, I—"

"I don't," Maverick said flatly. "But I do try."

"Sorry," Max said. "I'm just . . . tired."

It wasn't the sort of tired Losshnak had talked about. Max wasn't trying to be something he wasn't to keep morale high, nor was he trying to think of and then implement ways to keep his people's feet moving. He was just tired of the weight of expectations.

Christie, Freya, Erwin. They all had looked at him with scathing blame in their eyes. Like Max was supposed to swoop in and save the day. Every damn day. It was just too much. He didn't deserve this. He didn't deserve any of this. This had to stop.

He steeled his resolve and breathed in the cool night air.

I don't owe these people a goddamn thing.

"You're right," Max finally said. "I hate admitting it, but you're right, Maverick."

"Of course I'm right. What do you take me for?"

"That's a can of worms we are *not* opening," Max said.

Maverick sniffed. "Maybe your Dao is underhanded compliments."

"I think it's time to go back to basics. Start doing what made these idiots think that I'm some sort of savior in the first place. Go out there, me and my buddy. Sleep in a hammock, kill stuff, bring them back what I don't need. Rinse and repeat. We'll do that and search for our Dao."

"Hell, yeah," Maverick said. "You're starting to say sensible things again."

"Yeah," Max said. "Screw this. Screw playing Daddy for these people. Christie can lead them for all I care. Not like I'm welcome anymore anyway. I will still bring them shit, though."

"Why so charitable?"

"I can have multiple goals," Max said, finally feeling everything falling into place in his mind. The conflict he had been having between his Dao and protecting humans was unraveling, like a tight knot finally loosened. For so long, Max had been struggling with bloodied nails to force the knot open. With that obligation now released, he exhaled in relief.

"Now I understand," Max said. He got up and looked at the grasslands and hills before him. The creek bubbled and flowed idly below. "I need to follow my path, my Dao. But I can have sentiments. I can prefer things, as long as I never let them control me. They must never guide my actions. They must never set the path I walk upon. Only my Dao will do that. I must surrender to my Dao. I must discard everything else. This does not mean I can't ever eat cake, because cake is not part of my Dao. But if cake *ever* conflicts with my Dao, I must choose my Dao every time over cake. This I vow. I make a pact with the universe. I make a pact to follow my Dao. I will find it, define it, and follow it to its end. This is my truth."

Leveled Up Ruby-Level Cultivator (greater) to 4
+6 free Attribute points

"Holy shit!" Maverick said.

Max nodded to himself. He had felt it coming in the middle of his speech. Another insight based not on a concept or an idea but a feeling. A commitment. This hadn't been about saying the right words. It wasn't about knowing or understanding. It was about embodying an idea.

"Let's go hunt," Max said.

CHAPTER FIFTY-FIVE

Climbing Higher

Max enjoyed the sense of profound serenity as he flew above the grasslands and hills in the middle of the enclosed area. He had taken a drink upstream from the creek and was feeling good.

He wasn't elated, excited, or exuberant. They'd had a rough time. People had died. Despite his revelation and the relief that came with it, Max wasn't about to throw a party. There was anger. Anger toward the lizards. Anger toward the Grays and the ICCB. He would use that anger to push forward.

But the anger didn't take over Max's mind. Neither did guilt nor a desire to belong. They were all subservient to his Dao. He would destroy. Specifically the ICCB, starting with the Grays.

Max decided to fly over toward the enemy's side of the field. Neither Losshnak nor any other lizards were in sight. Max smiled. Could the enemy really be asleep, licking their wounds?

Such weak resolve.

Now, here was the thing: Max had flown over the fields so many times, he knew their layout as well as he did the back of his hand. In the middle was that one giant four-legged Boss-tier dinosaur. Surrounding it were other dinosaurs in metal plating along with giants of primitive minds. Max couldn't look at any of these monsters without feeling a sense of overwhelming disgust. This was what the ICCB did. They turned sapient creatures into beasts for sports.

But the monsters in the middle area were stronger. The T-rexes had thicker plating that was covering their scales in more places than in the outer areas. The giants were better equipped, wearing leather armor and stone tools, such as axes and hammers.

These will surely give more Experience.

The question was should he attempt to farm here? And if not, should he farm on the enemy's side? The latter would make resources on their side more scarce. But it would also open up a path to the stronger monsters faster.

With Losshnak's abilities, they can farm the harder monsters just as easily.

Which meant that sabotage wasn't the answer here.

"I can't believe it took you this long to ponder such an obvious question," Maverick huffed as he flew next to Max in the night air.

"That's because I sensed what you thought as soon as I started pondering," Max said, smirking slightly. "Your mind was basically going 'More Experience better. Me want more Experience. Me go now.'"

"That's because I'm not an indecisive little coward," Maverick said.

Max chuckled. "It's a good thing one of us is then. Otherwise, we'd have been killed a dozen times already."

"Pish posh," Maverick said. "We would have faced more adversities, but we would be stronger for it. I blame you for us not being Level Thirty yet."

"Well, let's go fix that problem right now."

It felt *excellent* to get back to basics. Simple farming. Fighting enemies. Killing them for Experience, **Cosmic Coins**, and loot. And it was all coming to Max in plentiful amounts.

The monsters were definitely a lot tougher than in the outer rim of the area. Especially the giants, but even the T-rexes were giving Max a bit of headache, due to their thick metal plating.

Max had started off by throwing a spear right at a T-rex's snout. Its large head towered twenty-five feet above the ground, and while the outer rim versions had been of a much more traditional variety, these seemed to be genetic freaks.

Instead of stubs for hands, evolved for balance while running, these beasts had long, spindly arms with a singular thick claw at the end of each. That meant they could reach up to sixteen feet in the air, and from the way they moved, the bones seemed soft and bendy, making the arms work like whips.

Max could fly, however, so he could keep out of reach of them. He wasn't so lucky, however, when it came to the tail.

Spikes. It's flicking spikes at me.

Max flew higher in the air to see how far the T-rex could aim and shoot its tail-weapon. As it turns out, pretty damn far. Even forty feet up in the air, Max still had to dodge the incoming spikes. He didn't want one to have to hit him in order to gauge how much Damage it could cause. For all he knew, the spikes could be poisoned.

And aiming his powerful kinetic projectiles from up here was starting to get tricky.

"Just fly down and risk it. Let me have a go at it," Maverick said.

Max shrugged and nosedived toward the great beast. He was floating a thin sword beside him.

He dove between the legs of the bipedal lizard as he had done a number of times before. But these beasts were not only augmented, they were also smart.

The T-rex anticipated Max's move. So it sidestepped and flicked its spiked tail at Max.

"[Phase Shift]!"

Max's skin turned translucent and the spiked tail smashed through him, as if he were nothing but smoke and air. A heartbeat later, his body rematerialized and 500 Mana was subtracted from his total, a reasonable tax to pay for his life. But a part of his brain not engaged in deadly battle wondered how he could keep up these costs once the Deathmatch was over.

Max pushed the thin sword between the metal plates shielding the monster's thigh and shin. Straight into the kneecap. The great beast roared and stumbled around as blood spurted from its wound. Max left the sword stuck in there as he flew upward. One of the spindly arms swiped at him.

Max wasn't hit by the spike, but the force of the swing overtook his control of **[Telekinesis]** and he was slammed to the ground.

His vision flashed red and he lost over 300 Health. His body weak from shock and pain, he tried to struggle up. The T-rex was barreling toward him, long arms outstretched, trying to hobble on its wounded leg.

"Up!" Maverick shouted. He was floating above Max and shooting.

"[Tether], [Tether]."

Max created two tetherings, one of them pushing the thin sword into the T-rex's wound. And another pulling it out. Since the standard spell was equally potent both ways, the sword didn't move.

But then Max started alternating the power levels with his Cultivation, making the pulling out of the wound stronger, just as he switched, pushing the sword back into the wound with a snap.

The seesaw motion hacked at the tendons and bone. The T-rex roared in anguish and fell to the ground. It scrambled toward Max, bloodshot eyes filled with pain and rage. Maverick shouted with mad glee and shot at those eyes.

Max scrambled up. The pain went deep inside his bones, but the Framework had protected him from fatal Damage or breaking a bone. Max kept the sword sawing at the T-rex's knee while he produced chain mail from his Inventory. With **[Telekinesis]**, he rolled it into a ball and started slamming it into the T-rex's skull. Eventually the monster stopped roaring and moving.

Defeated Level 32 [Tyrant Saurus (Special)]
You gained 38,500 Experience points

"Sweet baby Jesus," Max muttered.

"That was awesome!" Maverick said and hooted.

Max had to admit that it was. The adrenaline coursing through him. Fighting a dangerous, worthy enemy. Just doing what he did best. No obligations, no promises. Just unabashedly going toward the direction you know you were meant to. Max couldn't help but grin.

The loot was even juicier than the Experience.

31,500 Cosmic Coins. Not only would Max get to Level Thirty quickly enough if they kept this going, Maverick could be Level Twenty sooner than they had dreamed. Admittedly, if the coin requirement kept doubling, they would need a metric crap-ton per Level very soon.

This time there wasn't any equipment that Max could use. Just a **[Silk Sash of Nimble Assassins (B-grade)]**.

B-grade, though? Damn. That's no joke.

Max grinned. Oh, this was getting even better. If he could farm out here in peace long enough, he could upgrade all of his equipment to B-rank.

"Speaking of which," Max said carefully, "I have bad news."

"No," Maverick said, already sensing through their bond what was coming.

"You know I have to."

"I want to file a formal complaint."

"It's too cheap to ignore. I'll just bring the Cloak to Level Five or Six for now. But eventually I want to bring it to Level Ten. It's too powerful."

"Absolutely unacceptable."

"And every B-grade Item we get, I'll pump to five and probably leave it there."

"Dude!" Maverick protested and flew right in front of Max. Max trusted him like a brother, but it was still unnerving looking down the long barrel of a gun.

"That fight was hard," Max said.

"Just beeline me to Twenty. Do you have any idea how powerful I might become?"

"We need to push for power spikes," Max said. It will make getting coins faster in the long run, anyway."

Maverick grumbled, having no good counterargument.

Max turned back to the loot. There was no more equipment, but he found something *very* interesting.

Two thimble-sized vials of thick blue liquid: **[Potion of Mana Freeze]**.

"You think this does what I think it does?"

CHAPTER FIFTY-SIX

Driven

Max wasn't about to stop. No. He was just getting started. He flew above a pair of giants who were looking at him with overt distaste: a male holding a club with a round rock attached to the head, and a female wielding a massive bone bow. It was aimed at Max.

Max, having opted to stay at the safe altitude of over fifty feet, found that it wasn't as safe as he had thought. An arrow as thick as his arm whizzed right past him, soaring high into the air, at least up to eighty feet. Max followed it. The air got thinner and colder, but he flew toward the arrow and snatched it up with **[Telekinesis]**. It was a heavy thing.

Max made sure to not dillydally and turned around quickly in the event of another arrow. It didn't come, but if he was seeing things correctly, she was nocking another already. Max checked his Mana.

Still a sizable amount left, but this next maneuver would be risky. He had a feeling the giant woman was pretty accurate with the bow.

Max stopped with the six-foot arrow floating next to him. Maverick was fifteen feet below him, trying to get in well-aimed sniping shots.

Max produced a tiny blue vial of **[Potion of Mana Freeze]**.

"You think it will do what it says?"

"Probably," Maverick said distractedly between shots. "Either that or it's a poison that'll make you plummet to your death the instant you drink it."

"Thanks for putting that idea in my head . . ."

In truth, it would be best to not test this new potion mid-flight, but the situation warranted it. Max could, of course, simply escape, but he wasn't feeling like it, and his beloved companion would never let him hear the end of it if he did.

And so he shrugged and ingested the little potion. It tasted like mouthwash, minty and cool. Not bad at all. Max even indulged in swirling it around his mouth before swallowing. The effects were immediate. Max could feel it the way he sensed his Mana. It was like his senses were stretching out in every direction into infinity. His Mana had stopped ticking down.

Holy shit, this is powerful.

Wanting to waste no time, Max dove down, giving the giant arrow a deadly spin. As he fed Mana into it, he could feel that he could do it more freely. Using his Cultivation to power up spells always cost extra Mana. It required a certain precision to do it in a way that was not wasteful.

Now Max didn't need to do that. It was a luxury to simply pour Mana into the object, and soon enough, the spin turned into a blur. Additionally, he also charged the arrow with Mana. He would release it and push it forward, giving it further momentum.

With this plan in mind, Max flew downward and the next arrow flew toward him. This one was aimed with true patience and skill. Just as it was about to hit, Max activated his **[Phase Shift]**. The arrow passed harmlessly through him before he rematerialized. He checked his Mana. Still frozen at a bit over 4,500.

Okay, I'm not spending any more of these before I know how rare they are.

Max hurled the arrow toward the female giant, releasing all of the gathered Mana within it. It whistled through the air like a rocket smashing into the ground and leaving a little crater. Gore went flying in every direction. The maneuver had killed giants instantly.

Defeated Level 33 [Homo Gigantes (Special)]
You gained 40,000 Experience points
Level Up! [Level 28 Gravitician] You have gained + 2 Constitution, + 3 Intelligence, + 3 Wisdom, + 3 free Attribute points

Maverick hooted, but Max was already flying forward. He would loot the corpses later. He didn't know whether the potion's effect would last one minute or one hour, but he needed to use it to its fullest potential.

So he took another spear out of his Inventory. It was a good thing the Ishkarassi liked spears. Max had been able to loot several from the raiding party.

Max flew around forty feet in the air and started putting spin into the spear. He also overcharged it with Mana, making it brim with energy. Max could feel his Spiritual Energy was still being exhausted. He wondered about that. Sometimes Spiritual Energy and Mana felt the same. But according to the rules of the Framework, they weren't always. He decided to save that thought for another time.

The spear skewered through a T-rex's metal chest plate as if it were cardboard. The beast's ribcage exploded against its armor, and it collapsed as blood oozed out of its mouth as well as the hole Max had made.

Defeated Level 31 [Tyrant Saurus (Special)]
You gained 36,200 Experience points

Max moved on. Maverick was content to follow, but through their bond Max knew he was trying to suppress feelings of inadequacy. Max could sympathize. Maverick must be feeling pretty useless right now.

I doubt this potion lasts for long, buddy.

Indeed, in the midst of charging the third spear with an overload of Mana, Max felt the effect wearing off. To his horror, the Mana started to absolutely *plummet* from his active Abilities. It was draining at a rate of over a hundred Mana per second. Additionally, it was hard to control. Max chucked the spear at the nearest giant on the ground, but in his haste, his aim was off, and while the spear created a beautiful little crater behind the giant, it missed. The blast-wave from the release of the kinetic energy was enough to toss the giant off his feet, however—hurt but not dead.

Max swooped down and let Maverick go to town on the enemy. The gun laughed gleefully, finally being able to fulfill his purpose.

Defeated Level 32 [Homo Gigantes (Special)]
You gained 38,600 Experience points

"One minute," Max said to himself. "The potion lasts one minute."

"It's powerful," Maverick admitted hesitantly.

"Extremely so," Max said. "I think it was a lucky drop. We'll need to be really careful with the two that are left."

"Regret using it?"

Max shook his head. "Nah. We needed to know what it does and how to use it."

"The fact that it doesn't drain your Mana when you use that cloak can be a lifesaver."

Max grinned. He was sure it would be.

CHAPTER FIFTY-SEVEN

The Sweet Spoils

Max hunted long into the night. The fights were tough and often took a long time. Especially if there were two enemies attacking with projectiles. Max tried to avoid those situations. The Mana was draining fast. He still had a few **[Potions of Greater Mana Regeneration]** left, but his Mana costs had definitely increased recently.

Not only was he short on potions, but the kinetic projectiles he used were of a one-and-done nature. They slammed into the ground or against the enemies with such speed that it completely destroyed the Items. Max still had some left, but most of the sharp and heavy stuff had been used.

Regardless, he was giddy. It was a case of *gotta spend money to make money*. He was expending resources for faster advancement. And boy, were there advancements to be had.

Max didn't want to cool down and stop. He just kept looting and moving on to the next enemy. He saw glimpses of the amounts of **Cosmic Coins** he looted, as well as some flashes of interfaces when he gained a new Item. He just canceled them and moved ever onward, fighting the next enemy or planning an attack.

After several hours, they started to cool down. It was hard work, and not only physically and spiritually—although his meridians were definitely starting to throb with dull pain—it was also just plain mentally exhausting.

Naturally, they also eventually Leveled Up to Twenty-Nine. That spurred Max on even further, to push through his limits. To fight harder and longer than ever before. But it came with a price.

The strategy and tactics, the fear and adrenaline, and even the blood and gore took a toll. Maverick was also spent. Max even had to hold him to shoot intermittently, because the gun's Mana pool was still relatively small and when it ran out, he couldn't fly.

However, they did notice that Maverick regenerated Mana much faster than Max did.

"It's because of my endless Wisdom, of course," Maverick had said.

Max had opted for a slow nod.

After this Deathmatch is over, I will need to pour a bunch of points into Wisdom.

"So you agree?" Maverick asked. Max could hear the smug smile in his voice.

Max shrugged. "I think the Stat is poorly named, is all."

They sat down on a patch of grass next to their recent kill, a T-rex. Max figured he would cut off a haunch of meat for the group to eat with a saber of serrated blade he had looted earlier. It was just a D-grade weapon, but someone could surely make use of it, or Max could throw it.

"Keep it," Maverick said. "You're still thinking too much about the group and how to provide for them."

"I thought we agreed that I'm allowed to do that if it doesn't conflict with the Dao."

Maverick didn't say anything at first. There was hesitation. Max sent a pulse in the form of a question through their bond.

"I get the food," Maverick said. "But keep the saber, you idiot. Giving it away conflicts with the Dao."

"Oh . . ." Max said, realizing something.

"Yeah?"

"This is harder than I thought," Max said. "I keep fooling myself without even noticing."

"Probably just takes time," Maverick said soberly. Then he cheered up. "Especially for you. Pumping everything into Intelligence? Overcompensating much?"

"You always— I've— It's not—"

Max sputtered until Maverick started to laugh. Max joined the laugh and for a moment they shared a nice little breather.

"Alright," Max said. "If we're done, we might as well check out the loot."

"Ooh!" Maverick said. "Finally. The coins. The coins, Maximilian! How many **Cosmic Coins?**"

Max also wanted to know. He checked his Inventory interface. The total was always noted in the upper corner.

They had previously had somewhere north of **35,000 Cosmic Coins** before going on this moonlight rampage. Now Max had killed sixteen creatures in total, mostly giants, with a few T-rexes tossed into the mix.

The total was now **508,600 Cosmic Coins.**

"Holy shit," Maverick gasped. "That's at least—"

"I'm not going to pour it all into you without giving it some thought," Max said curtly. Maverick harrumphed.

But it was an amazing amount. Max hadn't had a stack like this ever. Not even close. It made upgrading Maverick to Level Twenty a real possibility in the near future. The required coins doubling every Level was still a very steep hill to climb. But if Max only focused on farming, he would accrue millions of coins in just a few days.

On top of that, the Experience was great. Max had gone up two Levels in total, which was no small feat, considering it got harder and harder every Level. A part of him wanted to continue. To push toward Level Thirty. It would take maybe five or six hours by his estimate.

But Max had to admit that he had been wrung dry. He was out of Mana, his meridians were aching with overuse, and he was rapidly running out of things to throw at his enemies. Using Maverick alone just wasn't fast enough.

Max sighed.

Tomorrow, then. I wonder what will happen at Thirty. Another Skill? A Class upgrade? Maybe both?

"Look," Maverick said. "Sorry not sorry to interrupt your wistful daydreams, but could we look at the loot closer? I caught glimpses. There are pieces with Intelligence in them. Wear them. Now. I want it!"

Maverick's manic hunger was contagious. Max poured all of the Items from his inventory onto the ground. Some of them were B-grade, he could tell just from their ornate or otherwise high-quality appearance. Max decided to save those for last. He would savor this fat haul.

There was a total of twelve Items. Six of those would go into ammunition reserves. That included a heavy two-handed mace, two shields, a spear, a hand axe, and a crossbow with a metal stock.

Maverick scoffed at the crossbow. "Inferior trash."

They all ranged from E- to C-grade—nothing spectacular. But Max was very happy to receive some ammunition. He had to admit that he had been pretty careless in his expenditure of resources tonight, using up pretty much all of his useful throwing weapons. He was especially happy about the spear and the shields.

Maybe I should also consider using the shields for defense. Float them around me to absorb projectiles. These tougher monsters might warrant that.

It would expend more Mana and require more control, but Max was starting to get ready to push himself further again. Especially considering the Stat boosts he was about to get. He looked at the veritable treasure trove of Items in front of him. Just the base Stats were enough to make him salivate. And he had a small fortune in **Cosmic Coins** to spend later on the Items.

Max took a look at the first one. They were a pair of thin dark-gray gloves. They went all the way up to his elbow. Max could imagine them being worn by some fancy woman in a shiny dress on a red carpet.

[Spidersilk Gloves of Insight (B-grade)]
+5 Intelligence
+10 Wisdom
+4 Charisma

I don't know if these look dashing enough for the Charisma boost. Rather feminine if you ask me. But they'll be hidden under my cloak.

"Don't worry!" Maverick said cheerfully. "I'll make sure everyone knows what a fine pair of gloves you found."

"Of course you will . . ."

Next up was the only useful C-grade Item Max had decided to keep. It was a simple ring, made from some alloy of silver or aluminum. He was no metallurgist or expert of any sense in these matters. It was studded with six small sapphires, the size of a grain of rice.

[Ring of Cunning (C-grade)]
+6 Wisdom
+6 Precision

It's alright. Those are my most important secondary Stats. Precision most definitely helps me aim my kinetic missiles and have a sharper control on **[Telekinesis]**. *I don't know if it helps, Maverick.*

"Actually it does," Maverick said. "You should pump more Stats into that Skill. I already hit plenty hard, truth be told. I'd like to hit plenty hard more often now."

"Good to know," Max said, nodding to himself. Then he moved on to the next Item. He had already gotten a glimpse of it, and could already tell it was going to be his favorite.

[Hood of Shadows (B-grade)]
+9 Intelligence
+9 Wisdom
+5 Constitution

Now this is awesome. Not only will it make me look like an edgy villain from a TV show, but it'll give me absolutely perfect Stats.

The last Item was a pair of heavy-duty combat boots made of iron and leather. They would fit better on someone like Jones, but Max decided he would keep them for himself. Maverick agreed.

[Boots of Stood Ground (B-grade)]
+5 Strength

+5 Constitution
+5 Resistance
+5 Toughness

Not too shabby. I could use some defensive Stats. Too bad about the Strength, though.

Max loved the way all the Items more or less matched, giving him an air of danger. Maverick sent a pulse of eyerolls through their bond.

After he was done equipping all of his new Items, he put his six free Attribute points into Wisdom and took a moment to admire his Stats.

Name: Max Cromwell
Cultivation stage: Ruby (greater)
Class: Gravitician Level: 28
Health: 8700/8700
Stamina: 8700/8700
Mana: 12200/12200
Alliance: Joshua's Group
Stats:
Strength: 80
Dexterity: 80
Constitution: 174
Intelligence: 244
Wisdom: 215
Charisma: 78
Precision: 117
Toughness: 108
Resistance: 118

Suddenly, a plastic jellyfish appeared in front of Max. It startled him slightly, but he wouldn't give it the satisfaction of knowing that. Despite his feelings toward the ICCB and the Zoos Collective, Max knew when to feign compliance.

[Greetings, Max Cromwell. We believe it is crucial to have an immediate discussion.]

And with that, without being able to do so much as inhale, Max was teleported away.

CHAPTER FIFTY-EIGHT

Revelations

Max appeared in a large, round room whose sloping walls were covered with thousands of panels and screens.

He wondered who was watching all of these screens. Then he looked up. Above him was an entity. Max could feel an immense Spiritual Power coming from it. It was so alien, so strange that it made him feel profoundly uneasy.

The creature was something resembling a shadow or a faint cloud. It had the basic outline of a jellyfish inside which translucent glittering dust swirled around like sand in the wind. It had many hanging tendrils, which intermittently reached for various panels, tapping screens to create various effects within them.

Then the jellyfish Max knew popped up next to him.

[That is our true form.]

"Wh—what are you?"

[We are the Zoos Collective. The cloud of matter you see above us is the remnants of one of our species from thousands of years ago when we ascended from our physical existence into a digital form. However, to use Cultivation, some form of physical body is required, and thus this remnant exists.]

Max said nothing. He only wondered if that was why the Zoos Collective was so keen on acquiring strong cultivators.

[There is a delicate matter we wish to discuss with you. We think you already know what it is.]

Maybe you should tell me so I don't have to keep guessing all day.

That was what Max wanted to say. But he knew better. It would definitely arouse suspicion if he had suddenly acted snarky toward the Zoos Collective.

"Please go ahead," Max said and smiled.

[Very well, Max. Let us be frank. We know that you know that the nature of the Cosmic Games is not what we told you initially. We lied to you. The real purpose of the Cosmic Games is nothing but a system to create and vet out powerful Cultivators for a war effort.]

Max didn't feign surprise. He just nodded.

[Very good. Now we can discuss. This is the local Zoos Mothership. It is a planetoid equipped with technology that we can't take the time to explain to you, protected by Cultivators that could erase your existence with the wave of a hand. You can speak freely here. We need you and we have plans for you. We will not obliterate you for speaking your mind. We would prefer cooperation but will use coercion if needed. What we are doing is of paramount importance.]

There wasn't exactly a change in demeanor. It was still the same voice and it was pleasant enough. But there was an undertone to it. No more bullshit. Max could roll with that.

"If you already knew that I knew, why am I here exactly?"

[We would like to explain our situation regarding this matter.]

"How many people can I save?" Max blurted out.

The jellyfish was still and quiet for a moment.

[It is variable. But we can run a simulation, projecting your growth. Assuming we average out your luck and gradually increase your competence and confidence over time . . . considering how long the Games will continue . . .]

"A number, please."

[Eight hundred, Maybe nine hundred people.]

Max nodded grimly like a man in court hearing his sentencing. That was a big number. Much bigger than the Tortanoids had gotten, which was admittedly encouraging. Max remembered hearing somewhere that during some Ice Age the human population plummeted down to somewhere in the thousand to three-thousand people range. He could be the one who got to plant a seed.

Maverick sent a snarky pulse through their bond. *Savior Complex.*

Ouch. Okay, you have a point. But we are really strong.

"Are there others like me?"

The jellyfish's tone in response was almost amused.

[There are none like you. There have been none like you in hundreds of years. Maybe ever, according to some of our projections. You are a Black Swan event, Max Cromwell. But to answer your question, yes there are some individuals who could pass the qualifications and be allowed to save a portion of your population. Quite a few people, actually. Humans are very adaptable.]

"Uh, thanks."

[But this is not a topic we are interested in. What we wanted to discuss is a further arrangement. If you cooperate, we can offer you more.]

I bet you're not interested in the insignificant lives of humans, assholes.

[Your appearance has created a unique situation. One that we wish to exploit. We were initially, of course, very excited to find a strong combatant in you, and one who had the patience and willpower for furthering his Cultivation as well. We were hopeful. Not to mention this very interesting Cultivation path the Framework offered you.]

"Hey . . ." Max said suddenly. "Where is Maverick?"

[We took the liberty of examining him. We have wanted to do that for a while, and this was the perfect opportunity. We have no intention of harming his functioning or other capabilities, nor alter his personality. We are simply curious and wish to learn more. Being able to replicate what you have become would be a giant boon.]

Max wasn't thrilled by the notion, but he had no other option than to trust these guys. They had said they needed Max and wanted him to cooperate, so they probably weren't doing any draconian levels of torture on his buddy.

"So what do you want me to do?"

[First we need to explain the Games to you more thoroughly. Henceforth you can think of yourself as our associate. You are now directly working for us. Consider this as a pre-contract. An agreement of an agreement.]

"I assume I don't have a say in this?"

[It is mutually beneficial if you do not attempt to complicate the situation for petty emotional reasons, yes.]

"That's a fun way of putting it."

[It has been four hundred and twenty-eight years since anyone has called us "fun." That was the Grays. They were ironic at the time, our Collective calculations say.]

Max snorted. Then he looked back at the floating jellyfish and waited for more.

[Indeed, the Games are a method of acquiring Cultivators from species that initially do not have the capability to Cultivate for a number of reasons. That is why the Framework was created. It is a weapon. It will enhance your capabilities and enable you to Cultivate.]

"A weapon? Against what?"

[Astute, indeed. The reason we need Cultivators is because of a war that has been waged for a very long time. Several thousands of years ago, before the ICCB was formed, this galaxy and a number of others were invaded. We have limited time, and we will keep this short.]

Max sat down. The white smooth floor hummed gently and it was warm, so all of this was actually rather comfortable.

[At first we did not know what had come out. They operated on a completely different wavelength, on a dimension that we had barely discovered. But there was no ICCB at this time. We knew of Cultivation, we knew of the other major species in the galaxy, sometimes trading, sometimes warring with them. But that all changed when the Outsiders came.]

Max didn't exactly have a seat, but if he had, he would have been on the edge of it.

[They are an entity that came from another time and another space. Why they came here, we do not know. But they immediately began hostile action. And we mean immediately in the literal sense of the word. They did not establish a base. They did not overtake a planet for its resources, nor did they take time to study their surroundings. Like beasts, they lashed out at the nearest thing created by a sapient creature.]

A swarm of insects suddenly flew at Max. They stopped right in front of his face. Max could now see they were little white bots, flying in the air. They got to work, glowing lights flashing within the body of the swarm, and suddenly a tasseled cushion plopped down next to him. This was promptly followed by a bowl of snacks.

Barbeque-flavored potato chips? My favorite. I'm as impressed as I'm creeped out.

Making himself even more comfortable, Max continued listening. The Zoos were still a collective of assholes, but maybe Max could deal with them.

[We quickly found the enemy was as powerful as it was aggressive. Even after thousands of years of war now, we still do not know the full nature of the enemy we are dealing with. Every capture results in the disintegration of their body. They are using Cultivation and Spirit magic as we are, but every time we try to capture or destroy it, it is recycled and teleported somehow. This is why the war is endless.]

"It goes back to the Source to power another enemy or something?" Max asked. "So no matter how hard you fight, the enemy doesn't get weaker?"

[Precisely. Faced with this calamity, the four major species controlling areas around these local galaxies quickly formed the coalition called the ICCB. But even our combined forces were not enough. We started to lose resources against an enemy possessing some kind of Dao of endlessness. And so to combat this we needed to create a supply of expendable warriors. Something that could be as endless and numerous as the Outsiders. And thus the Cosmic Games were conceived.]

The delicious chips turned to ash in his mouth.

[We are aware of the moral implications. However, you must consider that if the defenses of the ICCB break, everything, and we mean *everything*, will be destroyed by the Outsiders. We are forcefully recruiting and using species for this war who would be destroyed anyway if we were to fail.]

The explanation went on for a little while longer. The Zoos-Collective went on to describe how the war that they had been initially losing was now in a deadlock, as long as the Games kept going. Max learned that there were several Games going simultaneously. The brutal Darwinian calculation of watching to see which chick in the nest eats the most and kicks the other chicks out was something Max had a hard time finding palatable. They discussed this back and forth and the jellyfish gave the verbal equivalent of a shrug. The situation was serious, and they needed optimized methods.

They had tried mobilizing entire planets of people by showing up, telling them what was happening and giving them the Framework and means to Cultivate. It hadn't worked out, despite attempts to assimilate species with very different psychological templates. The result was always interplanetary civil war.

"I really don't know what to think of it all," Max said, shaking his head. "I'm inclined to believe you. There's no real reason for you to lie this elaborately. I would have been forced to fight and sign your shitty contract anyway."

[Yes. You would have.]

"And I can't understand the scope and significance. I get that it's large-scale and insanely expensive, but it's just a concept to me. I have an idea of war, but I haven't seen it or felt it."

[We understand this perfectly well. We do not require you to sympathize, nor do we expect you to forgive us.]

"So why exactly did you bring me here and explain all of this to me?"

The jellyfish was quiet for a while. Whether it was calculating something or considering its answer, Max couldn't say. But after a handful of heartbeats, it spoke.

[We urge you to cooperate. We have an idea of what your Dao might be. We have a very good idea of your psychological profile as well as your companion's, and the interaction through which you feed each other's emotions. We cannot read your thoughts, but we have a very good idea of what kinds of insights you have had in your Dao.]

"Oh," Max said, feeling like a schoolboy who got caught with his hand in the proverbial cookie jar. Of course they knew about his insights.

[We have no interest in punishing you for what sorts of fantasies you may have harbored. We only urge you to understand what kind of game is being

played here and your role as a piece on the board. If this whole war were a game of chess, the ICCB would be the king. We are the central processing unit, as well as the source of resources. We are the governing entity.]

"And I am a pawn, who is supposed to play nice, is that it?" Max spat out. He bit his lip and shook his head, regretful of his outburst.

[No, Max. What we are saying is that you can be the queen of this galactic chessboard.]

CHAPTER FIFTY-NINE

Truth Management

[Your circumstances, your psychology, and most importantly, the Dao that the Heavens have given you have all added up to a very unique entity in you. To say that you have talent or potential would be a massive understatement. To say you are a prodigy or a genius could be closer to the truth. You are singular, unique, a Black Swan event.]

Max swallowed. At some point, in the middle of all of this, he had stood up, and now, without even noticing, he tumbled back onto his tasseled cushion and buried his head in his hands.

"No . . . No, no, no, no."

The Zoos jellyfish didn't say anything. They only floated in the air, waiting for Max.

"Why?!" Max looked at the Zoos jellyfish with wild, bloodshot eyes. "Why did you have to tell me? I didn't need to know any of this! Not yet. Not for months. Maybe not for years!"

[We discussed it at length. While the timeline does not remove you from the Games for the time being, we thought it was paramount that you know in case your psychological state develops in an unwanted direction. We apologize for having to disclose information to you that we knew would cause distress. We know it will be hard to process. Our apologies.]

"No," Max said, tears trickling down his cheeks. "You don't know anything. You don't have the faintest goddamn idea what it feels like, do you? You only have a faint memory of normal feelings, you stupid plastic buckets. Why the hell did you have to do this to me?!"

This had to be the worst rug pull in the history of the universe. The Heavens sure had an interesting sense of humor.

Just as he had cast it all away. Just as he had felt free, powerful. Even happy, he dared to say. Taking care of humanity and protecting them had been good for him. It had helped him grow. It had helped him form bonds and keep relatively safe. He had done what had been right.

But nothing had been as sweet as letting go of that. To be able to focus on his own needs and wants. To be able to Cultivate his Dao. Selfish maybe, but he would have still achieved the same end goal. He would have reached the end of the Games and gotten to save a handful of humans. He had been able to enjoy the luxury of being responsibility-free and self-centered. It had been the right thing to do.

And it had felt so good. Following one's Dao. The certainty. The liberty.

And then came the Zoos jellyfish. In their endless wisdom, benevolence, and sacrifice, fighting a war to protect the galaxy or some shit. Whatever they wanted to call it. Max called it self-preservation. He could relate to that. He even understood the Zoos Collective's point of view. He just couldn't handle the weight of it.

He spoke in a trembling voice, trying to keep his breathing calm. "Just save the galaxy, Max. Just surpass your limits and become some kind of saint for trillions of people. No pressure, but if you fail, everything, literally everything dies. Don't worry. Just do your best. Ha ha. Haha . . . Hahahahahahaha . . ."

Max couldn't help it. His mind started swimming as the laughter overtook him. Quickly, the swarm of nanobots flying next to him fabricated a hypodermic needle with a purple liquid in it. They jammed it in his neck and he lost consciousness.

Max woke up again in the plains of the Deathmatch arena. The Zoos jellyfish was hovering above him. Max didn't really care. He just stared at the grass that wafted back and forth idly in the soft wind. He could feel Maverick materializing in his lap. The weight was a comfort.

[Good, you are finally awake. We have to return you to the battlefield. Because the Kiritus Corporation, better known by you as the Grays, are sore losers, they have spent an expeditious amount of veto points to complicate this Deathmatch. Therefore, the second phase now begins. We are confident you will handle it with the same adaptability and prowess you have done so far. There will be an arena-wide announcement shortly.]

And with that, the jellyfish blinked away. *An unlikely ally in an unlikely situation,* Max thought idly. If it could be even called that.

An unwanted ally in a really shitty situation.

But that didn't even start to describe it. The weight of it all was too much to deal with right now. Max got up and did his best to push it all to the back of his mind. It would seep through, but it was the best he could do.

The best thing I can do is get stronger and fight.

Max glanced at the upper-right corner of his vision. His Mana was restored to full. His meridians didn't ache either. This may have seemed like a minor thing, but it was actually quite significant. It meant Max could keep hunting. Keep fighting. That's what he was supposed to do. That was what he *needed* to do. He just felt so deflated. Through their bond, Maverick gave him the equivalent of a gentle pat and squeeze on the shoulder.

"You know?" Max asked.

"Yeah," Maverick said quietly. They fell silent for a while after that. Max looked up. The orange flare flickered in the sky. For once, almost serendipitously, the dark purple clouds of the Dreadlands weren't covering it all. It was clear. The stars looked just like they had on Earth. Max wondered how many planets out there were being fought over by warrior-slave Cultivators and the Outsiders.

"Screw it all," Max said. "I don't want any part of any of this. I don't want the responsibility. I just want to follow our Dao."

"Yeah," Maverick said, so solemnly it was almost uncanny. "Me too. Screw them all. Let's power up. Become a force to *abso-goddamn-lutely* not be messed with. And then we decide for ourselves what should be done."

Max nodded. Before they agreed on what to do next, two giant holograms appeared in the sky, one a plastic jellyfish, the other an angry gray alien with black eyes.

CHAPTER SIXTY

A Change of Plans

[The ICCB has decided to expedite this Deathmatch, moving it into its next phase. The purpose of the first phase was to select high-quality warriors and push them to be stronger versions of themselves. We are pleased to say that both parties have achieved said goal.]

Next, the Gray spoke. It had a cool voice laced with malicious indifference.

"The first phase was a test of combat prowess and resilience in a situation with limited resources and support facilities. The next stage will bring in more contestants to the arena: a hundred people from both parties. Thirty of those are allowed to be **[Combatants]**. *The nature of the match will change. It will no longer be a Deathmatch. Instead, you will need to build and protect your bases. You will be awarded points based on the speed at which the base is built and expanded, and its utility, comfort, and defenses."*

[This, however, is only one half of the story. You have fought hard with a small guerilla force, and now you will receive reinforcements. This will allow for larger-scale tactics and strategy for both combat and out-of-combat activities. Balance and prioritization will be key. You will get an individual assessment based on your baseline Class, as well as a total-point multiplier based on how well you function as a civilization.]

"The creatures in the middle of the plains will be made significantly more scarce. New enemies will spawn that will be programmed to attack the bases. You will need to remain alert for constant threats and work both preemptively and reactively to mitigate the damage accrued to your infrastructure and population. Additionally, attacks on enemy outposts are allowed."

Max chuckled to himself and Maverick sent a pulse of grim mirth through their bond. Now that he knew what the ICCB was really up to, these little games made a lot more sense. The first stage had been guerilla fighting. Who can tough it out? Days upon days of fighting with nothing but the most basic sleeping equipment with barely any rest and food. Max had high Cultivation and he was tired. He could only imagine how the rest of his team was feeling. Suddenly he understood Christie and her anger a bit better. How tired she must be.

And now they would get support troops. They would get **[Laborers]** and **[Artisans]** who were supposed to scrounge around the area and utilize the resources. Build a functioning outpost in the frontlines that can keep the fighting going.

And now the **[Combatants]** would have an additional mission. Protect the outpost. Destroy the enemy outpost. This wasn't a Deathmatch. This was a training exercise for the war.

Clever, clever.

"Do you like the ICCB more or less, knowing this?" Maverick asked.

Max chuckled. "Yes."

[If the match goes for long enough and reaches a stalemate, the winner will be assigned based on the points accrued. However, the total obliteration of the other party will also be considered a victory. A victory of this nature will grant additional rewards for the surviving species.]

Again, surrender is not an option. In line with how the Outsiders work, yeah? It's either an endless deadlock or death, Max thought.

"Now, the highest-Level individuals will be removed from the match until they have chosen the hundred individuals to participate. There will be a truce until this is done."

[Remote Teleport]

Again, Max felt himself being whisked away someplace else.

CHAPTER SIXTY-ONE

Back in Town

The Zoos jellyfish asked where Max wanted to go. He had forty-eight hours to assemble a force of a hundred members. They asked if he wanted to circle around and inspect the settlements to pick up particularly high-Level individuals.

Max declined. Building a team of star players was not the play he wanted to go for here. He needed one that was already established and highly cohesive was the play. Additionally, he needed people he knew he could trust. So he asked the Zoos Collective to teleport him to Joshua's village.

Max appeared there in a blink. The orange sun's first rays were just starting to light up the sky. The air was cool and there was a sense of serene stillness about the village. Max smiled wistfully. It felt like an eternity since he had last been here.

What had started out as a settlement of logs for seats around a firepit and a fortunate bucket, was now something else entirely. The village had changed and grown. It was now surrounded by a wooden stake wall. By the gate stood a pair of young men Max didn't recognize. One of them was holding a sword and shield and the other a slingshot. Neither of them seemed hostile, but they definitely seemed wary as he approached.

"I'm here to see Joshua," Max said.

The duo looked at Max and noticed the giant revolver in his holster, the barrel hanging down behind Max like a sword. Their eyes went wide and they gave him a nervous nod and let him through.

What Joshua and the others had done to the place was, in a word, remarkable. It was a bona fide village, no longer some scrappy camp, held together by sheer power of will.

After passing through the gate, Max stopped for a moment and took the view in.

On his left were stout little black bunkers that the obsidian dwarves had given to Max, around which a scaffolding of wood had been built from real planks, as good as from any factory. The scaffolding acted as both a shelter from the rain and storage for myriad items. There were hammers, saws, pieces of cut cloth, and a number of other useful items hanging from hooks made of bone and wood. It seemed like the bunkers were being used as a warehouse and a workshop.

This has Joshua written all over it. Those dwellings are too high-quality to give to some of our people and not others. So let's share them instead.

"Technically they're ours," Maverick said. Max scoffed and shook his head.

"What?" Maverick asked.

There were lots of houses. Dozens. Maybe a hundred in total inside. All of them were made by driving stakes into the ground, using wide and thin planks to create walls, sloping the roof, and putting branches and leaves on top. Some of the houses also had a piece of cloth covering the roof as well.

These might get a little moist during rain, but at least the weather is generally warm. Hopefully this hemisphere doesn't have winters.

Max continued on. There was a square filled with stalls and tables as well as the old fire pit and some worn-out logs for sitting around it. The stalls featured things such as spoons, simple clothing, fishing hooks, and knives crafted from bone. The items were displayed in such a way that they looked like they were on sale. Had Joshua established some kind of an economy?

This is where it all started. Damn, it feels like a lifetime ago. They sure have come a long way.

By the great oak-like tree near the firepit stood a house of a different design. Slightly higher, slightly larger. It was even painted—a faint hue of summer-sky blue—and had a window in front. Max crept closer and could hear a faint snoring coming from the house. He peeked inside. Joshua was sleeping on the floor under a piece of cloth, which was functioning as a sheet. He was bare-chested and his cowboy hat covered his eyes. Next to him lay an unfamiliar woman with wavy auburn hair, a hand on his hairy chest.

I'll let them sleep.

Max sat down on one of the logs. It had been smoothed out by a craftsman's hands along with intense wear. Comfortable. There had been a fire last night, possibly only a few hours prior. There was still warmth and the faintest wisp of smoke rising from the charred remains of wood.

"As soon as I pick Joshua and ninety-nine of the most important members of this community, it's going to break down, isn't it?" Max asked.

"What am I, a fortuneteller?" Maverick asked. "How should I know?"

It would, Max knew it. This small society was a good thing. These people didn't know about some galactic-scale war. They were happy selling their bone knives and trying to find love and friendship. These were just ordinary people that had lived ordinary lives on Earth, trying to live an ordinary life here.

But sometimes life was a bitch. Max felt some measure of guilt coming here and essentially taking a wrecking ball to the community. He estimated over 400 people lived here. Removing the hundred best of them would result in problems.

"It's just temporary," Maverick said. "The ICCB assholes said that the winner will have their species teleported to the Deathmatch area and given all sorts of resources."

Max shrugged. He wasn't sure what to believe anymore. It was clear the ICCB didn't mind yanking their chain if it meant getting their representative species to do what they wanted.

"Well, you got a point there," Maverick muttered.

Max heard shuffling from inside the cyan house. A few moments later, Joshua's groggy face peered out. As soon as he noticed Max, it spread into a happy grin.

"I thought I heard a familiar voice."

CHAPTER SIXTY-TWO

Joshua's Village

It felt good to be talking to Joshua again. The man had an inviting aura, for lack of a better word. Max knew he had a special status in the village and that Joshua respected him. Still, he was probably just one of 400 people who Joshua needed to deal with. That didn't matter. As far as Max was concerned, Joshua was a friend. He just hoped it would stay that way after the man learned what had happened.

Other than omitting the true nature of the Cosmic Games and some details of his Dao, Max told Joshua everything. From Day One to this moment. Every victory, every death, every turn of events. Max told Joshua of the stakes of their match with the lizards, what he was here to do, and what would happen after he left with his chosen hundred people.

Max was as candid and forward as possible for two reasons. One was simply practical. Joshua was going to be the de facto leader of the people who didn't fight, and, in a sense, the whole operation. He wouldn't have a say in anything relating to the fighting, but he would be the highest authority in the match. He needed all the information he could have. No bullshit. He needed to know what kinds of interpersonal dynamics were going on.

Max also wanted him to hear these things from him directly, rather than sleep-deprived, anger-blinded Christie, who might tell a less savory version of what had transpired.

Joshua looked down at his steepled hands most of the time, but sometimes lifted his gaze to look Max in the eyes, as if to verify that he was really telling him the truth. The older man's easy smile faded quickly as Max told his tale, but at no point did Max sense any sort of judgment or hostility coming from him.

"We sure demand a lot of you," Joshua said once Max was done and let out a little laugh. "I don't know all the details, and I won't make any judgment one way or the other before I hear from the other party."

"I just wish we could be of the same party," Max muttered.

Joshua smiled gently. "Not an easy lot you've got."

Max shrugged. It felt nice to have this reassurance, but on the other hand, what did Joshua know? Max pushed that darker thought down.

"I don't know about your people," Max said, switching the subject. "But you seem to have done a lot here."

Joshua smiled broadly and was about to jump into an explanation of his own. Then he stopped himself and gave Max a serious look. "Shouldn't we be choosing our hundred people? You sure we have time for this?"

Max nodded. "I have forty-eight hours. I want a proper night of sleep and to try some of Sid's cooking before getting back out there."

Joshua smiled broadly. "We'll make sure you get the choicest cuts of meat. Even though it has been months, I haven't forgotten who helped build the foundation of our little village. I may be the leader here, but it was always you who was our windbreaker at the helm."

"I appreciate that," Max said. "It's been intense out there. Seeing a friendly face after all this time means a lot."

Joshua clapped him on the shoulder and squeezed. Max smiled.

"This him, Josh?" the auburn-haired woman asked from the doorway. She was wrapped up in a blanket. She was tall and slender and had a beautiful, oval face with inquisitive green eyes.

"The one and only," Joshua said. "Max, meet Linda."

"A pleasure," Max said, getting up and shaking her hand.

"You wouldn't believe the stories I've heard," Linda said.

"You wouldn't believe the new stories I just heard," Joshua replied. Linda sat down in his lap and they shared a kiss.

"The camp has a lot of new faces," Max said, as soon as the lovers untangled.

"She was leading a group of nomads," Joshua said. "It was good luck that we found them. Lots of good fighters in that group. And seeing as you stole all our best fighting men . . ."

"And I need to do it again," Max said.

Linda frowned at that. Joshua squeezed her thigh and gave her a quick explanation.

"You need to leave some," Linda said. "These people need protection."

"I just need thirty," Max said.

"Well, we don't have that many to spare," Linda said. "Who's going to hunt or protect us from the [Werewolves]?"

"[Werewolves]?" Max asked. "Really?"

Joshua nodded. "Oh, yeah. Basically replaced the panthers. Their bite won't turn you into a lycanthrope, but boy is it nasty."

"It doesn't heal," Linda said, shaking her head.

"Just keeps bleeding," Joshua said. "Good thing Elena's so skilled with the salves. She just got to Level Twenty, and it's been a massive boon."

"That's amazing," Max said. "She's definitely coming with us as well. We'll need her."

"Hey what the hell is going on?!" Linda asked, now seriously glaring at Max. "You've come here to do what, exactly? Just steal our best people and leave us defenseless?"

Max stared her down. She had a solid glare, he had to admit. The old Max would have been fazed by her intensity, beauty, and maturity. Now he just looked at her, waiting for her to stop her glaring and aggressive attitude. He wanted to like Linda, because Joshua liked her, but right now he was getting tired of her shit.

"Just so we are clear . . ."

Joshua looked at Max differently now. He nodded more to himself than to Max.

Max raised an eyebrow.

"You've changed," Joshua said, his eyes giving Max a searching look. "For better or worse?"

Max shrugged. "This path I follow? Somehow it requires me to take on more and more responsibility with each step. It's not a question of whether I'm better or worse. I am better *and* worse."

Neither Joshua nor Linda had anything to say to that. Max got up.

"It's good to see you again, Joshua," Max said. "Now, you two are going to put together a list of the hundred most suitable people. Write down each one's name, Class, and Level, as well as their Cultivation. I need the highest-Level, highest functioning, most highly motivated people. The creme de la creme. Thirty of them will be [**Combatants**]."

"I'm not doing any of that," Linda said and crossed her arms.

"You'll do what you're told," Max said in a tone that brooked no argument.

"You can't have thirty [**Combatants**]," Linda said. "How many do you have in the village altogether?" Max asked.

"Thirty-three," Joshua said.

"Fine," Max said. "Give me twenty-five. I'll select the other five from different settlements, one from each of the five biggest settlements on this island."

Linda was about to protest, but Joshua jumped in. "That's good. But what about your list? What can we write it on?"

"I have something for that," Max said and grinned.

Then he reached into his Inventory and took out a stack of printer paper and a handful of graphene pencils. He had requested them earlier from the Zoos Collective and his wish had been granted.

"You can keep the leftovers," Max said and winked. Then he took off into the air, and Maverick flew out of his holster, shouting down at the two stunned humans.

"Which way are the [**Werewolves**]?" Max asked ten feet in the air.

With a slack jaw, Joshua raised a finger and pointed. Max thanked him, and Joshua let his arm limply fall to his side.

"Later, suckas!" Maverick cried.

CHAPTER SIXTY-THREE

All the Upgrades

I t didn't take long to find the [**Werewolves**]. There were some stray ones here and there in the woods, but Max wanted to find the nest. He had two days to spend here, and all of the enemy were placed in a truce, made to wait. Losshnak would certainly be finding things to kill in that time.

I wonder what kind of monster he's coming back as.

It seemed like the lizard population was much more willing to pool resources and make sacrifices. It was probably not so much them doing so willingly so much as it was Losshnak dictating what he wanted. Either way, Max was sure the paladin bastard would come back to the arena juiced to the gills with Experience and Cultivation materials.

Max wasn't sure how tough the [**Werewolves**] were, but he doubted there would be much trouble with them. He could fly.

"Uh, on that note," Maverick said, brushing against Max's Spiritual Energy, "notice anything . . . different?"

Max glanced at the corner of his vision. "Oh, shit."

The fivefold buff was gone. While Max had a sizable Mana pool, it was draining down at a worrying rate. It was a good thing he had a slew of new B-grade equipment. Those had given him a lot of Stats.

"Oh, Maximilian," Maverick said in a sweet tone, "before you descend, could you also explain to me why DO WE HAVE OVER HALF A MILLION **COSMIC COINS** UNSPENT?!"

"Oh," Max said and chuckled. "Yeah, maybe we should sort that out."

He descended, landing in the canopy of the tallest tree that he could see. He found a comfortable branch to sit on while leaning against the trunk and brought up his Inventory.

Maverick, meanwhile, silently hovered in the air beside him, as if listening.

"You think there's something out there?" Max asked as he swiped at the air with his fingers, bringing up the upgrade interface.

"Let's see," Maverick said and inhaled theatrically. "HEY! HEY ASSHOLES. YOUR MOTHER WAS A BITCH AND YOUR FATHER LEFT HER CAUSE YOU'RE AN UGLY MUTT!"

They heard a chorus of angry howls somewhere nearby and, soon enough, black hairy shapes with angry red mouths, watering at the sides, came barreling at them.

"You think they can climb?" Max asked idly as he upgraded his new cloak.

[1,000 Cosmic Coins spent]
[Cloak of Many Phases] upgraded to +2
+14 Intelligence
+16 Wisdom
+8 Resistance
+8 Toughness

"Probably," Maverick said between shots.
"Let me know if I need to get up," Max said.

[2,000 Cosmic Coins spent]
[Cloak of Many Phases] upgraded to +3
+15 Intelligence
+18 Wisdom
+8 Resistance
+8 Toughness

Maverick laughed gleefully and unleashed a barrage of ammunition at the mouth of the shape running closest to them. Max didn't bother to get a good look at the creature. He could do that later.

[4,000 Cosmic Coins spent]
[Cloak of Many Phases] upgraded to +4
+15 Intelligence
+18 Wisdom
+10 Resistance
+10 Toughness

The creatures seemed to be rather tough. It took Maverick half a dozen clear shots before the monster went limp.

Defeated Level 23 [Werewolf]
You gained 1,080 Experience points

Max glanced over at Maverick's fight.
Decent Experience.

[8,000 Cosmic Coins spent]
[Cloak of Many Phases] upgraded to +5
+18 Intelligence
+18 Wisdom
+10 Resistance
+10 Toughness

"Nah, you're good," Maverick said and started shooting at another one of the black beasts. "Besides, they're stupid enough to try chasing me around."

"Good," Max said, and swiped the confirmation to spend **Cosmic Coins** again.

[16,000 Cosmic Coins spent]
[Cloak of Many Phases] upgraded to +6
+20 Intelligence
+20 Wisdom
+10 Resistance
+10 Toughness

Stat boosts galore! Max kept swiping at his upgrade interface, like a schoolboy addicted to a game on his smartphone. The dopamine hit was real. Maverick was giddy as well. He had finished off the three **[Werewolves]** and was now hovering above Max's shoulder. Max wasn't sure if he could see the interface window or not. Max was in the process of upgrading his gloves to Level Five.

[8,000 Cosmic Coins spent]
[Spidersilk Gloves of Insight] upgraded to +5
+11 Intelligence
+20 Wisdom
+8 Charisma

"Put them on," Maverick urged after Max finished the final upgrade on the slick gloves. They were dark gray and so thin that they were almost translucent. They went all the way down to his elbows. As he put them on, he could feel the subtle increase in his Stats, as the gloves tightened ever so slightly against his skin.

"Damn, that feels good," Maverick said.

"It's not that much Intelligence," Max said.

"Maybe not," Maverick said, sending the equivalent of a shrug through their bond. "But they will make you less useless, and that brings joy to my heart."

"Asshole," Max said and chuckled.

Next they upgraded the **[Ring of Cunning (C-grade)]**. Only Level Five. It was cheap enough, as it was only C-grade. Maverick protested, calling it wasteful, but Max wanted to make sure they had every Stat imaginable for the coming battles.

[6,000 Cosmic Coins spent]
[Ring of Cunning] upgraded to +5
+10 Wisdom
+12 Precision

"Absolutely worth it for a few thousand **Cosmic Coins**," Max said.
Maverick grumbled.

Next up was the Item that Max was most excited for: **[Hood of Shadows (B-grade)]**. It offered the perfect Stat profile, sure, but it also just looked badass. It went beautifully with his robes. A black hood settled on his shoulders. When he pulled the cowl fully down, his face was just a dark silhouette.

"So edgy," Maverick said.

"I feel cool, what can I say?" Max said, trying out an ominous smirk from under the hood before he lifted it back behind his neck.

Max swiped up the upgrade interface for the hood and started pouring **Cosmic Coins** into it. Max knew it was only a B-grader, but he wanted to keep it. Maverick made it extremely clear that he would be extremely unhappy if Max poured more than five Levels into it.

"What is going on in that mushy monkey brain of yours?" Maverick exclaimed.

"Can't you read it?"

"I'm getting a headache just thinking about trying."

"Just let me live my life."

"At least upgrade the cloak before this ugly rag."

"You're an ugly rag," Max said.

Maverick was right, though. Level Five would be enough. If he wanted to spend excess coins, they should be put into the cloak. One could argue that Level Six or Seven would be a sweet spot in terms of Stats earned per coins spent. But their situation with the **[Path of Divine Soulbond]** was different. While Maverick was an outrageously greedy, vocal bastard, he had a point. The more resources they spent on him in the long run, the better.

But Max still thoroughly enjoyed looking at his cool new cowl at Level Five.

[8,000 Cosmic Coins spent]
[Hood of Shadows] upgraded to +5
+15 Intelligence
+15 Wisdom
+9 Constitution

Next up were the [**Boots of Stood Ground (B-grade)**]. They matched Max's outfit really well, which made him disproportionately happy.

Hey, it's alright to have some *vanity, as long as you don't let it control you.*

"Keep telling yourself that," Maverick said.

"Shut up."

The boots were made of dark iron and thick, black leather. They were clearly intended for a melee combatant. Probably someone who would swing a heavy axe in the frontlines. There was some Strength in them, but its stats were mostly defensive. Max liked that. They rounded out some of his weaknesses as a glass cannon.

The boots had two heavy clasps to tighten them. Max strapped them on, discarding his old worn-out leather boots. They felt a bit cumbersome, but heavy boots wouldn't make a difference with his [**Telekinesis**]. They'd allow for badass landings on lizard faces for style points.

He brought them up to Level Five, like the rest of his equipment. Max considered how reasonable it might be to Level them up to Seven, on the basis of them providing him with the heftiest boost in defensive Stats. Maverick was just about to launch into a tirade when Max decided against it.

The boots are pretty good at Level Five as it is.

[8,000 Cosmic Coins spent]
[Boots of Stood Ground] upgraded to +5
+8 Strength
+8 Constitution
+10 Resistance
+10 Toughness

"Finally," Maverick said. "Time for the main prize!"

Max still had a little over **400,000 Cosmic Coins** left. With some quick mental math, Max calculated that that would give Maverick a single Level, and one might argue that it was foolish to waste the coins on Maverick when there were still relatively cheap Stats to be acquired from the B-tier items and the cloak.

When he thought of doing it, it felt somehow *off*. Again, Max considered, Maverick all the while watching him silently through their bond. He didn't say anything, nor did he reveal what he was feeling or thinking. He just watched.

Max wasn't about to pry into Maverick's mind either. They had a mutual understanding.

And that was what spending points on [The Maverick] was about. It wasn't about the raw Stats. It was about their companionship. It was about their bond and their trust toward one another.

You live alone and die alone, huh?

But not Max, not Maverick. Despite his lonely fate, Max would always have his buddy. Someone who would always stay by his side. Max knew he'd left a lot of his humanity behind. He was already finding it hard to relate to others. He was just so ahead of them, and his fate was destined to be something entirely alien to what humans grow up to expect. And he couldn't share that with any of them. He was alone. Except he wasn't. Because Maverick was there. He had this special companion who would be with him through thick and thin, because it was engraved in their very nature through their Path and their Dao. And for that reason, Max decided to spend **400,000 Cosmic Coins** on his buddy, happily. Yes, he could be an unreasonable bastard, but damn it, he had earned those coins too. Maverick wasn't just a tool.

[400,000 Cosmic Coins spent]
[The Maverick] upgraded to +12
+42 Intelligence
+30 Precision

"Okay, yeah!" Maverick said slowly, almost slurring like an addict just after getting their hit. "That hits the spot."

Max gave his buddy an amused smirk and brought up the Stats screen. Damn, did it look good! The **Cosmic Coins** had been well spent.

Name: Max Cromwell
Cultivation stage: Ruby (greater)
Class: Gravitician Level: 29
Health: 1830/1830
Stamina: 1830/1830
Mana: 2650/2650
Alliance: Joshua's Group
Stats:
Strength: 83
Dexterity: 80
Constitution: 183
Intelligence: 265
Wisdom: 240

Charisma: 82
Precision: 130
Toughness: 113
Resistance: 123

These Stats looked good, but it only now fully occurred to Max how woefully low his Mana was again. It was great for spamming **[Tether]** until kingdom come and then some. But for the constant high-speed flight Max was used to? Woefully insufficient. But that was what he had to work with, and he resolved to make it work.

After closing the Stats interface, Max fell into thought. Level Twenty for **[The Maverick]** was close, yet so far away. Max wanted to hunt again. He glanced down from the tree at the furry black corpses on the ground. The **[Werewolves]** were reasonably tough, and he had almost two full days.

"Yeah, yeah, yeah, yeah," Maverick said, still reveling in the afterglow of the Level Up. "We'll go kill more stuff in a second. Just let me enjoy this for a moment."

Max scoffed. He felt Maverick's spirit through their bond. It had gotten so potent in such a short time. As the new power consolidated, Max could feel Maverick's spiritual body reaching outward from its core. After Maverick had reached Level Ten, it now seemed that every Level improved his Cultivation. The gun was getting more than just the Stats.

His spirit is absolutely identical to mine. But still different. How does that even make sense?

"I want to try something," Maverick said and zoomed forward. Fifteen feet, twenty feet, thirty feet. Maybe thirty-one and a half. Then the gun plopped down on the ground from midair like a rock.

"Not bad," Max said from his comfy branch.

"Help me up this instant, you dolt," Maverick yelled. Somewhere close by, a few growls responded to the shout.

"Sure, sure," Max said and jumped down.

CHAPTER SIXTY-FOUR

Back to Basics

I t felt strange fighting on the ground. Max had been so used to flying and maneuvering in the air, that he had almost completely neglected to use [**Tether**].

Now it's time to go back to basics.

When a [**Werewolf**] lunged at him, sharp claws extended, he instinctively used [**Telekinesis**] to first dodge and then fly ten feet in the air to stay out of reach.

I probably shouldn't do that.

"[**Tether**]." Max said and flicked a finger at the beast that had lunged at him.

It was violently thrown onto its back and pinned to the ground. The immense pressure was clearly hurting it badly. It writhed and snapped its jaw at Max, rage in its eyes. Max looked around.

Maverick was having fun. This was more for him, anyway. Now that Max was unable to throw kinetic missiles wantonly at enemies, Maverick got his moment to shine.

He was flying around in the air, cackling at the two [**Werewolves**] that were swiping and biting at him. Sometimes they caught the gun with a clawed paw, but Maverick recovered and flew around them in circles, enjoying his newfound range in motion. All the while, he kept shooting, and soon enough both of the lycanthropes were dead.

Defeated Level 20 [Werewolf]
You gained 850 Experience points
Defeated Level 23 [Werewolf]
You gained 1,020 Experience points

Max flew up to get out of reach. Then he released the [**Tether**]. Wasting no time, the [**Werewolf**] jumped and tried to swipe at him. Max was too far above him, however. He wanted to explore the limit of his abilities, now that they were back to swimming in the kiddie pool. Too bad the kiddie pool also had a kiddie Mana pool. Max kept glancing at the blue bar in his upper vision.

"[Telekinesis]."

The [**Werewolf**] was swiping wildly with its claws and fell backward, hitting its head on the ground before being hoisted to hover a foot over the ground, feet up.

Max grimaced. The [**Werewolf**] wobbled. While something like a spear or even a breastplate was manageable, it was *heavy*. The [**Werewolves**] were brutish and muscular, resembling a mutated man more than a wolf. Only their curved back and forward shoulders prevented them from walking upright. They ran on all fours and when they got close, they extended their spine to loom over enemies before clawing them.

This bastard must weigh like 250 pounds.

Max could have poured Spiritual Energy into the spell, but he opted against it. Mana had become a scarce resource again. He needed to be conservative with it. It was a great stroke of luck that the new Items he had received had greatly increased his Mana pool, but [**Telekinesis**] was an expensive spell. Max dropped the beast.

"You done?" Maverick asked, pointing his barrel at it.

"Yeah," Max said and opened his Inventory to make a list of how many Mana-related potions he had left. Meanwhile, Maverick finished off the third [**Werewolf**].

Defeated Level 22 [Werewolf]
You gained 990 Experience points

"Two [**Potions of Greater Mana Regeneration**], two [**Greater Mana Potions**], eight [**Mana Potions**], and one, almost useless [**Lesser Mana Potion**]," Max said.

"Don't forget the [**Potion of Mana-Freezing**]," Maverick said.

"How could I?" Max said. "But I'm going to save that for a very special occasion. I think it has Losshnak's name written all over it. I can use some of the rest for training."

"You think we're close to Level Thirty?" Maverick asked.

"Not close, not far," Max said.

"That is the most boringest answer I have ever heard."

"Most boringest?"

"Well, I'm trying to do *something* to make this conversation exciting."

Max shook his head. "How about we just go look for more [**Werewolves**]?"

"Works for me," Maverick said cheerfully. "HEY, YOU UGLY, HAIRY SONS OF BITCHES! WHERE ARE YOU? COME AND GET SOME!"

Soon enough, four more [**Werewolves**] barreled through the bushes and between trees at them with frothing mouths and rabid eyes. Max chuckled as he tethered two of them together.

Well, I can't argue with results.

They killed a few more stray [**Werewolves**] as they walked through the woods. Well, Maverick killed. Max mostly just protected himself from the attacks, locked down the enemies with [**Tether**] when they got too close, and, from time to time, dabbled with [**Telekinesis**] on a single enemy. He was trying to get a feel for lifting heavy objects.

It's not just the weight. As far as physics go, if I can throw twenty-pound objects with breakneck speed, I shouldn't struggle this much to lift 200 pounds. The reason this is harder is because they have a Resistance Stat.

They killed maybe fifteen [**Werewolves**] in total. The Experience was good, but no Leveling Up yet. It was getting close, though. The morning had turned into afternoon. It was a hot day, but fortunately the forest provided shade.

Wearing black is not ideal. Maybe that's why the ICCB initially gave us those white jumpsuits.

The loot was good too. Nothing crazy. The [**Werewolves**] were tough, but at the end of the day, just basic enemies. **4,000 Cosmic Coins** on average and a bunch of supplies. Two loot boxes with materials. D-graders both. Probably containing cloth, planks, tiles, what have you. Max wasn't interested. He'd give them to Joshua when he got back to the village.

"That is the stupidest thing I've had to suffer from you in a while," Maverick said.

"Huh?" Max said, snapping out of his thoughts.

"You somehow forgot what the next part of the Deathmatch or whatever will be?" Maverick said slowly, as if explaining something to a particularly stupid five-year-old. Max didn't appreciate it. "It's *base-building*. Why are you giving away free materials?"

"I just thought—" Max said trailing off. "I just thought it wouldn't be allowed."

Oh, Maximilian, ever the naive sidekick," Maverick said and sighed theatrically. "I will teach you something about life. A cheat code, if you will. Listen attentively, my trusted little friend. Always try to get away with anything you can, and if you're caught, just play stupid."

"That's— Yeah . . . actually, that makes sense," Max admitted grudgingly. "Let's do that."

The overwhelming smugness Max could feel through their bond made Max want to slap Maverick.

CHAPTER SIXTY-FIVE

Werewolves

The first thing Max noticed was the smell. He had gotten used to the faint, earthy scents of the forest, so the stench of rotten meat hit his nostrils so hard he almost choked. Highly Cultivated bodies had their downside. Holding his nose while trying to force down a retch, Max figured it was actually a good thing that he had gotten this whiff of decomposing bodies.

I'm upwind. It's better I smell them than they smell me.

Max crouched behind a tree and peeked at the camp where the lycanthropes had assembled. Max realized it was the same place he had faced the Stranger for the last time. A forest opening with a big rock in the middle and a hillside with caves underneath it. There were piles of bones, pieces of rotten meat hanging from them. One of them was clearly a human skeleton. Next to the big rock Max had fought by before, there was a small fire pit with a roast of some meat skewered on top of it. A bored-looking pup was idly turning the meat.

Curious. They don't seem intelligent enough to build anything.

As if to prove a point, two adult **[Werewolves]** bumped into one another, started growling, then swatting each other. In a few seconds, it turned into a full-on bloody brawl. A few **[Werewolves]** who had been passing by, paused, knelt down on their haunches, and watched, barking and howling at the fight.

"There has to be a Boss monster out there," Max said.

Maverick said nothing.

"Dude," Max protested.

"What do you want me to say," Maverick said, suppressing a giggle. "You make it too easy for me."

"Let's just go in and fire them up," Max said. "There's enough of them to give us a challenge."

Maverick scoffed disdainfully. "If you break a sweat, I'm disowning you."

"I'm not your—"

"DISOWNING YOU!"

The camp heard that one. The brawl stopped and all the wolfish faces turned to Max and Maverick. They dropped from their haunches to all fours, growling, the fur on their back bristling.

Then they all dropped into a prowl stance, stomachs low to the ground, and started approaching with predatory intent glinting in their eyes.

"How do you want to play this?" Maverick asked.

Max didn't answer. Instead he took off into flight just as soon as the front of the [**Werewolf**] pack started running toward them. Max flew over them. They jumped and tried to snap at him, but Max didn't want to take any risks—heavy, sturdy boots or not. A wound that didn't heal sounded like a bitch to deal with.

Max landed on top of the big rock in the middle of the opening and began to take his bearings. Maverick kept shooting.

This wasn't a simple scenario to consider. These weren't panthers with paws and claws, nor were they ordinary wolves. They had more human sort of hands than typical wolves, so they were able to climb. And they climbed *damn* fast.

Max only barely dodged a swipe at his ankle as the first [**Werewolf**] clambered on top of the rock. He took to flight again, chugging down his penultimate [**Potion of Greater Mana Regeneration**]. Combined with his higher Wisdom, it was strong enough to keep him in the air and out of claw range. Meanwhile, Maverick shot down the first foe.

Defeated Level 23 [Werewolf]
You gained 1,050 Experience points

Max's heartbeat was already cooling down when something struck him in the middle of his back. It punctured the skin and Max could feel a trickle of warm blood trailing down his spine. Max looked down as an arrow with a bone tip clattered down. Then another arrow struck him in the shoulder.

"Gah," Max gasped and flew higher, searching the battlefield for the [**Werewolves**] wielding bows. There were four of them. Two more arrows flew at Max, but now he was ready and dodged them. The one that struck his shoulder had made only the smallest of nicks, probably thanks to his high Toughness, but it still struck blood.

His stomach lurching at the potential implications, Max dodged again and checked his Status effects: a little red droplet icon with a "2x" next to it.

A bleed effect? A hemotoxin?

Maverick gunned down another one.

Defeated Level 20 [Werewolf]
You gained 650 Experience points

Max didn't feel weak. At least not yet. He had been hit with a few poisons before, and this didn't feel urgent. So, it must have been a bleed effect. That was what Joshua and Linda had meant about the wounds not closing. He wondered how long the effect would last.

One can hope they drop an antidote . . .

Defeated Level 22 [Werewolf]
You gained 975 Experience points

Max checked his Mana. Still plenty left. It was draining at a fairly low rate now that he had a Mana Regeneration Potion in him. The expenditure wasn't that bad if he was just flying around.

There were maybe twenty-five or so **[Werewolves]** left. It would take ages for Maverick to gun them all down. Although, he was making good progress already.

Defeated Level 24 [Werewolf]
You gained 1,190 Experience points

Max produced a spear from his inventory. He took control of it with **[Telekinesis]** and flew downward at the enemies, guiding the spear with flicks of his hand. It didn't quite skewer them, even though Max applied a bit of Spiritual Energy to accelerate the spear every time he tried to run it through a chest, but it did rupture a lung here, crush a ribcage there, and eventually spear a larynx. Maverick killed another one.

Defeated Level 20 [Werewolf]
You gained 700 Experience points
Defeated Level 22 [Werewolf]
You gained 970 Experience points
Defeated Level 21 [Werewolf]
You gained 835 Experience points

Max threw the spear, releasing the **[Telekinesis]** but adding a **[Tether]** to it, pulling it toward the chest of a **[Werewolf]** twenty feet away. It shot through the beast's torso like a bullet through butter.

Defeated Level 23 [Werewolf]
You gained 1,070 Experience points

I wonder if these guys were a species with a civilization sometime back, before the ICCB turned them into monsters. Probably. Well, no use thinking about it. Now they're something else. Maybe it's for the best that I end their suffering.

"Less pseudo-profound yammering, more shooting," Maverick shouted under the sounds of gunfire.

Max rammed the spear through the side of one of the **[Werewolves]**. Then he mostly dodged a small volley of arrows, other than one which managed to nick him in the neck. He gasped at the cold pain and noticed the debuff changed from two stacks to three. It seemed to have a long timer.

I didn't ask if the bleeding takes minutes, hours, or days to stop.

If it was anything longer than minutes, he couldn't take many more cuts, no matter how small.

Max threw the spear, utilizing **[Tether]** again; another **[Werewolf]**'s torso exploded from the force of the spear slamming through it. Max's high Intelligence was paying off.

Defeated Level 24 [Werewolf]
You gained 1,200 Experience points

Max flew to his spear and picked it up. It was starting to look like it was on its last legs. Max was about to throw it again, but then he stumbled and nearly dropped it. Something was coming out of the cave.

"What was that?" Maverick asked.

Max pointed, deaf to the barks and snarls below him. These little puppies barely mattered.

CHAPTER SIXTY-SIX

Fenrod, The Blood Glutton

It was a behemoth the likes of which Max had only seen once before. It wasn't quite as tall as the giant red demon he had encountered when he had arrived on Alpha Ludus, but it was *big*. It crawled out of the cave, dragging dirt with its stomach. But when it extended itself, Max knew he was dealing with something bad. It had better posture—less hunched than its smaller siblings. The giant spine cracked like a felled tree crashing to the ground, and the black-and-gray-furred, obscenely muscular frame extended to its full height of almost thirty feet.

[Fenrod, the Blood Glutton]
[Special-Grade Boss], [Level 55]

It roared. It was loud. So loud it hurt. But that was nothing compared to the *shockwave.* [**Fenrod**]'s roar rippled the air and physically struck Max. His vision flashed red, and he lost a 150 Health. It was so strong that it even knocked out his flight! He fell to the ground, losing further Health as soon as he hit it. At that, the lycanthropes began to converge on Max, who was lying on his back, helplessly coughing.

"**[Gravity Well]**!"

A swirling center of mass appeared above Max, collecting pebbles and leaves into a nexus. The [**Werewolves**] attacked him, swiping down on him, but they couldn't get through the altered gravity. Some of them got caught up in it, and one of the younger ones even got lifted off its feet and started yipping in panic. Max excluded himself from the spell's effect and so flew through it, back into the air. Along his way, he elbowed the young [**Werewolf**] in the face when it tried to snap its jaw at him.

Once he reached fifteen feet in the air, he had noticed it was a mistake. A claw the size of a bicycle was swiping at him. Only Max's honed instincts saved him.

"[Tether]!"

A repelling force between Max and the claw was created. It halted the swipe but didn't quite have the effect Max had hoped for. He had half-expected the claw to be swung back with force, unbalancing the Boss. Instead, it only managed to turn what been a murderous, crushing attack into a swat. The swat still hurt like hell, and it tossed Max out of the air again.

This time Max was lucid enough to activate the [Telekinesis] suspending him in the air. He didn't bounce from the ground, which was a bonus. But he had still lost a lot of Health in only a little time. Max landed on the big rock in the center of the forest opening. [Fenrod] watched him with the confidence of an apex predator. For the first time in the longest while, Max chugged down a [Health Potion].

At least Maverick managed to kill two more in a fusillade of magic bullets. It seemed like he was shooting in bursts. Was he enhancing his abilities with Cultivation?

Defeated Level 22 [Werewolf]
You gained 980 Experience points
Defeated Level 20 [Werewolf]
You gained 690 Experience points

[Fenrod] inhaled and Max knew what was coming. He barrel-rolled down to the other side of the big rock to dodge the shockwave. It still made his ears ring, but he took no Damage. A [Werewolf] was waiting for him on the ground, but he was alone, so Max simply tethered it against the rock and flew up in the air again.

Just when Max thought he was safe, [Fenrod] took a few earth-tremoring steps forward and swiped at him again. Max flew below the strike, and in response, the Boss turned and swiped with another hand. Max used two [Tethers] to bind up the great monster's hands. It worked. It didn't snap them together, but it made [Fenrod] struggle as if he was dealing with a particularly sticky glue.

That bought Max enough time to fly out of reach again. He circled behind the rock and turned in the air, just as he released the tether on the [Werewolf]. It growled and pushed itself off the wall, only to be kicked in the face by Max's new heavy boots.

Max had no acceleration or weight to crack its neck, but the [Werewolf] yowled and Max was sure he had done some Damage. Then he turned in the air again, dodging a smashing strike at the ground by [Fenrod].

Maverick killed another one. There weren't that many left.

Defeated Level 24 [Werewolf]
You gained 1,245 Experience points

[**Fenrod**] stopped and assessed the situation with a far more discerning eye than a mere beast should be able to. Then he let out a commanding set of barks. The remaining [**Werewolves**] yipped in protest. [**Fenrod**] let out a mighty, decisive roar that made Max's ears hurt and the other [**Werewolves**] whimper. They scampered out of the cave opening, watching the fight from there.

"So just you and me, big guy?" Max said as he descended on the rock. Maverick flew close to hover above Max's shoulder.

"The Boss is still at full Health?" Maverick observed. "With all due love, you really are a waste of space sometimes, Max."

"What do you want from me?" Max said and took off into the air when the giant paw smashed at the rock again. Maverick started shooting. They were instantly hit by another roar and a shockwave, this time striking them both down.

Max inhaled. This was bad. Maverick got up quickly and continued his barrage. The Boss was smart enough to ignore him, however. Instead, he walked toward Max with the confidence of someone who had never lost a fight.

Max decided it was time to go on the offensive. He flew at [**Fenrod**], dodging another claw swipe. He was anticipating the angle, so it was easy. Then he used [**Tether**] three times, pulling the great monster's legs together.

Where two had worked like glue, three worked like a hydraulic press. Slowly, despite the huge muscles of the wolf-man-beast pushing against them, plowing dirt out of the ground, its legs were pulled together and it toppled to the ground. It growled with anger.

Maverick blasted at the giant creature with wanton glee, swarming around [**Fenrod**]'s head like a mosquito hopped up on caffeine.

The Boss roared again, sending out a blast-wave. Max was half-prepared for that, but he still took Damage and it managed to cancel his flight. He was fortunately flying low enough to not take additional fall Damage.

He ran behind the big rock and caught his breath. Maverick was the one doing the Damage anyway.

"He's got a pretty chunky Health bar," Maverick remarked. "And he *will* struggle out of your spell."

"Just keep shooting!" Max shouted, trying to think of a way to deal with the situation. He could always use a [**Potion of Mana Freezing**]. Then he could unload an Inventory full of junk at full blast. But that would leave him with only one potion remaining.

I just need one, right? One minute to kill Losshnak.

But if he failed and had nothing to fall back on . . .

[**Fenrod**] broke free of the [**Tethers**]. Max could feel it in his Mana the moment it happened.

The shockwave is a problem. Let's try something . . .

Max took out one of the shields from his Inventory. It was actually a decent one. Max gave its Stats a quick glance. He figured he might want to keep it if possible.

[**Bulwark of Fortitude (C-grade)**]
+6 Constitution
+4 Toughness
+4 Resistance

Max had neither the time nor the intention to strap the shield on his forearm. Instead, he just grabbed one of the leather straps and took to the air just as a black, long-clawed paw smashed against the rock. Quickly, [**Fenrod**] moved and swiped again. Max dodged. It was a clumsy motion with the shield in his hand, but at least it was enough to keep his head.

Here it comes.

The roar came immediately. The pain rang in Max's ears immediately. He lifted the shield with both hands. He took no Damage, nor was his [**Telekinesis**] canceled.

"Oh, I like that," Max said and grinned.

"Finally you're doing something useful," Maverick said between gunshots.

Max drank down a [**Mana Potion**] and threw the shield with a Cultivation-enhanced [**Tether**] at the [**Werewolf**]. It struck it in its shoulder and it yowled, losing a chunk of its Health.

"Now the real battle begins," Max said, still grinning.

CHAPTER SIXTY-SEVEN

Synergistic Choices

It was the longest battle Max had ever waged, But after the last [**Potion of Greater Mana Regeneration**] and two more of both [**Health Potion**] and [**Mana Potion**], it was finally coming to its inevitable end.

It's been an expensive ride. But at least I didn't use the Mana-freezing stuff.

Max's breath was ragged. He was slumped down with his back against the big rock in the middle. Maverick was in his hand, having expended his Mana pool a while back, and he was now using Max's to fire.

[**Fenrod**] was crawling toward him. He was clearly as depleted as Max was by this point. He let out a shockwave, but Max blocked it with the shield. Maverick kept shooting.

Max glanced at the [**Werewolves**] huddled at the cave's mouth. He really hoped they just stayed where they were. He could fly away, but he really didn't want to have to. His meridians weren't simply aching; they felt like they were pumping hot magma through his body.

"Just . . . die . . . already . . ."

The Boss's massive Health bar was inching over to fully red. It had taken such a long time. There had been no tricks, no clever cheat cards. Just a brutal brawl, Max dodging, Maverick shooting. Using [**Tether**] to attack with the shield had worked like a charm. It did great Damage, especially when it hit the Boss's face.

Finally, the beast let out a mighty death rattle.

Defeated Level 55 [Fenrod, the Blood Glutton]
You gained 73,650 Experience points
Class upgraded from [Graviticist] C-grade to [Spatial Sorcerer] B-grade
Level Up! [Level 30 Spatial Sorcerer] You have gained + 3 Constitution, + 4 Intelligence, + 4 Wisdom, + 5 free Attribute points
Upgraded Skill Choice Available!

Max saw a glimmer of something in [**Fenrod**]'s eyes, almost like respect. It had been a hell of a fight. Max really hoped he wouldn't have to face this bastard in the next life. But there was something more beyond that.

Relief? Gratitude?

He shook his head. Surely he had just been imagining things. But another part of him disagreed.

Was it the first time they did it, or the first time you noticed?

"Rest in peace," Max said and patted the creature's automobile-sized head. It was rough and probably full of lice or the gods knew what. Max didn't care.

The [**Werewolves**] streamed out of the cave and sat on their haunches in a black furry row. Then in unison they lifted their heads toward the sky and howled a high note. After they were done, they turned all their eyes on Max.

He flinched, trying to will his legs to un-jelly themselves. His meridians absolutely *throbbed* with the sensation of being slowly burned. Grimacing, he brought [**The Maverick**]'s golden barrel up and aimed it at the wolves. Max took up a fighting stance he was prepared to die in.

Is this really it? I can fly to the top of that rock but not to escape. Maybe if I find a tree? But they can climb.

"Bring it!" Maverick shouted. Max could feel the bluff and bravado through their bond.

But they didn't bring it. The wolves kept on sitting on their haunches and looking at Max. Some of them laid down, some of them walked back to the cave. But most of them stayed and watched.

"Okay then," Max said and backed up a few steps. "I'll just get my stuff and, yeah. See you never."

He swallowed and hesitated but eventually turned to his side to loot [**Fenrod**]. He wasn't sure if it would trigger some primal hunting mechanism in the wolves that was for some reason currently turned off, but Max wanted to go home.

Home? Even after all this time away from Joshua's village . . . The idea of ripping away a hundred of its best members feels pretty shitty.

Things might get bad. Max wanted to trust that the spirit that Joshua's village was imbued with would save it from sociopaths or disasters. But who knew?

"Okay, Mr. Cool," Maverick said impatiently. "Can you just loot the Big Bad Wolf so we can skedaddle the hell out of here?"

Max did. They both liked what they saw.

81,711 Cosmic Coins
[A-grade equipment box]
25x [Greater Health Potion]
25x [Greater Mana Potion]

"God, yes," Max sighed. He was most excited about the Mana potions. They would actually let him fly again, at least in some measure. Maybe even throw some spears at people sporadically.

I really need another attack.

"Well, we did get a Skill," Maverick said excitedly. "And by 'we,' I mean you did, and so did I?"

"You did, huh? What's the Skill?"

"Still thinking . . ." Maverick said.

Max shrugged and opened his Skill choice interface.

[Space Rift I]
Create a rift in space, overlapping with reality. Anything caught in the temporary rip in space-time will suffer damage from the spatial distortion proportional to your Intelligence modifier.
Cost: 20 Mana

That's pretty damn awesome. I guess now that I'm a **[Spatial Sorcerer]**, *I get access to more than gravity stuff? Damn. I'd love to flex this in Losshnak's face. Literally.*

It was just what Max needed. Targeted Damage. The whole tossing-stuff-at-enemies thing was fun and extremely efficient, but it cost anywhere from one hundred to 180 Mana to toss one of those bad boys on full blast. But with this, Max could attack with rapid succession. He'd have a Damage Ability that would pretty much always hit.

I wonder how wide the rift is by default. I could expand it with Cultivation, of course.

It was time to move on.

[Singularity Strike I]
Conjure a small, intense singularity at a targeted location within 40 feet. The singularity lasts for a few seconds, pulling in nearby enemies and dealing continuous damage, based on your Intelligence modifier. The gravitational pull increases with proximity to the singularity.
Cost: 40 Mana and 5 Mana per second to maintain

Max shrugged.

Well, that seems pretty powerful. Seems like it does the same thing as **[Gravity Well]** *but better. I could use this to clump enemies together and follow up with area-of-effect spells. It's good, and I like that it does Damage, but I already have a tool like this.*

There was really no point in pondering this option further. It was a dud for Max.

[Gravity Storm I]
**Summon a tempestuous maelstrom of gravitational forces over a wide area,
affecting a radius of up to 50 feet (modified by Intelligence and Cultivation).
This chaotic storm randomly increases or decreases gravity within its bounds.
Enemies caught in the storm may find themselves suddenly rooted to the
ground or helplessly floating in the air. Additionally, the gravity distortions
within the area cause a damage-over-time effect. The strength and unpre-
dictability of the gravity fluctuations are influenced by your Intelligence
modifier.**
Cost: Variable Mana and variable cost to upkeep

*This spell is the Holy Grail of crowd control! This could be a real game-changer in
large-scale battles or against multiple foes. And that's exactly what's coming up. The
enemy will have an army thirty-five men strong. This spell could literally end the battle
right then and there.*

"Aargh," Max said.

That piqued Maverick's interest. "That good, huh?"

"They're good, yeah."

"Whatcha got in there?"

Max explained the two good options to Maverick.

"How is that even a question?" Maverick said. "You pick the **[Gravity Storm]**,
of course. You're the control and support and most importantly, the one who carries me. I'm the damage dealer!"

"Well yeah, but you're not . . ." Max trailed off.

"Not what?" Maverick said, already getting offended just in case.

"Not enough firepower," Max said and gave an apologetic smile.

Maverick drew in a breath. "You did not."

"It is what it is. You're an excellent, constant source of Damage. But see what
happened back there when you were the main source of Damage? It took a *long*
ass time."

"I have never felt so hurt in my life," Maverick said and sniffed melodramati-
cally. Max could just imagine him holding his chin up in a close-eyed pout. "Maybe
if you listened to me once in your life and asked what kind of Ability I got, we
could look at your Abilities in a new light."

"You didn't—"

"Silence!" Maverick snapped, reminding Max of the ugly green ICCB house-
fly. "I was simply waiting on my decision to choose before hearing what kinds of
Abilities you had available."

Max felt his ears redden. He hadn't even considered that they should syner-
gize their Abilities together.

"I heard that," Maverick said smugly.

"Shut up," Max said. "Tell me what you got."

"Well, I got Damage, then some Damage, and some more Damage," Maverick said, and Max could hear the grin. "You're in for a head-scratcher."

[Full Chamber Barrage I]
The revolver rapidly fires a barrage of six enchanted bullets that seek out targets within a 30-foot radius. Each bullet deals moderate Damage and has a chance to pierce through multiple enemies, dealing reduced Damage to subsequent targets.
Cost: 25 Mana per barrage

[Explosive Rounds I]
Enhance the revolver's bullets with explosive magic. Upon impact, these bullets explode, dealing area-of-effect Damage to enemies within a small radius around the target. This Ability is particularly effective against groups of enemies or fortified positions.
Cost: 15 Mana per shot

[Phase Shift Ammo I]
Load the revolver with special ammunition that can phase through obstacles. These bullets can bypass walls, shields, or other forms of cover, hitting targets that are otherwise unreachable. The phasing effect lasts for a few seconds after firing, reverting to normal bullets thereafter.
Cost: 10 Mana per phased bullet

Without thinking, Max brought a hand to the top of his head. He scratched.

"They're all so good . . ." Max said wistfully.

"They're as slick as their owner," Maverick said. "But yeah, I was waiting for you to tell me what you got before choosing."

Max smirked. He reached through their bond to Maverick's mind. The little bastard hadn't waited for him so they could synchronize their picks. He just didn't know what to choose.

"Hey!" Maverick said. "I want your opinion, not judgment."

"Gotta eat your greens, if you want dessert," Max said.

"What does that even mean?"

Max shrugged. "Anyway. Those **[Phase Shift Ammo]** could really do a number on Losshnak's shield."

"That's what I was thinking," Maverick said. "But will we need it afterward?"

"Being able to shoot through cover is always pretty handy."

"I like **[Explosive Rounds]** more," Maverick said. "I want to blow shit up."

"That probably has the most scaling potential," Max admitted. "Or the [**Full Chamber Barrage**]."

"That's a mean one," Maverick said, pulsing a nod through their bond. "But it's only good for cutting down enemies with no defenses."

"Yeah, good point," Max said. "The two others let you either destroy defenses or bypass them."

"Listen," Maverick said. "My Dao is that of destruction, so I'll pick [**Explosive Rounds**]."

Max nodded to himself, searching his mind for a counterargument. He didn't find any. He liked [**Phase Shift Ammo**] more, but it might just be fancy for the sake of being fancy. Sometimes it was just best to blow shit up.

"Yeah," Max said. "Do what you gotta do."

"Done and done."

Max nodded again, bringing back his own Skill choice interface. He hummed to himself, tapping an index finger on his lips.

"Anyway, you're an idiot stupid head if you think you should pick [**Gravity Storm**]," Maverick said.

"Yeah?" Max said, voice carrying a challenge. "And why's that?"

"Because," Maverick said slowly in his kindergarten teacher voice, "you have those potions that make your Mana cost null. So you can create an insane storm for a minute, absolutely ripping everything to shreds."

Max was about to argue, and then his brain registered what Maverick had just said.

"You, uh . . . ," Max said. "Yeah, I'll— I'll do that."

"You do that," Maverick said and sent a pulse of smugness through their bond.

Max grumbled to himself but ended up picking the [**Gravity Storm**].

CHAPTER SIXTY-EIGHT

The Last Push

Max was back at the village. They were preparing a little party for him. Once he'd returned and the word spread of what he had accomplished, everyone gathered at the giant oak tree by the fire pit and Joshua's house, an area that functioned as the town square. Everyone cheered Max's name. It felt good.

But not as good as it used to.

No. Max was a bit saddened to reach that realization. Even though Linda had come up to him and said she was sorry for being so aggressive earlier, Max just nodded and smiled. It felt good, sure. But it was also meaningless on some level.

Still, Max was at peace. His main goal and secondary goal were aligned. Protecting humans still felt good. Still felt right. But he had greater concerns now, and he would not be distracted. But still, he had to admit that having his cake and eating it too felt pretty good.

While the village prepared, Max went into one of the stout black bunkers. He set up his Cultivation formation on the floor and fed a few **[Celestial Illumination Pills]** into Maverick's bullet chamber. It felt almost nostalgic sitting in that room. He looked around and chuckled as he noticed a crack in the wall. It was *that* bunker.

Max fondly reminisced about Maverick spontaneously firing off in the hut when he had gleaned the first hint of the gun's autonomy. They had been at Quartz—no, Amethyst—Level back then, hadn't they? It felt like a lifetime ago. In a sense. it was. The life Max was living now was something else entirely than the one he had some months ago.

Alpha Ludus is the epitome of life in the fast lane. Grow now or die.

And so Max resolved to grow. He breathed in and out slowly, clearing his mind and gathering focus. Once he felt he was in the right mindset, he popped a pill of his own and Cultivated. It was time to reach the peak of the Ruby stage. Then they would only have the **[Breakthrough Insight]** to contend with.

They sat for hours. Between every [**Celestial Illumination Pill**], they had a short break, chatting idly with each other, mostly trying to figure out an angle to their insights, especially the final one. But when their ideas grew stale, they got back to work. Work smart? Work hard? Max would take either victory here.

Eventually, long into the evening, they broke through.

Leveled Up Ruby-Level Cultivator (greater) to 5
+6 free Attribute points
Advancement to Diamond-Level Cultivator (lesser) available

Max checked the System message. It said just what he expected.

[Breakthrough Insight required to advance]

"Whew," Maverick said. "That was a lot of work."

"But so worth it," Max said. He sighed and leaned back. His meridians were aching and his mind was reeling from the focus that had been needed. They had pushed themselves hard. Every moment of time was precious now. Max had never worked so hard in his life as he had recently. It was amazing to see what he could do.

He used to be such a loser with nothing to give to the world. Now he had something that he had always lacked and it energized him—it was more than motivation, more than drive, more than ambition. He had *purpose*, and that purpose gave him power.

Maverick agreed through their bond. There was a moment of mutual respect that neither wanted to mar with cheap remarks. Then Max got up.

He had followed his Dao in getting stronger. Level Thirty was a huge milestone. He and Maverick had both picked what they thought were the best available Skills for them. Max would have to test out [**Gravity Storm**] as soon as he could. He needed it to be ready for the upcoming battle.

There was not much more Max could do at this point. He had reached a high Level, he was at the peak of his Cultivation, just missing his [**Breakthrough Insight**], had accrued as many high-grade Items as he could, and had spent his **Cosmic Coins** wisely.

I've done all I can.

It was a liberating feeling. He really *had* done his best. Max looked back on the last few weeks. Sure, they hadn't been perfect. He'd made errors in judgment. He could have pushed himself slightly harder while grinding for Experience or Cultivating. But damn it, if this wasn't Max at his best, he didn't know what was.

I have never been so powerful, so capable. This is what it means to live your Dao? To be the best version of yourself? To have absolutely no regrets? I've done my best. Now I just have to trust that that is enough.

Maverick wasn't saying anything, but Max could feel his presence in his mind. His buddy was soaking up every word. Every emotion, every nuance, Maverick approved and agreed. That also felt good. The two of them were starting to find a stronger equilibrium as well.

I am ready.

"Sid, you have no idea how much I've missed you," Max said as he chewed on the savory, fatty meat. The eighteen-year-old kid with lazy eyes and hanging hair framing his face grinned back at him.

"Good to have you back, Boss," Sid said. "Try the roots with the sauce. I added something extra today."

Max punctured the food with a tool resembling a sharp chopstick. It entered the brown root easily and some steam came out. Max dipped it in a sauce of animal fat, egg yolk, and herbs. Then he finally tasted it and sighed.

"Dear Odin in Valhalla, it's like I'm in a restaurant," Max said and turned to capture the attention of other people at the table. "You guys don't know how good you have it!"

Sid's cheeks were blushing with pride.

"What Level are you, Sid?" Max asked.

"I'm at Twenty-Six," Sid said proudly. "I'm also at the peak of the Greater Amethyst stage in Cultivation."

"Damn," Max said and nodded in appreciation. "You haven't been fooling around. All this just from cooking?"

Sid nodded.

"I think Sid is the highest-Level person in the whole village," Joshua said and then tipped his hat to him. "For which we are all very damn grateful."

"With chow like this," Max said and shook his head as he savored another piece of meat, "it's no wonder why you guys have prospered so."

"Agreed," Martin said next to Bill, who nodded.

"Hear, hear," Joshua said and raised a mug. "To Max."

"To Max!" the table chorused. The other ones around them joined in.

"Hey, my contributions are just as important, if not more so!" Maverick exclaimed.

"I thought you didn't care about what others think," Max said.

Maverick sniffed. "I don't. But I am a staunch protector of truth."

"You sure are . . ."

Everyone at the table chuckled at that.

"I have to admit I misjudged you," Linda said leaning toward Max. "Maybe you are as good as they say."

"Eh," Max said and waved a hand. "Don't believe everything they say. Especially Joshua."

"Oh, believe me, I've learned not to," Linda said and grinned.

"Hey!" Joshua said.

The mood was jolly, and the food was great. Max enjoyed talking with all the old faces. Joshua seemed really happy and in love with Linda who clearly reciprocated his feelings fully. Max wasn't Linda's biggest fan, but he didn't need to like her. He just needed her to do her job. Max wasn't sure what that was, but she would come with the hundred chosen tomorrow. If, for nothing else, to make Joshua the most effective leader possible.

Elena stopped by to give Max a big hug. She had clearly gained in confidence. It was great to see her and exchange a few words. The bubbly girl had come into her own, her insecurity now gone. She knew who she was and what she had to do.

Unfortunately, that also meant she had to get back to the sick tent, instead of joining the party. They didn't have a proper [**Doctor**] in the village, which was a major drawback. Elena was a Level Twenty-Three [**Apothecary**] which meant she could concoct salves and elixirs to heal people, much like Ban.

The [**Werewolves**] had done a number on their people. A lot of the hunters and gatherers who had to go to the woods were in the tent, keeping their constantly bleeding arms and legs high in the air, as Elena tried to salve their wounds.

Max wondered why his nicks hadn't been that bad. Maybe it was Cultivation or some secret trick of the Zoos Collective unique to him alone? Who knew.

"I don't know what's more amazing," Joshua gushed on. "You taking care of the [**Werewolves**] or the pen and paper you gave us."

"It's him taking care of the [**Werewolves**], idiot," Linda said and nudged her man.

Joshua rubbed his neck in embarrassment and everyone laughed.

"Yeah, I can imagine the paper being useful," Max said.

"So useful." Linda said.

"It will allow me to draw schematics and plans for buildings," Martin said.

"Yes," Bill agreed. "We want a stack. We've got some ideas for two-story buildings."

"You think that's needed?" Max asked with a mouthful of roots and sauce.

Bill nodded.

"Let's assume the population grows from four hundred to one thousand," Martin said. "This will lead to two problems, fragmentation of the population being the major one. It's hard enough for Joshua to remember everyone's name and face as it is. If a leader can't do that, they need another way to keep track of the people orbiting him."

"I don't like the way you put it, Martin," Joshua said. "I don't want anyone 'orbiting' me."

"That's the way it is, Chief," Bill said. "Just eat your beef and listen."

"I've already heard this," Joshua said.

Martin turned back to Max. "So, with a bigger population being spread across a bigger area, I'm sure you can see the implications."

"Fragmentation, cliques, maybe even a mutiny."

"Exactly," Martin said. "Just like we almost had with that grunt. What was his name again? Bret?"

"Brian," Max said quietly.

"Brian! That's it. Good riddance, if you ask me," Martin said and went back to his explanation.

"Hear, hear," Bill said. "But I'm sure Max has him on a tight leash. Don't you, Max?"

Max didn't listen. He felt a pang of strong emotion flush his chest. Anger? Guilt? Something like that.

"Excuse me," Max said and got up.

Max quelled the people's protests and walked past Joshua's house and the great tree. Behind it was an eight-foot wall like everywhere around the village. Max floated over it to find himself in a field of grass, stout trees, and molehills.

"He didn't know," Maverick said. "Cut some slack for the architect nerd."

"Yeah, I don't have a problem with him," Max said.

"You sure?"

"Can't you peer into my brain with your Ability?"

"I've told you it's not that simple," Maverick said. "It's messy in there, so I only use my power when I'm sure you have something juicy, preferably embarrassing, in there."

Max gave a dry chuckle at that.

"So why did we come here?" Maverick asked.

"Well, I figured I'd try out the [**Gravity Storm**], for one."

"Ah, so you just abruptly left a party thrown for you to come practice your Skills?" Maverick asked drily.

"Good party," Max said. "I enjoyed the food. I enjoyed the people."

"But?" Maverick asked.

"This is also a choice," Max said. "I need to choose how to spend my time. Sure, I could spend it having some laughs and building camaraderie with these people. But that is not our Dao."

"Are you ready to be that lonely?" Maverick asked.

"Well, at least I have you, I guess."

"God, your life's a mess, dude," Maverick said.

"Shut up," Max said. "Let me open this loot box and then we'll have a look at our new Skills.

CHAPTER SIXTY-NINE

Serpent's Embrace

Max didn't want to allow his expectations to get too high for the [**A-grade equipment box**]. He had gotten fairly lucky with the first one. But he decided that at least he could stack the odds.

"You know, Maverick," Max said in an unnecessarily loud voice, "it sure would be great if I got exactly what I needed from this box. Sure wouldn't mind getting something that would help give me the best odds I could for these upcoming tough battles."

Maverick said nothing, but Max could feel the amusement through their bond.

Then he opened the box. A notification interface flashed in Max's vision, but it blinked out.

There was a strange pause which Max hadn't experienced before. For half a heartbeat, nothing happened. But then the Item appeared in his lap. It was a strange bracelet, made from a silver so white it practically shone in the evening's moonlight. It would coil around Max's hand from wrist to elbow. He put it on. On the wrist rested a snake's head, the eyes ornamented with tiny sapphires. Now that Max took another look, he saw that the whole bracelet was fashioned with an intricate pattern resembling scales. Any silversmith would have sacrificed their left eye to be able to craft that.

Impractical. Gaudy. But kind of badass. Let's see the Stats.

[Serpent's Embrace (A-grade)]
+15 Intelligence
+15 Wisdom
+8 Precision
+8 Constitution
Passive effect: When you defeat an enemy, you earn Mana.

Max could barely contain his laughter. He didn't want to express too much emotion, just in case the Grays were watching. They probably were. But with the strange pregnant pause before the Item appeared and its nature, he was left with no question about it. He was being watched.

Not going to lie. Feels nice to pretty much have a god on your side.

The passive effect was thrilling. Especially if they were going to go into larger-scale battles. Max had already seen how devastating his abilities could be against a host of significantly weaker enemies.

Wasting absolutely no time, Max poured in the **Cosmic Coins** he had earned from the adventure with the [**Werewolves**]. He decided to splurge a little bit and Level this perfect item all the way up to Seven. Maverick made some token grumbles about it, but through their bond, Max could feel that he actually understood why Max would go all in on this particular Item.

It's like it was made *for our Dao.*

[32,000 Cosmic Coins spent]
[Cloak of Many Phases] upgraded to +7
+24 Intelligence
+22 Wisdom
+10 Precision
+10 Constitution

"That seems hella useful," Maverick said. "You know, I'm kind of jealous that you get to equip Items. What do I have?"

"Don't you regenerate like ten Mana every second?"

Maverick scoffed. "Twelve Mana."

Max shook his head in disbelief. *The nerve of some people!*

"I heard that!"

Max smiled. "You were supposed to."

Maverick continued his grumbling, but Max ignored him and brought up that beautiful, beautiful Stat sheet. He had some free points to spend, which meant he would round out his Stats. Maverick insisted with vehement persistence that he should pour points into Intelligence and pass the 300 mark. As tempting as that was, Max figured a balanced approach would suit them best. They were already an absolute unit in terms of damage. But considering that they had a total of seventeen free Attribute points to spend, Max relented. He wanted to see that big 300 as well.

Name: Max Cromwell
Cultivation stage: Ruby (greater)
Class: Spatial Sorcerer Level: 30

Health: 2,000/2,000
Stamina: 2,000/2,000
Mana: 3,000/3,000
Alliance: Joshua's Village
Stats:
Strength: 83
Dexterity: 80
Constitution: 200
Intelligence: 300
Wisdom: 270
Charisma: 82
Precision: 140
Toughness: 115
Resistance: 125

Max hoped too many of the mole creatures scurrying around wouldn't be caught in his **[Gravity Storm]**. Maverick had no similar sentiment. The asshole on a leather handle flew up in the air and started blasting the ground with **[Explosive Rounds]**. Max followed and flew up next to him to get a better view.

The radius was decent—perhaps four or five feet of a blast zone. The blasts created a strange black and gray ball of energy which swirled into itself and then expanded before imploding. It made the sound of a percolating coffee maker or a sink being drained, only louder and more aggressive.

The implosion left a smoking hole in the ground.

"Not bad," Max said.

"Yeah?" Maverick said like a child wanting to impress a parent. "Watch this!"

Maverick flew higher and shot up the ground producing effects with different sizes and shapes. He was clearly using his Cultivation to enhance the Ability. He could even create an explosion of ten feet in radius, but it seemed to be less potent. He could also create small explosions, each the size of a baseball. Maverick shot one only a few yards away. Max could feel the heat emanating from it.

That actually gives me an idea . . .

When Maverick was done, he dropped down and plopped into Max's extended arms. Max had seen it coming. He could feel the equivalent of heavy panting through their bond.

"You altered the size?" Max asked.

"The more concentrated the area, the more Damage," Maverick said weakly. "At least, I'm pretty sure that's how it works. I'll have to test it out on real enemies to be sure."

"You sure made sure this field won't become an enemy of yours," Max said and chuckled. "You wiped out at least three generations. Rest in peace, little mole guys."

"I tried not shooting anywhere near the molehills," Maverick said.

"Eh, the village probably eats them anyway," Max said and descended back to the ground. He went over to the nearest crater Maverick had created and inspected it. The ground was blackened and brittle, with cracks trailing across the hardened earth like lightning.

"Your stuff burns pretty hot," Max said.

"As expected," Maverick said, extremely pleased with himself.

Max tried out his spell. It was his first time using it, which was always a little clumsy. He could feel it. The **[Gravity Storm]** had a different type of energy within his Mana than his other Abilities. This one was dense. The default spell would be costly, Max could already tell. But with his advanced Cultivation, he had the skill to adjust the intensity of the Mana in many ways. Max released a trickle of it ten feet away from them.

A strange phenomenon occurred. It was as if a fist-sized space in the air became distorted like an old television set getting bad reception. That point in space went gray and experienced *static.* It even made the expected noise—well, more like static combined with the suction of an ancient vacuum cleaner.

It isn't exactly a gravity spell. It distorts reality.

Max canceled the spell. That had been like two Mississippis. So, five seconds? Max immediately glanced at his Mana.

Thirty Mana spent. Manageable. He had no idea what the Ability would do if he placed it directly where Losshnak's head was. It would cause some Damage, that was certain. Would it disorient him? To what degree?

For the first time, Max wished he had a human guinea pig. He wanted to ask Joshua but wasn't sure if that was appropriate. Brian would have done it, but . . .

Max shook his head and continued.

A human-sized storm. Two Mississippis. One hundred and twenty Mana.

A spherical storm of ten feet in radius. One Mississippi. Three hundred Mana.

Max took a **[Greater Mana Potion]** out of his Inventory and chugged it down, regenerating 500 Mana. Then he flew in the air, looking down on the field with a hard, focused stare.

A field of **[Gravity Storm]** distorted reality below Max, ten feet high, thirty feet in length and width. The static flashed like a broken snowstorm. Max concentrated.

One Mississippi . . . Two Mississippi . . . Three Missis—

Max was knocked out of the air. For a moment, he lost consciousness and then found himself on the ground. His meridians ached and his Mana was completely drained.

I swear, if there's some Gray assassin hiding in the molehill, I'm personally filing a formal complaint to the ICCB.

"That was a pretty hefty storm," Maverick said.

"Thanks," Max muttered.

"Now we know your limits. Which are disappointing, as per usual."

Max just closed his eyes and tried to catch his breath.

"But with one of those stupid potions you have . . ." Maverick said. "Damn, that's gonna be scary.

"We're not even sure we know what it does yet."

"We aren't," Maverick admitted. "But you could feel it, couldn't you?"

Max nodded. He could. The storm was dangerous. There was something alien and terrifying about it. He wasn't sure what it would do, but it was a powerful addition to his arsenal. Power of a kind he hadn't ever wielded before.

The power to destroy.

CHAPTER SEVENTY

A Stranger Forevermore

Max woke up the next morning feeling pretty good. He was safe, he had a good meal digesting in his belly, and things were as they should be. The pieces on the board were all set. Or that was what he thought. But when he peeked his head out of the hammock hanging from the great oak-like tree, he noticed he had woken to the sounds of arguing.

"Wait, you expect us to just get up and leave?" an angry woman said. "Are we coming back?"

"We don't know," Joshua said and glanced over at Max's hammock. A hopeful, albeit wan smile came to his lips when he noticed Max had awakened.

Max grumbled to himself, strapped on his holster, and, rolling his shoulder, approached the mob.

"Morning," Max said. "Afterparty?"

"Not quite," Linda said, her lips drawing in a line. "I think you should talk to the folk, this being your idea."

"My—" Max burst out but controlled himself, pressing his hand into a fist.

His plan. The nerve of this woman. If it were up to him, they would all still be on Earth, happily oblivious to the horrors that the universe had to offer. What part of this was *his* plan?

Maverick sent a chiding pulse through their bond. Max nodded to himself. It didn't matter. Let her think what she did. Max needed to be above that. So he took a few steps forward, ready to address the crowd.

Why do I find myself in situations where I have to give these stupid sweeping speeches?

"I'm sure Joshua has told you what he can," Max said, increasing the potency of his voice with Cultivation. "I'll explain the rest. Humans are locked in a battle with the lizards, the Ishkarassi. This is a last-man-standing, winner-takes-it-all situation. It started off as something simple, but it has grown disproportionally complicated. You don't need to know the details."

"Tell us everything!" a bearded man Max didn't recognize from the crowd yelled.

"What you need to know is this: the victor of this fight will basically eradicate the other race from the island. One way or another, this village you have built will cease to exist."

"What?"

"You're serious?!"

"What the hell are you talking about, Max?"

"If we win," Max continued, his voice booming over the crowd, "our whole surviving population will be teleported to the middle of the Dreadlands, where there is a special zone full of resources. It's a very nice place with clean water, plenty to hunt, and forageable food as well. From what I understand, we are also given some form of a fortress that we can defend."

The crowd seemed to calm down, now listening intently.

"This means all humans will be in one easily defensible place with plenty of resources. It's an ideal situation. The game is designed in such a way that the winner will have such a solid, strategic foothold that they're almost impossible to kill. This will lead to a single outcome."

Joshua spoke. "The losing side will wither away."

"Correct," Max said. "The losers will perish. Either this village is reestablished in the fortified zone or it won't matter that we took one hundred members from this community, because the lizards won."

The crowd stood absolutely still. Max raised his voice further.

"And so I need to take the best hundred of this village. I don't want any bullshit or ego about it. I want raw Stats. I want the highest Leveled, the highest Cultivators, the most useful Classes. We need all sorts of people, but we only want the best. So please be honest with yourselves and with each other. Because if we don't get the absolute best of the best in this fight . . ."

Max paused and looked at the crowd with dead-set serious eyes.

"Otherwise we'll perish, and the blood will be on your hands. I don't want bickering. I don't want selfishness. I don't want ego. I just want the hundred best men and women. Am I understood?"

"You can't just decide who's superior!"

"You'll rip this community apart!"

"Max! This isn't you!"

Max sighed and rubbed his forehead. He wanted to yell at these idiots. But that probably wouldn't be the best idea. He gave Joshua a pleading look. But Joshua was looking at him in a curious manner. There was something new in that gaze.

As if he had just seen Max for the first time. Max was starting to get used to that look, but he sure didn't like it. He drew in a breath and addressed the crowd, his voice booming over everyone, overpowering them with the sheer volume and potency from his perfect Ruby Cultivation.

"Listen to me. Take it to the ICCB if you want to complain. I did not come here to ask. I did not come here to negotiate. I am trying to save your goddamn lives, and I want you to cooperate . . . This isn't corporate politics or some village hierarchy bullshit. This is life or death."

Max drew in a breath and let the dramatic pause linger.

"This is fucking survival. You need to take a hard look at what the human race is doing on this planet. You guys have had it pretty good in this village. Joshua has done a great job, but it's kept you from growing. Kept you *weak*. You're concerned with your comforts and the status quo. Good thing I'm here. The new status quo is this: if you don't cooperate with me, it increases the chances of our whole goddamn species going extinct pretty fucking dramatically. So just shut the fuck up, sit the fuck down, and choose the hundred best among you, *now*."

Max would have preferred a more upbeat ceremony as people bundled up in sullen groups, muttering to themselves. Joshua called out names and Linda jotted them down.

Max watched the crowd. They were not happy. Not one of them. Max recognized a good hundred people from the crowd from the times he had lived in the village. Not even they seemed understanding. Elena looked at Max from the crowd with a blank expression.

"How do you feel?" Maverick asked.

Max shrugged. "Tired. I'm just tired of holding people's hands and dragging them through this."

"I find it interesting that you keep doing it," Maverick said. "A lesser man would have just thrown their hands in the air and said 'Then just die, I don't care.' I'll have to begrudgingly give respect where respect is due."

"I need these people," Max said.

Maverick scoffed. "No, you don't. The Zoos guys are going to cradle your little testicles until you reach the finish line. Even if Losshnak killed you, they'd probably just reverse time or some shit to save your ass. We passed the finish line, dude."

"Maybe," Max said. "I wouldn't count on the Grays being so lenient. I'm pretty sure it's me versus Losshnak. The Grays know it, the Zoos Collective knows it, I know it, he knows it."

"My point stands," Maverick said. "You don't need to save these people."

"I guess," Max said. He looked over at Joshua calling out the next name. Joshua noticed Max looking, but he only blinked and didn't acknowledge it. "But it's turning out harder than I thought."

"So why do it?" Maverick asked.

Max was silent for a moment as he watched the crowd. All he could see were sullen glares and cold shoulders. "I suppose I'm just trying to retain a piece of humanity within myself."

CHAPTER SEVENTY-ONE

All-Star Team

After ascertaining that Joshua and Linda were handling everything well on their own, Max left the village and called for the Zoos Collective. The plastic jellyfish appeared in front of him immediately.

"I want to go out to other communities and pick humanity's all-star warriors," Max said. "Five of the best on this planet."

[Wise choice. We think it is wise to use your own village to build the majority of your camp. But as for the warriors, you have understood correctly how Cultivation works.]

"Not only understood it," Max said. "I witnessed it. I did it."

[Indeed. A single Cultivator who is powerful enough can wipe out mediocre warriors by the hundreds. This is why strong individuals are required. However, when it comes to warfare with the Outsiders, tactics and formations are needed. We appreciate your attempt at striking a balance.]

"Thanks," Max said. "Give me a list of people's Levels and, most importantly, Classes. We need the all-stars to have strong Classes . . . and not something like that one Ishkarassi had with the **[Trapper]** Class. That stuff is too situational, I don't care how smart the user is."

[Astute, as always. We will provide a list.]

Within a heartbeat, an interface appeared in front of Max with twenty names, Classes, Levels, and Cultivation stages. Max perused the list.

"What do you think we need?" Max asked.

"I've got the firepower!" Maverick said immediately. "You've got the control."

"We need frontliners," Max said. "But something like artillery or support wouldn't hurt."

"Two support, two frontliners, and an artillery?" Maverick suggested.

"Makes sense," Max said and looked at the list again.

He wasn't happy with what he saw. Most of the people on it had decent Levels. A large portion of them were even at Level Twenty-Five. But the Cultivation Levels were abysmal. Only three were in the Ruby Stage, and even those had only scratched the surface.

His first choice was Pierre Falieri. Level Twenty-Four, Ruby Cultivator, lesser Stage Two. The Class was interesting: [**Battle Medic**]. Max wasn't entirely sure what it meant, but it was probably a Healer with some support or even offensive capabilities.

Next up, Jasmine Jones, whose name sounded like she was a Marvel character. Max chuckled to himself. She had an interesting Class. Only Level Twenty-Two, at the peak of Greater Amethyst Cultivation. But the Class: [**Storm Witch**]. Not something as mundane as a [**Lightning Mage**] or some such. Max suspected Jasmine had gotten a Class Upgrade token somehow. He could use people who were prone to luck.

"Did you know," Maverick said, "that when Napoleon was recommended a new officer for his war efforts by one of his generals he allegedly said, 'Yes, yes. He is smart, brave and the troops love him. But is he lucky?'"

"Yes, Maverick," Max said, containing his exasperation. "I did know, because I just thought of it."

"Oh," Maverick said. "Well, yes. I was wondering how I came to know that in the first place."

Max shook his head and chose the third person. Amber Kovalchek. Level Twenty-Five, Greater Amethyst, [**Druid**]. He wasn't sure what [**Druid**] meant. Nature stuff. He had played plenty of games where Druids had multiple branching options. Max was hoping Amber had picked up supportive skills, because that's what he needed her to do. Taking her with this amount of information was a risk, but sometimes risks were necessary.

Now we just need the frontliners.

Ryan Jenkins, Level Twenty-Five, Ruby Cultivator, lesser Stage Four. Highest Level Cultivator on the list at first glance. Overall strongest person, but the Class was a little lackluster. Just a [**Knight**]. Maybe Ryan could make up for it with his higher power Levels. Anyway, he was a frontliner and that was good enough for now. Seemed like just like in video games, tanks were in short supply.

But then Max caught another tank Class on the list, [**Shield Maiden**].

Interesting.

Level Twenty-Four, peak of Greater Amethyst. Not bad. She was at the bottom of the list. Seemed like the names were set up in alphabetical order. Max glanced at the name.

Katherine Winters.

"No way," Max said to himself. "Kat?"

CHAPTER SEVENTY-TWO

An Insightful Moment

After Max confirmed the selection with the Zoos Collective, they teleported him back to the smog-fenced arena in the Dreadlands. Max was a little disappointed to notice that his Health and especially Mana didn't jump back to 500 percent of their normal values, but he had expected that.

He found himself back in the same field with high grass as he had been teleported away from. He wondered what he should do next. Go back to the camp with Christie and the others? But why would he do that? They didn't need him there, and he didn't want to go. But he did have some time to kill. Max doubted Joshua and Linda had managed to get all their ducks in a row yet.

"We could chase the [**Breakthrough Insight**]," Max said.

"Yeah," Maverick said. "Any ideas?"

"None," Max said and shrugged. "But we have to start somewhere."

Max felt for his meridians and the Spiritual Energy within them. He had been Cultivating like Ban had suggested, to strengthen himself. Everything felt ready. There was no uneasiness nor any other signs in his mind or body indicating that he may have been attempting the breakthrough prematurely. So all that was left was to find the correct insight.

Max plucked Durum's great leather-bound tome from his Inventory and leafed through it until he found some passages about [**Breakthrough Insight**].

There is little practical advice that can be imparted to the Cultivator seeking their [**Breakthrough Insight**]. *But there are some notions that are important to consider.*

Foremost, whereas the previous, lesser insights have been about understanding oneself or embodying ideas relating to the Dao, the [**Breakthrough Insight**] *is similar, yet different.*

Its acquisition is a milestone for transcendence into the super-mortal realms of Cultivation. We are not allowed to disclose too much, but we will say what we can. The [**Breakthrough Insight**] *is about a principle.*

As a Dao practitioner, you have a hidden purpose written into the tapestry of existence itself. The Heavens ordained that you were born to live your life in a certain way. That is your Dao. You exist for a reason. This reason is the principle.

The [**Breakthrough Insight**] *is different from the other insights, which are concerned with the question of 'What is I, that exists?' Now, the question is different. For a breakthrough into the super-mortal realm, one must ask the following:*

'Why is it, that I exist?'

"Ah, gee, great," Max said and grinned sardonically. "That's so easy. Just figure out the purpose of life. So simple!"

"Pfft," Maverick said. "Stop with passive-aggressiveness. We've figured out harder shit."

"Have we?"

"I don't know. Doesn't matter. We'll figure this out."

"So basically—" Max sat down in the grass, putting the book back into the Inventory (they had enough to chew on). "—there's principles."

"Goooood," Maverick said, stretching the word out. "Go on."

"Like love, loyalty—"

"Wait, I got it!" Maverick said gleefully. "So it's like being the best barber in the world? By the way, you need a haircut."

Max sighed. "That's not what it's like at all. It's not about being the best barber. It's about creating or protecting beauty. Beauty is the principle . . . I think."

They both felt a tug at their Spirit. Max wasn't quite there yet, but he had brushed the target.

"Ah, I knew I was close," Maverick said.

"Uh huh . . ."

"We already know our Dao," Maverick said, getting frustrated. "We destroy. We obliterate. All that cool shit."

That was true. That was clearly the nature of their Dao. They were something that destroyed.

"You weren't listening while I read," Max said. "It's not about the nature of our Dao. It's about *why* we have this Dao."

"Ohh . . ." Maverick said. "I get it. Wait. No, I don't. 'Why' in what sense?"

"Huh?" Max said. "*That* made no sense."

"Look," Maverick said, "the [**Breakthrough Insight**] is the answer to a question asking 'why,' right?"

"Sure."

"So *which* 'why' is it the answer to?" Maverick asked.

"You're overcomplicating this," Max said.

"Oh, *sorry*," Maverick said without a hint of apology in his voice. "I apologize. I didn't realize you had this figured out already."

"I don't but—"

"Just shut up and listen," Maverick said. "Is the question why the Heavens need this Dao to be fulfilled, or is the question why *we* have this specific Dao?"

Max fell silent. His mind went blank.

"Uhh . . ." Max started, grasping for answers. "Maybe the answer for both is the same?"

"Wouldn't that just be so frigging profound and convenient?" Maverick said.

"Shut up," Max said. "Any ideas, smartass?"

"Me follow Dao. Me destroy things. Me not ideas, only bullets."

"Thank you for your contribution . . ."

"Heh. Let's just put this all on the backburner. We'll figure it out."

"Yeah," Max said. "Let it simmer in the subconscious for now."

With that, Max got up. And just as he was about to decide whether or not to go back to the camp, the sky was once again dominated by two figures: the Gray and the jellyfish.

CHAPTER SEVENTY-THREE

The Final Phase

[All the participants have now been teleported into the area. There will be a twelve-hour grace period, during which the bases cannot be entered by beings other than one's own race.]

"We will be spawning new enemies into the area shortly. You are free to scout and attack them even during this grace period. Additionally, they will most likely find your bases and be stopped by the barrier. That does not mean they will go away. In fact, your bases will most likely be attacked immediately after the grace period has ended."

[Feel free to take any countermeasures you may require. Attacking the enemy base is also allowed as soon as the grace period is over. Good luck.]

And with that, the giant images in the sky vanished. Max looked around and found a leafy tree thirty feet away. There weren't too many trees around in the plains, but Max was glad one was so close. He flew to the tree and settled on the least uncomfortable branch. Then he watched.

Within a few minutes, he saw new creatures starting to spawn. There were a lot of them. And this wasn't like the giants and T-rexes from before. They had simply wandered around, a farmable resource. This was an army. A *horde*.

They came in a myriad of shapes and sizes, but they all shared common characteristics: black and sleek with oily membranes covering their sinewy bodies. No eyes, only slack-jawed maws brimming with sharp teeth.

A few of them were larger than the others and really stood out. Twelve to fifteen feet in height. Hunched forward by heavy, muscular arms that ended in various appendages. They had weapons for hands, with clubs for fists, and two long blades instead of fingers. When they lumbered forward in the horde, the smaller ones made way for them.

There were also a few different smaller creatures. The most revolting were the spiders. Eight spindly legs, a bulbous sack growing from each of their behinds, and a large mouth in the middle of their backs. Instead of eight eyes, eight stubby tentacles protruded from their faces, waving idly around, as if smelling the air.

There was also a dog type the same size as the spiders. They looked fast, like greyhounds. Slack-jawed maws, spikes and bony angles all along their bodies with ridged, protruding spines and muscular back legs. Max doubted he could outrun these nightmare dogs.

The fourth creature seemed more plant than animal with a black mess of vines opening up into something resembling a white sunflower. In the sea of black, the white drew the eye. They were tall but not as tall as the giants. In the middle of the petals was a maw which snapped open and close. From the tangle of vines branched out long whips. The vines were barbed with long thin spikes, like thistles, covered in a delicate white fur.

Probably projectiles. I wonder what the range is . . . Well if I can stay in the air, it won't be a problem.

And to Max's great dismay, there was a fifth type of monster. A grotesque fusion between a bat and a manta ray floated in the air, its black, slick body rippling like a wave. They had no eyes, no mouth, nothing. Just an empty head, like a flat triangle, giving them an otherworldly aura.

Idly they would flap their webbed wings and then glide like a manta ray. They also sported a ridged spine as well as strange sacks at the ends of their wings, which seemed to secrete some black substance. Max wasn't looking forward to learning what it was this time.

Acid? It's probably acid, isn't it?

"What the hell are we supposed to do against all of this?" Max whispered.

"Maybe they're weak," Maverick suggested.

"There's thousands of them," Max said. "How are we even supposed to fight that?"

These were likely a representation of the Outsiders, Max was fairly sure. If not the real deal, or even a good replica, they were an appetizer. A demo version, if one were inclined to think that way.

Could it be that this is no longer even about the fight between humans and Ishkarassi? Is it just a game to see who survives the longest? I don't know if either side can hold off a horde like this.

"What do you want to do?" Maverick asked.

Max thought for a moment, then nodded to himself and slowly and quietly dropped down to the ground from his tree. He crept through the tall grass with the greatest of care. The closest black dog monster was panting fifteen feet away. Its breathing was rapid, as if the creature was overheated or excited.

Max attempted to swallow down his nervousness. He could **[Tether]** the dog down if needed. He did his best to ignore the heavy panting and looked up at the sky. The mantabats were his major concern.

He looked behind and around him. He could possibly escape with flight, depending on how fast the mantabats were in the air. They didn't look fast, but Max didn't know enough yet. Still, he was going to take the risk.

Max plucked a spear from his Inventory. Then, using **[Telekinesis]**, he slowly and carefully lifted it into the air and set it spinning. After a few seconds, he exhaled and pushed Spiritual Energy into the spear. It shot at the closest mantabat.

It didn't even have time to react. The spear cut straight through its torso, ripping it open. The creature let out a high whine and exploded into black ink.

Defeated Level 25 [Outsider]
You gained 1,500 Experience points
Serpent's Embrace activated: Earned 120 Mana

From his hideout, Max couldn't make it out clearly, but it seemed like the creatures converged where the ink had dropped. There was a white-petaled vine monster there. To Max's great horror, the white petals stretched and the mass of vines grew a little taller.

Maverick sent a pulse of some tangled-up emotions through their bond. Max agreed, but there was no time to reply. The greyhound creature came to investigate where the spear had come from.

So they have some degree of intelligence, at least.

It quickly caught sight of Max, but he was ready, tying it down to the ground with two **[Tethers]**. Sure that it was about to cry out in alarm, Max used a third one to lock down the creature's jaws.

Maverick was about to blast it away when Max quickly shot him a message: *What in the hell do you think is going to happen when they hear the gunshots?*

Ignoring all of Maverick's dumb justifications and ridiculous excuses, Max focused on this new form of Mana he had acquired.

Max released a *very* local **[Gravity Storm]** directly at the creature's head. It enveloped it and the dog immediately started thrashing against the **[Tether]** holding it in place. After a few seconds, it went limp.

Defeated Level 23 [Outsider]
You gained 1,350 Experience points
Serpent's Embrace activated: Earned 120 Mana

Max watched the greyhound's skin bubble up. It burst into a spray of black, oily ink that hissed when it hit the ground and even melted the grass. Some of it got on Max's hands and face. It *burned*. Max started seeing red in his vision and his Health trickled down. By the time the Damage had ceased, just those few stray drops of the stuff had taken fifty Health from him.

"Oh, shit," Max whispered. Maverick sent a pulse of shock through their bond.

Max looked at the small oily puddles on the ground. This was certainly something new and different. And not the kind of new and different Max enjoyed. This enemy was complicated . . .

Well, it sure is good that I have a really powerful spell in my arsenal now, then.

[Gravity Storm] had done a *significantly* higher amount of Damage than Max had anticipated. He had thought he would have to suffocate the greyhound creature slowly, but this spell had snuffed it out as efficiently as a couple of shots from Maverick. But **[Gravity Storm]** was an expensive spell. Even that one cubic foot of storm had required high control through his Cultivation and it had cost a decent amount of Mana.

But now I can get a Mana refund for killing stuff . . .

For a moment, Max harbored a fantasy of flying up into the air and blanketing the horde with a massive **[Gravity Storm]**. Last time he had done that, had drained him in an instant though. It was risky. Perhaps he could use a **[Potion of Mana Freezing]** . . .

There was also the problem with the ink explosion. It would apparently make whatever survived even stronger. More information was needed, but if Max acted recklessly, he might simply create a threat that couldn't be taken down.

Maybe next time, when I know more . . .

A nearby section of the horde then turned their heads and sniffed the air. They were coming closer. An instinct took over Max's mind, and he immediately used a **[Tether]** to pull himself into the tree he had descended from. Quickly he hid behind the trunk and crouched to observe.

Another type emerged. This Outsider was a humanoid figure. A ghoulish abomination with a ridged spine of foot-long spikes protruding from its back. It was all but paper skin and bones, and it shambled on with the similar slack-jaw of all the other types of creatures. It bent its back and touched the oily puddles with its hanging skeletal arms, instantly absorbing the ink. As soon as it did, it let out a guttural groan, extended its spine, and looked up into the sky. It grew an inch in height, growing longer spine spikes and arms, and a more extended jaw.

It's like it gained Experience from that. They reabsorb their dead. Holy shit.

"What's up with the types?" Maverick whispered. "That one looks like it was a human."

"Sure does . . ." Max muttered.

Whether the shambler heard them, smelled them, or used some other sense to sniff out the traces of the oily substance on Max's skin, it turned its head toward the tree. With a determined, aggressive shamble, it walked forward on its skinny, wobbly legs and extended its arms like a hungry zombie.

Max didn't waste time. He activated **[Telekinesis]** and was about to fly away.

The shambler let out a high inhuman screech. Altering in pitch and intensity, it was something like a Nazgul's call from *The Lord of the Rings* but deeper. Max couldn't tell what the rest of the horde did, but the closest giant and two of the nearby mantabats stopped in their tracks and turned.

Max flew out from behind the tree, full speed ahead. It wasn't fast enough.

The shambler extended its mouth even further and a fat, gray tongue lashed out as quick and long as a frog's. It tightly wrapped itself around Max, snapping his arms against his sides.

"Shoot it!" Max said as he crashed to the ground. The tongue had some paralyzing agent which disrupted his Cultivation.

The eyeless horror shambled forward with its extended hands. Black nails on its fingers as sharp as knives were twitching with anticipation.

Maverick wasted no time with ceremony. He started blasting the shambler in the face with **[Explosive Rounds]**. It took four rounds before the creature collapsed and the tightness around Max's body loosened.

Defeated Level 28 [Outsider]
You gained 1,950 Experience points
Serpent's Embrace activated: Earned 120 Mana

That gave him half a heartbeat to breathe, because the next thing he noticed were blobs of some greenish-gray substance flying toward him in the air.

The mantabats had extended themselves to "stand" in the air vertically. Two of them lobbed balls of green something at Max.

"**[Gravity Well]**!" Max shouted and immediately used a **[Tether]** to get out of the way.

Two of the gray-green blobs got caught in the swirling vortex of gravitation, but the other two passed and splashed on the ground. The globules were not much bigger than two fists clasped together but several gallons of a sticky liquid splashed in every direction. It didn't burn when it landed on Max's skin. It *pulsed*. It started sucking on his skin. It was painful. Max used a **[Tether]** to dodge another barrage and he vanished into the long grass. He could hear the horde starting to mobilize. The screeches filled the air and a disorganized march began heading in his direction.

Max took to flight and pushed into his Cultivation to increase his speed and stability. He was weakening. His mind was fuzzy, his meridians burned, and his body ached. The green and gray goop was all over his clothes, and the fumes smelled like paint thinner. He rubbed the pulsating stuff off his hands and face. Flying around like a bee drunk on pollen, disoriented, and barely able to focus, he managed to dodge another barrage of the goop and stay ahead of the horde.

Maverick shouted something and tried to communicate through their bond, but Max could barely register it. He was fast losing his grip on consciousness.

Some spikes landed on his back, probably from the white-petaled vine creatures. Some Status effect appeared in the corner of his vision, and he could distantly feel warm blood trickling down his back.

Through his fuzzy vision, he saw a milky-white barrier ahead. That would be sanctuary. But these creatures would stay and prowl. Max willed himself to focus.

I am . . . not . . . this . . . weak . . .

Wake up! Snap . . . SNAP OUT OF IT. I AM NOT GOING TO LOSE!

He regained some of his mind, which meant a lot of pain came through as well. The fumes had made breathing hard and his vision weak. The spikes had some poison in them that was now ticking Max's Health down fast. Not all of the black horde was on him, but hundreds of shamblers, greyhounds, vine creatures, and spiders were. Even a giant had followed.

"I will not end here," Max said. "I will end you!"

He dodged another set of sticky globs and downed a [**Greater Mana Potion**]. Maverick was firing [**Explosive Rounds**] at the mantabats. One of them went down.

Defeated Level 25 [Outsider]
You gained 1,500 Experience points
Serpent's Embrace activated: Earned 120 Mana

If this didn't work, Max would drop down like a stone, be overwhelmed by the monsters, and die. He gathered the Mana inside him and infused it with his Cultivation.

"[**Gravity Storm**]!"

Suddenly a whole field was enveloped in a strange violently flashing static, forty feet in width and length, five feet in height. The black horde was inside it, screaming in pain.

Max's Mana was instantly drained. He fell from the sky.

Defeated Level 22 [Outsider]
You gained 1,150 Experience points
Serpent's Embrace activated: Earned 120 Mana

Defeated Level 26 [Outsider]
You gained 1,700 Experience points
Serpent's Embrace activated: Earned 120 Mana
Defeated Level 25 [Outsider]
You gained 1,500 Experience points
Serpent's Embrace activated: Earned 120 Mana
Defeated Level 24 [Outsider]
You gained 1,350 Experience points
Serpent's Embrace activated: Earned 120 Mana

Anticipating this, Max created a **[Tether]** pushing him and the ground further away from each other. He was suspended ten feet in the air. It beat getting crushed to death any day.

The horde of Outsiders was disoriented. Some of them fell, some of them backed away, some of them went completely still, some of them died.

Defeated Level 26 [Outsider]
You gained 1,700 Experience points
Serpent's Embrace activated: Earned 120 Mana
Defeated Level 25 [Outsider]
You gained 1,500 Experience points
Serpent's Embrace activated: Earned 120 Mana

Maverick shot at the army of monsters, alternating between normal bullets and **[Explosive rounds]**.

Defeated Level 23 [Outsider]
You gained 1,250 Experience points
Serpent's Embrace activated: Earned 120 Mana
Defeated Level 25 [Outsider]
You gained 1,500 Experience points
Serpent's Embrace activated: Earned 120 Mana
Defeated Level 28 [Outsider]
You gained 2,000 Experience points
Serpent's Embrace activated: Earned 120 Mana
Level Up! [Level 31 Spatial Sorcerer] You have gained + 3 Constitution, + 4 Intelligence, + 4 Wisdom, + 5 free Attribute points

Max snapped out of his battle trance with the Level-Up System message. His vision was alarmingly red. He was in danger. He needed to stop fighting. He made some distance, dodging globs of acid with a **[Tether]**. He was so weak. Now with the adrenaline waning, his mind was dimming. As was his life.

His Health was trickling down. He chugged a **[Greater Health Potion]**. It took him from 200 back up to 700. But it was still trickling down.

With the last dregs of his strength, sapped by the green and gray goop and the **[Gravity Storm]**, he managed to fly away. Upon crossing the milky barrier, he immediately collapsed to the ground. He tried to pick himself back up, but he couldn't. Max passed out.

CHAPTER SEVENTY-FOUR

Reacquaintances

Not so tough now, are you, big guy?" a gentle voice said from somewhere above.

Max sighed. Breathing was hard. He tried opening his eyes, but it was a tough job. As if the light had taken personal offense to Max and wanted to stab him in the eyeballs. He finally managed to force one open and catch a glimpse of the person working above him, rubbing something on his cheek.

"E—Elena?" Max croaked.

"Just rest," she said.

Max tried to lift his head but finally gave up. He felt numb. It was hard to move.

Is it the poison?

"I gave you a numbing agent," Elena said. "It'll wear off in an hour. I imagine there'll be more pain . . ."

"How— How much time we have?"

"I don't know," Elena said. There was a hard edge to her voice. She wanted to say something more.

"Elena?"

"You're an asshole, Max."

Max sighed. "I know."

"You don't know," Elena said. "I left five people in the healing tent back in the village. With wounds that wouldn't close. I left bandages and a salve they can rub but . . ."

Part of Max felt sorry, but the rest just felt irritated. It was always the same. People couldn't see the bigger picture. Max didn't want the five people who were bleeding out there dying either. But this was more important. Why was it so hard for people to wrap their head around that?

"You did that," Elena went on. "And now I'm here, saving your life, *cause it's so damn valuable or something.*"

"Sorry," Max croaked.

"Are you?" Elena snapped. "Are you really?"

Max scoffed. It turned into a little cough, but Max forced it down. Then he just gave her a wry smile. He cracked an eye open again. Elena was shaking her head and holding back tears.

"It's bad out there," Max said. "Real bad. You're going to have your hands full."

Elena said nothing to that.

"I chose you because you're capable," Max said. "As cruel as it sounds, it's what matters here."

Elena said nothing, just shook her head. Max didn't have anything else to say. But he heard several footsteps approaching.

"How is he?" Joshua asked.

"Awake," Elena said. "Alive."

"Tsk," Christie said. "Only the good die young."

"You'll be glad soon enough that I didn't croak," Max said.

"What in the hell is out there?" Linda asked.

"Something bad," Max said. He forced open both of his eyes. "Something really bad."

"What can you tell us?" Joshua asked.

"Build walls."

"What does that mean?" Linda asked.

Max let out a sigh. The pain was coming back. Distantly, he felt Maverick fly out of his holster. Joshua and Linda gasped. The gun was probably doing backflips or otherwise showing off.

Max only half-listened to Maverick's explanation of the situation. He could trust his buddy to give the people an accurate account. Max relaxed and let himself fall back to sleep.

When he woke up, he was feeling better. He had bandages over his hands and face. They felt squishy.

Probably imbued with some salve or whatnot.

Max got up and rolled his shoulders.

"You good?" Maverick asked.

"Never better."

"They're scared shitless," Maverick said.

"As they should be," Max said. "I don't know how to deal with this."

Max looked around. He must have been out of it for at least eight hours. Maybe more. The bamboo forest had been completely cut down, and a wall was forming around the border of the milky barrier. It sloped inward, with sharpened bamboo stalks pushed through the cracks to slow down a charge. There were also shelters—little huts with two walls and a roof facing the barrier.

They must have built those after Maverick told them about the mantabats.

A bunch of [**Laborers**] were digging a trench two yards away from the wall. If the wall were breached, the trench would slow the onslaught.

Not deep enough. Not wide enough.

Max sat down by the pond, laying his back against one of the rocks on the shore. It felt nice and cool. There was nothing for him to do except wait out the pain and lethargy. He heard a pair of footsteps approaching from behind. Max turned to look.

It was a woman the same age as Max, with pale skin, raven hair, and intense green eyes. She was tall and wearing leather pants and a chainmail skirt. Her top was also leather— black and sleek, and hugging her athletic form. Max gave her a tired smile.

"You look like shit, dude."

"Didn't think I'd ever see you," Max said. "Good to see you, Kat."

Kat sat down, her chain-mail skirt clinking.

"Yeah," Kat said. "You too."

Max didn't really know what to say. He used to be a bit flustered around Kat. He vaguely remembered having had a crush on her. That felt like a really long time ago.

"Your eyes," Kat said. "They've got a very different look now."

Max shrugged. "This place gave me a simple choice: change or die."

Kat nodded emphatically at that.

"You probably didn't need to change all that much," Max said.

Kat let out a humorless chuckle. "It's been something else, I'll tell you that."

Max took a closer glance at her shield. It was rimmed with silver and studded with black sharp spikes with red tips that looked practically molten and curved slightly inward from the edges. In the middle was an ornamental tiger.

"Nice shield."

"[**Boremang, Bulwark of Fury**]. I've had it since Day One," Kat said. "Unique-grade. Saved my life countless times."

"I can relate to that," Max said. "I also—"

"Hellllllooo, what have we here?" Maverick said and slid out of the holster. "Is this a high school sweetheart? Some old squeeze? She's quite the looker."

Kat scowled at the revolver. Max shrugged. She ignored the gun and turned back to Max.

"Looks like I got the better end of the deal," Kat said. "Mine doesn't talk."

"Wanna switch?"

"Hey!" Maverick protested.

Kat grinned and Max smiled back.

Maverick tried capturing Kat's attention for a while, but she just ignored him. Dejected, the gun eventually flew back to his holster and shut up.

"He's usually more . . . No actually, yeah, that's exactly how he is."

"My condolences."

Max smiled.

"I, uh—" Kat said, suddenly stammering for words. Were her ears turning red? "I heard quite a lot of stories."

"Half of them exaggerations, I'm sure."

"Dude, if it's even half, that's some crazy shit," Kat said. "Who are you?"

Max looked at her with a serious glare, trying to determine the nature of her question. She looked back, intent but curious.

"I am what I am," Max said.

"That's a bullshit answer."

"But it is the answer," Max said. "I became what I needed to become."

Kat shook her head and scoffed in frustration. "You sure have changed."

"You will need to as well," Max said. "If we survive this shit, I'll tell you more. Teach you what you need to know."

"Huh," Kat said and cocked her head. "It used to be me teaching you how to tie your combat boots back in the army."

Max shrugged. "That was never my forte."

"But this?" Kat said, waving a hand. "From what little I heard, you were born for this."

"It's cold and dark out there," Max said. "Someone has to keep the fire going."

Kat nodded but said nothing else. For a moment she just thumbed the edge of her shield thoughtfully. Max watched her sharp features and cool, intelligent eyes. He had missed her company.

"I heard it's bad out there," Kat finally said.

"It is bad," Max said.

"What do you think we should do?" Kat asked, genuine worry in her eyes.

Max looked at her, assessing if she could handle the real answer. Kat swallowed, and her ears reddened again, but she held her gaze. Max nodded.

"Fight," Max said. "Fight with every step you take. Fight like you're about to die. Because that is the only thing that will save us now."

Situation Analysis

Kat left and Max lay down in the grass, half-dozing, half-thinking. His body wasn't in pain anymore, but he was still exhausted. Max and Maverick spent one hour gently Cultivating with the help of a pair of [**Celestial Illumination Pills**]—merely an exercise to purify their meridians and replenish the Spiritual Energy. A Cultivation massage, as Maverick called it.

Afterward, Max returned to his ponderings. They only had a few precious hours left. They needed a plan. Just building walls and trying to hold out was not going to cut it. Those giants would barrel through. Max could certainly hold off a great horde for at least a little while, especially with the help of [**Potion of Mana Freeze**] . . .

But there are so many . . .

The Ishkarassi would definitely be better organized and have superior tactics and defensive formations. It was what they excelled at. Not to mention that Losshnak was perfectly positioned as a bastion to hold down a defensive line.

"We're going to lose if we just defend, aren't we?" Max said.

"Huh?" Maverick said. "You're really asking that? I swear, Max, sometimes you surprise me with your acute lack of brain cells."

"So we need to attack," Max said. "But here's the kicker: if we fly out there and attack the lizards and our forces defend without us, won't they all just get killed?"

"Does it matter if you kill all the lizards?" Maverick said.

"Cold."

Maverick sent the equivalent of a shrug through their bond. "They don't treat you with the respect you deserve."

"Kat's nice," Max said.

"So tell her to hide," Maverick said, keeping to his nonchalant tone.

"This is not the way," Max said.

"You say that because you're refusing to follow our Dao at the expense of your lesser goals."

"No," Max said. "It's not that. It's a bad approach."

"Well sorrryyyy," Maverick said. "Let me know when you magically conjure up a better one."

"I'm thinking."

"Don't. It's not your strong suit," Maverick said and flew up in the air. "Come."

"Hm?" Max said.

"Just come."

Max got up and followed. They walked along the perimeter of the camp. At the border of the barrier, a great construction effort was well underway. Fifty men and women were hammering and sawing and tightening ropes. They were tired and Max could see empty glass bottles scattered on the ground. Many a [**Stamina Potion**] had been spent here.

The wall of bamboo, planks, and bricks was flimsy at best, but considering it had been built in the timespan of ten hours or so made it more impressive than it looked. On the other side, people were slamming bamboo stakes into the ground as well as making the trenches deeper and wider either with spade, stick, or hand.

"And now come here," Maverick said and soared higher. Max activated [**Levitate**] and followed.

They pushed past the milky barrier into the open air. A horde of Outsiders was already converging. Not alarmingly huge yet but certainly in the hundreds. A giant was leaning against the barrier, glaring inside, waiting for the grace period to end.

"Look at that," Maverick said, pointing his barrel at the enemy. "And now look at that."

The gun pointed his barrel at the flimsy wall.

"What do you think is going to happen the minute this barrier breaks?"

"The wall will be manned," Max said.

"By *thirty* warriors?" Maverick said and scoffed in disdain. "They're not you, Max. None of them are."

"We can thin the horde with [**Gravity Storm**] and [**Explosive Rounds**]."

"Sure we can," Maverick said. "And what happens when we're out of Mana, but the horde still keeps pushing? Need I remind you that once these enemies die, they release their oily goop and make the rest of the horde stronger?"

Max descended back inside the barrier and walked toward the pond. He got a few looks here and there, but nobody bothered him. That was good. Max really didn't need any distractions right now. He needed to think.

CHAPTER SEVENTY-SIX

Unorthodox Tactics

It took him about an hour, but Max finally had some form of a plan of offense. Maverick was right. They couldn't simply defend. The Ishkarassi had superior defensive ability in Losshnak, and they were more organized fighters.

If the lizards are all about order, let's throw a very human specialty at them: Chaos.

Max flew out of the milky barrier that would go down within the hour.

"Max, where are you going?" Joshua shouted at him, but Max didn't have time to answer. A lot of worried-looking men and women watched.

If they knew even half of what I'm willing to do to save their lives over and over again . . .

Maybe they did and they were just scared. Or, Max was imagining, suspicious and angry. Either way, it wouldn't matter soon. They were two minutes away from midnight. Whatever happened, happened. But despite what Max kept telling himself, he was worried.

I just really hope this plan works.

"We're about to find out," Maverick said cheerfully. He wasn't worried. He knew he and Max would most likely be saved by the Zoos Collective even if they lost here.

"It's a crazy plan, though," Max said.

"Bah! We'll be fine," Maverick said. "Just don't screw this up."

"Uh huh."

Max flew over the fields and hills that were now covered by a dark monstrous horde. Maverick watched his back, so he could dodge the spines of the vine monsters and the acidic blobs of the mantabats. Max did his best to stay just out of shambler-tongue range. Maverick shot an idle bullet here and there to keep the enemy's attention on them.

Max needed to muster all of his focus and attention. Even a single misstep could be deadly. He needed to fly low and slow. It was a difficult feat. Max clutched a [**Greater Mana Potion**] in his hand as he carefully powered his flight with his Spiritual Power. He needed to be just enticing enough a target. To be just out of catching range, like a carrot dangling on a stick attached to a donkey's back.

It worked. A chorus of discordant screeches sounded below Max as the black horde of Outsiders started to follow his flight. This wasn't the whole horde, of course. Max didn't have the Mana, the time, nor the skill to collect the whole of the massive enemy body. This was maybe a third of their total grotesque population. That meant there were thousands of them altogether.

And Max had a single goal in mind regarding where to drive this horde. And so he drank his Mana potion to top himself off, and flew over the hills, driving the enemy into a clump against the flowing creek on his right.

But not far off, the creek ended into a waterfall and a steep slope downward to the forest's edge. A milky barrier surrounded the area.

Max smirked to himself and flew directly above the barrier, driving the monstrous horde against it. They screeched in anger as Max flew beyond their reach. The last globules of acid splashed on the milky barrier, which absorbed them, only emitting a light fizzle.

Max then flew over it and hid in the forest. He waited. He landed on the mossy ground and closed his eyes, panting frantically.

The adrenaline, the fear, and the strain of the feat demanded a rest. He leaned against a pine tree and breathed in deeply, trying to calm his mind. He inhaled the fresh, rich forest scent all around him. The pine tree's bark felt rough on his back, and an insect scuttled over his neck and onto his shoulder. Max didn't even bother to brush it off. He just breathed. And waited.

Maverick kept watch, but fortunately neither an Ishkarassi nor an Outsider came upon them. They were alone in the forest, their task a success.

After Max's breath had normalized and some of his Mana had regenerated, he got up and brushed himself off.

Could it really be this easy? Did I just outsmart them?

Max drank another [**Greater Mana Potion**] and flew up through the canopies and above the tree-line to inspect the situation. He landed on a treetop overlooking the milky-white barrier inside which the lizards were preparing some strange formation. Max paid no further heed to their business and instead looked upon his work.

It was exactly as Max had envisioned it. The horde of Outsiders was gathering and packing around the barrier. Some of the backline started to wander off back toward the plains, but *thousands* of the monster horde were now converging tightly around the barrier, completely surrounding it.

Checkmate.

Max and Maverick laughed and shared the equivalent of a high-five through their bond. They had done it. No matter how you sliced it, the horde would overwhelm some thirty [**Combatants**]. And from the looks of it, the Ishkarassi hadn't even prepared walls. What kind of miracle tactics they were going to use remained to be seen. Max grinned and got as comfortable as he could atop the tree. He was getting a front row seat for the show.

But something was off. The Ishkarassi really didn't seem to be concerned with defenses. But they were doing *something*. Max peered inside the barrier, enhancing his vision with his Cultivation.

"What are they doing?" Maverick asked.

"They've built an altar," Max said, suddenly feeling a chill run down his spine. "Look, there's Losshnak standing on top of it."

"What are the others doing?" Maverick asked.

"I don't know," Max said. "But I don't like it . . ."

CHAPTER SEVENTY-SEVEN

Overcharge

A re these really the hundred best?" Max said as he watched the lizards' formation.

"There's something wrong here," Maverick said. "They're all naked."

Max nodded. Indeed they were. Only Losshnak was clothed in his scale-mail armor, shining shield, and short sword. Max also took note of another, older lizard with graying scales. He was wearing a red robe and holding a staff made of white bone. He stood next to the altar and waved the staff in slow circular motions.

The other 103 lizards were on their knees. Many were arranged in a circle and within that circle the rest had formed a triangle. In the middle of the triangle was the altar upon which Losshnak stood.

Most of the lizards were looking at an empty space on the ground, their tongues flicking in and out nervously. Some had closed their eyes, as if patiently awaiting something. A couple of them were crying, their shoulders jumping up and down.

"What is going on?" Maverick asked. "This looks like a . . ."

"It looks like a sacrifice," Max finished.

"That doesn't make any sense," Maverick said. "Is it some religious thing? They're going to need everyone to fend off this fun little surprise we made for them."

Finally, the red-robed lizard slammed the butt of his staff down. A blanket of red mist formed around the elderly drake. It grew darker and thicker, until it was a cloud. All the while, the old creature was withering down into a gray husk.

"It's his blood," Max said. "That's some blood mage. He drained himself."

"What the hell is happening?" Maverick asked.

It didn't take long to find out. The blood mist passed the formation, gathering in size as it passed each Ishkarassi, taking blood from each. After it had gone through all of the naked lizards, the misty cloud had enough volume to settle over the formation. It started spinning and quickly turned into a vortex, at the center of which was Losshnak. Then Losshnak took his sword and cut his own throat.

Max gasped in disbelief.

"Whoa!" Maverick exclaimed.

Losshnak stumbled and held his throat, the sword falling from his limp fingers. The blood mist converged on him and entered through the bleeding cut at his throat.

Max could hear the collective groan of the hundred naked Ishkarassi. The blood mist was completely sucked up inside Losshnak, and for a moment, a blood red aura was upon him. It vanished and soon a trickle of red and blue energy started to trail through the air from all of the naked sacrifices.

The more energy that was drained from the other Ishkarassi, the smaller and more withered they became. Their scales turned gray and started falling off. Their eyes went dim and milky. They groaned and writhed.

And Losshnak grew stronger and bigger.

Max watched in stunned horror. Swirls of red and blue energy were trickling through the air toward Losshnak. Once the swirls were exhausted, each accompanying lizard fell to the ground and collapsed as if made from dust. They had been completely drained.

Some cried out, but most held their heads up high as they withered. And as they withered, Losshnak grew.

Max extended a sliver of his Spiritual Energy to see what was going on inside Losshnak only to discover he was charging up like a nuclear reactor heading into an overload. A halo of golden fire sprouted above his head as well as wings of red, white, and gold. He grew in stature inch by inch, eventually towering over all the other lizards at fifteen feet. His wings grew as well, and the intensity of his halo became so bright, Losshnak's face was no longer visible.

Max couldn't stop watching as the Ishkarassi gave their lives one by one for the greater cause. They only needed one survivor. Max kept his Spiritual Sense on Losshnak. It was almost impossible to describe the intensity of the power. He was still at Ruby, that much was clear. It wasn't that the ocean was getting deeper, but it was getting wider.

They're building a reserve. He will be able to go full-speed way beyond the point I'll be fully exhausted.

The final dregs of the last Ishkarassi was drained just as the horde of Outsiders crashed into the lizards. The milky barrier was lifted, ending the grace period. The Outsiders swarmed into the Ishkarassi camp.

Losshnak blasted them with a **[Holy Nova]** so intense, it blinded Max for a heartbeat. At least fifty of the Outsiders burned to death almost instantly.

"Ho-ly shit," Maverick said. "He must have gained a Level just off that.

Max nodded grimly. "He did."

Next, Losshnak conjured his trademark barrier of golden shimmering light. The Outsiders crashed into it and crawled on top of it in every direction, until the barrier looked like an anthill. A lance of light surged from inside the barrier. It was so thick and so bright, Max knew it was being augmented by Cultivation. It cut through the Outsiders crawling on the barrier.

"Shouldn't we attack the horde?" Maverick asked. "He's going to get more Experience."

Max shook his head. "We need him to exhaust some of that power. The couple of Levels and the Stats he gains won't make a difference. We need to wait for that candle to shine a little less brightly."

"We might have to wait a while . . ."

Maverick was right. Now was an opportune time to attack. But not the horde.

Max plucked a shield out of his Inventory. It had a triangular shape with a sharp edge on the bottom. Max turned it toward the golden barrier and started putting spin into it. He really charged the thing this time, feeling the slight strain of his meridians. He needed this one to break the barrier and do some serious Damage. He would still have the advantage of distance and the high ground, so drinking a Mana potion after all this would keep him topped off.

And I really need it.

After expending a total of 220 Mana, Max hurled the shield at Losshnak's barrier. At the same time, Maverick shot a few **[Explosive Rounds]**.

The shield hurtled through the air so fast, only a Cultivator's eye could follow it. It crashed into the barrier, almost off-handedly killing two Outsiders.

Defeated Level 27 [Outsider]
You gained 1,950 Experience points
Serpent's Embrace activated: Earned 120 Mana

Defeated Level 25 [Outsider]
You gained 1,450 Experience points
Serpent's Embrace activated: Earned 120 Mana

The shield broke through Losshnak's glimmering barrier, but instead of shattering it, it made a hole. Max could see the shield strike Losshnak, but he caught it with an arm and slid backward. Maverick shot a few blasts into the hole in the barrier, which was already knitting itself closed.

Defeated Level 23 [Outsider]
You gained 1,300 Experience points
Serpent's Embrace activated: Earned 120 Mana

The greyhounds jumped in and the spiders scuttled inside the hole. Even a shambler managed to get in. At least half a dozen of them managed to swarm in before the barrier closed. Max couldn't properly see what was happening inside, but he was sure this wouldn't stop Losshnak. But it wasn't supposed to. If it would just tire him out, that would be enough.

Max watched the copious amount of black oily substance bubbling. A few creatures grew big, but a particularly greedy shambler managed to gather most of the essence. It sprouted, growing up to twelve feet.

Max was sure it couldn't challenge Losshnak, as massive and powerful as he was now. But the shambler moved forward and started pounding the barrier with all of its weight. The creatures crawling on the barrier made space. The shambler's spindly arms packed a surprising punch, and the ripples on the barrier grew in intensity.

It's not going to hold up forever.

And as if on cue, a giant Outsider finally approached. It lumbered forward, making high-pitched screeches from its slack-jawed mouth, forcing the rest of the horde to make way. It had horrific-looking hands. One was in the form of a spiked mace, and the other a pickaxe.

Max knew Losshnak had seen it approaching, because the barrier grew brighter until two lances of light pierced the throat of the shambler, decapitating it. This was good. This was exactly what Max wanted.

Spread him thin.

The barrier strengthened, its shimmering light growing brighter. It ultimately burst aflame, causing the creatures scuttling on it to screech in pain and anger. They scuttled away and made way for the giant, who was now rushing toward the barrier. Max prepared another projectile.

With a strained effort, Max poured Spiritual Energy into the steel sabatons he had spinning in the air next to him. Maverick was already shooting at the barrier. Max concentrated. His meridians clearly weren't fans of this amount of strain, but Max needed this one to hit hard.

He poured energy into the sabatons until his Mana started ticking down dangerously fast and the hold he had on the [Telekinesis] spell became unstable. He launched the kinetic missile. Meanwhile, Maverick shot a barrage of [Explosive Rounds].

The sheer force of his spell nearly knocked Max into the creek. The large shambler, the giant, Maverick's explosive bullets, and Max's kinetic missile all struck Losshnak's flaming barrier. It resisted but ultimately couldn't hold. Max saw a blur of steel crashing into the barrier and striking Losshnak. He fell down, and the swarm of black monsters was upon him.

Max heard a bellow so mighty and wrathful he flinched.

"[Holy Nova]!"

A great ring of white flame erupted from Losshnak's enormous form. It tossed back all the smaller creatures, making them writhe in pain as they burned. The shambler was also thrown back, and it fell on its hindquarters. The giant was undeterred, simply pushing through the pain, even though half of its body was aflame with a white fire.

Losshnak slammed his mighty wings, making the giant stumble back. Then in a flash of white and golden light, he was in the air, fifty feet high. He turned and stopped as soon as he noticed Max.

He flapped his mighty wings once more, turned upside down, and crash-dived into him.

CHAPTER SEVENTY-EIGHT

A Super-mortal Cultivator

Without his highly-trained instincts and peak Ruby Cultivation, Max would have been utterly destroyed by the high-speed lance of light aimed directly at his heart. Losshnak blasted through a repelling **[Tether]** and a **[Gravity Well]** like they weren't even there.

Still, they might have bought Max the few extra milliseconds he needed. The lance only hit him in the shoulder. It flared and burned as Losshnak poured his Spiritual Energy into the attack. Max disengaged with a **[Tether]** and flew up in the air. Losshnak immediately followed, extending another lance of light ready to skewer Max.

Losshnak was faster, but Max was the more experienced flyer. He bobbed and weaved like a bee. But the wasp was keeping up. Losshnak kept blasting at him, but Maverick warned Max each time so he could dodge in time. That led to Losshnak repeatedly overshooting and then needing to course-correct, which gave Max the time to maintain the distance he needed.

"It's not working!" Maverick shouted over the wind. "He's using the Barrier Skill on himself. Just flicking it on and off when I shoot. I've only gotten two shots in!"

"Everything counts!"

Losshnak kept hot on Max's tail, giving him no room to pull off any offensive moves. It was a good thing Maverick was making the giant lizard dodge and expend Mana for his barrier.

Max was running really low on Mana. He could only stay in the air for maybe another minute. Less if he had to supplement his flight with Cultivation, which cost additional Mana.

I have to . . .

Max popped his last **[Potion of Mana Freeze]**.

Then he charged his flight with Cultivation to match Losshnak's speed. Max turned in the air and used a repulsive [**Tether**] on himself and Losshnak, who was charging him with a lance of light extending from his sword. He charged the spell with a massive amount of Spiritual energy.

First Losshnak slowed down, then he stopped. Then he was blasted backward in the air. Max soared after him, flying above Losshnak and tethering them again. Losshnak activated his personal golden shield, but it was a smidge too late. He was blasted down toward the ground.

Losshnak crashed into a hillside, throwing up a plume of earth and smoke. His wings had momentarily gone out, but soon he reignited them and they blazed brighter than before. A few stray Outsiders, leftovers from the horde, attacked Losshnak. He cut them down with the light extending from his sword, like they were nothing but annoying critters.

Then, with a blast from his massive wings, and he pulsed out a [**Holy Nova**], but instead of it spreading wildly around him, it concentrated into a ball in front of him. Max could faintly feel Losshnak building up Spiritual Energy and charging his spell. Then the gold, red, and white orb of flame shot toward Max with a devastating speed.

Max took a dive downward and dodged. Losshnak squeezed his fist and the orb exploded in a hot, bright fire. The edge of it singed Max, costing him 200 Health. But Max paid it no mind. Instead he extended his arms and pushed Mana out of them in the form of a spell.

"[Gravity Storm]!"

Losshnak was caught in the middle of it. An area of forty cubic feet in the air became a field of static. Max could see the Losshnak flinching, struggling, and writhing inside. Max intensified the severity of the storm, enhancing the spell with his Cultivation so intently that it started to ache his meridians. Even though he wasn't spending Mana, Spiritual Energy was not free.

Maverick blasted at Losshnak's shadowy form in the static with a concentrated rage, fueled by fear. There was no wanton glee, no maniacal laughter. Maverick was afraid and he was turning that into anger.

Losshnak finally managed enough control to cast his golden barrier on himself. That allowed him to flap his wings and push himself out of the static. Max tried to push him back into the storm with a Spiritual-Power-enhanced [**Tether**], but Losshnak pushed through it.

Damn it. He still has more Spiritual Power than me?

Max needed to let his meridians replenish, so he started flying around at high speed in the air. Losshnak followed him and tried twice to catch him with an orb formed from the [**Holy Nova**] spell. But now that Max still had some time with unlimited Mana left, he could keep up and create distance. But it was still hard to find angles of attack.

Max would fly in spirals and circles and toss out quick and dirty local **[Gravity Storms]** the size of a fist. They would flash into existence and disappear after a heartbeat, but they were all targeted at Losshnak's face.

The massive lizard grimaced and sometimes lost his bearings and some measure of speed, but he wasn't about to stop.

However, this tactic had worked. Losshnak was unable to catch Max. The great lizard stopped in the air to stare at him. Max found a high tree and landed on the top branch, grateful for the break. Then he drank a **[Greater Mana Potion]** and a **[Greater Health Potion]**.

Losshnak reached for a potion himself—most likely a Mana variant.

The two of them stared at each other, expressions unreadable. Both Max and Losshnak had naught but a stone-cold stare to offer one another between labored breaths. Losshnak crossed his arms. Then, if Max saw correctly, the giant lizard smirked and nodded to himself, making the flaming halo above his head bob.

The champion of the Ishkarassi threw a disdainful glance at Max as he sped through the air over him. Max watched him go and was first confused but that turned into an instinctive alarm in half a heartbeat.

He was heading right toward the human camp. Max knew exactly what Losshnak was about to do. Max had done something similar not long before.

Max pushed his Spiritual Energy into the **[Telekinesis]** providing him with flight. His meridians screamed at him in protest. His potion was running out. He didn't have much time. He didn't know what to do. He was at the end of his wits.

"We won't make it in time," Maverick said. "And even if we do, what can we do?"

"No," Max said, suddenly finding a certainty he didn't know he possessed. "We *have* to destroy him."

Something stirred inside both of their spirits.

"Say it again!" Maverick said.

"We have to destroy."

Slightly different meaning. More general. More abstract. It unlocked something inside Max. He could feel a power swell. A power so vast, so strange, that it scared him. He closed his eyes as he flew forward, reaching toward that space. Time itself seemed to slow down.

"Max . . . ?"

Max heard something. His Dao? The Heavens? Whatever it was, it was urging him on, giving him the right words.

"We are that which must destroy. We are the other half. We are the darkness and the night to life's light and day. Through desolation, we bring balance. We must eternally reap so that new can be sown."

Advanced to Diamond-Level Cultivator (lesser)
+50 to all Attributes
[Achievement: Super-mortal Advancement]
Reward: [Manual for Super-mortal Cultivation]
[Achievement: World First Super-mortal]
Reward: [Super-mortal grade weapon box]

Max opened the loot box immediately.

[The Scythe of Oblivion, Super-mortal-grade weapon]
+1 Speed
+2 Control
+1 Power

A large black scythe with a silver blade six feet long appeared in the air in front of Max. For a moment, he was afraid the weapon would fall, but it simply hovered in the air. He reached out with his Spiritual Sense, and there was the weapon. He commanded it. It shot out toward Losshnak's flaming figure in the distance. Max closed his eyes. He could sense the scythe. He could see through it.

Not normal vision. Spiritual vision. He could sense where everything was. Down in the outpost was a handful of humans. Still over eighty of them left. They fought the Outsiders encroaching on them. All of them felt like mice in Max's Spiritual vision.

And approaching them was Losshnak. Not exactly a mouse. More like a really big dog. But a dog Max would put down beyond a shadow of a doubt. He reached out with his senses and commanded the scythe to strike Losshnak down. The silver blade ignited with a black and gray Spiritual fire. It was met by Losshnak's flaming barrier. The scythe pushed in without effort, but Losshnak poured all of his Spiritual Energy into it.

It was as if the dog was fighting an iron chain. A futile struggle. With a simple flick of a suggestion to the scythe, Max changed the intensity and the angle of the Spiritual attack. The barrier shattered, the white-hot flames snuffed out by the cold black and gray flames of [**The Scythe of Oblivion**].

After the barrier was destroyed, the scythe's blade, still ablaze, struck true. The scythe moved with rapidity not fully visible even to Losshnak's eyes. Max could feel the sense of surprise emanating from his enemy. There was a light gasp, and then a long sigh.

The scythe's blade had entered Losshnak through the throat, piercing and rupturing every intestine on its way down. Max manipulated the black and gray flame. It spread throughout Losshnak's body, and soon he was fully enveloped by it.

Max reached out through his spirit to find Losshnak's. It was getting ever smaller, turning from a violent, large dog into that of a housecat. A scared housecat. Max could feel his form shrinking and his supercharged Cultivation dissipating.

It's okay. There is no pain. Relax. Go forth into the next journey, Losshnak. You were a worthy opponent.

Max could feel that Losshnak heard and felt it. His spirit shuddered, as if trying to answer. Max let the flame rage on and consume the Ishkarassi's spirit. It dissipated, as if it had never been. There was no trace of it. Max wondered where it went. Into somewhere beyond?

Defeated Level 32 [Ishkarassi]
You gained 37,900 Experience points
Serpent's Embrace activated: Earned 120 Mana

Max flew up with an almost effortless ease. He looked at his Mana. It was slowly trickling down. He poured his Spiritual Energy into the flight. It was like letting a drop of water trickle down his fingertip into the spell. He sent a surge of energy to the scythe, commanding it down to deal with the Outsiders.

Then he cast a spell down on them.

"**[Gravity Storm]**."

Max didn't invoke the spell. He *commanded* it. It was something close to a fifty-by-fifty-yard area. He needed it to be ten feet high to deal with some of the giants and other enormous creatures. Max observed his Mana. Sure, it was draining. He even needed to drink down a **[Greater Mana Potion]** to top it off. But the massive storm swept the Outsiders, attacking them, disorienting them, slaying them.

"I must destroy," Max said quietly. "It is my nature."

Defeated a combination of enemies simultaneously
You gained 270,000 Experience points
Serpent's Embrace activated: Earned 21,600 Mana
Level Up! [Level 32 Spatial Sorcerer] You have gained + 3 Constitution, + 4 Intelligence, + 4 Wisdom, + 5 free Attribute points
Level Up! [Level 33 Spatial Sorcerer] You have gained + 3 Constitution, + 4 Intelligence, + 4 Wisdom, + 5 free Attribute points
Level Up! [Level 34 Spatial Sorcerer] You have gained + 3 Constitution, + 4 Intelligence, + 4 Wisdom, + 5 free Attribute points

The stray enemies that had been left standing in the aftermath of the storm were cut down by the scythe zipping and cleaving here and there.

Defeated Level 26 [Outsider]
You gained 1,650 Experience points
Serpent's Embrace activated: Earned 120 Mana

Defeated Level 28 [Outsider]
You gained 2,000 Experience points
Serpent's Embrace activated: Earned 120 Mana

Defeated Level 24 [Outsider]
You gained 1,450 Experience points
Serpent's Embrace activated: Earned 120 Mana

All that was left was the stunned group of humans who were all looking at
Max and only now realized that he had an aura burning around him, black and
gray like the scythe's fire.

Max looked behind him to see if his companion had a similar aura. Maverick
did not, but something else had definitely changed.

Maverick had transformed. He had become something else. Whereas before
he had been a flying gun, now he was a . . . *drone?*

Next to Max floated a black and gold disk of ornate scrollwork adorning it. It
was the diameter of a children's swimming pool, only thinner. Under the disk
were two long, golden barrels that swiveled this way and that in excitement.

Max did the only reasonable thing he could do in that situation: he maneuvered himself in the air to land on top of his companion.

"You better get into the habit of wiping your dirty feet when you ride me,"
Maverick said, clearly the same personality as ever.

Max scoffed. He crossed his arms and looked down at the people looking at
them. He sensed a mixture of emotions emanating from them. Confusion, fear,
respect, awe.

"We did it," Max said. "We won."

"Hell yeah, we did!" Maverick said.

Both of the ICCB patron species had their hologram appear in the sky above
the human camp. The Gray had crossed its arms and clearly had no intention of
talking. It only glared at Max with the most vitriolic hatred. Max could feel it
through his new senses. It was a crushing pressure, like a blanket of heavy heat
trying to suffocate him. Max fought and pushed back, which was putting a serious drain on his meridians. Maverick was also affected, and Max could feel his
new disk form wobbling under his feet.

The Zoos -Collective noticed this, because they sent a pulse of Spiritual Energy
toward the Gray. The hologram turned to look at the jellyfish and the pressure on
Max relented. Max rubbed his throat and inhaled freely again.

So the Spiritual Energy can also carry messages. These guys are using it on a completely different level. I didn't even have the faintest idea something like that was going on.

[**The victor of this match has been decided. Humans have destroyed the Ishkarassi, thus earning all the rewards and boons appropriate. Your collective efforts will receive four hundred [B-grade Material Boxes] as well as two thousand [A-grade Food Material Boxes]. In addition, your whole race will be teleported into this area. We will expand the smoke to encompass the whole scope of this resource-rich area and to provide enough space for the surviving 5,324 humans on this island. Additionally, the smoke will protect you from any harm for thirty days. During this time, you are allowed to build a fortress here with the materials provided. You will, of course, be permitted to leave and re-enter the smoke at will, if you are inclined to acquire resources or Experience from outside the area.]**

"Let it be known," the Gray hologram said, *"that the enemy race will receive a full disclosure of your situation as well as the exact location of this area in the Dreadlands. Once your thirty days is up, you will face the consequences."*

[**Yes. There will most likely be a mobilization of the enemy forces into a collective siege. The Ishkarassi will be fully aware that their situation will become difficult if they let you prosper in the most resource-rich area of this island.**]

"The timer starts now," the Gray said and blinked out of existence.

The Zoos jellyfish stayed. It said nothing more. But it did send a pulse of Spiritual Energy to Max. It was difficult to decipher, a complex web of meanings, as if created by a master painter, every brushstroke holding multiple layers. A single pulse of energy stacked with emotion and meaning.

Thank you, it said. *We knew you could do this. We hope you will stay on course. Remember that we are allies. We have great hopes for you. Congratulations on reaching the super-mortal Cultivation realm. There will be further instructions.*

I really damn hope so, Max thought to himself. *I don't even know what being a super-mortal Cultivator means. I guess there's still some pages left in Durum's book. Something about following our Karma.*

"Eh," Maverick said. "We'll figure it out. Stop with this constant worry and analysis."

"One of us has to," Max said. "And I don't see it being you."

Maverick scoffed. "Certainly not. Now let's get down there and bask in the glory and adoration of those ants."

Max laughed and shook his head. "Don't call them that."

"You said it first."

"All I thought was that they felt like ants."

"Big difference," Maverick said and laughed. "Want to go explain it to them?"

CHAPTER SEVENTY-NINE

Aftermath

When Max and Maverick descended, people made room for them, settling into a loose semicircle, all of them looking at Max with his aura coming off of him like fire and steam.

They all had the same expression on their faces. Shock. Disbelief. Kat was in the front row. She looked at Max with an expression he had never seen on her face before. Pure, wide-eyed awe. She dropped her shield and took a step forward but stopped herself. Max nodded to her.

"Joshua?" Max called out to the crowd, strengthening his voice with his Cultivation. He overdid it, making his voice boom out like a cannon shot of command. People flinched.

Joshua advanced out of the crowd and took off his hat in an instinctive motion when he approached. "Max? Is that really you? You're . . ."

"Something new," Max said.

"Damn right we are," Maverick said. "Look at me. Just look at me. Do not dare avert your eyes, for I am perfection incarnate!"

Max scoffed and shook his head. This made Joshua relax, and he put his hat back on.

"Joshua," Max said, "you'll be stepping into bigger boots. Over five thousand people to lead. Can you handle it?"

"Me?" Joshua said, his eyes searching for an answer. "It's a lot. Surely there is a higher-Level leader somewhere. I'm just—"

"You are just," Maverick said. "And that is what is most important in a leader. You are *just* what we need."

The crowd laughed nervously.

"Yeah," Max said and rubbed his neck. "It wasn't the best pun."

"Max!" Christie said and pushed from the crowd, her face set in an apologetic smile. "You— I was— I'm sorry."

Max lifted a hand. "Save it."

Christie flinched, lowered her gaze, and nodded as he took a few steps back. Some distant part of Max felt bad. But her need for making amends wasn't his concern. She was a big girl; she could deal with it. Max didn't have the time. He turned back to Joshua.

"You will do it," Max said. "And Linda will help you."

"'Course I will," Linda said and came closer. She looked Max up and down. She was breathing heavily. Wound in the shoulder. She had been fighting. She nodded at Max, as if approving. Max liked that. She didn't cower. He found himself respecting this woman more. She must have noticed something shift in his gaze, because she gave a little smirk. He scoffed.

"You guys will be leading the other [**Leaders**]," Max said. "A community of over five thousand people will need some leading. I am sure you will figure it out. Just know this. If there is any question of your authority, any coup, any mutiny . . ."

The aura around Max grew darker and more intense. Both Joshua and Linda nodded.

"We will make laws and rules," Joshua said, rubbing his chin. "Most people will be reasonable, I'm sure. Especially given the situation."

"There will be trouble, dear," Linda said. "Some people will not abide by the law."

"I am the law," Max declared with cold confidence. "And they *will* abide."

Then Max nudged Maverick. It was time to go. The two of them soared high into the sky and flew through the wall of smog. It was time to see what a super-mortal Cultivator could really do.

CHAPTER EIGHTY

Epilogue

The tension in the room was so thick, a knife wouldn't cut it—you'd need a plasma torch to make any headway. The Zoos didn't mind. To say they were happy was an understatement. They were *ecstatic*. Their plans had come to fruition. All the risks and all the expended veto points had paid off.

This could be heard in the tight, restless buzzing of the Z'var. Azzzhtik'Likzirrruk was in the middle of the room at a round white table. He was still and seemed vulnerable, his green exoskeleton shining faintly in the dim lighting of the room. He was rubbing his front legs together and staring at the Zoos hologram.

It took a while for the Zoos to accurately remember how long it had been since they had seen Azzzhtik'Likzirrruk not flying around imposingly.

The Quarmak were calm, as per usual. They always played the game very differently from the Zoos. The Zoos had no aversion to the frog-people. Quite the contrary, they had collectively voted to recruit the Quarmak as an ally. The Quarmak knew this.

As did the Grays. They were sending shifty glances at every party at the table. The intelligence the Zoos had acquired had revealed that the Kiritus Corporation had agreed to ally with the Z'var under the table, if this scenario happened.

Max Cromwell had advanced.

He had won, too. That was good. But the conflict over the resource node was but a petty squabble. It had no significance in the bigger picture. For a representative to reach super-mortal stage of Cultivation so fast, on the other hand . . .

It was completely unheard of. Ruby bottlenecked most races. It was at that point where the relevance of the Framework was starting to fade. It could no longer support the Spiritual weight of a highly Cultivated soul. It could support the super-mortal stages of course, it had been designed to do that. But the speed at which Max Cromwell had shot to this level of advancement was preposterous. How serendipitous that the human race and this individual had fallen under the patronage of the Zoos. This would change everything.

And the ICCB knew it. That is why Azzzhtik'Likzirrruk had surrendered. That is why the Grays were nervous. That is why the Quarmak were silently waiting. They were waiting for the Zoos to make a move.

[The fate of the games is sealed. Max Cromwell had done something we thought unthinkable. This iteration of Cosmic Games is no longer a competition. It is a case study in how fast a super-mortal Cultivator can obliterate the other races.]

The Z'var buzzed with anger and frustration in a chorus of twisting metal. The Grays were looking particularly white but said nothing. The current state of the Games would devastate their position in the ICCB the most.

"Surely we weren't called here only to hear what we already know?" the leader of the Quarmak croaked. "You are going to offer a compromise or a compensation of some kind, yes?"

The Quarmak's choice of words was interesting. There were other factors too. The warmth of their skin, the dilation of their pupils—markers the frog-people were advanced enough to hide, but if they had chosen to hide them, there was something at play. Of course the Quarmak knew that the Zoos would know they were hiding something. Such was the nature of these Games.

Regardless this meant that the Quarmak were looking to oust the Zoos from their place of power. Did that mean they had some kind of an ace in the hole in terms of a candidate?

A part of the Zoos was assigned to investigate, while the main function focused on the council meeting.

"Yes," Azzzhtik'Likzirrruk said. His tone was still clipped and demanding, but it had lost the hardness of absolute authority. But he still played his part in this theater just as he was supposed to. "Obliterating the other representative races is a loss for the whole ICCB. Surely this isn't what the Zoos Collective has planned?"

[It is not. This is why we propose two options. Option number one: we let Max Cromwell reign as he pleases, and as he kills other representatives that hold potential we take custody of those representatives.]

"You would dare?!" one of the Grays said.

"Preposterous," Azzzhtik'Likzirrruk said. "You would take all of the recruits from these Games? You would cripple all of the other three parties in the ICCB for several weeks! Thousands would die and all factions would lose planets, even whole solar systems."

"Surely you understand," the leader of the Quarmak said, "that such action would be considered so heinous, it would make the Zoos Collective persona non grata within the ICCB. Surely you would not want to offend us to the point that we cut you off and leave you to fend for yourselves against the Outsiders."

A farce of a comment, and everyone knew it. They couldn't afford to cut the Zoos off—even less so now with Max Cromwell having reached a super-mortal stage of Cultivation.

[Understandable. The Zoos Collective does not want to take drastic measures either. But that is the price of declining our second offer.]

"Let's hear it then," Azzzhtik'Likzirrruk said. His voice was cold, but an undertone of defeat could be heard.

[We remove Max Cromwell from the Games and focus on expediting his growth. We will, however, require the equivalent of 20 percent of the expected winnings from each faction. After the transactions are done, we remove Max Cromwell and let you continue to fight over the rest of the prize resources. Additionally, we demand to be made head of council until further notice.]

This sparked outrage—half theater, half authentic. The additional 20 percent reward that the Zoos demanded was certainly greedy. But they had decided to attempt to get away with it. The expended veto points as well as the upcoming pour of resources into Max Cromwell made it a necessary gambit.

"You—" the Grays spluttered, "—dare ask for more than the head of council?"

Azzzhtik'Likzirrruk had flown up and joined the Swarm. They were communicating in their disgusting language, which the Zoos modified with a software into melodic music. The Quarmak had huddled up together in their translucent jelly and were burbling and croaking to themselves. They would capitulate, so the Zoos waited patiently.

Eventually the three other factions had a conversation that the Zoos wasn't privy to. This was standard. They could have attempted to weasel their way in, but it was risky. The barrier had been cast by Azzzhtik'Likzirrruk, the most powerful sorcerer alive. The Z'var's magical prowess was not to be disrespected.

"We choose to accept," Azzzhtik'Likzirrruk said and flew back down to the table. "You have played your hand well, Zoos Collective. See that you lead in a way that doesn't only benefit your own coffers but also ensures the continued survival of the ICCB."

[You will find us a wise steward. We do not intend to use our new position for personal gain alone. We will use it to enhance and realize the potential of Max Cromwell. Surely the ICCB can see the advantage to this.]

"If there is anything," the leader of Quarmak said and croaked loudly to make sure the focus of the conversation was on him, "that the Quarmak can help the Zoos Collective with, regarding the growth of this Max Cromwell, please only request a convenient time for us to discuss. Perhaps directly after this meeting?"

There it was. The offer of an alliance. It came from the weaker party, and it came immediately. The Quarmak both recognized their lesser position at the table as well as the potential for an alliance with the Zoos. The Zoos would accept, but it would cost the Quarmak. Nonetheless, it would be good to have an ally, as tenuous as that relationship might be.

[We would be happy to have this conversation right away, if the Quarmak have any spare officials.]

"Of course," the leader of Quarmak said, smiling sweetly with his plump frog lips as if having just swallowed a fat fly. Then he turned toward one of the people in his retinue. The frog nodded and leapt out of the ring of thick green goop in which the Quarmak resided. As he came above the surface, a membrane of the goop stuck to his skin, completely enveloping him.

The Zoos created a smaller copy of their hologram, which appeared next to the Quarmak representative, sitting at the edge of the ring of green gel. They teleported into one of the negotiation rooms in the local mothership.

"I do not approve of personal deals being struck in the council room," Azzzhtik'Likzirrruk said.

[Silence.]

The Zoos accentuated their air-piercing command by making the lights flicker and the room tremor. They would need to show authority now.

The Z'var buzzed with livid anger, but Azzzhtik'Likzirrruk simply sat at the table in silence. Eventually he got up and flew toward his Swarm. The Zoos blinked out of existence and reappeared to hover above the table.

[Now . . . We have prepared a list of changes in policy that we will have the authority to set in motion. We will additionally be providing a list of changes that we will require the ICCB to vote on. Furthermore—]

Something was wrong. They all sensed it. A klaxon sound suddenly blared and the council room's lights flickered red. The Zoos had long ago discarded physical form, but the effect still felt visceral on some level. Thousands of years of starflight in their corporeal form had ingrained it in the collective memory. This was danger.

The Kiritus Corporation would know the full picture first. Indeed, after a few seconds, one of the Grays spoke. Their eyes were hard and serious, their skin gone from gray to pure white. They addressed the room with utter solemnity.

"A new rift has opened," the Gray said. "In this local sector. Right outside the solar system."

"WHAT?" Azzzhtik'Likzirrruk screeched. The Quarmak and the Grays flinched.

"The Outsiders have spawned another rift. We have a visual on seventeen breeding constructs, as well as a hundred scout units."

"Where?" the leader of the Quarmak asked urgently.

"Outside the solar system. Eighteen point eight billion miles away," the Grays said.

This was beyond unfortunate for the Zoos and the ICCB. They were attacking the Games? Did they have intel on Max Cromwell? Surely a lowly Diamond-stage Cultivator wouldn't warrant an attack of this scale. And even if they could recognize Max Cromwell's potential, how did they know? Surely they had no intel on the location of any of the Games? Was this a coincidence? Unlikely. There had to be an answer. Only one came to the minds of the Zoos.

[We will have to stop using Outsider-DNA in the Games. Immediately. Send out a command to destroy any facility dealing with the DNA. They used it to gather intel. That is the only reason they are here. They are here to destroy Max Cromwell.]

"How long until they arrive?" Azzzhtik'Likzirrruk asked.

"Four weeks," the Gray said. "The scouts will be in the system in two. But the incubators will take a month to arrive."

"Do we evacuate?" the Quarmak leader asked.

The Swarm buzzed angrily. Azzzhtik'Likzirrruk spoke for them. "And leave three habitable planets and the local mothership? We have factories here. Eighty billion of our people live on Alpha Ludus. We have to defend."

[Agreed. The outsiders have come with only seventeen incubators. They are expecting an easy fight. They are expecting us to take Max Cromwell and evacuate, so they take our solar system easily. Or they are forcing us to risk losing him. A lose-lose.]

"I don't care if it costs all of our collective veto points," Azzzhtik'Likzirrruk said. "We are not taking key personnel and leaving. We will defend."

"Hear, hear," the Quarmak said in a croaking chorus.

The Grays nodded and watched the Zoos. The Zoos discussed the matter amongst themselves. This was an unfortunate turn of events. They would have to take even further risks. But if Max Cromwell could survive a true assault by the Outsiders . . .

[We will fight.]

About the Author

Wilbur Woods is an entertainer, coffee drinker, and story eater, as well as the author of the Cosmic Games series, originally released on Royal Road. He has loved stories since he was a kid, and when he asked himself what he really wanted to do, the answer was simple: write.

Podium

DISCOVER MORE

STORIES UNBOUND

PodiumEntertainment.com

www.ingramcontent.com/pod-product-compliance
Lightning Source LLC
Chambersburg PA
CBHW031057130726
47906CB00008B/613